Juliet E. McKenna has been interested in fantasy stories since childhood, from *Winnie the Pooh* to the *Iliad*. An abiding fascination with other worlds and their peoples played its part in her subsequently reading Classics at St Hilda's College, Oxford. While working in recruitment and personnel, she continued to read across all genres, and started to write herself. After combining book-selling and motherhood for a couple of years, she now fits in her writing around her family and vice versa. She lives with her husband and children in West Oxfordshire. *The Thief's Gamble* is Juliet E. McKenna's first novel.

Find out more about Juliet E. McKenna and other Orbit authors by registering for the free monthly newsletter at www.orbitbooks.co.uk

By Juliet E. McKenna

THE THIEF'S GAMBLE

A Tale of Einarinn

JULIET E. McKENNA

orbit

www.orbitbooks.co.uk

An *Orbit* Book

First published in Great Britain by Orbit 1999
Reprinted 1999 (twice), 2000, 2001, 2002

A CIP catalogue record for this book
is available from the British Library.

ISBN 1 85723 688 2

Typeset in Erhardt by Palimpsest Book Production Limited,
Polmont, Stirlingshire
Printed and bound in Great Britain by
Mackays of Chatham PLC, Chatham, Kent

Orbit
An imprint of
Time Warner Books UK
Brettenham House
Lancaster Place
London WC2E 7EN

For my sons, Keith and Ian.

ACKNOWLEDGEMENTS

Many people helped shape this tale. My heartfelt thanks go to Steve, for his constant support and inspiration; to Helen, for bringing so much to the original concept; to Mike and Sue, Liz and Andy, for invariably honest criticism. Also, an honourable mention goes to all at Castle Penar.

The writing is only the start. I am indebted to Emma, Val and Adrian for championing the cause, to Tim for invaluable editorial advice and to all at Orbit for their enthusiasm.

On a personal note, I would like to thank the various branches of the Rose family for their help during the Great Chicken-Pox Crisis. I would also like to thank my mother for the unforgettable phone-call: 'You know, it was just like reading a real book!'

GID

Wrede

Vanam

Oakmont
Hancher

Selerima

ENSAIMIN

Drede   Eyhorne
Ambafost
Friem

CALADH

Col

Gulf
of
Peorle

Believed position of
Hadrumal
(The Wizard's Isle)

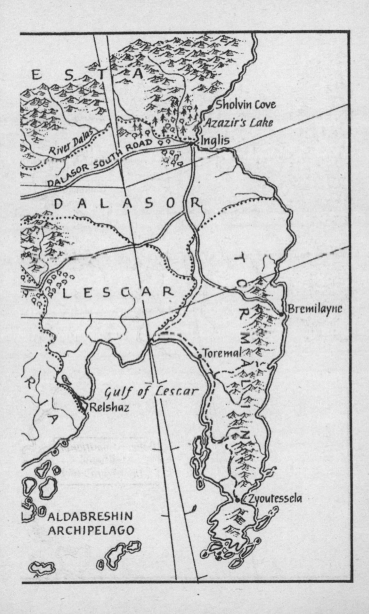

ESTA

Sholvin Cove

Azazir's Lake

River Dalas

Inglis

DALASOR SOUTH ROAD

D A L A S O R

T
O
R
M

L E S C A R

Bremilayne

Toremal

R

Gulf of Lescar

A

Relshaz

N

Zyoutessela

ALDABRESHIN
ARCHIPELAGO

CHAPTER ONE

Taken from:

Wealth and Wisdom
A Gentleman's Guide to their
Acquisition and Keeping

BY

Tori Samed

Gambling

Most gambling revolves around the runes of the ancient races, their use for divination and other such superstitions having long been discarded in civilised countries. Some games are based purely on randomly drawing a predetermined number of runes; others rely on casting combinations that earn greater or lesser scores. In either instance, cultivating a memory for what has gone before is recommended.

The best place to gamble is with friends, in convivial surroundings accompanied by a good vintage, provided that the stakes and means of redeeming debts have been agreed beforehand. When travelling, many of the better inns in the cities and on the major coach routes will have a permanent gaming table with a resident host. Such games are generally played fair and can run to very high stakes. If you have sufficient skill, you may rise from the table, your purse heavy with coin. However, any debts incurred in such company must be honoured instantly if you wish to avoid having your goods and luggage seized in payment.

Do not be beguiled into a casual contest in a city thronged at festival time. Beware the amiable stranger who offers you a friendly game to while away a dull evening in a back-roads tavern. Such men prey on the unwary, turning the game mercilessly to their advantage with weighted runes and sleight of hand. Turned away from hearth and home, disgraced or fugitive, they are little better than mercenaries and thieves.

The Packhorse Tavern, on the Col Road
south of Ambafost, Ensaimin,
12th of For-Autumn

Some opportunities ought to come labelled 'too good to be true'. Of course, ten years of living by my wits should have taught me how to spot them. You would have thought so anyway; so would I.

The night this particular opportunity came to wreak havoc in my life, I was sitting comfortably full of good dinner in front of a roaring fire, and listening to the wind tearing at the snug inn. I was wearing my usual nondescript travelling clothes and, with any luck, the other patrons in the tap-room would have been hard put to decide my age, sex or business. Being unremarkable is a talent I cultivate: middling height, middling build, nothing special – unless I choose differently. Feet up on a stool and hat over my eyes, I may have looked half-asleep, but mentally I was pacing the room and kicking the furniture. Where was Halice? We had been due to meet here four days ago and this unplanned stay was eating into my funds. It was unlike her to be late for a meet. On the few occasions it had happened before, she had always got a message through. What should I do?

I counted my money again; not that anyone else in the room noticed as I slipped my fingers into the pouch under my shirt and sorted the coin. I carry noble coin on me night and day; I've had to abandon my belongings a few times and being caught out with no money leads to bad experiences. I had thirty Caladhrian Stars, ten Tormalin Crowns and, reassuringly bulky, three Empire Crowns. They were more than enough to give me a stake for the Autumn Fair at Col and I had a heavy pouch of common coin upstairs which would cover my travelling expenses as long as I left in the morning. If I waited any longer, I'd have to pay carriers' coach fare and that would seriously eat into my reserves.

The problem was that I did not want to work the Autumn Fair on my own. Lucrative as it is, it can be a dangerous place and while I can take care of myself nowadays, Halice is still a lot handier than me with her sword and her knives. Working as a pair has other advantages too; when someone feels their luck with the runes is going bad, it's much harder to see why when there are two people adjusting the odds. As an added bonus, people never expect two women to be working the gambling together, even in a big city. I could hook up with other people but Halice is better than most as well as more honest than some.

Of course, the most likely explanation was that Halice was stuck in some lord's lock-up awaiting the local version of justice. I cursed out loud, forgetting myself for a moment, but luckily no one seemed to have noticed. There were only three other people in the tap-room, and they were deep in conversation with the innkeeper. They were merchants by their dress; this was a well-travelled business route and the chances were they were heading for Col. The filthy weather seemed to be keeping the locals by their own firesides, which was fine by me.

If Halice was in trouble, there was no way I could help her. Identifying myself as her friend would simply land me in shackles too. I frowned. It was hard to believe that Halice would get herself into trouble she could not get clear of. That was one of the main reasons we worked Ensaimin for the most part. Competition for trade guarantees a reassuring lack of inconveniences such as circulating reward notices or co-operative Watch commanders, which make prosy places like Caladhria so inhospitable. Here trouble is seldom so bad it cannot be left behind once you cross a local boundary, and we take care never to outstay our welcome.

So there I was, sitting and fretting and sipping rather good wine, when a very wet horseman strode into the bar and beckoned to mine host. I could not hear what they were saying, and that immediately piqued my curiosity, but I could not move closer without drawing attention to myself. The horseman passed over a small parchment and I heard the chink of coins. As he left, the innkeeper unfolded the letter or whatever it was and the merchants crowded round.

'So what does it say?' a thin man in a stained yellow tunic asked.

'Dunno. Can't read.' The innkeeper shrugged his fat shoulders. 'I'll need to know more before I tack it up though, money or no.'

I bit my lip with frustration. I can read, thanks to a mother determined I should have every possible advantage to offset my birth, but there was no way I was going to make myself conspicuous by offering help.

'Here.' The thin man's companion reached for the parchment and frowned at it. 'Where's the Running Hound?'

'It's the big coaching inn on the market in Ambafost,' the third merchant piped up, peering over the reader's leather-clad shoulder.

'Well, there's a trader staying there who's interested in buying Tormalin antiquities.' The bearded man smoothed out the notice and read it through, lips moving as he did so. 'This says he'll pay good prices and that he'll be buying on market day.'

'He must be doing well, to be paying to advertise like this.' The third merchant gnawed at a nail thoughtfully. 'Is there much doing in antiquities at the moment?'

The bearded man shrugged. 'Maybe he's got plans for the Autumn Fair. There are collectors in Col and there'll be traders from Relshaz and the Archipelago as well.'

The thin man stared at the parchment with greedy eyes. 'Perhaps we should try and get hold of a few good pieces if the prices are going to be favourable.'

They huddled together and the bearded man got out a map as they discussed the possibilities.

I drank the rest of my wine and pondered my next moves. I happened to know where you could find some very fine pieces of Tormalin Empire work, and if I could get anywhere near a realistic price for one, even allowing for a merchant's cut, I could wait for Halice until the very last hour, then hire a private coach to get me to Col and still have money over to stake me for a very high playing game. The trick would be getting the piece to the merchant without the original owner being aware of it and there it seemed that the gods were smiling on me for a change. I should have known better, but at the time all I could think of was the profit I could make. There was also the little matter of a very sweet revenge which would be a substantial bonus. Was it worth the gamble?

The merchants were absorbed in their discussion, and I went upstairs without anyone remarking on it. I unshuttered the window and peered out. Rain was still falling but the wind was slackening off and the waxing lesser moon was fleetingly visible through gaps in the cloud.

Should I do this? It would be risky but, then again, it could be very profitable. Well, I'm a gambler and no one ever struck it rich keeping their runes in their pocket, did they? The temptation was just too strong. I changed clothes rapidly, swapping homespun and leather for good broadcloth breeches and tunic, boots, gloves and hooded jerkin, all in charcoal grey. Black gives hard edges which can catch the eye even in the darkest night. The rough wooden beams of the inn made leaving through the window simplicity itself, as long as I took care not to mark the intervening plaster. I was soon jogging through the woods fringing the road to Hawtree.

It was cold and wet but the prospect of a little adventure warmed me. I did not do much thieving in those days. The difficulties of fencing goods in a strange place are formidable and while weighting the runes in a game of chance can get you flogged, getting caught stealing from a noble's house gets you the pillory at best and loses you a hand at worst. Unfortunately, only nobles have anything worth stealing. You may wonder why I was chancing it this time, but I happened to know this particular noble was not going to be at home, which did rather weight the odds in my favour. Raeponin's devotees can talk all they want about balance and justice and levelling the scales, but you won't ever find me making offerings at his shrine. After all, I gamble for a living, not for fun.

I had sat on my horse under a dripping oak tree earlier that week watching the gentleman and his entourage heading north with enough luggage to indicate a lengthy stay in another place. I would have recognised him anywhere, even after ten years. You do not easily forget the face of a man who has tried to beat and rape you.

Hawtree was not far and I covered the distance easily; staying fit is essential in my kind of life. I breathed in the damp green scent of the night happily. I love being out in the country at night, for all that the sun rules my birth-runes. It must be my father's blood coming through, despite my city upbringing. The village was mostly dark and a few of the wooden houses showed dim lights, but this was farming country and most folk here slept and rose with the sun. The larger brick and flint buildings round the market square showed more signs of life despite the fact it was now past midnight, so I ducked into an alley and waited to catch my breath. I walked noiselessly through the dark lanes, keeping an eye out for dogs who might advertise my presence.

The house was just off a garden square, a favourable position for a wealthy landowner's residence. The tall front showed heavy oak shutters barred with iron and a stout door with an expensive lock; this did not bother me as I worked my way round to the alley at the back. I found a dark corner and studied the kitchen and outbuildings round the yard. My mother said I was the most useless maid she had ever known but my years as a housekeeper's daughter had given me invaluable knowledge about the domestic arrangements of large houses. A scullery maid would be trying to sleep in the meagre warmth of the dying kitchen range while her more fortunate seniors would have chilled and cramped quarters in the garrets. The cook and chamberlain would have the better rooms overlooking the yard. I couldn't tell how many servants the bastard had taken with him so I had better avoid any of those areas. The room I wanted was towards the front of the house on the ground floor so ideally I needed to get in through a first-floor window. I studied them in the fitful moonlight and blessed the keen night-sight that my father had granted me. It did not look promising but I was reluctant to give up; I wanted the money this would provide and the more I thought about it, the more I liked the idea of finally getting my own back on the misbegotten swine who had first brought me to this house. I suppose, to be precise, quite a chain of events had brought me to this house; the bastard with the nice collection of silver simply happened to be the last link.

I had finally stormed out of what had once passed for my home after my mother had lamented once too often about the ruin of her life, saddled with the by-blow of a minstrel, one of the Forest Folk at that. I had already taken to gambling which I had always been good at and was working small deceptions to earn my meals. I had formed no real plans beyond some vague idea of trying to find my wandering father and, looking back, I am surprised it took so long for me to land in trouble. A panicking attempt to bluff my way out of an inn without paying had left me thrown on the road with a smarting arse and my few belongings taken in lieu of payment.

I had arrived in Hawtree two days later, tired and ravenous, dirty and desperate. Neither of the decent coaching inns had let me past their doors and I had ended up in a grimy hostelry next to the slaughterhouse. It had not taken me long to realise why there were so many women sitting around the tap-room and it was a measure of my ignorance and despondency that I decided to try for a customer myself. Lack of food must have softened my brain. It was not as if I was a virgin, I had thought, and my mother, ever determined I should not get caught like her, had taken me off to a reliable herbalist as soon as she had first caught the under-gardener fondling my bottom. It had not occurred to me to worry about disease and, looking at the competition, I had felt confident that I would be able to earn a meal at very least.

I combed my hair with my fingers as best I could – I wore it long in those days – and pinched my cheeks to heighten my colour. I was still using herbal washes to bring out the red in my hair and cosmetics to make my eyes reflect green rather than grey, and, despite its stains, my russet dress looked sufficiently exotic in the dingy bar. Chances were none of these yokels had ever seen a real Forest maiden so, their reputation being what it is, I decided to increase my asking price. The next customer to survey the waiting women was tall, dark and handsome in a sharp sort of way and he rapidly passed over the others to catch my eye. The other whores looked away and muttered among themselves. Naive as I was, I felt sure they were jealous.

'Well, well, you're not from around here, are you?' He came over and gestured for wine, which I drank thirstily.

'No, I'm just passing through.' I did my best to look mysterious and alluring.

'All alone?' His hand brushed mine as he poured more wine.

'I like to travel light.' I smiled at him and my spirits rose. He was clean and young and looked wealthy; I could have done a lot worse. As I said, I was very naive in those days.

'What's your name, sweetheart?'

'Merith.' Actually that's my oldest spinster aunt but who cared.

'This isn't a very comfortable inn. Could I offer you some hospitality?'

That was a new way of putting it but I wasn't going to argue. I smiled at him from beneath my dyed lashes.

'I'm sure we could come to some agreement.' After all, I wanted some coin out of this, not just a warm bed and food.

He offered me his arm and I flaunted out of the gloomy tap-room, attributing the sudden buzz of conversation behind us to disappointed hopes.

Ten years on, I stood in the dark and looked at the windows thoughtfully. That was the salon where he had taken me, I was sure. He had shown me in and told me to wait. My spirits rose at the thought of food and clean sheets and the business to come even promised to be quite enjoyable. I wandered round the room and noted the fine tapestries, the polished furniture and the superb Tormalin silver on the mantel shelf. Stories from the ballads I had heard my father sing began to echo in the back of my mind – virtuous maiden falls on hard times and is rescued by a handsome noble, that sort of thing.

When I heard the door, I turned with a welcoming smile but my host was not bringing the supper he had promised. He locked the door behind him and his lips curved in an ugly smile as he ran a dog-whip through his hands. He was stripped to shirt and hose and flushed with anticipation. I moved to put the table between us; from the glint in his eye, I would not have bet on my chances of talking my way out of this. I may have been naive but I wasn't that stupid. I realised I was in serious danger.

'Come here, whore,' he commanded.

'If you want something more lively than plain sex, I want more money,' I countered boldly. If he thought I was going to play, he might get careless and I would be out of there like a rat from a burning barn.

'You'll get what I decide to give you.' He was not talking coin; he lunged at me and the lash flicked my cheek.

I screamed as loudly as I could but all he did was laugh. 'My servants are paid well to be deaf, you slut. Scream by all means. I like it.'

I could see that he did too. He moved and so did I, we circled round the table and he began to frown.

'Come and see what I've got for you,' he leered, lifting his shirt.

I dashed for the window but he was too fast and grabbed a handful of hair. He threw me to the floor and raised the whip but I rolled under the table. He cursed obscenely and snatched at my ankle. I kicked and twisted as he dragged me out but he was too strong. He ripped at my skirts with his other hand and my head smacked against the chair legs. He laughed as he saw the blood and oddly, that was what finally made me lose my temper.

I went limp. As he relaxed his grip, I drew my knees up. He laughed again as he straightened up to unlace himself, then I brought both of my feet up into his stones. He collapsed, retching, and I scrambled to my feet. I grabbed a fallen chair and smacked it hard into the side of his head and ran for the window a second time. As I fumbled with the catches, I heard him groan and curse. I have never been so frightened in my life, utterly occupied with opening the window, not daring to lose a moment of time by glancing behind me. After what seemed like an age, I had the casement open and the shutter beyond. I risked a glance at the bastard on the floor; he had got to his knees but was clutching himself with screwed-shut eyes. I swung out of the window and dropped to the road. With the first stroke of luck I'd had in a long time, I didn't hurt myself, and I ran as far and as fast as I could.

The first time I'd told Halice that tale, she'd been astounded I could be so matter-of-fact about it. The memory could still wake me in a cold sweat if I was overtired or feeling low, that in itself was part of the reason I wanted some small measure of revenge. As for the rest, I'd learned I'd come out of it lightly if you could believe the broadsheets' lurid tales of mutilated bodies and the sad strangled corpse I'd once seen dragged from a river.

I stared at the window. I could still feel the terror but, more importantly for my present ambitions, I pictured the details of window- and shutter-catches, engraved on my memory. I had made it my business to learn a range of skills in case I should ever again get stranded with no money and I knew I could get in if I could find a place where I could work unobserved for a while. I walked round the house and saw a side window facing the blank wall of the stable-block; ideal. It took less time than I had feared and I found myself in a library. That was a surprise; who would have thought the ape could read. I opened the door cautiously but there was no sound or light from any direction. The house smelled of beeswax and possessed a chill that spoke of several days without fires. I moved along the corridor, my soft soles noiseless on the polished floorboards. The salon door was locked but that did not delay me for long. The darkness was troubling me by now, not even real Forest Folk can see in complete blackness, but I could still recall the layout of the room and put my hand unerringly on the mantel.

What should I take? The temptation was to sweep the lot into my little padded sack; I owed the scum for the scars on my cheek and temple and for the old man I had been driven to knock over for his purse further down the road. I dismissed that foolishness; I would take one of the smaller pieces, that would be enough. I ran my hand along the shelf and lifted a long-necked vase. No, too unusual, I could not price it reliably. Next along was a goblet, a coat of arms deeply incised on its side. Too easily identifiable. I passed over a platter and some spoons that felt too light to be genuine and then found a small lidded tankard. It was plain, apart from scrolls on the handle and lid, but had a reassuring weight. The handle was smooth and fit neatly in my hand; it was just the sort if thing I would have liked for myself. It was towards the back of the shelf, behind two ornate wine jugs; did that mean it was less likely to be missed? Perhaps, but I intended to be long gone before then. I pocketed the tankard and lifted the remaining pieces to dust the shelf; no point in leaving clues and a dozy maid might not notice the loss for a few days.

By now my eyes were aching from straining in the dim light and I left rapidly the way I had come. Refastening the window took some time and the sky was starting to lighten by the time I returned to the inn. It occurred to me that some hapless footman or the like would get blamed for the theft but I cannot say that bothered me; serve them right for working for such a turd. I only hoped his anguish when he discovered the loss was as deep as I wanted. My gamble was paying off nicely so far. I got into my bed for what remained of the night and slept deep and dreamlessly.

The Chamber of Planir the Black,
in the Island City of Hadrumal,
12th of For-Autumn

'Share a bottle with an Archmage and you'll either be ruined or made for life – that's what they used to say, isn't it, Otrick?' The stout man speaking held out his glass for a refill and laughed fruitily at his own quip.

'I think those days were already long past when I first came here, Kalion.' Otrick poured him a full measure and then topped up his own drink, his steady hand belying the wrinkles carved in his face and the white hairs now outnumbering the grey in his steely hair and beard.

'How long ago was that, Cloud-Master?' the youngest man present asked, taking the bottle with a creditable attempt at ease, given the exalted company he found himself keeping.

Otrick's close-lipped smile was as about as revealing as a masquerader's guise. 'Longer ago than I care to remember, Usara,' he replied softly, raising his glass. His vivid blue eyes glinted under his angular brows.

'Anyway, Archmage, what was it you wanted to discuss?' Kalion half-turned on the deeply upholstered settle to address the neatly built man who was shuttering the tall windows and drawing the thick green curtains precisely together.

'Oh, it's nothing vital, Hearth-Master. You were in Relshaz for Solstice, weren't you? I was wondering if the antiquarians there have turned up anything interesting lately?' Planir lit a couple of oil-lamps and their yellow glow warmed the deep oak panelling around the room, a few gleams here and there revealing choice pieces of statuary in discreet niches. The soft light blurred the network of fine lines around the Archmage's

eyes and made him look barely a handful of years older than
Usara. He set a lamp down on the table.

'Do we want a fire, do you think?'

'I should think so,' Otrick said emphatically.

Kalion looked a little askance at the skinny old wizard,
dressed neatly if unfashionably in grey wool broadcloth. He
contented himself with loosening the neck of his own maroon
velvet gown, new from the tailor in the latest style and shade
and richly embroidered with a border of flames.

'You see, Usara thinks he may have turned up something
new but, equally, it may just be a waste of everyone's time.' The
Archmage snapped his fingers on a flash of red and dropped a
flame into the fire laid ready in the spotless grate. He drew in
the silken skirts of his own black robe and seated himself in a
high-backed chair, warming his glass in his long-fingered hands
as he leant back against the rich sage brocade. 'Sweetcake? Do
help yourselves, everyone.'

'What exactly is it you're studying, Usara? Remind me,'
Kalion asked the youthful wizard indistinctly round a mouthful
of fruit-and-honeycake.

Usara's thin face flushed brightly, the colour clashing with
his sandy hair and somewhat cruelly highlighting just how thin
it was becoming above his high forehead. 'I've been working on
the decline and fall of the Tormalin Empire for some seasons
now, Hearth-Master. I met some scholars from the University
of Vanam last year when they came to use the library at the
Seaward Hall and they invited me to use their archives.'

Kalion shrugged with evident disinterest, the gesture creas-
ing his chins unappealingly as he reached for more wine.
'So?'

Usara smoothed the linen ruffles at his neck, glancing
fleetingly at Planir, who smiled reassuringly over the rim of
his glass and inclined his sleek, dark head slightly.

'Go on,' the Archmage encouraged him.

'Well, when Sannin was there over the Winter Solstice, she
went to a celebration where the wines were flowing pretty
freely and tongues started getting loose as well.'

Otrick laughed abruptly, his thin face alight with mischief.

'If I know Sannin, that's not all that got loosened. She's a fun girl at a party.' He subsided at a glance from Planir but continued to chuckle into his straggly beard as he munched on a slice of cake.

Usara shot the old man an irritated look and spoke with a little more force. 'They started talking about history. Someone noticed her necklace, it's an heirloom piece, Old Tormalin, and one of the historians wondered what tales a necklace like that could tell, if only it could talk.'

Otrick coughed on his mouthful. 'That was an old excuse for looking down a girl's dress when I was a boy!'

Usara ignored him. 'There were scholars from all sorts of disciplines there, and a couple of wizards, and they started wondering if there could be any way to find out more about the original owners of antiquities.'

'What good would that do anyone?' Otrick frowned as he shook the empty bottle. 'Do you have another of these, Planir?'

The Archmage waved him to a collection of bottles on a gleaming sideboard but he kept his own grey eyes intent on Kalion.

Usara continued. 'Once they got talking, Sannin said, they started coming up with some interesting ideas for research.'

'Did they still look like good ideas when the wine had worn off and the headaches hit?' Otrick's tone was sarcastic.

'When she told us all this, we started to think about it ourselves. There are some old variants on scrying that we could try and some fragments of religious lore that we might be able to incorporate. We're coming up with some promising lines for further enquiry.' Usara leaned forward, face intent, unaware of Otrick's indignation at being talked over.

'You see, Hearth-Master, if we can find a way to use Tormalin antiquities to somehow look back through the generations, into the lives of ordinary people, we could have no end of new sources of historical information. Don't you see how it could help my studies? In all recorded history, the fall of the Tormalin Empire was the greatest cataclysm ever to befall a civilisation. If we could find clues to help us patch together the fragments of the written record—'

'None of which is of any more than passing interest and is of no use in the real world.' Kalion's disdain was clear as he reached for more cake and refilled his glass now that Otrick had located the corkscrew. 'Thank you, Cloud-Master.'

'Understanding our history is an essential foundation for looking to the future.' Usara's thin lips nearly vanished altogether as he squared his shoulders to contradict the larger man.

'Don't get pompous with me, young man. I can remember when you arrived here in your clay-stained apprentice rags,' Kalion said crushingly.

'Knowledge always has a value, Hearth-Master. It is—'

'Knowledge only has a value if it has an application.' Kalion spoke over Usara mercilessly. 'Why are we even discussing this, Archmage?' he demanded with a hint of exasperation.

Planir shrugged again and rubbed a hand over his smoothly shaven jaw. 'I was wondering if we should put some resources into following it up.'

'Oh, surely not.' Kalion looked as appalled as a man so well wined could hope to. 'There's so much else the Council needs to consider. You heard Imerald's account of how fast smelting is being developed in the north. That's a real advance, something we should be involved in. Look at the ways Caladhrian cattle stock is improving now that most of the Lords are enclosing their pastures. I could give you a handful more examples of other sciences where more progress has been made in the last generation than in the previous five—'

'Spare us the full speech, Hearth-Master,' Otrick yawned theatrically. 'We were at the last session of the Council, remember. We were listening.'

'You can't deny that some of my predecessors did take the isolation of senior wizardry rather too far, Cloud-Master.' Planir's rebuke was light but still unmistakable.

'That's what I've been saying for I don't know how many seasons.' The florid purple tinge on Kalion's cheekbones faded a little. 'Given the rate of the changes we're seeing on the mainland, if we don't find ourselves a role, we'll be left behind.

This prejudice against getting involved in politics, for example, is outdated and meaningless—'

'I'm not prejudiced. I just don't see the benefit to me of getting tangled up in helping to organise the boring little lives of the mundane. If I'm to spend my time on things that take me away from my own research and studies, it'll be on my terms and to achieve something I need.'

Otrick passed Kalion the wine which effectively diverted him. 'Anyway, save the speeches for the next session of Council, Hearth-Master. That's the place for important debate. Now, as far as I'm concerned, Usara, you can spend as many seasons as you like finding out who did what while the Empire was collapsing round their ears. What I want to know is whether this little scheme of yours is going to tell me anything about magical techniques and skills that were lost in the dark generations.'

'Now that would be knowledge worth having.' Kalion nodded emphatic agreement.

'I suppose we might discover such things, if we could work with artefacts that belonged to wizards . . .' Usara looked uncertainly towards Planir, '. . . if we can find a way of scrying into their activities.'

The Archmage leaned forward and refilled the younger mage's glass. 'If I were to support this project, I think I'd want to give it more focus and looking for lost magic seems most relevant.' Planir paused for moment and looked thoughtful. 'I think you have a valid point, Kalion. The time has come for the Council to consider our role in the wider scheme of things in the modern world. Equally, there's something in what Otrick says; if wizards are to become more involved in matters beyond this island, to avoid the mistakes of the past, we need to do so on our own terms.'

'If we were able to rediscover some of the magic lost during the disintegration of the Empire, we would certainly improve our bargaining position,' Otrick allowed.

'We could establish useful contacts if we were able to offer scholars solutions to some of the questions thrown up by the collapse of Old Tormalin power.' Usara spoke up boldly. 'Most of the tutors and court advisors to nobilities all the way across the mainland come from the various universities.'

'That's a fair point.' Planir looked enquiringly at Kalion. 'What do you think, Hearth-Master?'

'It might be worth looking into. What do you propose?' the stout mage asked cautiously.

'Hall records could give us the family names of the early wizards. We could enquire if those families have minor heirlooms they would be willing to sell,' Planir mused. 'Usara and his pupils could concentrate their researches on them.'

'It'll be a waste of time and coin,' Otrick said robustly. 'You'd be better off sending some agents into the mountains and getting some decent information about this blast-furnace or whatever it is they call it.'

'That does sound as if it could be a significant development, Cloud-Master,' Planir agreed. 'Still, if I can spare a couple of men, it shouldn't be hard to collect a few Empire antiquities with decent provenance. Don't you think? We would find out sooner if Usara's project has any value. Who knows, we might even uncover some valuable information on lost magic.'

'We might do nothing more than push up the price of Tormalin antiques and land ourselves with a room full of old pots and statues,' Otrick snorted.

'That is also possible,' Planir admitted. 'So, it's something to look at when we have resources to spare but hardly a priority now. Do you agree, Hearth-Master?'

'I suppose so.' Kalion still sounded dubious.

A timepiece on the mantel chimed four soft strokes and Kalion looked at it in some surprise. 'You'll have to excuse me, Archmage, I didn't realise it was so late.' He drained his glass and rose to his feet with some effort.

'The longer night chimes always catch me out after Solstice,' Otrick agreed, but showed no signs of moving.

'We must make time to discuss your Council speech in more detail, Kalion. Ask your senior pupil to check with Larissa to arrange a convenient time.' Planir bowed Kalion formally into the escort of the lamp-boy who had been dozing on the stairs. He closed the heavy oak door softly and then rapidly stripped off his ornately embroidered robe to reveal practical breeches and a light linen shirt which he covered with a worn and ink-stained chambercoat.

'I meant to ask you when you started using the same tailor as Kalion,' Otrick chuckled around the last mouthful of cake. 'I always say gowns are for girls in garlands.'

This time Planir's smile showed his teeth and, with the gleam in his eye, he looked positively predatory. 'Details are important, Otrick, you taught me that.'

'So did we dance your measure correctly, Archmage?' Much of Usara's diffidence had departed along with Kalion. He crossed to the sideboard and helped himself. 'Cordial, anyone?'

'I'll have some of the mint, thanks.' Planir lounged in his chair and stretched his soft leather boots out to the fire with an air of satisfaction. 'Yes, I think that went very well. If any more rumours about our little project surface, that story should cover them.'

'You think so?' Usara passed the Archmage a little crystal goblet. 'Kalion didn't seem all that convinced.'

'He didn't think it was worth much interest,' Planir corrected him. 'Which is what I hoped for.'

'He's got a lot of influence among the Council, being the senior Hearth-Master and all that goes with it.' Uncertainty continued to colour Usara's tone.

'He has, indeed.' Otrick nodded. 'He's also the man most people round here go to for gossip, isn't he?'

Comprehension dawned and Usara laughed. 'So if someone gets curious about what we're doing, they'll check with Kalion and he'll tell them he knows all about it and it's nothing of any significance.'

'Whereas few things attract more attention than rumours of a secret project with the personal interest of the Archmage and the oldest Cloud-Master,' Planir agreed, sipping his drink contentedly. 'You see, Usara, people have all sorts of ideas about the proper role of an Archmage but very few realise it's spending most of your time persuading people to do what you want them to do while making sure they think it was all their idea in the first place.'

'You certainly moved Kalion like a bird on a game board,' Usara acknowledged.

Otrick grinned wolfishly. 'Don't ever play White Raven with this man, 'Sar, I swear he could end up with the forest birds serving the raven rather than trying to drive him out.'

'I haven't played Raven in years, Cloud-Master.' Planir shook his head in mock sorrow. 'It rather lost its challenge after a few seasons as Archmage.'

Otrick rummaged in his breeches pocket for a little wash-leather pouch. 'So when will you be telling the Council the truth?' He popped a couple of leaves into his mouth and chewed with relish.

'When I have a full story to tell or when someone senior enough brings me a rumour I can't ignore.' Planir fixed Usara with a keen eye. 'I'd prefer it to be the former. How close are you to finding out what I need to know?'

Usara swallowed his drink with a hint of his former nervousness. 'We've managed to refine the methods of identifying the pieces we need.'

'About cursed time. Sending so-called merchants out with a sack of coin to buy up every piece of Old Empire tat they could find is what attracted attention in the first place,' Otrick snorted.

'That was unfortunate.' Usara faced the old mage with dignity. 'However, I don't recall you coming up with any better ideas.'

Planir forestalled any argument with a commanding hand. 'Given we've had people working on this for close on two seasons, I'd have been amazed if we'd got away with it any longer. Now, what results are you getting?'

'The information we're getting is very detailed, almost too much so. We need to place it in a context; it's the gaps in the written records that are holding us back at the moment.' Usara's frustration was evident.

'I think it might be time to get one of the Vanam Histories brought here,' Planir said thoughtfully. 'I'd like to see progress on this sooner rather than later.'

'We have asked but we haven't been able to persuade the

Mentors to release one to us.' Usara shuffled his feet unhappily at this admission.

'I imagine I'll have more success. An Archmage has all kind of powers, 'Sar, and actual wizardry is often the least important.' Planir's eyes shone in the lamplight. 'Have you heard from Casuel Devoir lately? When's he due back?'

'Equinox, I think,' Usara shrugged.

'I said he was a bad choice for this kind of work,' Otrick sniffed.

'Do we have a lot of choice? Casuel's had no pupillage for three seasons, so no one's missing him. He's bright enough and quite knowledgeable about the Old Empire, isn't he? It's not as if we've told any of them the full story.'

Planir slid a sideways smile towards Otrick. 'You remember that business at Summer Solstice a few years back? His determination to outdo Shivvalan should give him the sort of edge he'll need.'

'Ha!' Otrick's amusement came and went in an instant. 'If we need answers before the Council starts asking awkward questions, we must move faster. We need more people.'

Planir reached round behind his chair to take a sheaf of papers from a desk. 'I think I should be able to find three or four suitable agents without attracting too much notice.'

Usara frowned. 'They'll need to work with a mage. We'll have to find a handful or so who could be trusted with this but who aren't anyone's pupil at present.'

'Not necessarily. I got Shivvalan Ralsere hooked when he came to ask me about a pupillage. I could take on at least one more and I think it's about time we got Troanna involved. No one's going to comment if she takes on a couple, especially if they're recent arrivals,' Otrick suggested.

'True, I'll give it some thought,' Planir said thoughtfully. 'You'll need to find some scholars who can identify these trinkets as closely as possible, 'Sar.'

Otrick yawned and rubbed his eyes. 'You'll owe me if I have a headache tomorrow, Planir, I'm getting too old to match someone like Kalion cork for cork.'

'I'll turn the wine-merchant into a lizard if you feel bad in the morning, Cloud-Master,' the Archmage promised solemnly. 'Given the coin he took off me for that vintage, it'll be a pleasure.'

Otrick heaved a sigh and the animation left his face, his years plain to see for the first time.

'So what do we do when we've got the full story then? If half what we suspect turns out to be true, the mainlanders will be able to hear the uproar from Council clear across the gulf. Anyone wanting to find this particular, mystical, hidden island will just have to follow the noise.'

'A shock's greatest when it's unexpected.' Planir looked untroubled. 'I think I'll give Naldeth's projects some personal attention. That'll stop everyone sniggering behind his back and if his theories gain a little currency, you can offer him some co-operation, 'Sar. Then we can control how and when any new information becomes common knowledge.'

'If you say so.' The youthful mage's uncertainty was apparent.

'You're juggling firebrands,' Otrick warned dourly.

Planir shrugged and rose to replenish his cordial. 'That's as good a description as any of being an Archmage. Anyway, that wolf may well be a dog in the daylight; we might have nothing to worry about.'

'I'd give you better odds on a winning spread of runes first throw,' Otrick muttered.

'So you think you've got everything under control.' Usara looked to Planir for reassurance.

The Archmage's smile glinted white and even. 'I do hope not, 'Sar, that's the last thing I want. I just set things in motion; what I'm watching for is the loose rune that can turn the game for us. We all have to look for that one opportunity and make sure we seize it.'

The Packhorse Tavern, on the Col Road
south of Ambafost, Ensaimin,
13th of For-Autumn

The noises of the inn woke me, the rattle of harness and stamp of hooves in the yard and the sounds of conversation and drinking below. I checked the sun as I dressed for my role as poor but comparatively honest villager; it was quite a lot later than I had intended to rise but I felt refreshed despite my night excursion. Cold water woke me up fully and I checked the pouch under my pillow to reassure myself that it had not all been a wishful dream. The tankard was there and in the daylight I could see I had chosen a fine piece. The silver had the rich sheen of old Tormalin work and the maker's mark was distinct and central on the base, another good sign. I did not recognise it but silver's not my thing; I'm better on paintings. Should I take it to Col myself if the market was rising? I thought about it but the whole idea had been to get some money so I could wait for Halice and, in any case, since it was such a good piece, I did not want to be the one left holding it if the theft was noticed and the local Watch came looking. This merchant, whoever he might be, could have it and welcome. All I wanted was the pay-off.

I breakfasted rapidly and, taking out my hired horse, rode for Ambafost, cursing the inconvenience of unaccustomed skirts. The road was busy now it was past mid-morning and the previous days of rain had given way to sunshine. Farm carts and local carriages were rumbling along, occasionally overtaken by horsemen in twos and threes or delayed by a plodding mule train. This was both good and bad; more potential witnesses to identify me if someone came looking, but by the same token more faces for me to get lost amongst. I wondered about changing inns but there was the problem of Halice; I didn't want to miss any message she might send. It was market day and the square in Ambafost was packed; stalls offered everything from vegetables and meat to Dalasorian glassware and Aldabreshin silks; some merchants were clearly trading their way down to Col. People jostled and shoved and shouted, the mêlée smelling of damp wool and leather mingling with the scents of baking bread overhead and animal dung underfoot. I like this kind of market; they offer excellent cover. A few beggars were trying their luck without much success but there was no sign of any Watch coming to move them on which I was happy to see.

I found the Running Hound easily and forced my way through the crowd. Several carriers' coaches had just arrived and there were passengers shouting at each other as they tried to find out when the next stage of their journey would begin: some needed to change routes, some wanted food, children were crying and one couple decided to start a major domestic dispute in the centre of the hall. A Rationalist was being completely ignored as she tried to find someone to bore with her theories on why advances in magic and science meant no one need bother with the gods nowadays.

'Where's the merchant interested in buying antiquities?' I grabbed a passing potman by the elbow.

'Private parlour behind the gentles' bar.' He shook off my hand and went on his way without even looking at me.

The clamour shrank to a murmur in the tap-room reserved for gentlefolk; there were settles here and sweet herbs among the rushes on the floor. The barkeeper gave me a sharp look but since I was evidently not a farmer or stockman, decided to give him the benefit of the doubt. I gave him my brightest smile, the one that says cute but dim.

'I just got into town and someone told me there's a merchant looking to buy antiquities. Could I speak to him please?'

'I'll let him know you're here. He's busy at the moment.' He polished the already spotless pewter of the goblet he was holding.

I did not want to force the issue so repeated the smile. 'I'll have a cup of wine while I wait then. Have one yourself.' I dropped a Mark on the counter and took the wine he poured, without waiting for change.

As I sat in a discreet corner, I saw two women come out of the parlour together; one with a smug smirk, the other trying to conceal her chagrin.

'It's a shame, dear,' the first said to her stout companion. 'Your father always swore those stones were genuine.'

The woman smoothed the blue brocade of her gown. 'The sentimental value remains. It's not as if I needed to sell like you.'

The first woman's lips narrowed. 'Times are changing, dear. There's no room for sentiment in business nowadays.'

They swept out of the street door together and I caught the barkeeper's eye as he put a flagon of wine and some goblets on a tray. He gestured to me and I headed over.

'You'd better not be wasting his time,' he warned as he opened the door for me.

'Good morning, my name's Terilla.'

I fixed on the bright smile again and looked at the three men sitting across the table in the small sun-filled room. In the centre a heavily built man in red broadcloth leant back against the wall and looked at me unsmiling. He was dark of hair and beard, his rings were heavy gold without gems and unless I was mistaken he had a knife up his left sleeve. I could not see his boots under the table but he struck me as the type to have more than one blade about him; unusual in a merchant. His companions were an ill-assorted pair; to his right sat a wiry type in rough leathers over green linen. It did not suit his sallow skin and long black hair but he did not look the kind to care. He was idly casting runes as he sat, one hand against the other, and my fingers itched. The other one looked as if he had wandered in here by mistake but he was drinking wine so he had to be part of the team. Perhaps he was an apprentice of some sort: he was certainly young enough. He was wearing sensible brown homespun, close-cropped fair hair and an earnest expression; I doubted he was carrying a blade, he looked the sort to stab himself in the leg with it.

The silence was getting awkward so I dropped the smile and opened my belt pouch.

'I just got in on the coach from Sowford. Someone said you were buying Tormalin pieces and I wondered what you might give me for this.' I put the tankard on the table.

The man in red looked at it but did not pick it up.

'Where are you heading?' The rune-caster swept up his bones and gave me a frank and friendly smile that I trusted about as much as my own.

'I'm travelling to Oakmont, to join Lord Elkith's Players.' Both places were several days' travel east and west respectively and he was welcome to try finding me later in a travelling troupe of actors. I held his gaze but out of the corner of my eye could see the quiet lad pick up the tankard and start examining it.

'Working with players must be exciting. What do you do?' He leaned forward, all interest.

Don't overdo it, pal, I thought, I don't look that fresh off the farm surely.

'I'm a singer,' I replied. That much at least was true, it's another of those skills I mentioned. Despite the shades of my mother's disapproval, I'd learned a good repertoire of ballads and some basic dance tunes for the lute.

'Will you be travelling to Col for the fair?'

The boss was looking expectantly at the lad. Was he some kind of expert? He looked rather young.

'I'm not sure.' I thought it was about time I asked some questions of my own. 'Are you looking to trade at the fair? Perhaps I should take Grandad's tankard there myself.'

I saw the shadow of concern cross the lad's freckles. He looked at his boss and something unspoken passed between them. It struck me as a pity I could not get him in a game, he'd lose his breeches with a face like that.

'It was your grandfather's? How do you come to be looking to sell it?' The boss smiled at me in what he clearly thought was encouragement. I giggled: wearing skirts does that to me nowadays.

'Oh it's mine all right,' I lied fluently. 'He gave it to me on his deathbed, for my dowry. I wouldn't sell it but you see, I need to get away from home. I want to sing but my father wants me to marry his partner's son. He's a clothier and fat and boring and only interested in wools and satins. I had to get away.'

Freckle-face's mouth was open and his expression was full of sympathy but the other two looked less impressed. Perhaps I'd laid it on a bit thick; I blame the dress.

'So how much would you give me?'

'What do you think it's worth?' The man in red leaned forward and I took a pace back, his gaze was uncomfortably piercing.

'Um, well, I'm not really sure.' Should I take a low price and get out or show them I knew its real value?

'I'll give you six Marks for it.'

'Caladhrian or Tormalin?' Either way, the offer was a joke.

'Tormalin of course,' he assured me; as if the six extra pennies would make any real difference.

'The reeve always said it was very valuable.' I looked up, wide-eyed and woebegone. 'Isn't it?'

Freckles shifted in his chair and would have spoken but Lanky in the green silenced him with a gesture. The boss sat back and ran a hand over his beard.

'It's worth what I'm willing to pay for it,' he said silkily, 'and that's six Marks, which I feel is more than generous, since I know it's stolen.'

Shit. Now I was looking to get out of there as fast as possible. Should I try and bluff it through? No point, I decided swiftly.

'Fine. Give me the coin and I'll be on my way. I've got a coach to catch.'

Lanky drew a swift pattern in some spilled wine. There was not a soul in the room beyond us four yet the bolts on the door slid shut behind me. A chill went right through me. Double shit.

'I'm sure you've got time for a little chat,' the boss said smoothly, making no move to get any money out. 'Why don't you tell us where you got this? You could tell us your real name too since we're here.'

'I got lucky in a game a few nights back. Some bloke in an inn wagered the tankard; I didn't know it was lifted.'

The skinny one poured me some wine but I ignored him. Catch me drinking with a wizard; not likely.

'Not good enough, I'm afraid.' The boss sipped his wine and wiped his beard. 'This tankard is part of a small but valuable collection belonging to a particularly unpleasant wool merchant in Hawtree. You see, we approached him but his price was too high.'

'Why did you choose this particular piece to steal?' Freckle-face could contain himself no longer and the boss scowled at the interruption. I looked at the windows but did not fancy my chances of getting out fast.

'Relax, we're not going to hurt you.' Lanky pushed the wine towards me again. That was all very well for him to say. I do not trust wizards; not at all. It's not that I believe all the ballads: the immunity to pain, the immense powers, the reading minds and so on. The few I've known have been handy with some spells but as vulnerable as anyone else to a knife in the ribs. As far as I'm concerned, wizards are dangerous because their concerns are exclusively their own. They will be looking for something, travelling somewhere, after someone to hear his news or just to find out who his father was, don't ask me why. Whatever they want, they'll walk over hot coals to do it and if you look handy, they'll lay you down and use you as a footbridge. I gave Lanky a hard stare back.

'We won't but the local Watch might have other ideas.' The boss lifted the tankard. 'He's an influential man. Catching the thief would do the Commander a lot of good.'

I was not going to reply; he had the air of a man making an opening bid and I would bet I had played in more high-stakes games than he had.

The silence lengthened. I could hear the din of the market-place outside; traders shouting their wares, beasts neighing and carts clattering over the cobbles. Two drunks lurched past the window, giggling helplessly, their shadows falling across us all waiting, motionless. The tension grew so thick you could have stuck a spoon in it and spread it on bread. The boss was impassive, Lanky smiled and Freckles looked frankly miserable.

'Of course, we need not tell the Watch anything.' Lanky grinned and lifted the untouched goblet to me in a toast. The boss scowled at him but went on.

'You see, there are other pieces we would like to acquire whose owners are not keen to sell and I wonder if we could come to some arrangement. You clearly have talents we could use.'

Good, we were down to business. 'Why can't your tame conjuror just magic them out for you?'

'I need to know exactly where they are and to get a sight of them,' Lanky shrugged. 'Can't always be done.'

So, no problem with ethics here. That made things easier.

'What you're saying is work for you or you'll hand me over to the Watch and let them cut my hands off.' Freckles winced and I marked him down as the weak link in the chains they were trying to lock on me.

'Basically, yes.' The boss's stare was getting distinctly unfriendly.

'We'd make it worth your while,' Lanky assured me. 'You'd get a good percentage of the value.'

'Fat lot of use that'll be if I get caught.'

'I'll be able to get you out of any lock-up. Once I know you a little better, I'll be able to track you like a trail-hound.'

That was a thrilling prospect, a wizard on my tail whom I would not be able to shake off.

'What if some outraged noble sticks his sword into me to save the Watch the worry?' I challenged. 'Can you bring me back from Saedrin's lock-up too? I didn't think wizards did resurrections.'

'If you're good enough to find this,' the boss picked up my tankard again, 'you're good enough to take the time and care to not get caught.'

He laced his fingers and cracked his knuckles with a satisfied air which gave me one more reason to dislike him. 'In any case, I don't think you're in any position to argue the point, are you?'

Sadly, I had to agree. We could spend all day trading clever remarks, with Lanky playing friendly house-dog to the boss's nasty street-cur but I was not going to get out of here before they agreed to let me go, whatever wild ideas keeping me in here gave the innkeeper. I could give them a flat refusal but I did not like the idea of being handed over to the Watch. I could probably sob my way to a flogging or the pillory but what if the Commander decided to hang on to me until Turd-breath the would-be rapist got home? I kept my gambling face nailed on but I was cursing myself: that's where revenge gets you, you dozy bitch.

'All right,' I said slowly. I took the wine, drained the goblet and refilled it. That made me feel better. 'So what's your business? You're not just buying and selling with a wizard and a scholar in tow. What's so important that you have to hire a wall-crawler?'

'You need not worry about that. My name is Darni and my companions are Geris and Shivvalan.'

'Shiv, please,' Lanky smiled. 'Your name?'

'Terilla, I told you.' That was my aunt who had married a baker and grown as round as one of his loaves.

Shiv shook his head apologetically. 'You're lying again.'

That could get tiresome; I decided to think very carefully before volunteering any information about myself. Still, they had to call me something. Why not the real thing?

'I'm Livak.' I raised my goblet in an ironic toast and Shiv returned it.

Darni snorted. 'Right, we'll get you a room here. We're moving on tomorrow; in the meantime, keep yourself to yourself.'

I shook my head. 'Sorry, I'm staying at an inn back up the high road. I'll see you in the morning.'

Darni looked at me contemptuously. 'Don't ever make the mistake of thinking I'm stupid.'

'I've got luggage there and a bill to pay,' I snapped back.

'I'll go with her to collect it,' Shiv volunteered and Darni's angry colour subsided.

'While I'm out, you can decide on a proper deal for my services. I'll owe you for not ringing the Watch bell on me over the tankard but don't push it. I want half the value of everything I lift, for a start.'

Darni evidently didn't like that idea.

'Be back before dusk,' he said curtly.

Shiv unbolted the door – normally this time – and waved me through with a courtly gesture.

'So what were your plans?' Shiv sat on his solid black cob like a sack of grain as we headed out along the high road. I noted the worn gear and the droop of the tired horse's head. My hired horse on the other hand was fresh and keen; I pictured the road ahead in my mind and thought about a good spot where I could kick into a gallop and lose him. I'd wager my abilities at getting lost against his tracking skills, whatever they might be. They were welcome to my luggage at the inn; they would find no clues about me in it.

We waited for a heavily laden wagon to negotiate a rutted wallow.

'I hope we haven't inconvenienced you too much, Livak.'

That nearly did it; he was setting himself up as a handy target for my frustration.

'Were you travelling to Col for the Fair? Wouldn't thieving there risk falling foul of the local talent?'

I ignored him. A donkey began making a fuss about something behind us and, as Shiv turned, I dug my heels into my job-horse's flanks. Fresh from days in the stable, he stretched out eagerly for a gallop and I lay down on his neck to avoid the branches.

Suddenly he came to a crashing halt and I hit the ground hard; I've never managed that 'relax as you fall' trick horse traders tell you about. For one awful moment I thought the horse must have put a foot in a rabbit hole; I did not want the poor beast's death on my conscience. After a moment he scrambled to his feet; I did the same. Nothing broken, thank Halcarion, but I'd be black and blue.

'Sorry about that, but I don't think Darni would be too pleased if I lost you.'

I looked up to see Shiv sitting alert on his big black steed with green light glowing round his hands.

'You bastard, I could have been killed.' I spat leaf mould.

'No, I made sure of that.' The concern in his voice sounded almost genuine. 'I don't blame you for trying, Livak,' he assured me.

'Easy for you to say.' I swore as the horse shifted and had me dancing on one foot, the other in the stirrup iron.

'Here.' Shiv caught the reins. 'Just give me your word that you won't try that again.'

'Thanks,' I said stiffly. 'All right, I'll swear.' I rattled off the standard vow to Misaen.

'I can appreciate you being annoyed at Darni dragging you into all this.' The wizard persisted in trying to be friendly. I was having none of it.

'Oh, can you really? Has he threatened you to get your co-operation? Have you had your plans completely ripped up? Are your friends going to worry themselves sick when you don't turn up as expected?'

He looked uncomfortable. 'We really do need your help.'

'Can't get rich enough? I thought wizards were supposed to keep honest with their magic. Isn't that what stops us ordinary folk from stoning you all as a flaming menace?'

'This is not about money. We're buying up special pieces for the Archmage.'

I could smell the scorching as those hot coals got closer.

'I don't want to know,' I snapped. 'I'll do a couple of jobs for your boss to even the scales, but if you come sniffing after me, you'll find trouble.'

He dropped his gaze in the face of my challenging stare. 'Fair enough. By the way, Darni is not my boss. I can overrule him if he tries to take unfair advantage.'

That could be interesting to see, a wizard's idea of unfair.

'What about the boy? Does he get a say?' Let him think he was winning me over, see what else he'd tell me.

'Geris?' Shiv laughed. 'He wouldn't dare.'

'Is he a mage or what? Is he your apprentice?'

'No, he's what you guessed, a scholar. He's from the University at Vanam, an expert on Tormalin art.'

The world can be a very small place at times; I'm from Vanam originally and I know the grim facade of the University. It's one of those places that only looks good in soft light or snow. I have no idea what the inside is like; it's strictly for the wealthy who can afford to send surplus sons and daughters off to learn Saedrin knows what useless stuff. I decided to cosy up to Geris if I got the chance and see what I could get out of him. I did not figure he would take much unpeeling.

'What about Darni, then? Is he a mage?'

'No, not really.'

'What's that supposed to mean? I thought you got born a wizard.'

'We do in so far as elemental affinity is innate, but it's not as simple as that.'

'I beg your pardon?'

Shiv had the grace to look abashed. 'Sorry. A wizard's power comes from the elements; the ability to affect an element is what makes you a wizard and that's something you're born with. It comes from within; we're still trying to establish how, and it varies in strength. Really powerful mages are quite rare in fact, and since most people only have one affinity, that limits them in any case.'

'So what about Darni?' I persisted.

'He has a double affinity which is unusual, but it's very weak. His parents live in Hadrumal; his mother cooks for one of the Halls and his father's a baker. If he'd lived anywhere else, no one would have noticed his talent. He'd just have been a chap with a knack for starting fires in difficult conditions and a better-than-usual weather sense.'

I'd never really thought about Hadrumal, fabled city of the Archmage, having cooks and bakers. It rather undermined all the tales told in lofty ballads; I wondered who did the cleaning!

'Once it was clear his talents were going nowhere, he started working for the Archmage's agents,' Shiv went on. 'This is his first mission on his own, so he's looking to prove himself on several levels.'

'What are Archmage's agents?' I exclaimed.

Shiv gave me a sideways look. 'Planir doesn't sit in a lofty tower in Hadrumal staring into a scrying bowl to get his information.'

Well, that was a cheery thought. One of the few good things about wizards is that the really dangerous ones stay safely out of the way on their lost island.

'So where do you fit in?' I eyed Shiv suspiciously.

'I am a wizard of the Seaward Hall, an adept of water with the air as my secondary focus. I am a member of the Advisory Circle to the Great Council.'

Well, that was all so much goose-grease as far as I was concerned. 'Which means?'

'It means most wizards around here will bow and scrape and do their best to find out just how close to Planir I really am. Back in Hadrumal, I'm a middling fish in a busy pond.'

The inn where all this nonsense had started came into view.

'You wait outside and I'll settle up and pack.'

Shiv shook his head. 'I'll come in. We'll eat before we head back.'

I glared at him, irritated; when I give my word, I keep it. Who knows, Misaen might really exist and I don't fancy fiery dogs chasing me through the Otherworld when I'm dead. I'm going to have to do enough fast talking to Saedrin as it is. I had wanted to see if Halice had managed to get a letter through and to leave message for her in turn.

'You're going to have to trust me sometime,' I snapped.

'I'm hungry,' Shiv said mildly.

I stalked ahead, feeling a little foolish. The tousled blonde wench behind the bar counter smiled at Shiv, who smirked back and trotted out some line calculated to appeal to that type. I left them to it and found the innkeeper tapping a cask in the cellar.

'I need to move on, so I'll pay my reckoning now. Can I leave the horse at the Running Hound?'

'Fair enough. Three Marks will cover it.'

I opened my belt-pouch and paid the man. This inn was not cheap but the landlord's determined lack of curiosity meant Halice and I had used it more than once before. Look on the bright side, I told myself, if you had got away earlier, you'd have had to leave a bad debt here which would have fouled the nest for the future.

'Have there been any messages for me?'

He shook his head.

'Saedrin's stones!' What had happened to Halice? Apart from anything else, I wanted someone I trusted to know what had happened to me.

'Can I leave a letter, and some money?' We had done this before and I knew the man could be trusted.

'Sure.'

I went to my room and packed swiftly. If it were not for the nagging worry about Halice, I would have been running my mind over all the possibilities in this unexpected turn of events. I wrote Halice a short note full of gambler's slang and private allusions and sealed an Empire Crown into the wax. It was the best I could do but I was still not happy.

'Writing to someone?' Shiv entered without knocking.

'Do I need your permission? Do you want to read it?' Being startled made me shrill.

'That's not necessary.' He flushed and turned on his heel. Interesting, I had managed to shake that irritating self-possession and I had not even been trying.

We ate in silence and rode out, Shiv kicking the cob into a trot.

'The letter was to my partner. We were supposed to meet up at that inn.' If I was stuck with this trio for the present, what with Darni's attitude and the lad's meekness, I figured I would rather have Shiv's friendly face back.

His back relaxed and he reined in until I drew level.

'Partner? Lover?' He raised an eyebrow.

I laughed. 'Strictly business. Her name's Halice.'

'So, does she . . . er . . .' he fumbled for words, 'dispose of your . . . um . . . acquisitions?'

About to take offence, I realised his error. 'No, I'm not

a window-cracker except in special circumstances. We play the runes.'

'I'll give you a game sometime.'

'Play with someone who can see right through the bones? Not likely!' I spoke before I could stop myself but Shiv did not take umbrage.

'If you make a living playing the runes and you work with a friend, I don't suppose the bones always fall without a little help,' he observed. 'You won't use your skills, I won't use mine. Deal?'

'Deal.' Actually the prospect was an interesting one.

'So when's your friend due?'

'Overdue already, I'm afraid. That's why I lifted that cursed cup; I was running short with the delay.'

Shiv reined to a halt. 'Would you like to know what has happened to your mate?'

I gaped at him. 'What do you mean?'

'If you've got something belonging to her, or something she's handled regularly, I should be able to find her.' I was relieved to see his smile again. 'It's part of the trail-dog act.'

'Sure.' This I had to see. I dug in my saddlebags and found Halice's preferred set of bones. 'These any good?'

'Fine.' Shiv caught the pouch as I tossed them over and turned his horse off the road.

I followed, consumed with curiosity as he dismounted next to a large puddle. He rummaged in a pocket and uncorked a small bottle of blue liquid. He squatted down and poured a few drops on to the surface of the water. I knelt beside him, wide-eyed as the puddle began to glow with a green light.

Shiv closed his eyes and grasped the runes tight; the same eerie radiance gathered round his fist and I shivered involuntarily. Magelight is what distinguishes the real from the fake and I had only seen it a few times before. I've seen a fair few more claim to be mages and it's remarkable what reasons they come up with to explain why they must suppress the outward signs of their magic. Shiv breathed deeply and the glow of the magic round his hand reached out to the pool.

'Look in the water,' he commanded, opening his eyes.

I obeyed and could not restrain an exclamation. 'That's her, that's Halice.' I stared at the image; it was like looking through thick glass, but she was clearly recognisable. I bit my lip; she was in a bed, eyes closed and hair tangled over her sweaty face. Her right leg was splinted and bandaged from hip to foot; this did not look good. Blood stained the dressings; that leg was a mess and no mistake.

'She's hurt,' Shiv observed unnecessarily. 'Can you tell where she is?'

I peered intently at the blurred image, searching for any clue, but could find none. 'It's an inn of some sort but I can't tell you where.'

Shiv drew some lines in the water, and the reflection shifted and moved. Have you ever been on a wagon looking backward when it's going at the gallop? You know the way everything gets smaller? That's as best as I can describe the way the picture changed. In a few seconds, we were looking at the outside of the inn. I breathed a sigh of relief.

'It's the Green Frog in Middle Reckin, I'd know that buttercross anywhere.' It was a good enough inn and more importantly, the small town had a reliable apothecary. Our associates, the brothers Sorgrad and Sorgren, had introduced us to him when a rather complex enterprise had left me with a gashed arm.

Shiv's brow wrinkled. 'That's on the Selerima road, isn't it? Just past Three Bridges?'

I nodded. 'Why?'

'I know someone who lives just beyond. I can ask him to make sure your friend's taken care of.'

Halice would hardly thank me for handing her over to a wizard but equally I did not think she would be too keen on dying of wound-rot or a fever.

'Could he take her some money and make sure the apothecary treats her? I'm good for it if he'll wait a while.'

Shiv nodded. 'Of course. He has some healing skills himself as well.'

I took a deep breath; this trust had to go both ways after all. I'd seen people crippled for life by breaks like that.

'Can you write to him? A carrier should be heading for Selerima today or tomorrow and could take the letter.'

'No need.' Shiv smiled and raised his arms above his head. Faint blue-green light hovered round his head and followed the breeze off down the road. His eyes were open but vacant; I waved a hand in front of them but he did not even blink, his mind leagues away. This was trust with a vengeance; I could have stuck a knife in his ribs as he stood there. Well, I could have tried, I thought; surely any wizard with a penny weight of sense would have some defence against that kind of thing. At very least, I could be mounted and lost in the trees in an instant. Let him try tracking me then.

There are times when I wish I had done just that. My mother always said curiosity would get me hanged one day. But I was intrigued by this whole set-up now, I wanted to know what was bringing together valuable antiquities, Archmage's agents and scholars from the University. I was not just a gambler; we had friends like Charoleia whose role as 'Lady Alaric the dispossessed noblewoman' had netted us handsome profits in various places. Information and especially advance knowledge of significant happenings could make me rich, and the Archmage's involvement had to be significant, didn't it? Halice wasn't going to be going anywhere for a good while and I make a rotten nurse, so I didn't see any profit to be made from sitting and holding her hand while her leg knitted.

Maybe this gamble would turn a profit after all.

The Old Tun Tavern, the Hanchet Road
east of Oakmont,
13th of For–Autumn

Casuel looked round the small room and sniffed. Adequate, he supposed, it would suffice. He stripped the soft, worn linen sheets from the bed and dumped them heedlessly in a corner. There was no sign of vermin, he was pleased to see, but it never hurt to take precautions. Examining the horsehair mattress carefully before remaking it with his own crisp linen, he sprinkled vinegar-water liberally around the bedstead.

He heard a knock and a muffled question through the door.

'I'm sorry, could you repeat that?' Casuel opened up, striving to keep his voice light and to hide his disdain for the grizzled peasant bowing and scraping before him. There was no point in aggravating the fellow, after all. One has to be courteous to the lower classes, he reminded himself.

The innkeeper made a rapid comment in incomprehensible dialect to the lad holding the jug of hot water and they both stifled a grin. 'I said,' the old man went on with heavy emphasis, 'will your honour be dining in the common room tonight or do you want to hire the parlour?' There was a lascivious hint in his smile.

'We will dine alone, as is customary when travelling with a well-born young lady.' Casuel spoke slowly to emphasise the purity of his own diction. The example of a native-born Tormalin should show these rustics what a bastard garble they were making of his noble tongue, he thought with satisfaction.

'As your honour wishes.' The old man gestured the younger

out of the bedroom, drawing the door closed but neglecting quite to shut it.

Casuel moved to latch it with a hiss of irritation and scowled to hear the two daring to discuss him as they clattered down the stairs.

'What do you think his business is then, Uncle? You reckon he's selling 'owt from those books and the like?'

'He won't do much trade unless he mends his manners, for all his fancy clothes. He couldn't sell garbage to a goat with that attitude.'

'So who's the lassie? Reckon he's dipping his quill there?'

'She don't look the type to me, too young, too quiet. Wouldn't fight a mouse for its cheese, that one.'

Casuel slammed the door to with a violence that made his candle flicker. He paused for a moment, deciding what he should have said to the insolent youth, then stripped off his shirt to wash away the grime of the day. Shuddering at the memory of the leagues spent crammed into a carriers' coach with Raeponin only knew what class of people, he scrutinised his white arms and rather narrow chest first, somewhat mollified at finding no flea-bites. Whisking soap to a foam with his silver-mounted brush, he lathered his face briskly.

Casuel held his polished steel mirror up, angling it to get the best light. He studied himself, drawing comfort from the aristocratic lines of his brow and jaw. The blood of Devoir still marked its sons with the faces of ancient power, he thought with returning good humour. He drew the fine steel blade down carefully, to make sure none of that noble – if no longer ennobled – blood marked his towel.

Turning to his bag for his toiletries, he looked at the modest selection of faded volumes stacked neatly on the scuffed table next to a smaller, uneven heap of parchments. His self-possession wilted a little; it would be better to have rather more to present to Usara on his return to Hadrumal, wouldn't it? He combed his wavy brown hair back thoughtfully.

A timid hand tapped at the door. 'Come in.'

Allin peered hesitantly round the door before entering.

'The inn-lady said dinner was ready to serve.' She bobbed a half-curtsey, caught herself and blushed furiously.

'I've told you, Allin, there's no need to do that.' Casuel tried to curb his impatience, not wanting to provoke another weeping fit in the girl, especially not when they were alone in his bedchamber, he with no shirt on.

'Sorry, Messire Devoir.' Allin ducked her head and smoothed her skirts unnecessarily but her voice stayed just about level, if all but inaudible.

'No need to apologise,' Casuel said in what he imagined to be a kindly tone. 'Remember, to be a mage is to command respect. You should accustom yourself to it.'

He pulled a clean shirt from his bag, frowning at the creases. 'Is your bedchamber satisfactory?'

'Oh, yes.' Allin twisted her plump hands around each other. 'Though I would be happy to sleep in the women's room, if that would suit better.'

'Your days of sharing beds with your sisters are behind you, let alone with strangers in the common dormitory.' Casuel brushed some dust from the sleeve of his coat. 'Let us go down to dinner. I'll show you the book I bought today.'

He picked up a couple of volumes and some notes.

Allin closed her mouth on whatever she had been about to say and took his arm obediently, scurrying rather to keep up with Casuel. No more than average height, he still topped her by a head or more. He smiled down at her and wondered again how much irritation he had let himself in for. Surely the girl should have been delighted at the prospect of a room to herself; she couldn't ever have had such privacy before.

He was pleasantly surprised with the parlour, which was neatly if plainly furnished. As they seated themselves at the old-fashioned table, the door opened and a fat woman swung it aside with her hips, hands occupied with a laden tray.

'Beg pardon, your honour.' The woman bobbed a perfunctory curtsey and swept Casuel's books and papers aside to make room for her burden.

'Let me do that!' Casuel snapped, snatching a precious volume away from the danger of slopping soup.

'There's broth, roast fowl, a mutton pudding, some cheese and an apple flummery,' the woman said with satisfaction. 'Eat hearty, my duck, you could do with some flesh on them shanks.'

Casuel opened his mouth but was unable to think of a dignified retort before the dame swept out again in a bustle of homespun skirts. The savoury smells from the table set his stomach clamouring with reminders about how long it had been since breakfast.

'This looks very good,' he said with some surprise.

Allin leaped to her feet and went to serve him some chicken.

'Do sit down!' Casuel snapped, immediately regretting it as her eyes filled. She ducked her face, leaving him with a view of braids neatly coiled and pinned around the top of her head.

Casuel heaved a sigh of exasperation. 'You must understand, Allin. You are mage-born, you have a rare and special talent. I understand this is all new and somewhat alarming, but I will take you back to Hadrumal with me and you can apprentice to one of the Halls. Your life has changed and for the better, believe me. I know it will take time to accustom yourself to the idea but you are no longer the disregarded youngest daughter whom everyone orders about. Now eat some supper.'

He pushed the tureen towards her and, after a long moment, Allin dabbed at her eyes with the edge of her shawl and hesitantly ladled herself some soup. They ate in awkward silence.

Allin broke it with a hesitant murmur which Casuel didn't quite catch, her Lescari accent still oafish to his ear.

'Sorry?'

'I wondered when we would be going to Hadrumal.' Allin peeped up from under her fringe.

A gust of wind rattled the shutters, and the gold embossed on the tattered spine of one of his recent acquisitions gleamed in a flicker of candlelight. Casuel's mouthful of mutton pudding suddenly tasted leaden and fatty. It was an undeniably old copy of Minrinel's Intelligencer. The notes in the margins looked interesting, but it was hardly a rare book. He pushed the mutton aside.

'I don't think it will be until after Equinox.' He spooned up flummery absently. 'I need to have something worthwhile for Usara.'

'Is he a very great mage?' Allin asked with some awe.

Casuel could not help a laugh. 'Not exactly. He's not that much older than me, and hardly what you'd call a commanding personality, he's a senior wizard in the Terrene Hall, where I study, but with a seat on the Council and rumour suggests he has the Archmage's ear from time to time.'

'And you work for him?'

'It's not as simple as that.' Casuel sipped some ale with a shudder of longing for a decent wine. 'He's probably testing me to see if I'm worth a pupillage, the opportunity of working with him on a special project.'

He nodded confidently to himself. 'I'm Tormalin-born, the earth is my element, as is his. Who better to help him research the end of the Empire? I'll wager I'll know more about the last days of the Empire than any five Council members he could name.'

'The books you bought from my father are for him?'

'That's right.' Casuel stifled the unworthy thought that the price for those undeniably desirable volumes was proving higher than he had anticipated. He had thought he was getting a bargain; after all, the man had been desperate to turn what valuables he had salvaged into solid coin before winter set in. Driven out of their Lescar home by the uncertain currents of the summer's fighting, Allin's parents were struggling to provide for their numerous brood when they had heard about the travelling scholar interested in purchasing books.

Still, once Casuel had realised that the child who was always called to light the stove was mage-born, he could hardly have left her there. Besides, having one mouth fewer to feed was as good as coin in the hand for her harried father. Especially this particular mouth, he noted, watching Allin finish the flummery with inelegant haste.

He took another drink and leaned forward, succumbing to the temptation to confide in someone.

'The problem is, I rather think I'm not the only one being

sent to the mainland in connection with Usara's projects. Once he'd approached me, I made it my business to keep a weather eye on him as well as his acknowledged pupils. Various people had conversations which could have meant something or nothing, it's hard to tell.'

He poked at the cheese with his knife and sniffed it doubtfully; it looked too much like the stuff his mother used to bait traps for his peace of mind.

'I can't decide what to do for the best. It might be to my advantage to be the first back, with a modest start and some good leads, because then Usara might retain me on a more formal basis, sign me to an acknowledged pupillage. On the other hand, with the Equinox coming up, there'll be all the various fairs, people buying and selling all manner of things, scribes with stocks of random volumes and so forth. It might well be worth waiting. I could find something really impressive.'

Casuel jabbed his knife into the cheese with savage irritation and pushed his chair back abruptly, rocking the table violently.

'Though I'd probably return to find Shivvalan Ralsere had come up with the self-same thing the day before.'

'You don't seem to like him very much,' Allin ventured timidly.

'I have nothing against the man personally,' Casuel lied firmly. 'It's just that things seem to fall rather too readily into his hands. It's simply not just. Shivvalan hasn't done half the work I have but, inside three years of arriving in Hadrumal, he was rag-tagging after mages like Rafrid and even Shannet. The woman hadn't taken a pupil in ten years and all of a sudden, she lit on Shivvalan Ralsere, overlooking mages who've spent seasons putting together a proposal for study, waiting for the offer of pupillage.'

The surface of the ale in the flagon stopped slopping and gleamed in the candlelight. A sudden thought diverted Casuel from that particular set of oft-rehearsed grievances.

'You see, I rather suspect Shivvalan's being a little underhand, using his powers for his own advancement. Scrying, for example. That's what Shivvalan's supposed to be so good at.

That's what Shannet had been working on, locked away in her tower, according to all the gossip at least.'

'Will I be able to scry?' Allin's rather small eyes brightened.

'Well, mages with an affinity for water are best at scrying. Your talent is for fire, but you should be able to master it. I have.'

Allin looked up at Casuel with an awe that flattered his bruised conceit.

An unaccustomed boldness gripped him. Trying to ignore the fluttering in his belly at his own daring, Casuel reached for a dish and poured water into it.

'Let me show you.'

He rummaged in his writing case for ink, and let fall a few careful drops. Amber light flickered stubbornly around his fingers before he could raise a muddy green to dimly illuminate the water. Biting his lip Casuel concentrated on picturing Shiv's seal-ring, something he could do easily. After all, he'd worn the reverse image printed on his jawbone for long enough after that disgraceful incident at Solstice.

The recollection distracted him, and he had to start again. The fresh trails of ink eddied in the water and then Casuel had it, a blurred image of Shivvalan sitting in an inn, evidently a far better one than this pest-hole, he noted with irritation.

'That's Ralsere.'

'Who's that with him?' Allin peered into the bowl, mouth open.

Casuel frowned at the lively-looking redhead sharing the ale flagon and playing runes.

'Some Forest maid fresh from the woods and fancying her chances,' he muttered. 'She'll have a surprise if she's got plans for tonight.'

'Pardon?'

'Nothing,' Casuel said hastily. Actually, the trollop wasn't bad-looking. Why did he never meet women like that, he wondered, glancing sideways at Allin's immature, dumpy figure, her plain, round face and snub nose.

The passing surge of lust faded when he recognised a man on the far side of the room.

'Darni Fallion? What's he doing there?'

Casuel watched open-mouthed as Shivvalan crossed the room to exchange a few brief words with the mercenary before returning to the girl.

His agitation conveyed itself to the water and the vision dissolved in a confusion of mossy greens and browns. Casuel ignored it and the ink now staining the crackled glaze of the bowl.

'Who is he, that other man?'

'He's one of the Archmage's agents,' Casuel said grimly. 'This could be serious. I mean he's fairly insignificant as agents go, but if Shivvalan is travelling with Darni, that means Planir must be involved somehow.'

There was no way Casuel could let an opportunity like this slip through his fingers; he had to know what was going on.

'Wait here.'

Casuel left Allin sitting wide-eyed at the table and left the room, returning rapidly with his mirror. Moving with unaccustomed purpose, he opened the shutter and set a candle on the sill, ignoring the chill blast of the weather. Allin shivered and wrapped herself tighter in her shawl, kept quiet by the ingrained habits of her scarcely passed childhood.

Settling himself on his stool, Casuel snapped his fingers and orange fire at once lit the candle with a flame burning steadily in defiance of the wind. He angled the mirror to catch the image and it began to glow with an inner radiance of its own, reflecting a golden light back first into Casuel's intent face and then Allin's eyes as she came to peep over his shoulder at the revelations in the shiny surface.

'*So where are we heading for next?*' The voice of the little image sounded both tinny and muffled in the silent room.

'Who's that?' Allin whispered hesitantly.

'Geris, some irritating boy from the University at Vanam. Saedrin knows what he's doing there!'

Casuel kept his eyes fixed on the mirror where he could now see Darni clearly

'*Drede, Eyhorne, then Hanchet.*' Darni tapped the map by way of emphasis.

'*How far are we taking the girl?*' Geris lowered his tone, looking uncertainly across the room.

Darni shrugged. '*As long as the Watch don't come looking for her, she can come as far as she's useful. A lot'll depend on whether she can acquire that item for us or not. If she can and my contact in Hanchet comes through, we'll double back for Friern. She can earn her cut of the coin properly, greedy sow.*'

'*Are you sure? It'll be very risky.*' Geris was clearly unhappy about something, his eyes flickering between Darni and the others on the far side of the room.

Darni took a long swallow of ale before answering in a low, even tone. '*If that herbalist is right, those are books that we need and there's no way we'll get them out of Armile any other way. You heard the apothecary; he's sure the chamberlain's living in Hanchet now and will be only too pleased to give us the layout of the library in return for a little coin and the promise of revenge. You knew I've been wondering where we might find an upper-storey man without attracting too much attention.*'

'*What if she's caught?*' Geris' voice rose and Darni scowled blackly at him.

'*As long as he's got someone to clap in the pillory and hang if it suits him, Lord Armile won't bother looking any further. Who's going to believe her if she starts talking about wizards hiring her light fingers?*'

'*I still don't like it,*' Geris said defiantly.

'*You don't have to like it; it's not your decision.*' Darni's voice rang harshly against the metal of the mirror. '*Either she's good enough to keep out of trouble or she just has to take the runes the way they fall. Anyway, if she makes a complete pig's arse of the first job, there'll be no point taking her to Friern, will there? We'll pay her off and dump her.*'

Casuel gaped at the mirror, appalled at what he was hearing. 'I don't believe it! That girl isn't just some slut with a taste for the long grass, she's a common lockpick!' He shook his head.

Once again, agitation unravelled Casuel's spell. He cursed and slammed the shutters closed against the cutting wind.

'They're planning to rob someone?' Allin looked at him, aghast.

'That's not the worst of it! Think about it, they could very well succeed! I've always suspected Shivvalan used intrigue to advance himself, and that Darni is no better than a common blade for hire. A season and a half of my painstaking work is going to be overlooked yet again because that pair have all the morals of wharf-rats!'

Casuel looked down with surprise at his hands, shaking with impotent frustration. 'Raeponin pox the pair of them!'

'What are you going to do about it?'

Casuel opened his mouth to deny any such idea but stopped, open-mouthed, staring at nothing for a moment. He coughed and took a reflective sip of ale.

'Well, if they're prepared to use such despicable tricks, I have a duty to do something about it, don't I? What if it all goes wrong? If a plot like that is traced back to a wizard and an Archmage's agent as well, the reputation of Hadrumal will be strung up on the gallows along with that red-headed bitch!'

Allin's trusting, respectful gaze spurred him on. Casuel lifted a long, thick book from his bag.

'What is that?'

'It's a set of itineraries, maps of the coach roads,' he replied with satisfaction. 'Be quiet a moment.'

It took him a few moments to locate the roads he needed, and cross-referencing wasn't easy, as he had to unfold several of the lengths of paper at the same time. Casuel cursed under his breath. Hanchet, there it was. It was a small place, wasn't it? Only really there to serve the bridges on either side as two rivers drew together, not a real town in the Tormalin sense of the word.

'You know, we could be there by the day after tomorrow, look,' he breathed at last.

He refolded the maps of the roads with trembling hands. 'No, we have to be realistic. We have no idea of whom we would need to contact, for a start. All we know is they're looking for someone who used to be chamberlain to Lord Armile.'

'If it's anything like back home, that should be enough to

find him. Everyone knows everyone else's business in a village that size,' Allin said timidly.

Casuel looked at her thoughtfully. 'Local gossips would make hay with something like that, wouldn't they? I know my mother and her sewing circle would. I suppose there would be an inn where I could ask a few questions without arousing too much suspicion.'

Indignation rose in Casuel's throat and he washed it away with a long draught of ale. 'How dare Ralsere and Darni think of robbing Lord Armile? Friern's one of the few fiefdoms between here and Col where the roads don't leave coaches bogged to the axles and horses muddied to the hocks! They're some of the safest roads around too, come to that; remember those footpads we saw being pelted in the stocks outside that market-hall?'

'Yes I do!' The edge to Allin's tone surprised Casuel until he realised what value a family driven from their home by the chaos of civil war would place on the rule of law.

He stared across the room, eyes looking far beyond the lime-washed walls. After a long moment, he straightened up in his seat.

'I could make some enquiries of this chamberlain fellow, there could be no harm in that. If it turns out that Lord Armile has some of the books Usara wants, why shouldn't I approach him openly? Raeponin rewards the ready, that's what they say, isn't it?'

'Is it?' Allin looked blankly at him.

Casuel began to pace back and forth across the uneven floorboards, audacity born of long-held resentments gradually winning over his natural caution. 'I've got to bring myself to Usara's attention, I've just got to, and that means throwing the runes at a venture, doesn't it?'

He stopped, turned on his heel with a decisive air, and reached under his coat for a fat pouch of coin. 'It'll be squandering the Archmage's coin in lush coaching inns that leaves Ralsere having to steal books rather than buy them like an honest man.'

He sorted the noble coin in front of him with a sneer on his face. 'I can simply ask to look at his library and then offer a fair price for those things we're looking for. Why not? Lord Armile's sure to be a reasonable man. He's nobly born after all, even if he is just some Ensaimin hedge-lord.'

A superior smile curved Casuel's full lips. 'I don't think we need complicate matters by telling him we're wizards. I find travelling as a dealer in books is sufficient explanation.'

His smile faded a little and he frowned. 'You know, Allin, I wouldn't want you talking to anyone about this when we get to Hadrumal, not until I've had a chance to speak privately to Usara. This sort of thing could reflect very poorly on the dignity of wizardry if word got around. Obviously I have a duty to make sure action is taken to prevent Shivvalan and his associates making such a reckless design in future, but I wouldn't want it to look as if I were simply bearing tales about a fellow pupil. I'll need to choose my moment carefully. Usara's project must be important if the Archmage is involved, however peripherally, and that means it warrants co-operation rather than confrontation between mages. Do you understand?'

She nodded hastily. 'Of course. I won't say a word to anyone.'

Casuel smiled approvingly at her unquestioning obedience.

'You'll do very well in Hadrumal, my dear. You have a quick mind and the right attitude. I will make sure you get tuition at one of the best Halls.'

That should be easy enough to arrange, once he had impressed Usara, hobbled Shivvalan's horses for him and secured the proper recognition that had unaccountably eluded him for so long.

The echo of a remembered ache stirred in Casuel's jaw. There was still the question of Darni. Hadn't he been the last one left standing in one of Hadrumal's dockside inns when those sailors had challenged all comers to a free-for-all fist fight? It might be better if Usara kept his name out of things when he reported this disgraceful business to Planir. But then, how else could Casuel come to the attention of the

Archmage? He would have to give the matter some careful thought.

CHAPTER TWO

Taken from:

The Geography of the East

being a description of lands formerly provinces of
the Tormalin Empire, compiled by Marol Afmoor,
Mentor and Scholar of the University of Vanam,
including comprehensive recital of the principal
towns, industries and wares of each.

Ensaimin

*The name Ensaimin is a corruption of Einar sai Emmin, 'the land
of many races' in the tongue of Tormalin antiquity. The plural
Einarinn is of course more familiar, being the ancient word for
'world'. Historians concerned with enlarging the reputation of that
lost Empire represent it as a province held with the sure grip that
characterised Tormalin rule of Dalasor, Lescar and Caladhria,
but this is not the case.*

*In the subjugation of Caladhria, Tormalin power pushed as
far as the White River, the natural boundary between the upper
reaches of the Gulf of Peorle and the mountains of the Southern
Spurs, the narrowest stretch of defensible terrain in that region. At
this juncture, formal contact was first made between the Tormalin
Empire and the Kingdom of Solura. King Soltriss, having laid
claim to all lands west of the Great Forest, sent emissaries into
that as yet unclaimed territory beyond. In their travels among the*

indigenous inhabitants, these delegates encountered diplomats from the Emperor Correl the Stalwart, who at that time was considering the annexation of lands beyond his existing boundaries.

It is indeed fortunate for those innocently dwelling on the broad plains of this fertile region that these mighty rulers each recognised the perils of attempting to expand their domains. Correl was already pushing his Cohorts north across the Dalas to possess himself of the mineral wealth of the Gidestan mountains and for his part, Soltriss was rightly doubtful about the viability of a province that would be separated from his other domains by the impenetrable mysteries of the Great Forest. It is undeniable that the Forest Folk would have seen such encirclement as a threat and resisted with all the arcane means at their disposal.

Thus the happy land of Einar Sai Emmin accrued much benefit as trade between the Tormalin Empire and the Kingdom of Solura developed in stead of conflict. Pack-horse routes became major highways east to west, Forest Folk began to travel and trade on their own account, and both Gidestan and Soluran exploration into the Dragon's Spines brought metals and gems from the north to the sea. Even traders from the wastes of Mandarkin beyond those forbidding mountains risked the dread passes to bring furs and amber to the markets of the south.

Fiefdoms ruled by lordlings with self-bestowed titles rose, interspersed with the self-governing cities grown up around the unions of road and river and the few safe anchorages along the coast, to produce the patchwork character of modern Ensaimin. Rivalry in a land dependent on trade discouraged unification, and many scholars make a convincing case for seeing the subtle hands of both Tormalin and Soluran nobilities in this, alert to the benefits of maintaining a buffer between such mighty powers.

The Running Hound Inn, Ambafost,
14th of For-Autumn

I had some vague idea of rising at dawn and heading off at the gallop; that's what people do on quests, isn't it? Not these three. When Shiv knocked on my door, it was well past sunrise and for a good long while I had been fully dressed and half-wondering if I should make a run for it. My promise not to make a run for it only applied to the day before, as far as I was concerned. We ate a leisurely breakfast in the private parlour, Darni wading through beef and onions, beer, bread, honey, more bread and sweetcakes. I asked for porridge and ignored Darni's amusement. I like porridge, and I also like to be able to walk after a meal rather than waddle. Still, it started me thinking; these three weren't scraping by and I wondered what an Archmage's agent earned in pay and expenses.

When we finally set off, Shiv and Darni rode while I joined Geris in a neat two-horse carriage. I sat up front with him as the back was loaded with a couple of iron-banded coffers and everyone's baggage. The coffers looked interesting, and I wondered if Shiv had taken any precautions or whether a quiet session with my lockpicks might prove fruitful. I can get very curious about locked boxes. I concentrated on the road ahead; the last thing I wanted was for Darni or Shiv to notice my interest.

Geris drove well; his hands on the reins were relaxed and he spoke to his bay horses with ease. Evidently he'd been driving for years, probably since childhood, which almost certainly meant noble blood; commoners like me are lucky to get the use of a mule. I'd been on the road for a couple of years before it was worth my while even learning to ride, and I don't suppose I'd ever have learned to drive if it hadn't been essential for a swindle Halice and I had worked in Caladhria.

'They're a nicely matched pair,' I commented after a few miles of companionable silence.

'I picked them up last spring,' Geris smiled. 'They are pretty, aren't they? Still, their paces are so good I'd have bought them if one was black and the other white. I'm not bothered about a stylish shade of coat.'

I like friendly, open people like Geris; they tell you so much more than they realise. In Vanam, it's only the wealthy who can afford to be so choosy about the colour of their horses, or who have the confidence to ignore fashion for that matter. So, wealthy as well as noble, two conditions not always related. Wealthy, noble, trusting and naive; why could I not have met him on his own? A less happy thought occurred to me; perhaps he was financing this gentlefolks' tour, not the Archmage. Still, I could be less careful not to win too much off him next time we played the runes.

'Shiv tells me you're from Vanam?' I commented idly.

'Yes, that's right.'

'That's quite a coincidence. That's where I come from originally.' I gave him my warm, sisterly smile. Geris smiled back, reminding me of one of those eager Aldabreshi lapdogs.

'Whereabouts do you live? Perhaps we have acquaintance in common?'

It was quite funny to watch his brain catch up with his mouth. As a gambit for polite chit-chat, that was a fine question, but was it really what he wanted to ask a woman from whom he had bought stolen property? His face reflected his dismay as he saw the conversational pit he had just dug ahead. I was tempted to claim a handful of city notables as people I had robbed. Would that count as acquaintance?

'I doubt it.' I took pity on him. 'My mother is a house-keeper.'

'Oh, for whom?' Still not the most tactful question but this time he didn't seem to notice.

'Emys Glashale. He lives east of the river, off the Rivenroad.'

Geris shook his head. 'I don't really know that part of the city. My family live on the Ariborne.'

'Oh?' I didn't have to fake a tone of interest. The Ariborne means money, but not necessarily old money. Some very shady characters try to purchase respectability with that address.

Geris glanced at me and then concentrated on a bend in the road which was badly rutted and boggy with the recent rain. His face showed eagerness to chat was warring with instructions to be discreet, doubtless from Darni. I sat patiently and we negotiated the curve without accident. Geris looked sideways at me again, and I saw his eyes brighten as they lingered on my breeched legs. I stretched them out and leaned back in the seat, which also helped to pull my jerkin tighter over my breasts.

'There are some beautiful houses on the Ariborne,' I said wistfully. 'Have you lived there long?'

As I hoped, the social code could not let Geris ignore a lady's conversation, even one as dubiously qualified as me.

'My father built the house about ten years ago, when he—' Geris broke off and hesitated. He laughed. 'Oh well, you might as well know. My father's Judal Armiger.'

'Never!' I gaped at him. 'The Looking Glass man? That Judal?'

Geris blushed but I could see he was proud of his parentage and no wonder.

'Why are you so shy about it? Judal's the greatest actor Vanam has known in three generations!' I let my enthusiasm have full rein. 'My mother told me how he formed his own company rather than seek a wealthy patron. She says everyone was astounded. And then, to build his own playhouse rather than use the temples like everyone else, well, that was a stroke of genius.'

'He's a clever man.' Geris sat straighter on his seat as pride filled him.

'Clever hardly fits it! People are still talking about the first time he staged a Lescari romance. It made the priests livid. How did he find the nerve to go and buy in a Soluran masquerade after that, just to show them what he thought?'

I laughed; I'd seen the masqueraders as a child on a rare day out with my father and I could still picture them vividly.

'He writes his own material too,' Geris boasted. 'He's survived mockery, sabotage and imitation to set the standard by which any troupe is judged.'

That had the sound of one of Judal's own lines to me but I wasn't going to quibble. He is certainly a remarkable man. Incidentally, he has made a great deal of money.

'My mother and I queued all afternoon to see *The Duke of Marlier's Daughter*, you know.'

Geris turned eagerly. 'Did you enjoy it? What did you think of it?'

'My mother said she'd never realised one mother putting a switch across her daughter's backside could have stopped the Lescari wars before they'd got started.' I laughed in sudden remembrance of her dry tone.

'I don't think that's entirely fair.' Geris looked more than a little put out.

'I thought the play was very fine,' I assured him. 'I really admired the way the princess stood up to them all and refused to let them rule her life, no matter what.'

Geris looked mollified so I didn't elaborate; I may have admired the stubborn Suleta as a bloody-minded girl myself, but nowadays I'd be more of my mother's opinion, unlikely though that sounds.

'Well!' I shook my head in wonder. 'So how do you come to be jaunting round with that peculiar pair?' I waved a hand at the backs of Darni and Shiv.

Geris relaxed a little. 'My mentor at the University is an expert on Tormalin Empire history, especially Nemith the Seafarer and Nemith the Reckless. Something – that is, when Planir needed someone to help with some – when he wanted to know more about that period, he contacted my master. He recommended me to Darni and Shiv.'

I hoped no one was trusting Geris with anything vital. With all his hesitations, he couldn't have been more obvious with 'I've got a secret' chalked on his back.

'Didn't you want to go into the Looking Glass?' I would

have sold all my aunts and cousins for a chance like that. Well, to be honest, I would have sold my aunts and cousins for a lot less, but I still could not understand how Geris could have walked away from something so exciting.

'Not really. I could never be a player.'

Well, that was true enough.

'I got interested in history when Father was writing *Vamyre the Bold*. I did some writing for the stage but it wasn't very good. I liked the studying best, trying to make sense of the old sages, shrine records, chronicles from the Empire, that kind of thing. Did you know the Tormalins reckoned a generation was twenty-five years, but the Solurans say it's thirty-three; that's why tying up their histories is so difficult.'

'And your father doesn't mind?'

'Father always said that we could choose our own path; he'd had to run away from home to be able to do what he wanted and he says he vowed not to be so hard on his own children. Most of the time he manages. Anyway, I've two brothers and a sister who act, a brother who writes really well and a sister who keeps things organised, so I don't think they miss me.'

He smiled, serene, content with his lot. I wondered what a strife-free family was like.

'This must sound stupid but I never knew Judal had a family; I don't think anyone ever thinks about Judal's life off-stage.'

'He'd be delighted to hear that.' Geris urged the horses to a trot as Shiv and Darni vanished into a wooded stretch of road. 'He never wants his own repute to interfere with our lives. My mother and my younger brother and sisters can walk around town without being recognised, and that suits her just fine.'

How many children did that make? 'She must be quite a woman.'

'She is,' Geris said proudly.

I smiled; I doubted he meant it in the way I did.

We passed a waystone and I frowned as I realised we were on the Eyhorne road.

'Where are we headed? I'd have thought you'd have been heading for Col, if you're dealing in antiquities.'

Geris' smile faded and he looked at Darni's stiff back uncertainly. I persisted.

'You must have seen an Almanac, surely? They're putting an extra day into the Equinox, you know, to keep the Calendar right. It's going to be the biggest fair in years. You could find all sorts of dealers there.'

'Of course, they use the Tormalin Calendar there, don't they?' Geris frowned. 'Didn't they add a day at the same time as the Solurans, three years ago?'

I shrugged; I did not want Geris distracted by errors in the various methods of measuring a year; keeping track of who uses which system and making sure you're working from the right Almanac is enough of a pain as it is.

'So where are we headed?'

'Oh, Drede,' Geris said absently. 'Are the Tormalins adding any days at Solstice, do you know?'

'What's in Drede?' This made no sense. Drede is the sort of place that only exists because there's only so much countryside people can take before they get an overwhelming need to build a tavern.

Geris shook himself and abandoned calendar calculations for the present. 'I'm not sure I should be talking to you about it,' he admitted.

'If I'm going to be doing a job for you there, I need as much time as possible to plan it.'

'I don't see how I can help.'

'Well, what am I supposed to be lifting? Who from? Why are these things so important?'

Geris shifted on the seat. 'It's an ink-horn,' he said finally.

'A what?'

'An ink-horn. You keep ink in it, it's made from horn.'

'Yes, I know what one is. What's so special about this one? Darni could buy a handful in Col.'

'We need this particular one. The owner won't sell so we've been wondering how to get hold of it. You came along at just the right time.' He gave me a wide-eyed smile.

Geris could keep his attempts at charm as far as I was concerned. The timing could not have been more wrong from my point of view. I was suddenly tired of this game.

'Look, either you tell me what's going on or I'm off this cart and into those woods before you can pick your nose. Try explaining that to Darni.'

He blinked at the hard edge to my tone.

'Darni said he'd tell you what you needed to know,' he pleaded.

'Geris,' I said warningly. 'I can be out of sight before you can get Darni's attention.'

'It's complicated,' he said finally.

'We've got half a day before we're anywhere near Drede and I'm a good listener, so talk.'

He sighed. 'Did I say my mentor at the University was an expert on the end of the Empire?'

I nodded. 'Yes, Nemith the Reckless's reign.'

'He collects old maps, temple ledgers, contemporary records, anything he can get his hands on. Dealers know him, and a few years ago he started picking up antiquities too, mostly things to do with scholarship – pen-cases, magnifiers, scroll-ends. Nothing very valuable, you understand, but interesting for their own sake.'

Where was this leading? I kept quiet.

'This is going to sound really peculiar.' Geris looked reluctant so I gave him a glare.

'He started having dreams. Not just ordinary dreams, but really detailed, vivid ones. He said it was like living in someone else's life and he could remember every detail once he woke up, for days afterwards. I don't suppose anything would have come of it if he hadn't been at a mentors' convocation at Solstice last winter where they all got drunk. He started talking about these peculiar dreams, and it turned out two other mentors were having the same. Now, Ornale, that's his name, was thinking he was just working too hard, his sleeping mind was getting involved in his studies. He was telling the story against himself really, but the two others were actually quite relieved to hear about it. One's a geographer who's investigating weather patterns, and the other's a metallurgist who's trying to find out just how the Empire mints purified white gold.'

Him and several thousand others, I thought. Life will get very interesting if someone rediscovers the secret of the white gold that makes Tormalin Empire coins the only unforgeable currency around

'So?' I prompted.

'Well, their studies had nothing to do with Empire history as such. The geographer was starting to wonder if he was going mad, I mean, he's a Rationalist and a real extremist; he says he doesn't even believe in the existence of the gods. The metallurgist was putting it down to too much exposure to mercury fumes. Anyway, they got talking and it soon became clear that these dreams featured people and events that Ornale recognised from his studies but that the other two had never even heard of. You see, the records about the end of the Seafarer's reign are pretty incomplete and Nemith the Reckless's reign was so short, what with the Empire falling apart around his ears, that there's virtually nothing to find. Anyway, there was a governor in Califer and Ornale, because of his studies, is just about the only person who knows anything about him, but Drissle, that's the metallurgist, he was able to tell him the name of his dogs and things like that.'

I could see why Geris would never make a playwright. I broke in as he paused for breath.

'So how do we get from weird dreams to stealing an ink-horn in Drede?'

'You see, they couldn't find anything in any sources about dreams like this. There are some temple traditions about using dreams for foretelling, but that led nowhere. There's a Gidestan legend about a man who had visions in his sleep but—'

'Geris, I don't want to know all this,' I interrupted. 'Why am I supposed to steal an ink-horn?'

He looked a little sulky and was silent for a moment, collecting his thoughts. 'They decided to see if they could find a common factor which might have some significance.'

The scholarly mind, I thought, a complete mystery to the rest of us.

'It turned out they each had a small collection of Old Empire artefacts. Drissle had a money-scale, some seal matrixes and an alchemy chest, and Marol had maps, cases and a model of Aldabreshi, showing the way the currents move through the islands and change with the seasons. It's really interesting, you see—' He bit his lip. 'I don't suppose you want to hear about that either. They found they each had one thing that they felt really attached to, that they wouldn't sell for any money. All these things dated to within a few years of each other, just before the fall of the Empire, and they all cropped up in the dreams. They decided to experiment and swapped the artefacts with each other, but once the things were out of their possession, the dreams stopped. When they had them back again, the dreams started again.'

I looked ahead, we were catching up with Darni and Shiv. 'Get to the point, Geris,' I pleaded.

'They couldn't find an explanation so they decided there must be magic involved. They asked around, and found out that one of the mages, Usara, is researching into the fall of the Empire and the founding of Hadrumal. He thinks these dreams could produce valuable information, so he's organising people to find more of these antiquities.'

'And this ink-horn is one of them?'

'It's the right period and it's the sort of small personal item we find is associated with these dreams. The real clincher is the old boy who's got it really doesn't want to sell. That's generally significant.'

'He could just be greedy, looking for a high price, like over the tankard.'

'I've been meaning to ask you about that.' Geris grew more animated and his tone rose. 'Why did you choose that particular piece? That merchant had quite a few things we were interested in; that was the really likely one but it's not the most valuable. Did you handle it for long? Did you feel anything when you took it?'

'Geris!' Darni and Shiv had halted, waiting to cross a

toll-bridge. 'What did I tell you?' Geris subsided into silence as Darni rode up.

'I'll tell her what she needs to know, when she needs to know it.' He rode forward to dispute the toll with the bridge-keeper and I stared at his back with real dislike.

We crossed into Friern and I let Geris drive us on in silence. I had plenty of questions but they could wait. Friern was not the place to have a major argument with Darni which might end up with me leaving the trio. We passed a tavern, the Grey Stag, and some while later stopped at a coaching inn, also the Grey Stag, to rest the horses and eat. I really don't like places where every inn is called after the local lord's badge. Lord Armile's militia were well in evidence as usual, galloping down the road with scant regard for anyone else. Enclosing the land had gone much further than the last time I'd been down this road: things were not looking good for the peasants here, significant numbers of whom were breaking rocks at the sides of the road for the work-bread. I was glad to realise we would only be cutting across the corner of the district.

It was late afternoon when the waystones listed Drede as our next destination and the road started to climb up into the downs. When we were still a little way short, Darni called a halt under a stand of willows and we let the horses drink.

'Now, Shiv and Geris will wait here,' he instructed me curtly. 'You and I will go into Drede. I'll show you the house and you can find your way in once it gets dark. As soon as you've lifted the horn, we'll be on our way.'

'Where to?' I asked mildly.

'I know a place we can stay, a private house not an inn. We should make it by dawn if we push it. Lesser moon's at three quarters, so there'll be enough light.' He addressed this last to Geris who was clearly about to object on his horses' account.

'What's the butt's house like?'

'The what?'

'The target, the victim?'

'It's a small place, a street house near the shambles.'

'And the man?'

'He's an old eccentric, an antiquarian. He's sixty if he's a year and in poor health, must be knocking on Saedrin's door every night.'

I shook my head. 'I'll need to see it first but I can tell you, I'm not doing it at first dark.'

Darni looked angry. 'You'll do as I tell you.'

'Not if you want this piece as badly as I think you do. Even with only a lesser moon there'll be people about until it sets at least, even in a small place like Drede. It's a street house, no yard, built up against the ones either side? That's not easy. If he's an old man, he won't be a heavy sleeper and let me guess, the house is packed full of oddities, floor covered, tables and books everywhere?'

'That's right.' That earned Geris a sour look from Darni.

'I'll go in just before moonset. You lot should go right through the town and put up at the first inn on the Eyhorne road. I'll meet you at dawn and we can set off like innocent travellers, keen to get a full day on the road.'

'I think—'

Shiv cut Darni off short. 'Livak's the expert here, so we'll do it her way.'

Darni shot him a filthy look but kept quiet. Interesting, I thought.

'So, who went to see the old man when he wouldn't sell?'

'Me and Geris,' Shiv replied.

'Then Darni's right, he'd better show me the place. Let's eat now and we can go in for an evening ale.' I flashed him a smile, doing my best to keep any triumph out of it, but he wasn't impressed. Sulk all you want, I thought, no skin off my fingers.

We ate fast and left Geris and Shiv playing runes under the tree. They were going to move on a little later when the roads were quieter and Geris seemed to want to improve his game for some reason. I'd told them to try and avoid any contact with anyone. The old boy might be halfway to Saedrin's table but I bet he'd make the connection between a memorable couple like them wanting to buy his ink-horn and it walking out of its own accord. The Watch round here weren't particularly bright but there was no point in risking witnesses who could identify them and their route.

We strolled into town and I considered taking Darni's arm, mainly to annoy him, to be truthful. I decided against it; he wasn't really worth the bother. I looked around as we walked, getting my bearings as it was a while since I'd been there. Drede is a nice little town, jumbled lines of houses of the local yellow stone, roofed with neat stone slates.

'Green door,' he murmured in conversational tone, 'alley to the right and ivy on the gable.'

I looked sideways under my lashes at the place he meant, scanning it for crucial information.

'He lives downstairs pretty much, from what Shiv saw,' Darni continued. 'You can go in through the eaves window.'

'I could just put the door in with an axe,' I offered. 'That would be quicker and make about the same amount of noise.'

Darni was about to snap something back at me but I silenced him with a gesture to the other people in the street. I was getting very tired of him and his arrogance.

'That window hasn't been opened since it was built, by the look of the cobwebs and the ivy.' I kept my tone level and reasonable. 'Trust me to know what I'm doing, Darni. Isn't that why you dragged me into this masquerade?'

We moved on to the modest little inn on the market square and shared a flagon of ale. It is not a hostelry I'll be recommending to any of my friends but, to be fair, it may have been the expression on Darni's face turning the beer sour.

The sun set and the lesser moon rose pink and gleaming in the south. I got up and Darni had the wit to follow my lead. We sauntered along the Friern road and into the darkness; I matched my steps exactly to Darni's.

'Keep going, don't look around and I'll see you at dawn.' I slipped down an alley towards the shambles and Darni walked easily on his way, his pace not altering a beat. I shook my head with mixed exasperation and admiration.

The alley smelled of old blood, fresh dung and frightened animals. Not the sort of place where any courting couples would be trying their chances, so just the sort of place for me. I worked my way round the back of the slaughteryard and up another lane. I squatted down and made myself comfortable to watch the old man's place.

The mean glow of a single candle moved about from time to time and then the front went dark. The houses on either side went through the usual routine of cooking, eating, throwing out the slops and shuttering the windows. The chimneys stopped smoking and two lads from next door on the left went down to the inn, wandering unsteadily back as the moon rode high in the sky. There was a minor disturbance when they discovered the door had been bolted against them and their mother let them in with shrill rebukes.

I sat and waited. The little town grew silent and still. Soon all I could hear were rats foraging in the middens behind me and the occasional scuffle as a hunting cat was successful. I crossed the street and moved stealthily down the alley. Woodsheds, privies and pigsties were tucked into the narrow space that divided the uneven lines of houses. The old boy's sty was vacant judging by the lack of smell, which was a relief; pigs have good hearing and more than their fair share of curiosity as well as the ability to make an ungodly row. I ducked into the shadows and studied the door and windows. Not good; the casements were as warped shut as the front ones and the ivy just as rampant too. I didn't like it but I was going to have to try the door. I knelt and studied the mud by the step; no claw marks or paw prints, no dog hair caught in the frayed wood of the door jamb. So far, so promising.

I looked closer and blessed Drianon for looking kindly on her wayward daughter. The old boy had gone to the trouble and expense of a lock. Praying that he'd abandoned bolts on the strength of it, I pulled out my picks and went to work. I can shift bolts but it's slow work at best and often noisy.

He'd paid good money, I realised as time crept on. It was a complex lock, could even have been Mountain Man work. Finally I had the last tumbler shifted and I tried the latch as slowly as I could. It moved reluctantly against rust and grime, but there were no bolts. I slipped inside and paused to get my bearings. The room was stuffy with wood smoke, urine and sour milk. Rattling breaths came from the far side of the room and the dying embers showed a hunched-up shape in a chair by the range. My Forest sight was growing used to the dark and I could see a table laden with unwashed vessels and half-eaten food, logs heaped carelessly on the floor, rags and rubbish everywhere. I approached the door to the front room, then entered another world.

Books lay everywhere but all were organised by subject and author. No dust marred their leather and the central desk bore a stack of parchment covered in neat script. A gleaming spy-glass rested on a meticulous drawing of the night sky, and the bench by the window held herbs and flowers with detailed notes on their uses and habitats. The ink-horn sat on a small table beside quills, knife and dyes. It was a beautiful thing, a pale honey-coloured horn that I could not identify, mounted in red gold, the bands chased with delicate decoration. I reached for it and hesitated. I did not want dreams from the dark ages invading my sleep and I half wished I'd stayed ignorant about the whole affair.

Coughing from the kitchen startled me and I grabbed the piece, my heart pounding. What if he was in the middle of one of these uncanny dreams? Would moving it wake him? I shoved it back on the table like a candle dripping hot wax. My heartbeat drummed in my ears as I stared at the cursed thing.

Pull yourself together, I commanded myself silently.

I drew a deep breath, carefully picked up the ink-horn and held myself motionless, waiting for any reaction next door. I heard a blanket rustle and the creaking of the chair, then the old man's breath settled back to a rhythmic rasp. His lungs sounded bad. I wondered how he would manage the winter.

I scanned the piles of books quickly while I waited for him to return to a deeper sleep. If Geris and Shiv were searching for information about the end of the Empire, there was too much here to risk losing if he died in his sleep and the local peasants cleared the place. One small stack was devoted to the last emperors of the Nemith line so I tucked them into my tunic, drawing my belt tight. Once I was sure the kitchen was calm again, I slipped out. I took the time to relock the door, ignoring my accelerating pulse and the sweat that itched between my shoulder blades. There was no way the scholar was going to miss the theft but if there was no sign of entry, with luck the Watch would dismiss him as a confused old idiot.

Satisfied with my work, I trotted through the dark streets and out along the high road, leaving Drede to its sleep. What I had trouble leaving behind was a feeling of being somehow soiled by what I had done. Yes, I know that sounds stupid for someone like me but I couldn't help picturing the wretched old man's distress at his losses. This wasn't thieving for profit, or revenge, like taking the tankard. It wasn't even stealing out of necessity from some cream-fed cat who could afford the toll. The old boy lived in his mind more than his body, and I wondered what vivid dreams of a distant age had meant to him in his straitened life as his body and senses failed with age.

'Pull yourself together, you nanny goat!' I scolded myself. 'He could be the sourest old bastard since Misaen organised the sun and moons.'

I'd tell Geris to ask some sympathetic mentor from the University down here to take care of the old boy; he did not belong in that hovel. I increased my pace and my qualms receded with the road behind me.

The sky was paling with the first hints of dawn when I reached the inn. I walked openly but silently into the yard, wondering how I was going to find the others. I need not have worried; Darni was sitting by the carriage-house door, snugly wrapped in his cloak and comfortable on a bale of straw. His eyes opened as I approached.

'Got it?'

I nodded and handed him the purse with the ink-horn. 'Have you been out all night? Are you going to be fit to ride?'

'I got enough rest. It's a skill you learn soldiering.' His mood seemed better than before.

'Any chance of something to eat before we get started?' I was tired now the night's stimulation was wearing off.

Darni handed me bread and cheese and small beer from the floor next to his straw bale and then passed me his cloak. 'You need to rest. I'll get the others moving and we'll be off as soon as the sun's up.'

I was not going to argue with this unexpected cordiality. I wrapped myself in the good wool, still warm from his body, and curled up on the straw.

CHAPTER THREE

Taken from:

The Duke of Marlier's Daughter

**A Tragedy in Five Acts by Awlimail Kespre
Act Two, Scene Three
The bedchamber of Suleta**

[Enter Tisell.]

Suleta	*Tell me, tell me, does my father yet breathe?*
Tisell	*Oh sweet mistress, he does, but one hears the rattle of Saedrin's keys in every breath he takes. The door to the Otherworld will soon unlock to welcome that noble shade.*
Suleta	*I cannot bear it!*
Tisell	*For his sake, you must bear the burdens that fall so heavily on your slender shoulders.*
Suleta	*Alas that I was ever born to such sorrow!*
Tisell	*Curse not your birth, dearest child, but rather the faithless jade that has so besmirched her husband's bed!*
Suleta	*Speak not so of the Queen's grace beyond these walls, Tisell, or I will not be able to save you from the lash.*
Tisell	*I speak the truth as all men know it, my lady. Queen she may be, but trull she has proved herself and worse, she has dragged her children through the filth of the kennel with her.*

Suleta   *Do not remind me of my cousins' grievous sufferings!*
The taunt of bastard will be no less cruel a lash
than that which flogged their mother naked before
the rabble.

Tisell   *You are all goodness, my chick, to think of others*
when you face such a choice.

Suleta   *What do you mean?*

Tisell   *Has your lady mother not spoken with you? I had*
thought—

Suleta   *I have not seen her since they bore my father home—*

[Enter Albrice, Duchess of Marlier.]

Tisell   *Your Grace [curtseying].*

Albrice   *Leave us, I would be private with my daughter.*
                                  [Exit Tisell.]

Albrice   *Your father has not yet turned his face from this world*
but the surgeon tells me he will do so ere dawn. No,
there is not yet time for tears, dearest child, we have
not that luxury. In marrying for love, I set aside my
rank as princess but with one brother dead at your
father's hand and the other taken in adultery with
that bitch, I am alone the living child of King Heric.
Now I must answer the demands of blood and family.
That blood flows pure in your veins alone, daughter,
and whose sheets it stains upon your wedding night
will decide the fate of this unhappy land. Their Graces
of Parnilesse and Draximal have claims to the throne
that would weigh equal in Raeponin's very scales.
It is your hand that will tip that balance to one or
the other.

Suleta   *I am to be portioned out like so much meat?*

Albrice   *Speak not so saucy to me, lady! Have I raised you so*
wanting in wit?

Suleta   *Draximal is a vicious sot whom three wives have*
already fled in Poldrion's barque, while Parnilesse
treads the lady's measure with his dancing masters
nightly! You tell me I must wed one of these and say
I want wit when I recoil? I tell you plainly, blood or

*not, royal in my veins or shed upon the thirsty soil, I
will have none of this!*

[Exit Suleta.]

East of Drede on the Eyhorne Road,
15th of For-Autumn

I did not expect to sleep but the next thing I knew Shiv was lifting me into the carriage and Geris was trying to arrange space for me between the baggage.

'It's all right.' I wriggled free of the cloak's folds. 'I can sit up front.'

Shiv smiled at me. 'Are you sure?'

I yawned. 'I can doze as we go, I've done it before. Ow!' The hard edge of a book dug me in the ribs and I yelped.

'What is it?' Geris looked around wildly.

'These.' I reached into my tunic and pulled out the books. 'I must have been tired to sleep on this lot!'

Shiv's eyes brightened as he saw the titles of the volumes but Darni reappeared as he was about to open the first one. He tucked them inside a linen sack and put them in this saddlebag.

'I've paid the reckoning, so let's be on our way. No one's seen Livak so let's keep it that way and leave everyone thinking we're the dyestuff traders we claim to be.'

That made sense of the locked coffers and setting a guard. I looked at Darni with the faint stirrings of respect; maybe he had hidden talents.

Geris drove off and I dozed. I can sleep anywhere as long as I feel safe, with the possible exception of the top of a carriers' coach, but this was no trouble since Geris was driving as if he had a cargo of eggs and the road was in good repair. By the time we stopped to rest the horses at noon, I was well refreshed and interested to see what the next stop on this deranged trip would be. I did not have long to wait.

We were not far short of the Eyhorne border when Darni

led us off down a side road. We crested a rise to see a small
knot of buildings beside a tree-fringed lake. The squat bulbous
chimneys of kilns rose above the roofs of workshops and trailed
plumes of dirty smoke into the blue sky.

'Darni!' A heavily built man in clay-stained shirt and
breeches emerged from a low shed and waved to us. He
turned and yelled across the water to a lad fishing from a
low bough.

'Seyn, come here! My son will see to your horses,' he
explained. 'Come on inside.'

He registered my presence and acknowledged me with a
courteous nod. 'I'm Travor, welcome to my home.'

He helped Darni with the first coffer while Geris and Shiv
took the second into the solid brick-built house at the centre
of the cluster. I trailed on behind into a large kitchen where
a pink-faced woman about my own age was kneading bread
at a well-scrubbed table while a bevy of equally well-scrubbed
children played around her feet on the tiled floor.

'Shiv!' Her pleasure at seeing him was obvious as she kissed
him on the cheek, carefully holding her floury hands to one
side. 'Hello Darni, and Geris, how are you?'

'Very well, thank you.'

'Geris!' The children swarmed round him and I saw there
were five of them, ranging from a slender blonde miss who
reached his waist to a determined crawler who seemed certain
he could walk despite evidence to the contrary. One a year by
the look of things, and from our hostess's thick waist I'd bet
the potter had a firing in her kiln again. She wiped her hands
on her apron.

'I'm Harna, you're very welcome.'

'Livak.' I offered my hand and she shook it.

'So, how long are you stopping?' She put the dough aside
to rise under a clean cloth and turned to Darni.

'Tonight, then we'll be on our way.'

Shiv interrupted. 'We could do with a little longer, I think,
Harna. Livak acquired us some books as well as the item, Darni.
They could be very useful and I'd like Conall's opinion.'

Darni shot me the first sour look of the day. 'I see. We'll

discuss it later,' he said in a tone which promised unpleasantness. He paused for a moment then stalked out into the
yard.

Harna ignored him and looked at me more closely. 'You look
tired, let me show you to your room. How about a bath?'

'That would be wonderful.' I followed her eagerly, leaving
Geris sharing sugar-fruits out among the children and Shiv
busying himself with bread and cold meat from the pantry.

'Everyone seems at home here,' I commented as we went
up the narrow stairs.

Harna laughed. 'I've seen more of Darni in the last two
seasons than I have in the last six years. I don't mind, it's for
a good cause.'

I resisted the temptation to probe further.

'What are you doing with them?' She clearly had no such
qualms.

'Oh, this and that.'

She nodded and let the matter drop.

'Here's your room.' Harna opened a low door into a small
chamber tucked under the eaves. I breathed in the lavender
scent of the spotless linen and nearly fell asleep on the spot.

'It's lovely, thank you.' It was too. The washstand had a jug
and bowl of lustre ware that would have commanded top coin
in Vanam, the walls were lime-washed a subtle pink and the
small casement was framed by neat linen curtains.

'The bath's this way.' Harna showed me down another stair
to a tiled room with a huge tub and a drain cunningly set into
the floor.

'This is very fine,' I observed. She smiled.

'Travor likes to make things efficient. When you're bathing
seven children, it can be like a ford on the Dalas in here.'

Seven? Drianon save me!

Travor entered with a huge kettle of steaming water. 'I'd
say more like a storm on the Caladhrian Gulf myself.'

He poured the water into the tub and I looked at it greedily.
'Thank you. Are you sure I'm not taking too much hot
water?'

Travor shook his head. 'The are kilns working today and I

built coppers beside them to use the heat. We can bathe you all and still have plenty over.'

He left and Harna reappeared with soft towels. 'Enjoy yourself,' she said as she closed the door.

I certainly did. There were bottles of scented oils on a shelf and I found some essence of Grassgild, one of my favourites. Soaking in the fragrant water and being able to wash my hair improved life enormously. When the water grew cool I dragged myself out reluctantly and dashed in a towel back to my chamber, where clean shirt and linen completed my transformation.

The house was quiet. I could hear the children playing somewhere off in the distance and a cart rumbled out of the yard. I stretched out on the goose-feather bed and reached into my scrip for the book I'd held back from Shiv.

On the Lost Arts of Tormalin. Sounded promising, I thought.

I opened it and began to pick my way through the narrow script; it was not easy going. We all speak Tormalin in Ensaimin but it's the common tongue. This text was in the Old High dialect, the language that had held the Empire together. I frowned over the oddly accented words, trying to decipher the intonation marks over and above the lines. I yawned and rubbed my eyes. This was too hard so I contented myself with looking at the section headings: On Astronomy, On Mathematics, On Refining Ore, On Oculism, On Pharmacopoeia, On Oratory.

Not exactly intriguing. I'm not sure how soon I fell asleep but when I woke to a gentle knock on the door the sky outside the window was soft with the pink and orange of dusk.

'Livak? It's Harna. I'm just going to call them all in for dinner. Are you coming down?'

'Yes, thanks. I'll be with you in a moment.'

As I went down the stairs, I could hear Shiv and Darni in the kitchen. I waited to hear what they were saying.

'I don't like her making decisions on her own like that,' Darni was grumbling.

'Well she could hardly come and get our approval, could she? That old man was going to notice the thing had gone, wasn't he? Taking some of the books might just make the

Watch think it was a chance robbery, someone trying their luck. Recluses like that always get the reputation of being misers; I bet half the town reckon he sits on secret chests of Empire Marks. With any luck, they'll decide someone broke in and just grabbed the nearest things that might be valuable.'

'You think she thought that far ahead? Anyway, how many people in Drede would know the value of books like these?' Darni's tone was scornful.

'Who cares? She knew enough to realise these books could be useful and that's just with the half-tale Geris told her.'

'That's more than she needs to know anyway. She's a thief, remember, that's all we want her for.'

'I disagree.' Shiv's tone was calm but firm. 'She's good at stealing but she can think fast too. The more she knows, the more chance we have that she'll come up with something the rest of us might miss. Planir told us to use any means we could find.'

I grimaced in the gloom. Did I want to get any deeper into this? This was some wizards' chicanery after all. I caught a mental whiff of those hot coals I had started to forget. On the other hand, there was going to be money in this; half the value of that ink-horn would make a tidy pile of coin for a start. Information always had value too.

Darni started to speak but the opening door and a riot of children interrupted him. I stamped on the spot for a few paces then made my way loudly down the remaining stairs and joined them.

The meal was excellent and plentiful. Harna clearly had a lot of practice since, as well as our party and their seven children, she was feeding two other men, whom I gathered were Travor's journeymen in the potteries. If Ostrin ever decides to disguise himself as a mortal and go around testing hospitality like the legends say he used to, Harna won't have anything to worry about, other than the possibility of a permanent divine houseguest. The journeymen ate, thanked her and left for their own quarters, and Harna started threatening the children with bed.

'Please can we see Geris do some tricks?' the oldest girl pleaded, blue eyes wide open in appeal.

'I'd be happy to,' Geris offered.

Harna smiled. 'Just a few.' She began to clear the table while Geris proved remarkably competent at sliding coins round his fingers and making them appear out of the baby's ears. I resisted the temptation to join in and turned to Shiv.

'Are you sure those two won't gossip about their master's strange visitors over their ale?' I gestured to the door after the journeymen. 'Harna said you've been here a lot since Spring Equinox.'

Shiv shook his head as he took a long drink of Travor's excellent mead. 'They won't talk.'

'Can you be certain?' I didn't even attempt to conceal my scepticism.

'Absolutely.' There was no doubt in his voice.

Rather to my surprise, my instincts told me to trust him.

'Shiv, Shiv, can you do us an illusion?'

I stared at the boy who was asking and choked on my mead.

'Harna?'

'Oh, all right.' Harna smiled and filled a large flat bowl with water. Shiv rubbed his hands together and green magelight gathered round his fingers. My eyes must have been as round as any of the children's as I watched a pond appear, grassy banks, reeds round the fringe, lilies dotting the surface.

'Do ducks, do ducks,' one of the little ones begged. Shiv obliged with an improbably yellow bird with a tail of ducklings following her. The image flickered suddenly and the ducklings began hiding in the reeds and leaves, the mother trying in vain to round them up again.

Shiv suddenly burst out laughing. 'Harna!' he protested. I looked up to see green light flickering in her hands and amusement in her eyes.

Shiv got the ducks under control again. 'Right, that's enough. Bedtime for you lot.'

The children obeyed with remarkably little protest. Well, the trick with the ducks certainly left tales of the Eldritch

Kin looking pretty dusty as bedtime entertainment. Harna and Geris chivvied them upstairs and Darni and Shiv went out for a last check on the horses. I wondered in passing where the chests had disappeared to.

'Come into the study.' Travor rose and led me to a neatly furnished room next door. He lit the fire, laid ready and waiting, and then opened a polished cabinet and offered me a delicate ceramic cup.

'Wine? It's heathberry, we make it ourselves. Or there's some juniper liquor, or more mead.'

I've had some bad experiences with fruit wines. 'Juniper, please.'

He poured me the hefty sort of measure you only get from someone who doesn't drink the stuff himself then stole a sideways glance at a desk where a large slate lay covered in neat diagrams.

'Are you working on something? Don't let me stop you if you want to carry on with it.'

'If you don't mind.' He sat as he spoke, relieved to abandon social niceties.

'What is it?' I peered at the drawing but could make no sense of it.

'There's a new way of smelting being developed in Gidesta; the Mountain Men have come up with something called a blast furnace.' He frowned at some calculations, wiped a patch of his slate clean and started afresh.

I peered over his shoulder. 'Is Harna a mage then?' The liquor had me speaking before my brain caught up with my mouth.

'That's right.' Travor seemed unconcerned.

'So . . .' I could not think how to frame my next question.

He looked up and a grin relaxed his square, rather harsh features. 'So how does she come to be married to a potter in the arse-end of nowhere?' Clearly a question he was used to.

I laughed. 'Something like that.'

He shrugged and returned to his mathematics. 'She has the talents but what she really wants out of life is a good marriage, a happy home and lots of children. We met when she was travelling with another mage, we stayed in touch and when she fell for Seyn, we got married.'

I drank my juniper; it was quite beyond me.

A sudden commotion of dogs outside made Travor look up. 'I'd better go and see to the hounds.'

As he left, Shiv reappeared. 'Any problem?' I asked.

'A fox or something sniffing round the ducks.' Shiv poured himself a small measure of barley spirits and sat down with a sigh.

'So, how long are we going to be here?'

'I've sent a message to a chap called Conall who lives over in Eyhorne. He's been working with some of the early records from Hadrumal and I'd like him to take a look at those books you found. That was good thinking.'

'If you tell me what's really going on, I might be able to pick up more useful things,' I said casually. 'Unless Darni won't let you.'

Shiv laughed and ignored the bait. 'We'll probably be here for a couple of days, so make the most of the rest. We'll be heading into Dalasor next so it'll be camping and cooking on open fires not feather beds and clean linen.'

'I thought all Dalasor had to offer was grass, sheep and cattle.'

'Have you never been there?'

'I make a living gambling and moving on, Shiv.' I refilled my glass. 'There's not a lot of use me getting into a game where the minimum stake is ten goats.'

Shiv laughed again and took a sip of his drink. I looked at him in the soft lamplight and felt a warm quiver. He was quite handsome really, even allowing for the not inconsiderable glow I was feeling from the mead. I crossed the room and joined him on the settle by the fire.

'Harna was saying she's seen a lot of you since Spring Equinox. That's a long time to be away from home.'

Shiv stretched out and closed his eyes. 'It is,' he agreed, 'but Pered's very understanding.'

I blinked. 'Pered?'

A faint, fond smile curled round Shiv's lips. 'My lover. He's an illuminator for a copyist in Hadrumal. We've been together for six years now, so he's used to my being away.'

I took another drink to cover my confusion and sought wildly for a way of turning the conversation. At least I hadn't made a fool of myself.

'You're not from Hadrumal originally though, are you? Your accent's nothing like Darni's but I can't place it.'

'No, I'm from western Caladhria, the fens beyond Kevil.'

I remembered something Halice once told me; where everyone else tells jokes about Caladhrians, Caladhrians tell jokes about Kevilmen.

'Drianon! You must really have been a fish up a tree there!' My mouth was definitely running away with my brain tonight; I put down my goblet.

'What do you mean? Because I'm a mage or because I'm . . .' Shiv opened his eyes and gave me a wicked grin. 'How does a lady put it in Vanam nowadays? One who scents his handkerchiefs? A man who doesn't cross the dance floor? Or do you favour the more literal descriptions? Rump–rustler? Sack–arse?' he said with relish and a flash of his eyes.

Well if he wasn't bothered, why should I be? 'Both, I suppose.'

'Oh, Caladhria's not as backward as you people think.'

'Come off it,' I scoffed. 'Half the Caladhrian houses I've been to don't even have chimneys. How many people in your village used oil-lamps?'

'Rush-lights work perfectly well. Why should they change?' His serious tone nearly fooled me but I saw the glint in his eye. 'But you're right; my family did not know what to do with me. There was no unpleasantness, I just felt like a pig in a cowshed. My uncle had a cousin whose wife was able to recommend me to a mage in Kevil and he sent me off to Hadrumal.' Shiv's eyes looked inward. 'That was fifteen years ago, half a lifetime.'

I'd forgotten Caladhria was like that; if your grandmother knew a man whose brother's sons had once sold your cousin a horse, you're as good as related. It makes for a difficult place to work my sort of business but it has its good points; I've never seen children begging on the streets there. A memory struck me.

'Why've you been chatting up every serving-girl we've met, if you're – er – otherwise inclined?'

'They tend to expect it and a friendly girl can tell you useful things.'

That was fair comment; I've batted my eyelashes at enough men I've no intention of touching let alone anything more.

'Can you imagine Geris trying to spread a little charm around? Or Darni?'

I laughed at the picture. 'What about Darni? Just what is his problem? Does he have any family?'

'Oh yes. He's married to an alchemist who came to do some work for the wizards who specialise in fire magic.'

There was little to say to that. 'Oh.'

'They had their first child just after Winter Solstice and I think Darni's not too happy to be doing so much travelling at the moment.' Shiv's tone was sympathetic.

I sniffed. 'No need for him to take it out on the rest of us. So do you know Harna because she's a mage then? Is that why you stay here?'

'That, and she's Darni's cousin.'

'Isn't that awkward? I mean, if Darni couldn't be a real mage and she's . . .'

Shiv shook his head. 'There was a time when Darni would have given his stones for half Harna's talent, but he's moved on. Meeting Strell helped him realise there's a lot more out there than magic.'

He yawned and rubbed a hand through his hair. 'I'm for my bed. See you in the morning.'

I wondered about going up too but with my afternoon's sleep I wasn't really tired. I went to look at Travor's slate and was absorbed in trying to follow his calculations when the door opened. I jumped.

'Sorry, I didn't mean to startle you.' Geris looked apologetic.

'Never mind.' I stared in fascination at the drawing of Travor's furnace. 'Have you seen this?'

'What? Oh, yes, it's very interesting, don't you think?'

I looked up; for someone who seemed to gather any stray scrap of useless information, Geris did not sound very keen. He was standing awkwardly by the fire.

'Everything all right?' I was curious.

'Oh yes.' Geris helped himself to a large measure of the wine and blinked a little as he drank it down. It apparently gave him the courage he was seeking. 'I really wasn't sure you'd be able to get that ink-horn, you know.'

'I'm very good at what I do.' I heard an unexpected edge in my voice.

'No, I didn't mean I thought you . . . that is, I thought it would be impossible for anyone.' There was no mistaking his wide-eyed admiration and I hid a smile under my gambling face.

'Oh?'

'Do tell me about it,' he urged.

Maybe this was my chance to feature in one of Judal's plays, if only at second hand. 'All right.' I smiled at him and we sat on the settle.

'Well, we went to look at the house first, and then we went for an ale . . .' I may have exaggerated the difficulties a little and I don't suppose Darni featured much in the tale but Geris' appealing face was hard to resist.

'I think you did marvellously,' he breathed as I wound up my somewhat colourful yarn. 'We can't thank you enough.'

'Sure. You're the only one who's thanked me at all.' The realisation hit me harder than I had expected and a tremor in my voice surprised me.

'No, we're all grateful.' Geris sounded quite distressed. 'When Shiv said he couldn't get to the piece, we thought we'd have to go back without it. Darni was furious.'

'And then I walked in and solved all your problems,' I snorted. 'Darni could show a little more gratitude.'

'I'll speak to him about it,' Geris said firmly and I could not help laughing.

'Don't worry about it, I've met his type before.'

'Have you?' Geris looked eager for more tales and I obliged, flattered by his interest and enjoying the chance to boast of some of my more spectacular successes.

I wasn't too surprised when he put a friendly arm around my shoulders as I was explaining Charoleia's latest plan to separate the Relshazri authorities from some of their revenues; I snuggled encouragingly into his side. I was quite happy to let him kiss me as we compared notes on the various ale-houses in Vanam; his breath was sweet with the wine and his lips firm and dry. I don't think he had expected to end up in his bed quite so soon, nicely brought-up boy that he was, but I had been sleeping alone for quite a while and I decided I'd passed too many solitary nights. It did cross my mind that, the last time I'd mixed business and pleasure, there had been tears all round but Geris's delicate hands and eager kisses soon saw off my reservations.

He may have been naive in some ways but there had been a few lucky girls back in Vanam, if I am any judge. He was a good lover, new enough to the pastime still to treat it with an awe I found quite touching, but experienced enough to know that pleasure shared is pleasure doubled. He was sensitive and responsive, and even did his best not to just roll over and fall asleep when we were done.

'Go to sleep.' I brushed the hair from his sweaty forehead and kissed him. He tucked the crisp linen around me as we nested together like spoons. I drifted off to sleep with his soft breathing in my hair.

Hanchet Marketplace,
15th of For–Autumn

'Hold it, you beauty.' Casuel gritted his teeth as he hauled on the reins. The sudden shock of cobbles underfoot helped, and the horse skidded to an uncertain halt, snorting its disapproval.

'That's better.' Casuel applied the gig's brake and looked around the marketplace for the principal inn. He pursed his lips in surprised approval. 'This is an improvement on what I had imagined. And we made good time too,' he commented to Allin good-humouredly.

'This is much more comfortable than travelling by carriers' coach.' The last stage in an open carriage had given her pasty cheeks an attractive colour for a change.

Casuel glanced round, hesitating about which way to take; the tail-end of the day's market was still cluttering up what passed for a town square.

'Clear the road, mester!'

The horse shied as some peasant waved an irritated staff in their direction and Casuel was about to tell the oaf what he thought of him when he realised he had stopped, in fact, directly in front of the water-trough. He clicked his tongue and slapped the reins on the horse's rump, looking disdainfully over the head of the impatient farmers waiting to water their beasts before setting out for home. He lurched before he remembered to loosen the brake so that they could move off.

An urchin spoke up hopefully from somewhere near Casuel's knee.

'What did you say?' This mangled dialect was even thicker in these hamlets off the main coach routes, he realised with a shock.

'Hold your horse for a copper quarter, sir?'

Casuel narrowed his eyes at the lad but after a moment reached into his pocket for the coin. This was hardly Col, after all. He held up a whole penny and the youth's eyes brightened.

'Where can we get rooms and stabling for the night?'

'Over yonder at the Stag Hound.' The urchin bobbed an attempt at a bow. 'Follow me.'

Casuel directed the horse awkwardly through the bustle 'You see, I don't have much need to drive in Hadrumal,' he explained to Allin, but she was too busy looking round. The inn yard was busy, but the sight of such a well-dressed driver soon brought an ostler to the gig's side.

'We require accommodation and livery for the night.' Casuel reached round for their bags and handed them down. 'Take these and bespeak us two chambers.'

'I can see to it, sir.' The groom clutched Allin's tattered valise to his chest, looking a little startled.

Casuel descended and grimaced as shoulder muscles unused to the demands of driving protested. He looked at the crowd growing around the water-trough and beckoned to the urchin

'Walk the horse till he's good and cool, water him, and then bring him back here, and the penny's yours when I leave in the morning.'

Stalking a little stiffly into the inn, Casuel was satisfied he had cowed the child into obedience. Allin scrambled down awkwardly in a confusion of petticoats and followed, bumping into Casuel as he halted, taken aback to find the bar counter three deep in thirsty peasants. He hovered uncertainly for a few moments then gritted his teeth. His future could depend on what he learned here, he told himself.

'Excuse me. By your leave.' Politeness was going to get him nowhere, he realised, as an elbow caught him agonisingly in the ribs and a burly farmer shoved past him to reach for an ale.

'Service!' His unfamiliar accent rang out over the hum of the busy tap-room and he fought a blush as the suddenly silent throng stared at him.

'I would like a jug of ale, if you please.' Casuel shook the dust from the folds of his caped cloak and coughed to cover his embarrassment.

The buzz of conversation resumed around him and the innkeeper shoved a jug and cups across the bar. Casuel took a seat at the end of the counter and looked suspiciously at the oily surface of the brew. Allin examined it dubiously.

'I know. I'd have preferred wine but there's no point even asking outside the larger towns in Ensaimin.' Casuel heaved a sigh of homesickness for his neat rooms in Hadrumal or better yet, his parents' well-ordered house.

'Excuse me.' He caught at the sleeve of a maid hurrying past with a tray of bowls.

'You can order food at the kitchen door.' She tried to shake her arm free without losing her load, not even turning her head towards him.

'No, I'm looking for someone,' Casuel began.

'Try the wash-house next door,' the maid snapped, twitching her elbow out of his reach.

Casuel sipped his drink and immediately regretted it. The barkeeper was at the far end of the counter and there was no sign of the pace of business slowing.

'I'd say we've got a rat in a dog-pit's chance of managing a quiet conversation here,' he muttered to Allin.

She nodded, momentarily silenced as thirst overcame caution and she tried the ale. She screwed up her eyes and coughed.

'Do you think they might have some milk?' She blinked.

'Not drinking?' A sour smell assaulted Casuel's nostrils and he turned to see a creased and dirty little man hovering by the yard door, eyes darting from side to side.

'Not this swill,' Casuel grimaced.

The ragged man's eyes brightened and he reached for the jug.

'Not so fast.' Casuel lifted it out of reach for a moment. 'I'm trying to find someone . . .'

'Wash-house next door,' the old vagrant said promptly, eyes still fixed on the jug.

'What's so special about this wash-house?' Allin wondered in an undertone.

Casuel shook his head, exasperated. 'We might as well go and find out. We'll get nothing here but a night in the privy.'

He caught the barkeeper's eye and dropped some coppers on the counter, only too happy to abandon the ale to the gleeful vagabond and to leave the heaving tavern. He stood on the step and took a long breath of fresh air. Allin squeaked behind him and squeezed her way under his arm, rubbing her rear.

'Where do you suppose this wash-house is, then?'

'There's steam coming from those shutters.' Allin pointed across an alley.

'Come on. I suppose the washerwomen will know who lives where.. Women always know that sort of thing, don't they? My mother generally knows the life history of anyone moving into the square before they've even unpacked their trunks.'

Allin smiled uncertainly. Casuel led the way but then hovered uncertainly by the door as he heard giggles from inside. He'd never really been at ease with women, especially not when they gathered together. He looked at Allin; perhaps she could do the talking. No, perhaps not.

Casuel squared his shoulders and went inside. He nearly stepped straight out again when he found himself facing a girl wearing an extremely low bodice over little more than a shift. She greeted him with a very frank smile.

'Can I help you?' A woman of about his mother's age looked up from a wash tub.

'I'm looking for some information.' Casuel tried to ignore the sweat beading on his forehead. Of course, it was bound to be hot in a wash-house. Obviously women working here would wear light clothing.

A smile twitched the corners of the matron's mouth. 'What kind of information would that be?'

Casuel removed his cloak, fearing sweat stains in his coat, and loosened the neck of his shirt. 'I'm trying to find a man who was once chamberlain to Lord Armile of Friern.'

'That'd be Teren, I'd say.' The speaker was a blowsy type with hard eyes and improbably russet hair loose around her shoulders. She looked past Casuel at Allin and a faint frown wrinkled her brow.

'Can you tell me where I might find him, madam?' Casuel asked with stiff politeness, gratified that this was proving so easy.

The redhead exchanged a rapid glance with the washer-woman. After a still moment, she looked at Casuel, amused. 'You know the track to the Dalasor high road?'

'I can find it,' Casuel said confidently.

'Cross the bridge beyond the coppices, carry on till the third ride on the left, there's a shrine to Poldrion next to a red-oak.'

'I'll find him there?' Casuel was puzzled.

'Fifth niche on the right, middle shelf.' The redhead laughed heartily and took a drink from a leather flask she'd been holding among the folds of her skirts. She smiled warmly at Allin.

'I'm sorry but he's dead and burned, two and a half seasons gone.' The washerwoman gave her linens a half-hearted stir with a copper stick.

Casuel nearly turned on his heel, outraged to be the butt of such tasteless humour for such women.

'It's no joke for his poor wife.' The lass with the loosely laced bodice emerged from a back room with a basket of bread and cheese which she shared around, offering some to Allin after giving her a long, considering look. 'Come in, girl, no need to wear out the step.'

A flash of inspiration struck Casuel. 'He has left a widow?'

The woman with the flask looked serious for a change. 'Poor bitch, her with five to bring up and no family closer than a three-day walk.'

'It's hard to be so far from your own at such a time.' The washerwoman's tone was sympathetic and she sighed as she chewed on her bread.

'If I cannot do business with her husband, I can at least do what I can for the poor unfortunates he has left behind,' Casuel announced loftily. 'Charity is the duty of all Rational men.'

The redhead muttered something which he didn't catch, what with her mouth full and her dialect suddenly thicker than before. The washerwoman nodded and her expression was thoughtful. Casuel ignored this irrelevance.

'Where would I find this lady?'

'You might catch her at the buttercross about now,' the younger lass volunteered, after checking for a nod from the redhead. 'She sells cheese for Mistress Dowling most days.'

Casuel nodded his thanks graciously. A thought struck him. 'How much would it cost for you to brush and sponge my cloak?'

The women exchanged a glance and the redhead suddenly hid her face in her apron with a sudden fit of coughing. The washerwoman's smile quirked again but she managed to reply civilly enough.

'Four pennies should see to it, your honour.' She smiled at Allin. 'You look like you could do with a freshening, lassie. Why not wait here while his honour's busy?'

'That would be nice.' Allin hesitated, clutching her shawl to herself.

'I'll call later.' Casuel handed over the garment and left, a little bemused by the burst of laughter he heard behind him.

He had no time to waste on the odd behaviour of laundresses, he chided himself. The market square was nearly empty now, the last few wagons either heading out along the tracks to the farms or waiting, canvases laced down, for their owners to quit the taverns which were now bright with lanterns and ringing with noise. With some distaste he picked his way between the straw, dung and fallen vegetables that littered the cobbles, heading for the neat thatched roof of the buttercross. He quickened his step as he saw several women packing up their baskets and leaving the broad stone steps to a few foraging thatch-birds.

'Excuse me, ladies.' He bowed formally and the women halted in startled surprise.

'I am looking for the Widow Teren.' He tried for a winning smile.

'Why's that, then?' one asked cautiously.

'I had business with her late husband.' Casuel decided a

masterful approach was called for, since charm seemed to have little effect round here.

The women spent a long moment exchanging glances which conveyed nothing to Casuel. One of them looked round the square and the people going about their business; she nodded to her companion.

'She's with her children, round the far side.'

'Brown dress with a blue apron,' the second added. The two of them moved away, crossing over to the well where they stood in apparently idle conversation, empty baskets swinging loosely on their arms.

The widow was not hard to find as Casuel walked briskly round the buttercross. She was about his own age, thin face tired as she packed her panniers with some heels of bread and vegetables that Casuel's mother would have rejected as unfit for her pigs.

'Just sit down and stop Miri rampaging around, will you?' she snapped at a ragged little boy who was chasing pigeons with his younger sister. The child opened his mouth to protest, wisely thought better of it and grabbed the girl by her tattered skirt, plumping down his skinny behind on the lowest step.

'Shouldn't those children be in bed?' Casuel frowned, looking at the length of the shadows.

'What's it to you?' The woman did not snap at him. She simply sounded defeated, not even looking at him, pushing ineffectually at wisps of hair escaping her headscarf as she tied the little girl's apron strings.

'I'm sorry, let me introduce myself.' Casuel bowed low. 'I am Casuel Devoir. I understand you are the Widow Teren?'

'Pleased to meet you, I'm sure,' the widow replied, standing and looking at him, bemused. The children simply stared at him, mouths open.

'I had been hoping to see your husband . . .' Casuel halted at the sight of the numb pain on the three faces before him. 'I heard of your loss,' he went on hurriedly, 'and was hoping I might be able to assist you somehow.'

A spark of life returned to the woman's dark eyes. 'Drianon knows we could do with some help. Here.' She passed a frayed basket to Casuel and slung the yoke of her panniers over her shoulders. 'Like you said, this pair should be in bed. Walk me home and we can talk there.'

Casuel opened his mouth to protest but shut it again. He had to have that information, he told himself. If it was important to Darni, it was doubly so to him. He walked after the woman and children, awkwardly trying to hold the basket to prevent the sharp spikes of wicker damaging his clothing. To his relief, the widow soon turned down a narrow entry and knocked on the door of a neat row-house. An older child with a squalling infant in her arms opened up, using her foot to foil a determined toddler's attempt at escape.

'Get your supper and take it in the back.' The widow settled herself on a low settle near the fire and opened her bodice. The children obediently filled bowls with thick soup and helped themselves to the coarse bread, filing out through the narrow door.

'I beg your pardon, I'll wait outside while you nurse your child.' Casuel turned to go, scarlet as the baby suckled with evident enjoyment and no little noise.

'I've my family to see to and I've been up since before dawn.' The widow's voice was uncompromising. 'This is the only time I get to sit down, so talk to me now or leave.'

Casuel cleared his throat and concentrated on staring into the meagre fire.

'I understand your husband used to be in the household of Lord Armile.'

'That's right. What's it to you?'

'I am interested in doing business with his lordship, I deal in books and manuscripts. Do you happen to remember your husband ever talking about the library at Friern Lodge?'

He turned his head despite himself at hearing the widow's tired laugh.

'It was me did the telling to him, what with me dusting the cursed place every other day.'

'You were a servant too?'

'Upper housemaid, until my lord decided to turn us both out for daring to wed without his permission.' Venom thickened the woman's voice and she blinked away tears as she hushed her startled baby.

Casuel did not know what to say. Women were enough of a mystery and crying women were completely beyond him. To his intense relief, the woman shook her head after a moment and sniffed.

'What do you want to know?' she asked.

'I'm interested in works dealing with the fall of the Tormalin Empire. Do you know what I'm talking about? Do you recall anyone perhaps mentioning any books on that subject?'

The widow lifted the child, laid it over her shoulder until it belched loudly and settled it to the other breast, her face thoughtful. She reached up and unknotted her head scarf, shaking loose fine dark hair sprinkled with white at the crown. 'I think we'd get on a lot better if you stopped treating me like some lackwit, Messire whatever your name was,' she said tartly at last. 'I'd read a good number of those books myself before we were turned out, so I should imagine I can tell you what you need to know. Before I do, I'd like to know why you want to know and what that might be worth to you.'

Casuel hesitated, not wishing to antagonise such an unexpected source of information, but struggling for a reply. He opted reluctantly for as much of the truth as he dared. 'I have a customer interested in literature dealing with that period of history. If Lord Armile has any such, I could then approach him and see if he might be interested in selling. Do you remember any titles, names of authors?'

'Hoping he doesn't know the value of what he has and working your way round to it like an afterthought.' There was a hint of laughter as well as a sharp edge in the widow's voice. 'Not so honest, are you, for all your fancy graces? Not that I mind. I'll serve his lordship an ill turn if I can and glad to, Drianon rot his stones.'

Casuel opened his mouth to defend his honour then shut it again. 'What can you tell me?' He took a waxed note-tablet from a pocket.

'Let's agree a price,' the woman countered, fixing him with

a stern eye that made Casuel feel about five years old. 'I want to take my children back to my own village. I need carriers' fare and the price of a cart for our belongings.'

'Will five Marks cover it? Tormalin?' Casuel reached for his money pouch.

The widow blinked. 'That would do handsomely.'

She kissed her sleeping baby's fluffy head and laid the child in a wicker crib, then to Casuel's profound relief laced her bodice, looking up at him with a smile teasing her lips. 'Bargaining prices for books not the same as haggling for horses then, is it?'

Casuel made a half-bow. 'I can drive as hard a bargain as any man, madam; my father is a pepper merchant and taught me his trade well. However he is a man of honour and has also taught me that one should offer charity, not seek advantage, when encountering widows and orphans.'

Besides, the money would put some decent clothes on their backs so the widow needn't present her family to her relations as beggars, he thought with some satisfaction.

'And you don't get drunk on holy days and you remember your mother at every shrine to Drianon, I take it.' There was more humour than irony in her voice now. 'Let me get the children to bed and then I'll tell you what I know. All I ask is you stitch that bastard up tighter than a festival fowl's arse.'

She looked at the pot over the fire and bit her lip. 'You'd better step out for something to eat; we've nothing to spare, I'm sorry.'

The third chime of the night was sounding before Casuel finally made his way back to the marketplace and the inn, elation filling him as he strode along, despite the repeating taste of a pie which he now suspected had contained horsemeat. A breeze blew a gust of warm soapy air across his path.

'Allin!' he exclaimed, remembering her with a guilty start. 'No matter; she can't have come to much grief in a wash-house.'

Nevertheless he quickened his step but was held up by a man at the door, whom it appeared, having drunk rather too much, had inexplicably decided this was the time to dispute the cost of his laundry.

'Excuse me.' Casuel pushed past to see Allin deep in conversation with the washerwoman.

'If he's taking advantage, you can stay here. Just to do the linens, nothing more. We'll look after you.'

'Evening, your honour.' The redhead greeted him loudly and stepped into his path, his cloak over her arm.

Allin scrambled to her feet, cheeks red, her hair freshly dressed with ringlets coiling in the damp air.

'Are you ready?' Casuel enquired curtly, taking his cloak and handing over a Mark. 'I think we should return to the inn. I want to make an early start tomorrow.'

The washerwoman gave Allin a rough kiss of farewell. 'You know where we are, dear.'

Casuel tutted impatiently as Allin tied her shawl about her.

'Did you find the widow?' she enquired as they picked their way back to the inn through the dim moonlight.

'I did.' His good humour returned. 'You know, this should be quite straightforward. According to her, Lord Armile barely knows what he's got on his shelves. He simply inherited the collection along with the title. I think I should find something to impress Usara, and perhaps even Planir.'

Almost as satisfying, an extra Mark had persuaded the widow to deny all knowledge of the library should anyone else come enquiring, Darni or Shiv, for instance. Casuel decided not to burden Allin with that detail.

He strode into the inn and halted on the threshold, surprised to see it as busy as before.

'Excuse me, I bespoke a room earlier.' He held up a hand to intercept the maidservant, her hair now coming loose from its pins and her apron stained with ale and food.

'Yon's the door to the stairs. Find one of the maids up there to bother.' She brushed past him, sweeping up a handful of flagons from a table as she went.

'Excuse me—' Casuel began indignantly but the girl was gone.

'Come on,' he snapped at Allin crossly and pushed through the carousing farmers to the stairs. Once upstairs he was none too pleased to find his bag shoved under a bed in a room crowded with nine others.

He went into the narrow corridor and beckoned a harassed maid with an armful of well-worn blankets.

'That's right, your honour. You in there and the lady in the women's room upstairs.'

'We bespoke two chambers,' he began indignantly.

'There's none to be had on a market day.' The woman made to push past him, annoyed when Casuel prevented her. 'There's no use kicking up about it. If you don't want the bed, I can let it five times over.'

Casuel coloured at her tone. 'Oh all right then.'

He escorted Allin up to the long garret above, relieved to find a group of clean, decently dressed farmwives already there. He returned to his own bed and dragged out his travelling bag, deciding to make some notes before he settled down.

Casuel drew a shocked breath, his grievance at the petty annoyances of the inn evaporating.

'Raeponin pox the lot of them!'

Someone had been going through his things! He shuddered with distaste at the thought of grubby sneak-thieves pawing through his linen, however slight the disturbance. He checked his various volumes, laying them on the bed, and reached down to the bottom of the bag for his packet of papers and letters. It was still sealed with his own signet but as he brought his candle closer Casuel could see the tell-tale smudges where the wax had been lifted off with a hot knife blade. He cracked the seal and sorted through his notes, hands shaking with indignation.

'Greetings.'

Casuel turned, surprised to be addressed in oddly formal Tormalin. A blond man in neat travelling clothes had taken the bed next to him.

'Good evening,' he replied curtly.

'You're a long way from home.' The stranger shook out his blankets and smiled.

What business was that of this undersized fellow? 'I travel in the course of my trade,' Casuel replied repressively.

'You deal in books, I see?' The blond man's eyes were blue and cold, despite the warmth of his smile.

'Among other things.' This curious character could answer a few questions himself, thought Casuel. 'I don't recognise your accent, where do you hail from?'

'I have travelled from Mandarkin.' The man's smile broadened. 'I find it much warmer here.'

If you're Mandarkin-born, I'm an Aldabreshi, Casuel thought. That lie might satisfy peasants who've never travelled more than ten leagues from their homes, but he had met several Mandarkin in Hadrumal and this man's accent was nothing like theirs. Something was not quite right here.

He yawned ostentatiously. 'Excuse me, I'm for my bed.'

Casuel took off his boots and breeches and got beneath the soft blankets, promising himself a thorough bathe and complete change of linen when he returned to a civilised hostelry.

'Raeponin only knows how anyone's supposed to sleep with that row going on,' he muttered to himself as the hubbub from the tap-room continued unabated.

Men in various states of drunkenness and undress began entering the room and Casuel huddled under his blankets in an attempt to isolate himself from the unsavoury gathering. The room gradually quietened, the thick darkness broken only by intermittent snores, usually interrupted by a kick from a neighbouring bed.

Surprisingly, it seemed Casuel had barely closed his eyes before the morning light was streaming through the shutters and the maid was hammering on the door to announce breakfast. He dragged himself reluctantly from the blankets, temples pounding and eyes gritty, unrefreshed after a night of unexpected and peculiar dreams. Conversations with Usara, other people he knew in Hadrumal, that scrying he'd done of Ralsere and Darni, all manner of inconsequential nonsense and memories had jumbled together, rolling over and around in his sleeping mind.

Allin soon gave up trying to engage him in conversation over breakfast and they departed shortly after in gloomy silence.

Travor's Pottery, the Drede Road,
West of Eyhorne,
16th of For–Autumn

I woke early, a little cramped, but I'm not complaining. Geris was still deeply asleep so I dropped a kiss on his tousled head and slipped out. Cold water soon had me fully awake and I began to hear movement in the rest of the house. I reached under my pillow for the book; I didn't fancy explaining why I'd held on to it. I wondered where Shiv's room was; if I could put it with the others, I felt sure he would not say a thing.

A heavy tread passed my door and I opened it a crack to see Darni's back heading for the staircase.

'So what are you doing about Conall? Do you know when he's coming?'

I couldn't hear the reply but it was clear he was talking to Shiv further down the stairs. I closed the door silently behind me and tried the next room along. It had Darni's kit in it so I moved on. Shiv's room not only had the books on the dresser but also the mysterious coffers at the end of the bed. I sniffed and rubbed a hand over my mouth.

Curiosity got Amit hanged. My mother had told me that jolly little tale for children often enough but it had never seemed to take. Caution, however, was a lesson I had learned. This was one time in my life when I wished briefly I did know more about wizards. Would Shiv have some magic woven around these boxes that would have him charging back up the stairs if I so much as touched them? Had Darni been standing guard at the inn to protect the boxes, or was that just a subterfuge to explain his presence in the yard as he waited for me?

My palms itched and I fingered my lockpicks. Saedrin's

stones; what did I have to lose? It wasn't as if I was going to take anything and even if Shiv did find out and threw me out of this masquerade, which I somehow doubted, I was no worse off than I had been the day before last. He would not renege on the deal over the ink-horn and half the value of that would see me happily on a coach to Col. Sorgrad and Sorgren would be there by now and I could work with them.

I closed the door and settled myself to work on the nearest lock. It was a good piece but nothing I could not handle and I soon had it free of the hasp. I raised the lid of the coffer; it was full of neat velvet-wrapped bundles. I reached in for a handful and unrolled a couple. I let out a slow breath of mystification. There were certainly some valuable pieces in there, rings and necklaces of old gold with gems cut ten generations out of fashion, but they sat next to trinkets you could pick up for a couple of Marks: a little crystal jar with a silver lid, a chatelaine's waist-chain with keys, scissors and pomander, a needle case for the obsessed embroiderer. There were a couple of daggers, but while one was decorated with filigree and gems to an extent which made it unwieldy, the other was a plain and serviceable knife that you'd use to cut your meat and bread. Strangest of all was a broken sword. The shards of blade were lost but the deer-horn handle was as carefully wrapped as the priceless bracelet next to it. Tales of lost swords proving rights to kingship and broken blades reforged are the stuff of Lescari romances – and Lescari politics come to that – but I could not see Shiv falling for that kind of nonsense.

High-pitched voices and running feet went hammering past the door and I hurriedly replaced everything and locked up the box. The children seemed to have descended on Geris so I was able to slip downstairs under cover of the commotion. Breakfast was a chaotic meal with people coming in and out so it was a while before I realised we had been joined by a grey-haired old man with a fussy manner at odds with his serious face.

'Shiv?' I nodded an enquiring eyebrow in the newcomer's direction.

Shiv swallowed his mouthful. 'Sorry, I keep forgetting you don't know everyone yet. This is Conall.'

'Pleasure.' I shook the hand he offered.

'Conall, this is Livak. She's a gambler by rights, but she's kindly been helping us get hold of some of the more difficult pieces.'

It was better than simply being introduced as a common house-breaker, I suppose, but what was this 'kindly helping'? I let it pass.

'You had the wit to pick up some books, Geris tells me?' Conall's eyes were bright with interest.

Saedrin save me from wizards and scholars, I thought. When would I ever be able to get back to decent, ordinary folk: horse copers, swindlers, gamblers and the like?

'Can you use the study, please? I want to get on.' Harna started whatever it is that mothers of small children do all day and we retreated next door.

'Now these are very interesting.' Conall rubbed his hands together with glee. '*Heriod's Almanac*. I've only seen one other copy of this version and it was badly corrupted.' He leafed through it, scanning the cramped script eagerly. 'Have you checked on the phases of the moons for the changes of season? What about the festivals – are there any clues there? Can we pinpoint the generation at all?'

'There's a *D'Isellion's Annals* with an appendix I haven't seen before.' Geris handed him another volume and Conall looked momentarily distressed, like an ass between two bales of hay.

'Could you have a look at this one first.' Shiv passed over a thin blue-bound volume, its pages darkened by age. I peered across the table but could barely make out the script, let alone read it. Conall frowned and took an enlarging-glass out of his pocket, humming softly as he studied the book.

He looked up with an expression of wonder. '*The Mysteries of Misaen*?'

Shiv nodded. 'It seems to be a journal of some sort, an initiate's work, I think.'

Geris produced a sheaf of parchment from somewhere and began searching through it.

'There's a lot here on the farseeing,' Conall breathed. He

looked up at Shiv. 'Am I reading this right? Does it say they could hear as well as see?'

'I think so. Look at the next page.'

'Here!' Geris pulled a sheet out of his notes. 'There's a reference to *D'Oxire's Navigation*. What do you think? Is it the one we found last winter?'

He and Conall bent over the table while Shiv and Darni watched patiently.

'Would anyone care to tell me what this is all about?' I asked acidly.

Darni opened his mouth but Shiv got in first. 'I think we can trust you.'

'Oh, yes,' Geris chimed in with a fond gaze that I found somehow disquieting.

'You see, there's rather more to this than strange dreams that might tell us more about the fall of the Tormalin Empire.'

'That's important though.' Conall raised a peremptory finger. 'We're only just beginning to piece together what really happened. So much knowledge has been lost.'

'True, and not only historical knowledge.' Shiv hesitated.

'I'm listening,' I prompted him.

'We did a lot of work in Hadrumal trying to find out why certain items were making people have these odd dreams. We don't have a spell that would command this sort of effect nowadays, but we've always known the Old Tormalins could do much that we've yet to find out how to duplicate. This looked like a good chance to do some serious investigation. We had plenty of material.'

Shiv rubbed a hand through his hair. 'I shan't bore you with the details . . .'

'Thank you so much,' I murmured. 'Sorry, do go on.'

'It's starting to look as if this is a whole new – or rather, ancient – form of magic.' His expression was that of a man who had just lost his inheritance on the wrong runes.

'I don't follow.'

'It's completely different from all that we nowadays know as magic. It's not based on the elements at all.'

'I'm sorry but I'm not with you.'

Shiv clicked his tongue in exasperation. 'You know magic relies on manipulating the constituent—'

'Not really, no.'

They all stared at me and I felt very uncomfortable. 'Look, I've never had anything to do with wizards,' I said defensively.

'Air, earth, fire and water.' Darni spoke up from the corner of the room. 'Wizards are born with an innate ability to comprehend and manipulate one of the elements. With training they can learn to manage the others. That's magic.'

'Well, there's more to it than that but basically, yes, that's how it works.' Shiv fixed me with a serious eye. 'But the magic surrounding these things has nothing to do with the elements at all.'

'So what is it?'

'If I knew that, I'd be in line for the Archmage's chair.'

'We know it draws on some kind of power.' Geris spoke up eagerly. 'It's stronger in some places than others, but we haven't been able to find any common factors. We're calling it aether, the source of the power, I mean. I've got a reference here . . .' He shuffled his notes.

Aether. A nice, impressive scholarly word meaning, if I remembered right, 'thin air'. I suppose plain language would not instil the same kind of confidence.

'So what do you really know?'

'The only clues we have are fragments in Old Tormalin writings and the garbled traditions of the mystery cults.' Conall leaned forward earnestly. 'That's where I come in. I'm an initiate of Poldrion. It's a family priesthood, the shrine's on our land and the older people round here are quite devout so we've kept it up. I broke an arm last year and it festered, so I was laid up for nearly a season; I amused myself by collating all the records.'

Some people certainly know how to have a good time, I thought.

'I came across some instructions on what the priests called miracles, and I found I could actually make things happen by following them.'

'I know that sounds incredible—'

I waved a hand to silence Geris' interruption. 'No, not really. Most religion's a sham as far as I'm concerned but I've seen a few priests do things I couldn't explain. Go on, Conall.'

'Let me show you.'

The old boy was clearly dying to do his festival trick. 'Go ahead.'

He placed a candle in the centre of the table and recited a complex mouthful of gibberish. I frowned as the candle-wick began to smoulder.

'Talmia megrala eldrin fres.' He repeated himself and the flame jumped into life. I stared as it died.

'But what's to say Conall's not really mageborn and just hasn't realised it before?' I looked up at Shiv.

'You can't hide magebirth; it usually comes out in childhood.'

'You find yourself setting fire to your bedclothes or making the well overflow,' said Darni, his lack of emotion remarkable in the circumstances.

Shiv nodded. 'It'll come out somehow, even when people do their best to suppress it. Some talents appear later but the oldest age of emergence on record was still only seventeen. Conall's more than fifty. Anyway, I could tell if this was elemental. I'd feel it.'

I stared at the thin trail of smoke winding up from the candle. Something was tugging at the back of my memory.

'Do it again.'

Conall obliged and I found my lips moving along with him.

'What is it?' Geris was watching me intently.

'The rhythm,' I said slowly. 'Can't you hear it?'

I picked up a quill and tapped it out. 'One two-three, one two-three, one-two, one.'

'What are you getting at?'

I repeated the nonsense words, stressing the metre, wondering why no one else was getting it. I've always had a good ear for rhythm, having the harp in my lucky runes. The quill I was holding burst into flames.

'Shit!' I dropped it and we all gaped stupidly for a moment as it burned a scar into Harna's polished table.

'Shit!' Shiv quenched it with a brief green flash and we all began to cough on the acrid smoke of burned feather until Darni opened the window.

'All right, I'm convinced,' I said a little shakily.

'What was so important about the rhythm?' Geris was looking more than a little piqued.

'I'm not sure,' Conall said slowly, eyes narrowed in thought. 'We'd better look into it. What made you pick up on it?'

'My father was a bard,' I said reluctantly. 'I suppose I've got his ear. Anyway, a lot of the old elegies he used to sing me to sleep with had that kind of lilt.'

'Did they?' Conall was rummaging through his parchments to find a clean page and began making notes. 'What were they? Can you remember the titles?'

I shrugged. 'I've no idea. They were old Forest songs that he used to sing to me.'

Conall looked at me as if he were noticing my red hair and green eyes for the first time. 'You're Forest blood?'

'Half-blood. My father was a minstrel who came to Vanam, where he met my mother.'

'Where can we find him?' Conall poised his pen eagerly.

'Not in Vanam, that's for sure,' I said shortly. 'He stayed for a while, then went back on the road. He came back from time to time but less and less frequently. I haven't seen him since the Equinox I was nine.'

'What was his name?'

'What is this? Why do you want to know?' You learn to live without a father; this was not something I wanted to get into.

'We know so little, almost anything could be significant,' Shiv said calmly. 'We should follow this up. Forest Folk travel widely but their traditions are kept very close. They could have something the rest of us have lost over the generations.'

'If we knew your father's name, we could identify his kindred at very least.'

'Jihol,' I said curtly.

'Jihol?' Conall looked at me expectantly. 'And his epithet?'
'Sorry?'

'The descriptive part of his name. It's important if we're to find him.'

I stared at him and something stirred in the depths of my memory. 'Deer-shanks,' I said slowly. 'That's what my grandmother called him.'

Well, spat would be a more accurate description. I squashed the recollection of her contempt breaking into a rare family afternoon in the sun.

Conall was busily writing things down. Geris frowned and then smiled.

'That would make you . . .' He paused. 'If you're half-blood, that would make you Livak Doe-daughter.' He said this as if he was announcing my right to a Lescari throne.

'It makes me nothing of the kind,' I snapped, disliking the way this conversation was exposing my ignorance of what I suppose you could call my heritage. He looked hurt but I had no time to waste on his romantic notions.

'Let's get back to the game, Shiv. So you've found a different sort of magic, what's so important?'

'I don't know.' He spread his hands. 'It could be just a curiosity, or it could be potentially earth-shattering. We just don't know what we're dealing with and ignorance can kill.'

'What you mean is, you wizards don't like the idea of other people using magic, do you?' I sniffed. 'What's the problem? You still seem to know more about all this than anyone else.'

'But wizards can't do this sort of magic.'

'Geris!' Shiv and Darni spoke together in a rare moment of unity and Geris blushed.

'They can't?' That was an interesting throw of the bones. I looked enquiringly at Conall.

'Um, no. Even people with minimal elemental talent have proved absolutely unable to work the few things we've discovered.'

I laughed until I saw Darni's expression. They had found a new type of magic but his useless mage talents were still enough to bar him from it; what a kick in the stones. I suppose he had some excuse for acting like a dog with a sore arse at times.

'But other people can? Who can and who can't?' I was getting interested in this.

'We don't know. We can't find any common trait.' They all looked solemn and fell silent.

A question that had been nagging at the back of my mind popped its head up again.

'Does this have anything to do with why you couldn't get that ink-horn for yourselves?'

'Pardon?' Shiv was singularly unconvincing as he tried to look blank.

'You said you could get things by magic if you had seen them and knew where they were, Shiv. You and Geris had visited the old man, so why did you need me?'

'You said she was sharp!' Conall laughed and I threw him a quick grin.

'There does seem to be a conflict with the two sorts of magic,' Shiv admitted. 'It's not always the case, but certainly, over really strongly enchanted items like the ink-horn, I can have real problems.'

Geris opened his mouth to elaborate but I waved him to silence.

'So now I know all this, how about telling me where we're going and what we're doing? The more I know, the more I can help.'

Darni looked as if he was going to object but decided to go with the run of the runes. He pulled out a map from Geris' now chaotic heap of parchment and spread it on the table.

'We're going through Eyhorne and up the high road to Dalasor. There's a man I need to see in Hanchet; he may have some information we can follow up. What we do next depends on how that goes. I certainly want to head for Inglis before winter. There's a merchant from there who outbid us on a piece we're particularly interested in, and I want it back. That's where you come in.'

I looked at the map and estimated the distance involved and the time it would take.

'Are you serious?' I asked incredulously.

'Absolutely.' Darni's tone was flat and hard.

So no chance of the Autumn Fair at Col this year. Oh well, if this was important enough for the Archmage to send people clear across the Old Empire, who was I to argue? I could keep quiet and wait for my coin. I wondered about trying to negotiate a daily rate.

I looked at the map again, 'What about Caladhria? There must be plenty of nobles with nice trinkets in there?' Caladhria was a lot closer and has nice things like real roads and inns and baths which Dalasor is notoriously short on.

'That's in hand,' Conall assured me. 'I've been working as an enclosure commissioner there for some years and I've got plenty of contacts.'

I'd bet he had, given the Caladhrian love of bureaucracy. A ruling council made up of the top five hundred nobles keeps ink- and parchment-makers in luxury there. It's always amazed me they ever managed to come up with the idea of enclosing the land but then, when you realise how much it's done to improve their stock-breeding, it becomes clearer. Have you ever known an aristocrat miss a chance to make more coin?

'So we're off to the delights of Dalasor; as much grass as you can eat and sheep as far as the eye can see.' Shiv clearly welcomed the prospect as much as me.

'Conall, it's market day in Eyhorne, isn't it?' Darni looked at me with a measuring eye. 'We'd better try and get you your own horse. I don't want to waste too much time crossing Dalasor, so we'll buy some remounts as well. Come on.'

We left Geris and Conall to peer excitedly at blurred ink, and Shiv to his efforts to restore Harna's table-top. Muttered curses were an essential part of both processes.

Eyhorne was not a long ride and the market was in full swing when we arrived. When it came to bargaining, Darni's 'cross me and I'll rip your arms and legs off' expression proved a real bonus and we soon picked up a sturdy-looking mule, cooking gear, blankets and tents. Darni clearly knew exactly what he was looking for, as much an expert in his field, literally in this case, as I am in mine. I relaxed and amused myself watching the local pickpockets at work.

'So what do you like in a horse?' Darni led the way confidently to the pens.

'No teeth and an inability to kick?'

He looked at me curiously. 'You do ride?'

'Hire-horses, as and when necessary.'

'So we needn't bid for that?' He pointed to a pen where a black and white brute seemed to be doing its best to eat the auctioneer's assistants.

'Not on my account,' I said fervently.

Darni looked at the vicious beast with faint longing. 'Shame; I'd like to get my hands on one of those Gidestan types.'

For my personal horse we eventually settled on a nicely behaved gelding with a coppery coat and kind eyes. We also found remounts for all of us and a spare carriage horse. The final price made me blink, but Darni paid up without visible pain.

'Time of year,' he commented as we saddled up and prepared to leave the town. 'It's a sellers' market at the moment.'

'Is he part of my payment or what?' I rubbed the horse's silky shoulder.

Darni shook his head. 'Call it a bonus. Planir can afford it.'

I started to wonder again about a longer-term association with the Archmage's agents.

We left the next morning and headed north. Darni set a brisk pace and I found myself enjoying riding a well-bred, well-schooled horse for a change.

'So, what are you calling him?' Geris asked as we waited our turn at a ford.

'What? Oh, I don't know.'

'He's got a noble head; how about Kycir?'

I laughed. 'Geris, it's a horse! You sit on it and it gets you places faster than walking. Anyway, why should I land it with a name like that?'

'What's wrong with it? He was the last undisputed King of Lescar.'

'He was also a complete plank!'

'He was a hero!'

'He died in a duel defending his wife's honour and when they went to tell her they found her in bed with his brother!'

'Kycir died believing in her!'

'He was the last one who did. That heroic tale left Lescar ten generations of civil war!'

We bickered away happily and, when we finally worked our way back to the horse, we settled on Russet as a name.

We travelled on for several days without incident to that stretch of heath between Eyhorne and Hanchet which runs up against the Caladhrian border. There was a slightly awkward moment when Darni realised Geris was planning to share my tent and hauled him off into the trees, supposedly to collect firewood.

'I'll get some water.' I casually picked up the kettle.

'Of course you will.' Shiv did not look up from the meat he was spitting.

I grinned at Shiv and moved quietly into the woods. Darni was ringing the curfew over Geris and no mistake.

'And how is she going to be climbing into attics with a two-season belly on her? Had you thought of that?' he hissed.

Geris mumbled something indistinct. Should I tell Darni I had thought of just such an event and taken appropriate action? No, it was none of his business. Let him ask me himself if he had the stones for it.

His voice rose in exasperation. 'Look, I don't care if you two are playing stuff the chicken ten times a night —'

I winced at the smack of fist on flesh and judged it time to leave. Darni and Geris appeared a little while later, carrying a good supply of firewood, which was something of a surprise. Nothing was said, I didn't ask and the evening continued in good enough humour so I suppose they must have sorted themselves out. I sighed a regret for the simple life of working with other women.

We made Hanchet a couple of days after that, just as the lesser moon passed the full and the greater waxed to three quarters. I for one was looking forward to a real bed and a bath. Unfortunately, Hanchet proved a disappointment in more ways than one. It's low-lying so most of the houses are wooden-framed withy and daub; the recent rain made the whole place thick with mud and stagnant-smelling. The bridge up the road had been washed out in an earlier storm and the town was full of travellers and traders waiting for it to be repaired. Even the Archmage's coin could not get us rooms anywhere decent and I was forced to renew my acquaintance with the various wildlife that thrive in cheap hostel beds. Our inn had no baths and, given the tension in the town, I didn't fancy the wash-house over the way, which had far too many 'laundresses' hanging round it. Hanchet's current ruler is a dry old maid who inherited unexpectedly and who has a particularly censorious attitude towards commercial sex. All the brothels had been cleared, but her ladyship had not yet caught on to the reason for the sudden boom in places to get your clothes and your body washed, if you get my drift.

Next morning Darni left us sitting over indifferent ale and worse food in the tap-room and went to find his contact. He returned unexpectedly fast with an expression that would have soured wine.

'Trouble?' Shiv pushed the jug towards him as he seated himself with a sigh.

'He's dead.' Darni scowled into his ale and fished something out.

'How?' Geris' eyes were wide with concern.

'Abscess. The surgeon pulled the tooth, but it was too late. The poison was in his blood and two days later . . .' Darni shrugged.

I ran my tongue round my own teeth, grateful to my mother for the gap I had there. I'd bet the others were doing the same; it's a story we've all heard, after all. I frowned at Geris, who was looking inappropriately cheerful, and he blushed and ducked his head.

'Did he leave any word, anything for you?' Shiv asked hesitantly. 'Your letter . . .'

Darni shook his head. 'Not that I can find out. The widow's

sold up and gone back to her own family. You can't blame her, he's left her with five to bring up.'

He glowered at his ale and went off to start an argument with the potman about it.

'So who was this man? What was Darni hoping to get from him?' I asked, curiosity pricking my neck.

'It's not important.' Shiv managed to combine smiling at me with a warning glance at Geris.

So that was that. I let it go; if there was no information and as a result no risky job for me, they could keep their little secrets if it made them feel important. Still, distracted men make poor gamblers. I took my runes out and smiled cheerfully at them both.

At least we could leave muddy Hanchet and, although we had to make a long detour to the next bridge, we were still in Dalasor before the full dark of the night.

CHAPTER FOUR

Taken from:

Thoughts on the Races of Antiquity

Presented to the Antiquarian Society of Selerima by Weral Tandri

I am sure, gentlemen, that, as children, you and I were entertained and on occasion chastised by our nurses with tales of the Eldritch Folk. Did any of you lose a fallen tooth, as I did, and lie awake that night, afraid lest some little blue man step out of a shadow and demand one from my mouth in place of his rightful offering? We can all laugh now and, as grown men of learning, we might feel such subjects too trivial for consideration. I will not argue with those who do so, but I have chosen to search for whatever seeds of truth may have nourished such flowers of children's fancy.

With the increasing popularity of antiquarian studies among gentlemen of breeding and fortune, several Eldritch rings have been excavated in recent years. Some fascinating discoveries have been made; from their bones, we learn these people were indeed shorter than modern men by some hands-widths. A warrior found buried on Lord Edrin's lands near Ferring Gap was found to have black hair and possibly swarthy skin, although this may have been a result of the remarkable preservation of his remains in ground akin to a bog before drainage allowed cultivation. Tales of little dark men do not seem so very far from the truth.

The Shadow-men were said to ride upon the wind. Well, a ring opened in Dalasor last spring found a woman of rank, by her garments, buried with six horses, bones all draped with the remains of richly ornamented harnesses. More workaday effects included tents, quilts, distaffs, a quern and a brazier, but there was no sign of any wheeled conveyance; indeed none such has ever been found even depicted in Eldritch art. Consider the vast windswept plains of Dalasor even today, and it is not so hard to imagine a race of people living and travelling with those herds of horses that we know once roamed the lands.

Gentlemen, the time has surely come to gather and examine the evidence in a more scientific manner. Our ancestors, in their ignorance, could not see beyond conflict with the ancient races of wood and mountain. Consider, however, the benefits accrued now that miners of Gidesta work with the Mountain Men of the Dragon's Spines; the very knives you use at table benefit from skills and techniques lost to our smiths for generations. When the Crusted Pox struck Hecksen last winter, their apothecaries could soothe and save many sufferers with simples learned from their commerce with the Forest Folk.

Our tales for children credit the Eldritch Folk with many miraculous powers but, alas, they have left no descendants in modern times. Their burials and artefacts are all we have to study, so I am here today to ask for your co-operation and yes, it is true, your coin. If we can establish a proper programme of study, we can add inestimably to our knowledge of antiquity and may even discover lost marvels to benefit ourselves and generations yet to come.

The South Road, Dalasor,
38th of For-Autumn.

I shivered as I stood looking across the grasslands early in the morning. The grass was damp with dew and silvered with icy fingers wherever the few scrawny trees gave shelter.

'Cold?' Geris opened his arm and I stepped inside his cloak gratefully.

'How long is it to Equinox?' I frowned. 'Isn't it a bit early for frost?'

Geris pursed his lips as he rummaged in a small trunk, typically emerging with three assorted Almanacs. The rest of us make do with one to a household, if we're lucky.

He flipped over the pages and compared the charts of the waxing and waning moons.

'It's five days if there's no lesser moon tonight,' he said finally. 'We've come a long way north, don't forget.'

I dug out my own cloak. 'So we won't get to Inglis until we're into Aft-Autumn then. Have you got an Almanac covering Inglis? What'll be going on?'

Geris consulted one of the other books but shook his head after a moment. 'It's all guild business, fixing prenticeships and the like.'

That tweaked my curiosity and I was about to ask for a look when Darni called us over to get mounted. As we moved out, I decided I really didn't like Dalasor. Among other things, there's almost no cover and that makes me seriously uncomfortable. I always like to have a discreet route out of any situation but out here you could be seen for leagues. As we rode, I found my back prickling like a child who's convinced there's a monster in the well-house or the privy.

We reached a turning off the high road and I was surprised

to see Darni take it. I kicked the horse, sorry, Russet, into a canter and caught up with him.

'Aren't we going to take the river? I thought that's the fastest way to reach the coast.'

Darni shook his head. 'All the miners and trappers will be coming out of Gidesta at the moment; winter comes early to the mountains. The boats will be full of them and they're rough company at the best of times. I want to steer clear of trouble.'

'Oh, oh well.' I tried to hide my disappointment.

Darni grinned at me. 'Looking forward to a game, were you?'

'They say you can make a killing on the bigger boats if you manage to get out without a knife in your back,' I allowed.

'Sorry. You'll have to try and win a few head of cattle off some herders instead.'

It was all very well for Darni to laugh but, a few days later, I did manage to win us half a beef and a load of fodder when we stopped to spend the night with some drovers taking beasts south for slaughter. I slept well despite the noise of the cattle shifting around us but that was my last decent night.

'You're very jumpy,' Darni observed neutrally as we crossed yet another featureless stretch of plain and I kept looking over my shoulder.

'I'm not used to being so conspicuous,' I admitted. 'The sooner I feel cobbles under my feet and can see a wall to hide behind, the happier I'll be.'

He smiled broadly and took a deep breath of the bracing air. 'I like it up here.'

'Well, I don't. I know this sounds daft but I'm sure I'm being watched.'

Darni considered this. 'Maybe we should ditch the last of that meat. We might have some wolves on our tail, I suppose. There are a lot of animals and birds up here, haven't you seen them? Aren't you Forest Folk supposed to be sensitive to animals?'

I shrugged. 'I've no idea. I don't tend to notice dogs unless they're biting my leg. All I know is I've got crawlers running up and down my spine.'

'Sure you didn't bring them with you from Hanchet?'

It was all very well for him to joke but I was serious. I went to help Shiv when we stopped to eat, trimming the meat while he lit the fire. Wizards do save you a lot on tinder and flint.

'Do you have to look for something specific when you're scrying, like you did with Halice?' I asked casually. 'Or can you just have a general look around?'

Shiv nodded. 'Why do you ask?'

'This may sound stupid but I can't shake the feeling we're being watched. Darni thinks I'm just getting the creeps from the local wildlife but I don't think that's it.'

'You're sure?'

'Certain.' I realised just how certain as I spoke, and Shiv heard it in my voice.

'That's good enough for me. I'll check back along our trail if you like.'

He took out his oils and worked his spells and we all gathered round to look into the fascinating images he drew out of the water. He found the herdsmen we had met and we watched as they forded a stream, tiny horns nodding as the cattle plunged through the water.

'All right, let's work backwards,' Shiv breathed.

The image sped along and I wondered if this is how the land looks to a bird, a tapestry of green and brown, laced with glinting waters, dotted with the darker green of trees and spotted with the last flowers of summer. My stomach lurched as the ground fell away down a valley.

We saw a few deer racing across the plain with lithe grey shapes in pursuit, their passage startling a bevy of fowl into the air. A raven was picking at the remains of a wild horse come to grief in a gully but, other than that, we saw no signs of life. Shiv brought the image back to us.

'Nothing you wouldn't expect to see,' Darni said as the picture showed four figures, bent heads together while the horses grazed. I blinked as the image dissolved in a dizzying spiral.

'I looked all around, not just on our trail,' Shiv agreed. 'There's nothing out there.'

I shook my head. 'I must be imagining it,' I said reluctantly.

'We'll try to find better cover when we camp,' Geris said comfortingly but I saw a gleam in his eye. Oh well, I thought, nothing works like good sex to give you a decent night's sleep, not an unpleasant prospect. I winked at him and stifled a smile when I caught Darni's expression.

'I know a place we can use.' Darni pushed on the pace and by late afternoon I realised he was heading for an earthwork that rose out of the grassland ahead like a small, flat-topped hill.

'Isn't that an Eldritch ring?' I gaped at him. 'Is that where you're planning to camp?'

'That's right.' His eyes challenged me. 'What's the matter? Frightened that shadow-blue men will step out of a rainbow and shoot you full of little green arrows?'

'They're copper, you know, Eldritch arrows,' Geris piped up. 'All their metalwork was.'

His flow of inconsequential information covered the fact that I was at a loss for words and I was able to keep a level face as we found the way through the ramparts of turf and made our camp.

After all, the Eldritch kin are just tales for children and, while those with their feet still in cow dung might believe in them, we more sophisticated city types are above such things. That's what I kept telling myself anyway, sounding about as convincing as a huckster selling baldness cures.

'They were real people, you know,' Geris said helpfully as we unpacked and I had just about got myself persuaded that I really should ignore such childish worries.

'What, little grey men who can step into shadows?' I managed a shaky laugh.

'No,' he said seriously. 'But people lived here and in places like this. One mentor took his students to dig up a ring near Borleat. They found a man buried in a boat with treasure all around him.'

'You're joking!' I frowned. 'That's a long way from navigable water. You can't get barges any higher than Tresig, can you?'

'Maybe they used to be able to. There are dry wharves nearby, aren't there?'

Shiv came over at this point. 'It's nearly Equinox.' He pointed at the last faint sickle of the greater moon. 'Is it anyone's birth festival?'

Geris shook his head. 'I'm a For-Winter baby.'

'Darni and I are Aft-Autumn.' Shiv shrugged. 'Oh well, I expect we can come up with something to drink to.'

'Er, well, it's my birth-festival actually. I was born in Aft-Summer.' I felt a little shy about admitting it for some daft reason.

'Not much chance of celebrating out here.' Geris looked really worried which both touched and concerned me. 'It won't be much of a festival for you.'

'Oh well, we'll—'

Shiv's plan was lost in a shattering scream from one of the horses and for one heart-stopping moment I really believed the Eldritch kin had woken.

'Backs to the fire!' Darni's bellow brought us back to reality and I saw men cresting the rampart, drawn swords glinting in the firelight. Their helms and mail chinked as they ran and their studded boots thudded into the soft earth. None of them spoke but they moved with a unity of purpose more chilling than any battle cry. The effect was slightly spoiled when some of them slipped on the slope, now slick with dew, but thank Saedrin, it gave us a breath to collect our wits and to realise we were badly outnumbered.

I fumbled in my belt pouch for my darts and stepped back to get distance for throwing. I felt heat on the backs of my legs; I didn't have much room before I would be treading in the embers.

'Kiss Saedrin's arse,' Darni snarled as he stepped out to meet the first attackers. Their air of confidence was terrifying and the first swept up his hand to bring his sword down into Darni's head. I watched the attacker's hand rise, and then carry on rising as Darni took it off at the wrist with an explosive strike. His mate was momentarily distracted by a faceful of blood and his troubles ended with Darni's short sword in his guts. When a third went down to a boot in the stones, the attack lost a little of its impetus and we were able to form a defensive circle before they hit us.

Swords met in a flurry of sparks, slash, parry, feint, lunge, hack. Darni's sword flashed in the light of the flames until he managed to reach in over a guard and rip into his opponent's throat. Blood sprayed across him, but he simply blinked it clear and kicked the bubbling corpse aside.

The dancing shadows from the firelight were confusing my aim. I threw a dart and for one gut-wrenching second, it looked as if the victim was unaffected. He staggered forward then sank to his knees clawing at his arm, dying in seconds with a choking cough. What a relief; the poison hadn't lost its strength after all.

My darts took out a couple more but I was soon running low. Darni was fighting like one of Poldrion's own demons and I kept him between me and our attackers. I glanced over my shoulder to check we weren't being encircled and saw Shiv and Geris were back to back with us. Geris had the reflexes and speed for swordwork but was making a slow job of finishing off his opponent. Even I saw a chance which he had just failed to follow through. The vicious face attacking him knew it too, and teeth shone in a triumphant sneer. Too many years fencing like a gentleman, whereas Darni had been killing for real; blood was running down the sleeve of Geris' off arm and I realised he was used to fighting with a shield.

He must have realised he was in trouble as he suddenly kicked himself to a quicker pace. He drove the attacker back with rapid slashing strokes. Confused, the man let down his guard and Geris split his skull; I saw his grimace as he turned his head to avoid the shower of brain and blood.

Back at our side of the fire, I used my last dart then found myself facing a bearded heavy, who thought I was now unarmed. His mistake; I slid a dagger down my sleeve and as he came in for a downward smash I got him through the armpit. I couldn't get the dagger loose as the bastard fell and began to feel cold fingers of fear as I screamed at Darni's back.

'I need a weapon! Darni, I haven't got a sword!'

He kicked a loose sword backwards, nearly taking off my toes. Shrieking obscenities, he drove his distracted opponent back a couple of paces. Blondie facing him made the mistake of thinking he saw an opening and came in to meet the blade in his guts. He sank to his knees, screaming wetly, and Darni kicked him in the face.

I moved to Darni's side and began to relearn my swordsmanship very speedily indeed, blessing Halice for insisting I practise with her and wishing for her skills.

A big bastard with a yellow beard came round to me, looking to take the weaker option. He was strong and quick and it was all I could do to match him until he slipped in the slime of his friend's entrails and I was able to smash my blade through his ugly face. Teeth and bone gleamed for an instant in the firelight as he fell headlong into the fire. His hair blazed with a revolting smell as his arms flailed wildly. I stamped frantically on the back of his head until he stilled.

Darni dropped another with a low sweep that took out his knees and then finished him with a thrust into the eyes. Our gazes met in an insane instant of calm.

'Get behind me. How are the others doing? What about the horses?'

The horses! If we lost those, it was a long walk home. I looked round and saw why Darni had not bothered hobbling his mount. The brutish-looking chestnut was rearing, kicking and biting with the controlled savagery of the trained warrior's horse, and several figures bled writhing under his hooves.

Shiv was using a beam of amber light like a halberd and the attackers screamed like pigs whenever it made contact. He dropped two of them, who went down as if they'd been poleaxed, not even twitching, the only movement the blood streaming from under their helms.

'Shiv!' Darni bellowed like a rutting bull and Shiv spared us a glance.

Acid fire tore into my leg and I nearly paid the ultimate price for being distracted. I shrieked like Drianon's own eagle and this bought me a second to recover myself. Darni was fighting two on one now, and I was facing serious trouble. He was not as big as the others but he was quick and strong and whipped his blade around mine with terrifying ease. I was being driven back step by step until I felt the fire crunch under my boots and scorch my legs.

The man I fought sneered at me with savage glee. I honestly thought I was lost. Sapphire light ripped past and the triumphant face exploded into a blackened ruin as it shot backwards. I gaped stupidly; we all did in a mad moment of stillness that seized friend and foe alike.

'Move!' Darni shoved me through the dying fire and the three of us bracketed Shiv as he wove coruscating, multi-coloured light round the ring of earthen ramparts.

A flash like forked lightning knocked two more backwards into scorched hulks of flesh and brilliance shot from Shiv's hands to the embers of the fire. Red light, bright as a new day, flashed across the ground to finish off the wounded and then shot through the air to crown the crest of the ring with flames where reinforcements died in screaming agony. Saedrin, how many were there? How many were waiting outside? I thrust away rising panic with real difficulty and concentrated on my own private mayhem, realising with some unoccupied fraction of my mind that I was whimpering. Piss on that, I thought. I joined in with Darni's litany of curses at the top of my lungs.

Down in the blood and death of the ring, another fell as his sword exploded into red-hot razors which tore his face apart. Those remaining now realised they were trapped and redoubled their efforts, defence giving way to desperation as they fought to get to Shiv and kill the magic. Now they were screaming back at us, my ears only hearing nonsense but recognising the vicious hatred in the tone. Terror built in the pit of my stomach and threatened to come howling out at any second. Now I was screaming at myself as much as the enemy.

Darni yelled something I missed but Shiv dropped his

handfuls of blue fire and began to weave a multihued web of power. In an instant, black shadows began to ripple down the length of our swords, vanishing like smoke in the air. I landed a blow on the man in front of me: the mail on his shoulder parted, the flesh beneath melting like tallow and smoking with a revolting stench. Geris moved to follow up when his opponent shrank away from the deadly darkness and nearly took a thrust in the ribs from the side. Shiv saw the danger and the man screamed like a girl as his arm fell apart under a blast of green light, the small bones of his hand and wrist scattering like runes. He sank to his knees and I finished him through the back of the neck.

It took me a few maddened moments to realise the fight was over, my ears still ringing, disoriented. Crazy shadows ran round the ring as Shiv's wall of fire flared one last time and then died. We braced ourselves for new dangers but none came. Darni broke from our frozen group and ran up the rampart, yelling defiance into the night.

Sudden terror flashed through me as a hand gripped my arm but it was only Shiv. I caught him as he sank to his knees, face deathly pale and eyes dark shadowed like a man in a fever, his breath coming in tearing gasps.

'Darni!' I shrieked, my voice rising, scant moments from hysteria. He looked back from the crest of the ring.

'Geris, help Livak, it's Shiv!'

Geris came and helped me lay Shiv down. I dragged the corpse out of the fire, my stomach rising at the sickly roasting smell. No time to be sick, I threw more wood on the embers and stood, not knowing what to do.

'Spirits, the red bottle.'

Geris carefully poured a mouthful down Shiv and he coughed weakly.

'Wine, no mead. Thanks. Now, get some wine and heat it with some honey.'

I obeyed with shaking hands. Shiv's colour improved a little and his breathing slowed. Geris tended him with single-minded concentration, loosening his shirt and checking him for wounds, ignoring his own bloody arm.

A dark shadow came over the top of the ring and I had my sword ready before I realised it was Darni, his eyes bright as a wild dog's.

'Well?' He kept his face to the night as he returned to the fire.

'He's exhausted but a good night's sleep should see him right.' Geris' tone was calm and confident as he went to his leather case of parchments.

'What are you doing?' I asked in bemusement.

He looked at me as if only just realising that I was present.

'Something to help Shiv sleep.' He showed me a sheet of neatly written couplets and then spoke the complex syllables over the fallen wizard. His breathing became deeper and more normal as the tension left his long body.

'Is that this aetheric magic?'

'Yes.' Geris frowned. 'It's never worked that quickly before. I wonder what it is about this place?' Frustration edged his tone.

'What else can you do?'

'Not much. Shit! The old books say they could heal wounds, cure fevers, all kinds of things. All I can do is put him to sleep. If only—'

'If a bitch had balls, she'd be a dog. Don't knock it, sleep's what Shiv needs.' Darni stripped off his blood-soaked tunic and shirt and began to wash the worst of the gore off himself.

'Are we safe?' I asked stupidly.

'For the moment. I couldn't see any sign but they might be regrouping.' Darni glanced round the carnage. 'I'd be surprised if they came back but we'll be ready.'

As he wiped himself dry with the remains of his shirt I saw several broad purple scars on his shoulders and chest. A fresh cut on his arm was oozing slowly and his knuckles were bloody and raw on both hands. He turned and I saw there were no marks on his back.

'There's a small green bag in my kit, Livak. I'd rather not get everything bloody . . .'

I fetched it for him and winced in sympathy as he poured neat spirits on his wounds before trying to dress them.

'Here, let me.' I worked fast and he grunted approvingly. 'That's fine. Now, let's look at that leg.'

I had forgotten my own wound, crazy as that sounds, but as soon as he mentioned it I felt as if I'd been kicked by a plough horse. I sat and watched numbly as he cut away my breeches to reveal a deep gash. The fire had scorched my leg as hairless as a high-priced whore's but there were no burns, which was a relief given the way they fester.

'This'll need stitches,' Darni said in a matter-of-fact tone. 'Do you want to do it yourself?'

'Hang on.' Geris finished cleaning the long, shallow slice in his own arm and came over.

'This is going to hurt,' he said unnecessarily as he clamped his hands on my thigh.

Darni wiped it with a spirit-soaked wad of lint; I managed not to vomit or faint but it was a close thing. He worked fast but, by the time he was finished, I was shaking and dripping with sweat.

'Get some sleep. Geris and I will stand first watch.'

'Um.' I could not trust myself with words and rolled myself in my cloak next to Shiv. Slowly my heart stopped pounding and the terror and elation of the fight receded. The shakes took longer to subside, just leaving me with the thumping pain in my leg. I closed my eyes and listened to the crackling of the fire. It reminded me of childhood illnesses bedded down in the kitchen and I screwed my eyes shut on sudden tears.

'Livak?' I was amazed to realise Geris' low question had woken me. I blinked up at his face, bleak with strain and tiredness in the grey light of dawn.

'Could you keep awake for a while? I've got to sleep.'

I sat up and rubbed my face, grimacing at the ache in my leg. 'Surely.' I looked round. 'Where's Darni?'

'Here.' Darni was sitting at the top of the slope keeping watch, tense like a good hound.

'Don't you want some rest?'

He shook his head. 'I couldn't; a fight like that leaves fire in the blood for hours. I'll rest later; I don't think they'll be back.'

'Who were they?'

'Bandits, I suppose. Probably out of Lescar, a group whose Lord came off second-best in some challenge.'

I squinted up at him, hair and beard still matted with blood, face cheerful and relaxed.

'Poldrion's ferry will be busy today,' I observed at last.

He grinned. 'I don't think he'll take many of these without fixing a price first. I wonder how many he'll tip over the side halfway.' He surveyed the corpses littering the grass with an untroubled air.

'I hope he'll credit you with a commission. Where did you learn to fight like that?'

'Lescar, fighting for the Duke of Triolle ten years back.'

'You're good.'

'I've got to be good at something.'

I let it go. 'What's wrong with Shiv?'

'He exhausted himself. You can't throw power like that around without paying for it.'

'I didn't realise,' I said in a wondering tone. 'I really should learn more about wizards.'

Darni stretched his arms above his head, grimacing as he tested his injuries. 'Before they realised I had no power as a mage, I attended some of the lectures. There's a dangerous old bastard in Hadrumal called Otrick; he's about the best there is with air magic. Anyway, he gives a lecture posted as "Why don't wizards rule the world?"' He gestured at Shiv's motionless frame. 'That's one reason.'

I wondered what the others were but did not like to ask.

'Otrick gives new students practical lessons too; I've seen some carried out of his hall.' Darni looked at me and smiled. 'Not being a mage isn't all bad, you know.'

The sun rose higher, Geris woke and we ate a breakfast made tasteless by the blood-soaked surroundings. Flies began to gather and we set about the revolting task of shifting the dead so we could get out without the horses going hysterical on us. Shiv slept on but his colour was back to normal, he stirred from time to time and his twitching eyes showed he was dreaming.

'We might get more trouble so we'll take some armour,' Darni ordered and we wrestled with the less mangled corpses. When I finally got a mail-shirt off, I was surprised to realise it was nearly right for me in length. I looked at the bodies with new interest.

'Stumpy lot, aren't they? You'll need to put two of these together for Shiv.'

Geris paused. 'Shiv can't wear armour; all that metal round him screws up the magic.' He put down the sword he had been cleaning and began to inspect the bodies more closely, pulling his dagger out. 'Yes, they are all rather short.' I wondered queasily if his academic interests included anatomising, but to my relief he contented himself with cutting away clothing.

'Darni, this is all rather peculiar.' He moved round the dell, removing helmets and coifs.

'How do you mean?'

'They're all very similar; they're all yellow-haired for one thing. How often do you see that?'

Darni peered at a few of the faces, bloodless with livid purple lips and tongues or revoltingly mottled depending on the way they had fallen. He shrugged, uninterested.

'So they're all related. Bandits often work in families, you know that.'

'So many of them? So close in age?' Geris looked puzzled.

'They're just robbers trying their luck.' Darni produced a pair of snips and began taking some of the excess out of the hauberk I had selected.

'Looking for what? We're hardly a merchant's train loaded with coin.' Geris sat back on his heels. 'All we've got worth stealing is the horses and they weren't their target.'

'That's because anyone who went near them got their head stamped on,' Darni grinned.

Geris did not look convinced. 'I'm going to have a look around.'

'Don't go far and be careful. Yell if you see anything.' I

watched him leave with concern, half inclined to go too, but Shiv chose that moment to wake.

'Is there any water?' he croaked. 'My mouth feels like the inside of a muleteer's glove.'

I fetched him a cupful. 'How are you feeling?'

He propped himself on one elbow and wrinkled his nose at the leathern taste of the water. 'I've felt better but I'll recover.'

'You scared a season's growth out of me.' It was supposed to be a joke but it did not come out right.

'I think I used up a season's growth.' He sat up and looked around. 'Saedrin! What a mess!'

Geris reappeared, looking dissatisfied. 'They didn't have any horses.'

'Their mates will have taken them back to wherever they are hiding out. I don't suppose we got them all.' Darni threw the mail at me. 'Try that.'

I draped it round myself, grimacing at the prospect of that weight on my shoulders. 'Good enough.'

Darni began lacing the rings together with leather thong. 'I should be riveting this, you know,' he muttered with dissatisfaction.

'No, listen,' Geris persisted. 'They did not have horses; I'm telling you they came on foot.'

'Out here? We're leagues from anywhere. You must be mistaken.'

'I've been looking at their tracks. I know what I'm talking about,' Geris insisted with uncharacteristic force. I looked up from the swords I was trying for weight.

'Go on.' My own sense of unease was returning.

'There are no signs of horses anywhere. Look at them, none of them are booted or spurred for riding. They were on foot!'

'So they're holed up somewhere close and watching the road.' Darni was not convinced. 'We'd better get out of here before they come back. Let's get working.'

Now Geris had got me wondering. As I went round searching for my darts, I looked more closely at the nearest body and shoving aside my revulsion, pulled apart the remnants of the clothing.

'This is odd.'

'How so?' Geris came over and Shiv looked at me with interest.

'Well, these clothes are certainly old and worn but he's all clean underneath.' I bent closer. 'Look, there's old blood here on the linen, I'd say from lice or fleas.' I ran a finger over the marble-cold flesh below. 'He's spotless, not a bite anywhere. He's clean too, scrubbed.' I moved to the next roughly intact corpse. 'This one's the same.'

'So they've got rid of their vermin. Where's the mystery? Have you ever had lice? Believe me, you don't want to keep them.' Darni concentrated on his work.

I sat back on my heels. Darni was probably right, but I didn't think we had read the runes right here. What was I missing? I searched further.

'None of them have any coin on them.' I rummaged in a few belt-pouches and pockets, brushing aside the flies and trying to ignore the smell of blood. 'None of them are carrying anything personal at all. No rings, jewellery, nothing. What's this?'

I showed Geris a patch of raw skin on an arm. He looked on the others but could not find anything similar.

'A stray shot from Shiv?'

'They're all dead, that's all I need to know. Come on, I want to get out of here as fast as we can.' There was an edge to Darni's tone that forbade further investigation or speculation. Geris muttered something and returned to cleaning his sword and Shiv started to get slowly to his feet.

We were soon packed up and ready to return to the road.

'Are we going to do anything about all this?' I paused on our way out of the ring and looked back at the pile of dead.

Darni shook his head. 'It'll take too long to get fuel to burn them.' He gestured to the far side of the rampart. 'They'll take care of it.'

I looked at the waiting ravens and swallowed hard. Thirty or more bodies should see the birds well fed for half a season.

* * *

Back on the road the clean air blew the scent of death out of my nostrils, and I felt better. We paused at the next ford and all stripped to wash the last of the blood from ourselves and our gear. Geris tried to get me to use a pool further down the river for modesty's sake, but I was having none of it; not with Drianon knew what bandits lurking in the area.

'I still think that was all a bit strange,' I murmured to Shiv as I dried my hair, one eye on Darni whose ears where muffled in soap as he scrubbed at his beard.

'I agree.' Shiv pulled his shirt over his head. 'I can't think why I didn't pick them up when I did that scrying. If they weren't on horseback, they should have been in the area I covered.'

'Maybe they rode in so far and then came in on foot,' I said dubiously.

'Why would they do that?'

'I've no idea.'

We rode on in dissatisfied silence.

Friern Lodge,
40th of For Autumn

Casuel grimaced as he stepped carefully out of the coach, alert for muck; it was going to be important to make a good impression. He tugged at the skirts of his coat to pull out some of the creases and frowned at the scuffs on his boot where some overladen yeoman had trodden on his foot.

'Is this it?' Allin looked round at the huddle of little brick houses.

'Well, I don't think we need to ask directions,' he replied tartly.

They stared at the broad brick frontage of the manor standing four-square and imperious behind the tall iron gates on the far side of the road.

'That's a lodge?' Casuel couldn't blame Allin for sounding incredulous. Lord Armile's dwelling might have started life as a hunting residence but he doubted if any of the original building was left by now. He looked thoughtfully at a straggle of cottagers waiting by a door in the paling where hard-faced men in grey livery rested on halberds and periodically let a few through, palms brushing briefly.

A horn sounded behind them. 'Make way!'

Casuel stepped into a handy doorway before a coach rattled past, wheels spraying Allin's skirts with mud from the rutted road. The horses' hooves crunched briskly up the gravelled driveway and Casuel watched with a qualm of regret. He would have made a far more imposing arrival if he'd hired a vehicle, he realised belatedly. Still, the expense could not have been justified, could it?

'Come on, Allin.'

He picked his way across the road and approached the

guards, head high and back straight, ignoring the curious glances of the peasantry. Allin copied him, Casuel pleased to see she was finally managing something that approached fitting dignity.

'Good afternoon. I wish to see Lord Armile's chamberlain.' Casuel made a carefully calculated half-bow and looked expectantly at the man with a ribbon sewn around the stag badge on his jerkin.

'Expecting you, is he?' the gate-guard asked cautiously.

'I do not have an appointment, no.' Casuel smiled politely.

'Then wait your turn.' Arrogance clearly came more easily to this militia than courtesy.

Casuel's smile did not waver as he reached into his pocket for a letter prepared earlier.

'Please present this with my compliments. He will see me.'

The guard looked uncertainly at the letter, at Casuel and then back up at the house.

'Here.' He gestured to a nervous-looking lad whose grey livery had been cut for a man at least a hand's-width taller. 'Take this to Armin.'

The lad ran off up the drive, slipping on the gravel in his haste.

'Is it the custom here to remain seated while ladies stand?' Casuel raised his eyebrows at two guards lounging on a bench.

'Get up!'

The two scowled at their leader but obeyed. Allin bobbed a curtsey and sat down, tucking in her skirts nervously. Casuel broadened his smile somewhat and took a note-tablet from his pocket, making a few jottings which he was pleased to see substantially increased the air of awe around him.

'He'm to come.' The lad soon reappeared breathless and sweaty despite the cool day.

'Thank you.' Casuel took his time, acknowledging the militiaman on the gate with a gracious nod of the head and a silver penny.

'You see, Allin, you have to know how to deal with these people,' he murmured.

He stifled a smile at the buzz of speculation behind them as the gate closed but his satisfaction soon evaporated as they walked towards the manor. Curbing underlings with their petty abuses of power was one thing; the man who lived here was going to be a horse of quite a different mettle.

'Why does this look like a Lescar noble's house?' Allin enquired tensely.

The ground-level windows had been recently reduced to narrow embrasures and they could see men working on the roof to add crenellations and a watch tower. A line of pinkly dusted peasants were stacking bricks to one side of the main gateway and logs lay ready for scaffolding. The ringing of hammer and chisel rose from somewhere over the back.

'Oh, these petty lordlings like to impress their neighbours with their fortifications,' Casuel said airily.

'This way.' They followed the nervous lad around a dry ditch where a gang of burly men in grey were fixing sharpened stakes. A side door stood open and a flat-faced man in dark blue was waiting expectantly with a maid who dipped a curtsey and took their cloaks.

'Good day.' Casuel was pleased to receive a practised bow in reply to his own and followed the man, his spirits rising as they were led through a panelled and polished hallway, steps ringing on the spotless flagstones. Allin looked around uncertainly, clutching her shawl.

'This way, please.' The lackey opened a door and ushered Casuel through with immaculate courtesy.

He paused for a moment to admire the fashionable room then turned to address his companion.

'May I ask—' His words tailed; the menial had closed the door behind him, leaving the two of them alone.

'I don't think we're very welcome,' Allin whispered nervously.

A faint chill breathed across the back of Casuel's neck; he ignored it.

'Ah, refreshments!' He headed for a sideboard, gratefully pouring himself a full goblet to settle a little commotion in his stomach. 'Here you are, that'll put some colour in your cheeks, my dear. I expect you're suffering from a touch of carriage-sickness.'

He raised appreciative eyebrows as he sipped the wine. 'Now, I would not have expected to find Trokain vintages this far west, Allin. Lord Armile is certainly a man of excellent taste.'

He turned slowly, taking in the room, its elegance carefully understated to form a backdrop to the full-length portrait over the fireplace. The standing figure in formal dress was half turned, one arm resting on a pedestal where a small statue paid lip-service to the family's hereditary priesthood.

'Is that him?' Allin breathed in awe.

'I imagine so. That's the latest Tormalin style, you know, quite the height of fashion.'

The face was hardly flattering to Casuel's eyes. The piercing gaze and harsh set to the full mouth presented an uncomfortable challenge but the vital realism of the painting made it stand out from the other, smaller, portraits around the panelled walls, their older, flatter style awkward and clownish by comparison.

'I had to pay the fellow a sack-weight of coin to come so far from home, but I think it was worth it, don't you?'

Casuel started and turned to see the picture's original emerge from a door concealed in an alcove.

'Who—' He coughed and cleared his throat. 'Who is the artist?'

'Some fellow Messire Den Ilmiral recommended.' Lord Armile's Tormalin was polished and marred only by a slight lisp betraying an early tutor's Lescari accent. He looked Allin up and down before bowing to her with a faintly puzzled air.

'It is an impressive work.' Casuel sipped his wine, realising that the artist had indeed worked to flatter his client in softening the harsh lines around mouth and eyes and reducing the sneering nose.

'Such an accolade from a man of education is praise indeed.' Lord Armile smiled with broad good humour and unfolded Casuel's letter.

'Now, you say you have business which will be to my advantage?'

Casuel smiled in return. For all his manners and decor aping Tormalin fashions, this was still an Ensaimin hedge-lord he was dealing with, no subtlety or decorum to him.

'Indeed.' He took a seat. 'I deal in books, writings, antiquarian documents. I have heard that you have a fine library.'

'From whom?'

Casuel hesitated for a breath. 'Does that matter?'

'I always like to know who's talking about me.'

Casuel failed to notice Lord Armile's smile did not reach his eyes.

'I did not catch the fellow's name, we were simply conversing in a hostelry.' Casuel took a sip of wine. 'The thing is, I have clients interested in purchasing various texts and I wondered if you might have some of those I'm seeking.'

'Who are your clients?'

'Scholars and antiquarians, the details are not important.' Casuel stumbled a little over his attempt at unconcern.

'Details are always important.' Lord Armile remained standing. 'I have no wish to sell any of my library. Be on your way.'

He turned back to the concealed door.

Casuel gaped for a moment then scrambled to his feet. 'Sir, I do not think you realise . . . that is, I can offer you significant coin.'

'I have sufficient sources of income.'

'You could earn the gratitude of powerful men,' Casuel said desperately.

Lord Armile turned to look over his shoulder. 'I am a powerful man,' he said softly. 'And you are not the first spy who has tried to gain an entry into my house and my business.'

'I am no spy.' Casuel's voice rose in indignation.

'Then who are you?' Lord Armile pulled twice on a bell-rope and Casuel heard booted feet scrape outside the door.

'I am a travelling dealer in texts and documents, I told you.' The flare of indignation burned away, leaving Casuel suddenly cold, the wine souring in his stomach.

'Are you indeed? Have you visited any of my neighbours? They have fine libraries, after all. No, you have not, I would have been informed of it. You have come straight to me, fresh off the coach from Market Harrall, not even a bag between you! Tell me, how is Lord Sovel?'

'I have not the honour of that gentleman's acquaintance,' Casuel said stiffly.

'No, I don't suppose you have. That scut of a son of his does his dirty work these days.' Armile clapped his hands and two thickset men in the ubiquitous grey livery slammed open the door. Allin squeaked in alarm and gripped Casuel's sleeve.

'You are making a grave error.' Anger thickened Casuel's tone. 'I am no spy, I am a mage.'

Armile raised a hand and the men halted. 'Are you indeed? Prove it.'

Casuel blinked and pried Allin's fingers from his arm. 'I beg your pardon?'

'Prove it!' The threat in Armile's voice was unmistakable and Casuel's meagre courage fled.

Feeling his hands shaking, he rubbed them together before weaving the amber lights of his power into a close net. Emboldened by the murmurs of awe he heard behind him, he drew deep on his resources and flung the power out into the form of a gigantic hound, eyes blazing, jaws dripping foam which sizzled as it hit the floor. Allin clapped her hands to her mouth to stifle a squeal.

Lord Armile stared unmoved at the phantasm. 'A pretty festival trick, I suppose.'

Casuel narrowed his lips, the beast bayed deafeningly and he was gratified to see that Armile's hands moved involuntarily towards his ears. Allin was now as white as the flagstones.

Perceiving a threat to their master, the men moved towards Casuel but he turned the hound towards them, setting it snarling, looking from one to the other. They exchanged dubious glances, each unwilling to find out how real those finger-length teeth might be.

Laughter startled Casuel, but he held the weave together.

'I am impressed. I must apologise, but these are troubled

times hereabouts.' Lord Armile moved to the sideboard, keeping a wary eye on the hound as he filled a goblet and handed it to Allin, who sank it in one draught.

'Please, let us start afresh.' Armile gestured to the men, who retreated all too willingly.

Casuel froze the hound for an instant then let it unravel into a gout of flame which rushed towards the ceiling, then through it. Lord Armile forced a smile once he saw his expensive plasterwork was unmarked.

'Will you do me the honour of staying to dine?'

'Thank you, I would be delighted.' Casuel smoothed the front of his coat; this was more like the reception he was entitled to, even if he had been forced to obtain it through such a vulgar display.

'Let us go through to the library. We can see what books might interest you. My lady.' He offered Allin a courteous arm with a winning smile.

Casuel nodded, straightened his shoulders and followed as Lord Armile led the way.

The library was a long room along the side of the house, the deep windows separated by bookcases and facing a wall lined with even more volumes.

'This is most impressive.' Casuel did not scruple to disguise his awe. 'I have rarely seen a private library of this quality outside Tormalin.'

'Thank you; my father was something of a scholar.' There was an edge to Lord Armile's voice which escaped Casuel. 'Please look around, I must let the kitchen know we will be two more for dinner.'

Lord Armile left through another panelled door and Allin looked after him, puzzled. 'You'd think he'd have someone to run his messages for him.'

'Do be quiet, there's a good girl.' Casuel was eagerly searching the shelves and scroll racks, checking against the list engraved on his memory.

'Oh yes, this is an excellent copy of *Mennith's History*. Look, here's the *Selerima Pharmacopoeia*, *Tandri's Yesteryears*. This is all very encouraging.'

He soon identified a handful of other texts in varying states of repair and annotation and sat at a handy desk to make some rapid calculations. Allin came to look over his shoulder and gasped.

'Oh, I knew this would not be a cheap transaction but I have inferior copies which I can sell on,' Casuel reassured her airily. 'Besides, I'm not exactly short of coin. Now, please let me work without interruption.'

Allin plumped down on a sofa, twisting her fingers in the fringe of her wrap.

It was some while later when Casuel looked up with a start as the blue-liveried lackey opened the door.

'Dinner is served. Please follow me.'

Casuel glanced at the window and was surprised to see dusk deepening above the trees.

'Yes, thank you. Come on, Allin.' He tucked his notes into a pocket and followed the servant.

He was surprised to find dinner served in a smaller salon with older, heavier furniture. Evidently Lord Armile's taste for the up-to-date had not reached this part of the house. Casuel stifled a smile; the profits from the sale of the books could be usefully spent here.

'Did you find much of interest?' Lord Armile gestured to the footman, who began to uncover the various dishes.

Casuel helped himself to a pigeon and some bread. 'Thank you, yes. I think I should be able to fulfil several of my commissions.'

'Who did you say you were acting for?' Armile nodded to a second lackey, who began to carve from a thick joint of beef. Casuel was pleased to see Allin relax as she filled her plate.

'I am assisting some of the Council of Mages in their research,' Casuel replied easily. He had established his position sufficiently to adopt a more friendly approach, he decided. 'Wizardry is a co-operative discipline.'

'These mages have antiquarian interests, you mentioned?'

'Among others,' Casuel said with as lofty a tone as he could manage with a mouthful of pigeon leg.

'Do try some of the game pie.' Lord Armile raised a finger to the footman, who quickly filled their goblets. 'Do you return to Hadrumal soon?'

'That depends.' Casuel reached for a dish of cutlets. 'I have various tasks to complete first.'

'But you are a free agent, you have discretion over your duties?'

'Oh, quite.' Casuel nodded. 'I am entirely my own master.'

Lord Armile smiled broadly, though this deepened the harsh lines around his mouth and made him look almost sinister. Casuel's admiration for the portrait artist increased still further.

'So, what did you find of interest in my library?' Lord Armile leaned back in his chair and sipped at his wine.

Casuel swallowed hastily and wiped his mouth with his napkin. 'There are certainly some interesting texts there, although I'm not sure how many my funds will allow me to purchase.'

Lord Armile raised a hand. 'My dear sir, I would not dream of taking your coin, not if the Council of Mages needs these books for their research.'

Casuel gaped. 'Well, that is, I mean, obviously I appreciate your generosity but—'

'You can repay me in kind, with a small service.' Armile inclined his head, unsmiling.

'What kind of service would that be?' Casuel asked uneasily. He looked across the room at the burly footman who stood by the door, arms folded across his broad chest.

'You do not know my neighbour, Lord Sovel, I believe?' Lord Armile snapped his fingers and the second lackey poured small glasses of white brandy. He was also unusually well built for a house servant, Casuel noticed belatedly.

'Well, you see, he has a gravel pit, and I wish to buy it. I have made him a fair offer for the land but he refuses to deal with me.' Armile shrugged. 'You can persuade him.'

'Why do you want a gravel pit?'

Casuel looked at Allin in some surprise, although grateful for the interruption.

'To reduce the costs of maintaining my roads, my dear.' Armile offered her some brandy which she declined with a blush.

'You certainly have excellent highways, my lord.' A little flattery would not come amiss, Casuel judged. 'Your merchants and tenants must be very grateful.'

'Curse the merchants; I simply want to know I can move my militia where and when it's needed,' Lord Armile replied, his expression stern. 'I believe in ruling with a firm hand.'

Casuel shifted in his seat. 'I certainly support the rule of law, but I'm afraid it is simply not done for wizards to involve themselves in local politics. I'm sorry.'

'So am I.' Lord Armile snapped his fingers and Casuel found himself seized from behind. Heavy iron manacles were clamped around his wrists as he struggled ineffectually in the grip of the footmen.

'This is an outrage!' he spluttered. 'Anyway, how in Saedrin's name do you think I could persuade Lord Sovel of anything?'

Armile stood and leaned over Casuel, who sank back in his seat. 'Threaten to render him impotent, immolate his entire household, I don't care.' His voice was low and infinitely threatening. 'Do whatever you must to convince him that the dangers of denying me outweigh the disadvantages of selling.'

He turned and made a deep bow to Allin, who was sitting, frozen, a half-eaten tartlet in her hand. 'Consider how best to assist me. You have until the midnight chime.'

He swept out of the room with his henchmen and they heard the key turn in the lock.

'Oh no,' Allin whimpered. 'What are they going to do to us?'

Casuel closed his eyes and took deep breaths until he felt in control of bladder and bowel once more.

'Do be quiet, you silly girl,' he snapped in awkward Lescar.

This at least startled Allin into silence. There was a long pause, in which they heard low voices outside the door.

'What are we going to do? Shall I try the window?' said

Allin after a while, her voice still quavering but no longer edged with outright hysteria. Casuel was relieved to see she was using her wits as well as her mother tongue.

'I think Lord Armile needs to learn that he cannot order a wizard around like some housemaid,' Casuel said shakily.

'But you can't work magic in chains; all the ballads say so.'

Casuel forced a wavery smile. 'That's a hedge-wife belief we've never felt the need to correct. Certainly a wizard with air talents wouldn't be able to work in these manacles and you'd better never try working standing in water but I am an earth-mage.'

He closed his eyes and concentrated, tendrils of amber light crackling over the manacles. Allin held her breath but nothing happened. Casuel opened his eyes and looked down at his hands in dismay.

'I shouldn't have put so much energy into that cursed illusion,' he muttered woefully.

'I thought wizards were supposed to be able to disappear and walk through walls and things like that?'

Indignation tinted Allin's tone and sparked an answering anger which started to burn through Casuel's incipient panic.

'A Cloud-Master might be able to; all I can touch at present is my innate element,' he snapped.

'So what can you do with it? Can you get us out of here or call for help somehow?' Allin crossed to the window and peered out into the darkness.

A qualm gripped Casuel's innards and he looked longingly at his glass of brandy. 'Give me a moment. I should be able to get these manacles off in a little while and that lock'll be no problem but I don't see how we'll get past those ruffians.'

Allin stared at him. 'Are you going to have to do what he wants? Do you think he'll keep his word?'

'I can't do it, in any case,' Casuel replied miserably. 'I mean, even if I could come up with something to scare Lord Sovel into agreement, once the Council got to hear of it – and they would – I'd be in more trouble than you can imagine!'

Allin began to rattle the shutters. 'Help! Help!' she yelled in desperation but the only answer was laughter from outside the door.

'Shut up, you silly girl!'

'Then do something yourself!' Allin turned and the branch of candles on the table flared head-high, as her anger reached the flames.

They both stared open-mouthed as the magical fire consumed the candles, leaving a puddle of wax ruining the finish of Lord Armile's table.

'Do calm down, my dear,' Casuel said shakily, suddenly grateful the hearth was unlit.

Allin's knees buckled and she dropped on to the window seat, her face ashen.

Casuel made as if to speak but snapped his mouth shut. Too late, Allin had noticed.

'What is it? Have you thought of something?'

'No, I mean, not really. It doesn't matter.' Casuel cringed at the thought of following up the notion that had just come to him. The humiliation did not bear thinking about.

'You have, you've got an idea.' Allin rose to her feet. 'What is it?'

Casuel hesitated; humiliation had to be preferable to disgrace, didn't it? 'Well, if you can conjure me a flame, and we can find something shiny, I could scry for help.'

Allin turned to the table and shoved crocks and plates aside wildly. She grabbed for a platter a breath too late and it crashed to the floor. She froze and they both held their breath but no one opened the door.

'Here.' Allin rubbed the sauce from a silver dish-cover. 'How about this?'

'Bring it here and find a candle.' Casuel drew a deep breath. 'Hold it up, that's right. Now, concentrate on the wick, very gently now. Focus your mind and bring a little fire.'

They stared at the candle, which remained obstinately unlit.

'Concentrate!' Casuel urged in frustration.

'I am!' Allin pursed her lips and bent closer. A sudden gout of flame leaped up and Casuel coughed on the stink of burned hair as one of her ringlets vanished into smoke.

'Hold it, hold it, that's right. Bring it down, calm down, you're doing very well,' Casuel gabbled hastily.

Allin managed a tremulous smile and the candle flame took on more normal proportions.

Casuel gripped his shaking hands together and focused his talents on the reflection. A surge of power startled him until he remembered the mass of iron around his wrists. Who should he try to contact? He searched his memory desperately for any wizards in the area. A sinking feeling came over him. With the range he could manage now, Usara was the obvious person to contact, wasn't he? Well, at least he might have some chance of keeping this sorry business quiet if he made a clean breast of it to a Council member straight away.

The dish-cover filled with a brilliant amber light and an image snapped into view. Casuel took a deep, reluctant breath.

'Usara!'

The sandy-haired mage looked up from his crucibles and gazed around curiously. *'Casuel?'*

Allin stared. 'Can't he see us?'

Casuel ignored her. 'Usara, please, I need your help.'

The wizard rolled up his tattered sleeves and gestured, the radiance of the spell darkened and the air crackled with power. Now he was looking straight at them.

'Where are you?'

'Being held by Lord Armile of Friern, who wants me to use magic in his service,' Casuel said baldly.

'How did this happen?'

'I'll explain later.' Casuel cringed; only if he couldn't find a way to avoid it. 'Please, if it were just me, I'd face him out, but I have a girl with me, a mage-born I was bringing to Hadrumal. I think she's in some peril.'

Usara spared Allin a glance. *'This Lord Armile has actually imprisoned you?'*

'Well, sort of,' Casuel began.

'I think we'd better make him think twice about this sort of

trick,' Usara said grimly. His face peered out from the image. '*Get ready to run.*'

'What—'

Casuel's question was lost in a shattering crash as the window wall exploded outwards in a cascade of masonry and glass.

'Come on!' Casuel's order was unnecessary; hampered by his fetters, he scrambled over the rubble after Allin, who had gathered her skirts above her knees and was running like a hare started by hounds. She halted, hesitating, rubbing her eyes as the darkness confused her. Shouts rang out from the house and from buildings ahead, doors slamming and dogs barking.

'This way.' Casuel flung a bolt of desperate amber energy against a garden gate. They ran for the jagged hole and plunged into a tangle of shrubs.

'Wait, let me get these off,' Casuel cursed but the manacles slid open after a few moments. He gripped Allin's shoulder as she stood, shaking, her breath coming in ragged gasps.

'Pull yourself together.' He wove a faint blue aura. 'I can get us out of here unseen if you keep quiet.'

She nodded in mute terror.

'We'll return to Market Harrall, get our things and take the first coach out.' Casuel forced more confidence than he felt into his tone. 'Once we're out of the district, we can head back to Hadrumal.'

Where he was going to have some explaining to do, he thought dismally, as they picked their way through the soaking vegetation. This was all Shivvalan's fault.

Inglis,
6th of Afi-Autumn

The rest of our journey was uneventful and both moons were waxing to a double full when we finally crested a line of hills to look down the sinuous length of the river Dalas as it met the ocean. Sprawled around the mouth was the city of Inglis, the only civilisation for leagues in any direction. I drew in a deep breath of satisfaction and said farewell to the endless grasslands.

'This looks like my kind of town, Geris. Things are going to happen here, I can feel it in the bones.'

He smiled back at me. We took the high road along the river down into the city. It was hard not to gape like a Caladhrian fresh off the farm at the huge rafts of logs being poled down the stream and the wide hulks of the riverboats coming down from the forests and mountains of Gidesta. We could hear the sounds of singing, drinking and in one case fighting coming across the water; my fingers still itched with regret at not having a chance at one of the famous games on board. I suppose Darni had a point when he said the boats were trouble, but it was not as if our journey through the plains had been all wildflowers, was it? Yells from a boat tying up made the horses shy as a man was thrown bodily over the rail. We left him cursing as he tried to climb the crumbling logs of the wharf. There were shipyards along each bank above the scour of the tide race, echoes of sawing and hammering rang back from the hills which ran down towards the ocean. I could smell fresh-cut wood and pitch and, hovering above it all, a wild salt freshness. I listened hard and could just make out the low murmur of waves below the din of the city.

Of course I had seen the sea before; I've been to Relshaz a

couple of times as well as spending time on the Spice Coast between Peorle and Grennet, but the sheltered waters of the Caladhrian Gulf are a far cry from the open ocean. I was standing in my stirrups as we wove our way towards the eastward docks where the tall masts of the Dalasorian clippers swayed against the early morning sun. The road took us along the docks and we paused while Darni and Shiv discussed what to do next. I did not bother listening; I was staring at the surf breaking against the rocks of the headland, the massive bulk of the sea defences, the sun glinting on the calmer waters of the estuary and the sleek lines of the ocean-going ships. They looked like racing hounds set against spit dogs when I thought of the lumbering galleys that trade between the Sea of Lescar and Aldabreshi. No wonder the Tormalins forbid the Dalasorians passage round the Cape of Winds; let loose in the southern waters, these could hunt down anything they chose.

A foul smell and the rattle of chains broke my thrall as the wind shifted. I coughed and turned to see a row of gibbets decorating the dock. Bodies in varying stages of decay swayed in the breeze, cages frustrating birds looking for a meal.

'What do you know about Inglis then?' I moved next to Geris, who was staring around like a farmwife at her first fair. 'Who runs the city?'

Geris shook his head. 'I'm not sure; I've never been this far north. Darni will know.'

He looked back at the sound of his name. 'What did you say?'

I repeated my question.

'Later. We'll get settled first and then sit down to do some proper planning. I've got some contacts here.'

'I need to know what I'm up against if I'm to do that job we were discussing,' I warned him.

'Oh, the merchant is called—' Geris' words were drowned as I shoved Russet into his horses and scowled at him to shut up.

'Not in the street and not so loud,' I hissed. He blushed and I resisted the impulse to reassure him; he had to learn some discretion or we could all end up rattling for the seabirds' amusement; Inglis had that sort of atmosphere.

Shiv led us through the busy streets into the heart of the city. The buildings were of good white stone and the main streets were well cobbled with water running through to sluice the gutters. As we rode I saw most of the buildings were very similar in design and age; there were few haphazard roof-lines or awkward street corners. This place positively reeked planning, order and money and I wondered again who exactly was in charge.

'Piss off!' Darni raised his whip as we entered a wide square and beggars started towards us from their seats round an elegant fountain.

I threw a few pennies to one man scrambling forward on legs twisted under him by childhood disease; you can't fake that. I regretted my generosity as others headed towards me.

'Spare copper?' A thin man waved uncoordinated hands at Geris' reins and I saw he had the vacant green-tinged eyes of a tahn addict. I kicked him in the back and raised my dagger, glad I was wearing gloves when I saw the mucus oozing down his face.

'Get lost before I cut you.' He was not so lost that he did not get the message, and he stumbled off.

'He didn't touch you?' Shiv called, concerned.

I shook my head. 'Don't worry.' Having spent three days emptying my guts down to the blood after once lifting a tahn addict's purse, I won't make the mistake of getting that muck on me again.

The Archmage's coin got us clean and airy rooms in a respectable inn. As I relaxed in a steaming tub, I decided I could get used to travelling like this. Drianon, it was good to get that chainmail off; my shoulders were killing me! A knock on the door saved me from drifting off to sleep in the scented water.

'Who is it?'

'Darni's got us a parlour on the first floor.' Shiv stuck his head round the door. 'He's gone out to find the contacts he was talking about, so you needn't hurry. Come down when you're ready.'

I dragged myself reluctantly out of the tub and dressed in clean clothes, my mood brightening with the realisation that this style of inn would have a laundrymaid. Sluicing linen in rivers is better than nothing, but you still end up smelling like a frog. I frowned over my stained clothes from the Eldritch ring; I'd done my best but you could still tell it was blood. A laundrymaid would probably have better luck, but handing these clothes over would cause talk, so I decided I'd have to dump them. That did not please me; the jerkin I'd ruined was one of my favourites. Elk-skin, it would not be easy to replace. A thought struck me and I hurried to Geris' room.

'There are bound to be some good spice merchants here, aren't there?' He smiled as I entered. He was sorting his collection of little polished boxes and canisters and I could see he would not be satisfied until Inglis added something new to his range of tisanes. Our campfires were enlivened most evenings by Geris blending and sipping and fussing over the temperature of his kettle. He shared the results round very generously, but none of the rest of us shared his capacity for excitement over a cup of oddly scented hot water.

'I need more coppersalt,' he frowned. 'It'll be expensive up here, don't you think? I'll just get a Crown-weight, that shouldn't cost too much.'

I considered pointing out that, even at Vanam prices, that much coppersalt would cost my mother most of a quarter's wages but there did not seem to be much point. Still, a trip to a herbalist might be worthwhile to see if Inglis offered any interesting 'spices' for my darts. I remembered what I had come for.

'Don't send your clothes from the fight to the laundrymaid; we don't want anyone to take any special notice of us here.

'Oh, I burned them one night while I was on watch,' Geris said easily. 'Do you think I'll be able to get fresh ale-leaves here?'

He'd burned them just like that, just like so much rubbish. A brushed silk shirt, broadcloth tunic and tailored breeches. What it must be to have the habits of permanent wealth.

'Come on, let's find Darni's parlour.'

'Just let me work out what I need to buy.' Geris continued sorting through his paraphernalia while I propped up the door post.

It could have been worse; we could have been in Relshaz where tisane mania is running riot. Apparently you can make a fortune there with a sufficiently startling box of herbs. Even a couple of incidental poisonings do not seem to have dampened the enthusiasm. Having said that, I was once in a high-stakes game with one of the more prominent victims and you'll never convince me his death was accidental.

'I'll take you to my favourite merchants when we get back to Vanam.' Geris took my arm as we went down the stairs. 'There's one just off the Iron Bridge who's brilliant; my mother gets all her herbs there too. You'll like her.'

He chattered on happily enough but I could see I was going to have to find a way of letting him down gently. Geris had the kind of nest-building urge you rarely see outside a hen-house. We were just too different, in too many ways. We'd passed the Equinox in a cattle-camp, one of our stops to trade for fodder and remounts, and Geris had made us all get out of bed to listen to the Horn-chain being sounded across the frosty grasslands. He'd stood there, reading out bits from his unnecessarily detailed Almanac, burbling on about the ancient origins of the rite and sun-cycle traditions. As far as I was concerned, it was just a handy way of learning how far-off other camps were and in what general direction, and I could have heard it just as well from the warmth of my blankets. I may be laying my hair on Drianon's altar one of these days but I knew it was certainly not Geris who would be doing the cutting. Still, plenty of time to worry about that later, I told myself.

'It's the last one on the right.' Shiv came up behind us and we opened the door to find Darni and a strange youth sitting in an elegant withdrawing-room, tastefully decorated in green brocade.

'This is Fremin Altaniss.' Darni waved a hand at the youth, who looked at us all uncertainly and opened his mouth.

'Wait.' I turned to Shiv. 'This strikes me as the wrong town to get overheard in. Can you do anything about that?'

'Surely.' He sketched some runes in the air with brilliant blue flashes, then sparks flew round the windows and walls, which glowed briefly.

'Now then.' I sat myself at the head of the table. 'Good morning, Fremin, and who exactly are you?'

'He's an agent assigned to watch over the merchant we're interested in.'

'Can he speak for himself, Darni?'

'He reports to me.'

The poor lad was looking like a mouse between two cats but I was not about to back down.

'Darni, when it comes to chopping people into bloody chunks, you are the best I've seen, no question. But believe me, I'm the best you're likely to see relieving people of their property. I need to know certain things which I don't think you'll appreciate, so I can ask you and you can ask him if that makes you happy but I really think it would be simpler if I did the asking myself.'

Shiv opened his mouth and then shut it as we all waited for Darni to make up his mind. The silence was made even more tense by the lack of outside noises.

'Go ahead.' He nodded, unsmiling, at Fremin, who decided he could breathe again.

'So, how well do you know Inglis, how long have you been here?'

'I followed Yeniya, that's the merchant, from Relshaz. We've been here since just before the end of Aft-Summer.'

'Ever been to Inglis before?'

He shook his head and I stifled a sigh. This job was going to be hard enough and I had hoped for better local sources.

'So what can you tell me about the city? Who thinks they run it and who really runs it?'

'The merchants' guilds run everything,' he said confidently. 'They really are in charge; different guilds do different things but their leaders organise it all between themselves.'

'Any sort of council or electors to give the people a voice?'

'No. Anyone who lives here permanently has to be a member of one of the guilds so I suppose they can get their concerns aired through their mastercraftsman.' He looked a little dubious.

'How does that work?'

'I'm not really sure; each guild has its own systems.'

I frowned. 'How tight is their control? There must be some people who want to strike out for themselves.'

Fremin shook his head again; I had a sinking feeling that he was going to do that a lot. 'Anyone who doesn't join is driven out. Anyway, there are benefits to belonging, free freight for goods to the south being the most important one. The guilds take care of running the city too.'

'There must be some who don't want to pay up,' I objected. 'Guild dues cost money and that means less profit.'

'No, it's all part of the set-up; the guilds don't take coin from their members. They pay their dues in services – street-cleaning, fire-watching and the like.'

Someone had thought this all through very thoroughly. An idea struck me.

'How efficient is the fire-watching? What's the attitude to fire-raising, come to that?'

'Livak!' Geris was outraged as he saw where I was heading.

'Look, it's not like Vanam here,' I reassured him. 'Nearly everything's built of stone for a start.'

Fremin looked unhappy. 'They'll hang you for it, just the same. Money and goods are at risk.'

'I could always raise a fire from a safe distance,' Shiv observed. 'Are you looking for a diversion?'

I nodded. 'The trick here is not just getting the job done, but getting away with it afterwards.'

'Can you do it?' The worry on Darni's face was a surprise.

'I'm not sure,' I said frankly. 'I'll need to find out much more before I can tell you. So, Fremin, or do you prefer Frem?'

'Frem's fine.' He relaxed a little more and I smiled at him; it wasn't his fault he was as much use as a eunuch in a brothel.

'How does this merchant fit in? What's her business and status?'

'She deals in furs and cloth; she buys furs from upriver and wool from Dalasor. She has a deal going with a family who do the weaving and fulling, and then she sends the cloth south to Tormalin as well as selling to trappers and the like when they come down from the hills. She also imports linen and silks from Tormalin and Aldabreshi.'

'Rich?'

'Very. Still quite young, not yet thirty certainly, and she's very pretty.'

'What do you know about her personal life?'

'She's a widow; her husband was one of the clothier family but he died of septic lungs last winter. She's being courted by a handful of men at the moment, all in the same sort of businesses and high up in the guilds.'

'How did you find all this out?'

'I found out where her servants drink and got friendly, asked around, the usual thing. I told them I'm making enquiries for a group of goatherders who are looking for new markets.'

Shiv must have seen through my gambling face. 'Is this looking too difficult?'

'Well, we have the kind of prominent citizen who will be able to call in all sorts of favours when she has a problem, such as the theft of a valuable necklace, for example. More than that, five powerful men are going to be eager to help out as a way of getting between her sheets. People will be asking questions as soon as she misses the piece and I'll bet they'll all be looking for the short southern lad with blue eyes and brown hair who's been asking so many questions and dresses in last year's Relshaz fashions.'

Frem looked a little sick and I felt sorry for him, especially when I saw Darni's expression.

'Next time, take the time to find out as much as you can just by watching. Be a beggar, filth and all, or, better yet, a madman. People might remember there was some imbecile drivelling on about the blue cats following him about, but they won't remember your face.'

'Is that what you do?' Shiv asked curiously.

I grinned at him as I sat back. 'Oh, I have a very nice line in looking for my lost children. I insist they must be around somewhere and people come out with all sorts of useful things when they're explaining why they can't be in this house or that. Once I've got all I can, I start getting odder and odder, explaining that one of the children is a goat and the other's a piglet. They can't get away from me fast enough.'

'Are you going to try that here?' Darni looked dubious.

'No. I'm staying well clear until the actual job. Frem, you can do one last thing for me then you're on your way home. Meet your drinking pals again tonight and find out all you can about these suitors. I especially want to know who's losing the race, and if she's fallen out with any of them over anything recently. Spend as much as you need to, tell them all you've made top coin on a deal for the goats and you're going home tomorrow. Book yourself passage down to Tormalin first thing in the morning and make sure you're seen getting on the boat. Pick a fight with someone on the docks or something.'

'I'll do that with you.' Darni clearly meant to reassure Frem but he looked as if he'd rather take his chances with a docker.

'Shiv, there must be wizards here. Can you find out what they do and how the guilds regard their activities? If you're going to be using magic, I'd like to know what the Watch are likely to make of it.'

He nodded. 'I can do that.'

'Right, I'm off out to see what I can find out for myself. I need to get a feel for the place before I can come up with any sort of plan.'

'I'll come with you.' Geris rose to his feet.

'I'll be less conspicuous on my own, trust me.' I'd be less conspicuous with a mule painted green but I didn't want to hurt his feelings.

'This is a rough town. It could be dangerous,' he objected.

'I can look after myself,' I said as gently as I could. 'I've been doing this kind of thing for a long time now, Geris.'

'If Frem's heading back to Hadrumal, I want to send a report. I'll need your help with that,' Darni stated firmly. 'You and I can stay here, then if Livak needs us to create some kind of diversion later, our faces won't have been seen too much.'

Geris brightened at that. I made my escape and left unobtrusively through the stable yard. I decided to walk; Darni had taken the stitches out of my leg a couple of days earlier and, although it was tender, I'd have more freedom on foot.

I breathed more freely the further I got from them all. Working at someone else's orders still felt oppressive, and it was good to feel at least the illusion of freedom once again. The faintest suggestion of hopping on a ship hovered around the back of my mind, but by now the challenge of the theft was just too enticing. This was going to be the most difficult job I'd ever tackled on my own, and I stifled a sharp regret for Halice, Sorgrad, Sorgren and Charoleia. If I had them to work with, I'd be in and out with half the lady's wealth and she wouldn't even know it. No point cursing over a rotten egg.

I strolled through the town, keeping a careful eye open to avoid anything that might get me noticed. The invisible woman, that's what I wanted to be. Now there was an interesting idea; now I was working with a wizard, I could have all sorts of advantages not open to the ordinary wall-crawler. I would have to ask Shiv more about that.

I was looking for some part of this city less obviously under guild control; in most coast towns it would have been the docks, but with trade the reason for Inglis' existence, that seemed to be the most tightly controlled area of all. I wandered apparently aimlessly, a trader newly arrived, seeing the sights. It was certainly an interesting place; metalsmiths of various sorts each had their own quarter, copper, silver, gold. Close by were gem-buyers, cutters, jewellers and craftsmen. Furriers and tanners worked together, their workshops well downwind of the clothiers and tailors whose warehouses formed most of the central district, interwoven with all the other trades of a major town. There were fruit-sellers, butchers, potters, carpenters, and all were doing brisk trade. Their customers ranged from harassed mothers in plain smocks towing reluctant children, to elegant ladies in flowing silks fawned on by obsequious merchants. Pedlars with trays of trinkets and food wove among the crowds.

I had more trouble spotting the pickpockets and cut-purses. I thought I saw one; I didn't catch him make the lift itself, but he started moving away from his victim faster than the general pace of the crowd. As his face turned towards me, I saw the expression of a rat in a bear-pit; not what the dogs are after but something they'll kill all the same. I scanned the square covertly for the hounds and saw several lightly armoured men circulating round the shops and stalls. Something else struck me. You'll find a Rationalist or two in most places these days, arguing that worshipping the gods is pointless in the modern age. Not in Inglis, it seemed; now was that policy, or just a sign that new ideas had trouble travelling this far?

I kept moving and finally found the horse fair. This was more promising; festival garlands of fruit and flowers still hung on some doors and lay in the gutters. If these people weren't so conscientious about their street-cleaning duties, they might have a more relaxed attitude to other things. I saw a priest actually handing out alms of bread and meat here too; his shrine was as unusually well kept as all the others I had passed but he was the first religious I'd seen in Inglis without a collecting box. There were a few inns across the broad dusty expanse of the sale meadow. The Rising Sun was obviously a brothel and the Cross Swords could only be a drinking den and nothing more. The Eagle promised better and I wasn't disappointed. There was plenty of merriment but no obvious drunks and a lively game of runes was being played to one side. I left them to it; no one wants to chat and gamble. There were tables with White Raven boards by the window and I looked for a vacant seat; I like playing Raven but neither Darni or Geris knew how. Shiv did, but after a few games I could tell he was not really keen, which makes sense when you think about it.

There was an empty seat across from a tall, wiry man with the dark curly hair and olive skin you see most often in southern Tormalin. He sat, seemingly relaxed over a goblet of wine, not a care in the world. I knew better; I could see the alertness in his eyes as he scanned the horse traders and every passing stranger.

He was wearing a business-like sword and sitting half-turned so that nothing would get in his way if he needed it in a hurry. Alert but not predatory, he struck me as interesting.

'Are you looking for a game?' I gestured at the board.

'I'll oblige you if you want to play.' He straightened up and beckoned to the potman.

'Do you want to play the White Raven or the Wood Fowl?' I began sorting the well-worn pieces.

'Whichever. Wine?'

I nodded and began placing the trees and bushes on the board. Let's see how good he was.

'Interesting,' he murmured and I sat back to sip an excellent Califerian red as he selected which birds to set out in the open.

'Just arrived in Inglis?' He did not look up as he set out apple-thrushes and pied crows, a polite man just making polite conversation.

'This morning.' Why should I lie when there was no need?

'Downriver?'

I shook my head and leaned forward to study his layout before placing the raven on the board. It was deceptive in its simplicity and he'd kept back corbies and owls for the next play; this might be one white raven that did get driven out of the forest if I was not careful.

'Are you in from Tormalin then? What's the news?'

Now why did he want to know where I was from? 'No, I came along the south road through Dalasor. I'm up from Ensaimin. How about you?'

'I came up the coast from Tormalin; I'm running some errands for a few people. I've been here ten days. Perhaps I can help you out, tell you where to find a good inn, the better merchants.'

'That could be useful.' We understood each other nicely.

We played a few rounds and I forced his songbirds off the western edge of the board before he used the hawks to drive me back.

'It's a long trip from Ensaimin,' my new friend observed, refilling my goblet. 'What brings you here?'

'Looking for new opportunities, the usual.'

'It's not a town that welcomes individual enterprise, if you get my meaning.' He glanced up from the board and I could see his friendly warning was sincere.

'It looks very well organised to me,' I observed as if agreeing. 'I hear the guilds run all the services, the Watch and so on.'

'That's right and they do it very well. The Watchmen aren't the usual bunch of losers with a mate on the town council; the guilds hire out of Lescar each winter when the fighting slows down. They're well paid and well trained; there's plenty of money moving round Inglis and the guilds are very keen that everyone knows it's safe.'

'Do they patrol regularly? How good are they at following up on trouble? Suppose I got my room rifled, for example?'

'They patrol everywhere, dawn to dawn. What trouble they don't catch, they hunt down, and I'm pleased to hear they can't be bought off either. They have wizards working with them too.'

'A pretty thorough lot by the look of the gibbets. Does everyone get hanged, or do they have a lock-up as well?'

'There's a keep where they dump drunks and so on.'

'Nice to know the streets will be safe to walk at night.' We both sounded thoroughly pleased with the situation. I betrayed myself with a clumsy move and nearly fell to a hidden group of owls.

'I've not seen many Forest Folk this far east.' He drank his wine and sat back as I studied the board; things were looking increasingly complicated.

'Oh, we get about.'

'It must be a bit of a nuisance, everyone able to pick you out by that copper-top of yours.'

I grinned despite myself. 'Oh, it's surprising what you can do with herbal washes. I can be as black and curly as you if I need to be.'

He smiled back appreciatively. 'I bet you'd look good in it too. The best I can do is shave my head and grow a beard.'

That made for an interesting picture. 'Had to do that often?'

'Now and again. I'm always interested in new opportunities, like yourself.'

We each made a few more moves.

'Blond must be a good colour for hair if you need to dye it.' He was very good; it really sounded as if it had only just occurred to him. 'Not that you see real blond very often.'

'No.' I gazed round the bar at the usual variety of middling brown and darker heads and beards. 'That maid's colour is straight out of an alchemist's crucible for a start.'

'You know, I don't suppose I've ever seen more than a couple of really yellow heads together.' Casual conversation over a friendly game, that's all it was, wasn't it?

'I met someone on the road who said they'd seen a whole troop with corn-coloured hair.' Fair exchange; he'd told me the important things about the Watch. Anyway, I'd be interested to know the reason for his curiosity.

'Oh? When was that?'

'A couple of days before Equinox, just before the drove-road that turns south to Lescar.'

He studied the board, seemingly intent on his next move, but I'd bet I'd have seen an Almanac if I'd been looking through his eyes.

'How are the cattle looking this year?' He made a swift move and boxed my raven in.

'Pretty fair, the rains kept the grass good through the summer.' So our yellow-haired attackers were not the ones he was interested in.

We continued the game and chatted idly about incidental things. It was a good contest and I eventually won, which pleased me more than I expected.

He rose and offered me his hand. 'Thanks for the game. Have a good stay; Inglis is a pleasant town, as long as you don't attract the wrong sort of notice.' He flicked the raven with a finger.

I finished my wine and left a few moments later. Finding the lock-up was easy enough and I studied it for a while before making my way to the district where Yeniya the merchant lived. Despite what I'd said to the others, I wanted to see it for myself. I was glad I did, when careful pacing of the streets and studying the roof-lines suggested her luxurious three-storey house backed directly on to the trading-house she owned in the avenue beyond. I'd have bet all my noble coin on there being a connecting door, and I marked it down as a potential route in or out. I was starting to see a workable plan.

I spent the rest of daylight studying in just as much detail a weaver's guild-house, the farmers' market and two more private houses and in striking up conversations and a game of runes in a couple more inns. I have absolutely no idea if I was being watched but this was neither the time nor the place to take chances. I made my way back to the others with my purse nicely full just as the bells of the city were sounding the first chime of the night. It was so comforting to hear them again after so long in the wilds; town bells mean civilisation, hot water and decent food.

'There you are!' Geris struggled to conceal the extent of his relief and I was touched at his concern.

'I told you I'd be fine.' I gave him a quick kiss. 'Now, let's get some dinner and when the others get back we can do some planning.'

My incidental winnings bought us the best meal in the house and we were laughing and flirting over the end of the wine when Frem and then Shiv reappeared. It was the most natural thing in the world to retire to our parlour with spirits and liqueurs but once the door was locked behind us, it was down to business.

'So, Frem, what do you have to tell us?'

It turned out that Yeniya was playing all of her suitors with a skill that made me glad she'd not taken up the runes professionally. They were all keen, eager and convinced they'd be cutting her hair for Drianon within the year, if not sooner. In the meantime, she was negotiating contracts for her various businesses to increase her already considerable wealth.

I grimaced at this news; I could not see how I could turn any of that to our advantage.

'There was something more.' Frem took a drink of wine. 'There's a nephew of her dead husband who's been making trouble. He took a case to the jurists' guild over the will. He reckoned his bequests were too small and wanted more shares in the business.'

'Did he have a case?'

Frem shrugged. 'That's hard to tell, but he's been telling anyone who'll listen that he only lost because one of the key judges is after Yeniya's hand.'

I grinned; that was just the sort of thing I had hoped for.

'What are you planning?' Geris asked curiously.

'Never mind, I'll tell you later. Shiv, what can you tell us about the wizards?'

He frowned. 'They're well enough respected and fairly represented in the usual trades, but they have to be guild members just like anyone else. I have to say, I think they will have divided loyalties. My authority will make sure they turn a blind eye to anything we do – none of them will point the Watch our way, for example – but I don't think we'll get any active co-operation. Any wizard stepping over the line here is on the next boat out, never mind where it's going.'

'That shouldn't be a problem,' I reassured him. 'Just as long as you can do some magic without everyone pointing the finger.'

'What do you want?'

'If I get myself locked up by the Watch, can you get me out and then back in again?'

'Yes, if I have time to study the building.' Shiv was looking intrigued.

'Can you make me invisible?' This was the big one.

'Yes. It'll last about two chimes – will that do?'

'Good enough.' I leaned back in my chair and smiled at them all. 'I think we can start planning now, gentlemen.'

It was simple enough really; I needed to get in and out without being seen and we wanted a good smelly scent for the Watch to follow when Yeniya started screaming theft, as well as a defence hewn in stone in case I was somehow spotted. Frem told us when her servants were due their next night off and Darni and Geris spent the intervening evenings striking up a drinking friendship with the aggrieved nephew, encouraging him to pour out his complaints ever more loudly and extravagantly. I watched all this one evening from a quiet corner. The pair of them could have taken their act to the Looking Glass; I really had not thought they had it in them, but they were brilliant. I followed our diversion home a couple of nights, and soon had the measure of his small house and its simple locks. Once he had a handful of Yeniya's jewels hidden in his chimney, he should keep the Watch entertained long enough to let us make a casual and completely unremarkable departure a couple of days after the Watch stopped quizzing everyone leaving the city.

CHAPTER FIVE

Taken from:

The Yeoman's Almanac for the Ocean Coast

Sostirc Heriod
*Containing comprehensive schedules and instructions for
all farming, husbandry and household tasks*

Schedule of Seasons as Governed by the Moons
and Notable Customs thereof

Winter Solstice
Sacred to Poldrion
Greater and Lesser Moons Full
Gidesta: White pelt sales. Inglis Frost Fair (Wolf-bounty paid).
Dalasor: Mistle Fairs. Riding the Bane-horse.
Tormalin: Coin taxes. Winter Assizes. Soulsease Night.

Aft-Winter
Sacred to Misaen
Lasts until end of Second Dark of the Greater Moon
Gidesta: Skull-setting to 20th day; Sled-motes thereafter.
Dalasor: Marking and blessing the herds. Marrying the Mares.
Tormalin: First-flower maidens crowned. Patrons' market-doles.

For-Spring
Sacred to Halcarion
Lasts until end of Second Dark of the Lesser Moon

Gidesta: Rite of Dastennin's Step when ice breaks. Inglis fur sales.
Dalasor: Horning the Ram-lamb. Forage sales on the Drove Road.
Tormalin: Plough-dressing, seed-blessing. Fixing the doorthorns.

Spring Equinox
Sacred to Raeponin
Greater Moon waning, Lesser Moon waxing
Gidesta: Mining Contracts sealed, Inglis. Apothecary Fair.
Dalasor: Minstrel Day. Lots drawn for summer water-rights.
Tormalin: Herd taxes. Convocation of Houses. Blossom-singing.

Aft-Spring
Sacred to Arrimelin
Lasts until Greater and Lesser Moons are both Full.
Gidesta: Riverboats commence. Mountain-mote at Gerrad's Peak.
Dalasor: Paying the Eldritch Wayleave. Ishelwater Races.
Tormalin: Tenure services due. Blessing the hulls and nets.

For-Summer
Sacred to Ostrin
Lasts until Last Quarter of Second Greater Moon.
Gidesta: Wool sales and Dyestuff Mart, Inglis. Dock festivals.
Dalasor: Shearing. Smoking out the Tick-King. Ring-feathering.
Tormalin: Hay-making. Crop-riding days. Rushing the Shrines.

Summer Solstice
Sacred to Saedrin
Greater Moon Dark.
Gidesta: Guild Elections in Inglis. Pacifying the Mountains.
Dalasor: Dairy fairs and cheese-racing. Whitenight fires.
Tormalin: Summer Assizes. Land taxes due. Emperor's Dole.

Aft-Summer
Sacred to Larasion
Lasts until Second Full of the Greater Moon.
Gidesta: Apothecaries' Markets. Cloth-sales. Shrine-ales.
Dalasor: Crowning the Stones. Dousing the herds.
Tormalin: Rose Mart. Shrine Wake-nights. Corn-plaiting.

For-Autumn
Sacred to Dastennin
Lasts through Full Dark until Greater Moon waxes.
Gidesta: Close of mining season. Ore-tithe to the Mountains.
Dalasor: Herd-motes. Smith-motes. Foster-motes.
Tormalin: Harvest. Selling Ostrin's Pig. Sea-salt sales.

Autumn Equinox
Sacred to Drianon
Greater and Lesser Half-Moons.
Gidesta: Metal and Gem Fair, Inglis. Rock-salt sales.
Dalasor: Cattle fairs on Drove Road. Sounding the Horn-chain.
Tormalin: Meat, milk and wool taxes due. Boundary walking.

Aft-Autumn
Sacred to Talagrin
Lasts until Second Full of the Lesser Moon.
Gidesta: Sale of Guild prenticeships. Journeyman quit-rents.
Dalasor: Planting the Winter-stake. Hide sales. Nut-fairs.
Tormalin: Wheat-queening. Last Calf feasts. Open wood-gathers.

For-Winter
Sacred to Maewelin
Lasts until Second Full of the Greater Moon.
Gidesta: Candle-auctions for trapping tracts. Ice races, Inglis.
Dalasor: Burning the Ails-faggot. Dressing the Sentinel-trees.
Tormalin: Green-branching the Shrines. Cording the roads.

Inglis,
10th of Aft–Autumn

The night for our little enterprise arrived and Shiv and I set out. Later Geris was going to bring the hapless nephew back to the inn for a friendly game of runes. Shiv had left a few spells to guarantee no one would be able to remember seeing the man and I had left Geris a rather special set of bones to make sure he could control the game. I'd spent a few evenings teaching him some tricks and the combination of his nimble fingers and naive manner could be quite devastating. I almost found myself wondering if we might not have a longer-term future after all; cosy nights together in a feather bed did a lot to encourage such ideas.

It was chilly and dark out, but the streets were lit by the flambeaux at wealthy doors and the linkmen with their lanterns. I took a swig of the juniper liquor I was carrying and then poured a little over my clothes and hair. I had to be careful; there was no point in being invisible later on if everyone was wondering where the smell of a pot-still was coming from. We found a quiet tavern in the kind of respectable neighbourhood that Watchmen like to look after and I launched into my celebrated impression of a drunk, maudlin and argumentative by turns. Perhaps I should audition for Judal too. It was not long before the taverner sent out a boy with a message.

'Come on, sweetheart, let's find somewhere for you to have a nice lie-down.'

'He said he loved me, he swore it.'

'I'm sure he did.' The Watchman half carried me out and escorted me firmly to the lock-up. I judged him Lescari, by his accent, and keen, by his shiny breast-plate.

I didn't see Shiv following but the cell door had not been

long shut when I was caught up in a dizzying invisible spiral of air. I felt completely disoriented and not a little sick so I shut my eyes to find myself standing next to Shiv when I opened them. I managed not to vomit on his shoes; I did not think that would be much of a thank you.

'Come on.' We moved as fast as we could without attracting attention.

'I've left an illusion of you sleeping,' Shiv whispered.

'Good thinking.' There's always something that doesn't occur to you and I was beginning to wonder if Shiv might be amenable to working with me and Halice in the future.

We found the discreet alley by Yeniya's house where Darni was waiting.

'She came back at seventh chime and hasn't gone out again yet. The servants left just before dusk.'

I frowned. We knew Yeniya was due to be dining with her jurist and we were counting on the fact that she'd never yet been seen wearing the chain with evening gowns.

'All right, get back and help Geris.'

Darni left and Shiv worked his magic on me. It felt really odd, I could see myself but dimly, as if I were a shadow. I took off my cloak and when I dropped it at Shiv's feet, he jumped as it became visible.

'Get back to the inn,' I whispered.

'What if there's a problem? What if she's not going out after all?' His gaze went somewhere past my right ear.

'I'll deal with it from here. We don't want anyone seeing you hanging about.'

He left and I crossed the street to take the steps down to the kitchen yard. It rather took the fun out of it, not having to watch, wait and hug the shadows. Should I go in or not? I was invisible, after all, and we knew the servants had left. Should I risk trying to find my way around the house if Yeniya was still in there? What could she be doing alone in an empty house? I could think of a few things; one at least would mean she was not actually on her own. Was that so bad? If she was busy playing stuff the chicken with some handsome lackey, they'd be unlikely to hear me playing house cat. I only hoped she had a separate dressing-room and did not keep her jewellery in the bedchamber. Good sex may make you think the earth is spinning, but it doesn't make caskets open of their own accord or things float through the air. I made up my mind to go inside anyway; if it all looked impossible, I'd just sneak out again and we'd have to come up with something new.

The kitchen and basement were dark and the locks soon gave in. I crept through the echoing darkness of the kitchen, sliding my feet along the smooth flagstones. The lingering smells of laundry and baking mixed with the hot metal scent of the range, teasing my memory; I had been reared in a place like this. There was no sign of food preparation, so Yeniya and her swain were apparently not dining in. That was a relief, but what was going on? We'd been watching her for days now, and she was usually as regular as the rains in Aldabreshi. Something was starting to feel very wrong as I skirted the long scrubbed table and headed for the door. I was starting to wish Shiv was still waiting outside or, better yet, in here too.

I crept up the stairs and into the richly furnished hall. Even in the gloom, it made the house where I'd grown up look tawdry; Yeniya or her late husband had taste as well as coin. Lustrous vases shimmered in alcoves, passing flashes of light through the windows threw splashes of colour on to the pictures that lined the walls. Dried flowers in silver stands scented the air; the house was confident, beautiful and serene. I stole silently up the carpeted steps to the first floor and found that the lady herself was now anything but these things.

Whoever they were, they'd shown no mercy. Her elegant and painted fingers had been brutally snapped, with the broken bones worked savagely against each other, ivory splinters gleaming in the ruin of the flesh. Blood on her once flawless face showed how she'd bitten right through her lip, silently eloquent of her agony, while tears made a sorry mess of her fashionable make-up. Clumps of her lustrous brown hair had been ripped out bodily leaving the rest stickily matted. The stains of bruises round her neck had stopped darkening when death finally released her but I could see the pattern of repeated strangling and release clearly enough. Her wrists and ankles showed the prints of vicious hands, and the blood and pale stains on her green satin shift told me why. Had the rape been part of the torture, or a bonus for the boys? A dagger thrust through one eye had ended her torment but the other, glazed and rimmed with blood, stared straight at me, the bright blue dimmed in death. That eye beseeched me; why had this had happened to her?

I pressed my hands against my mouth until I got a grip of myself. This was a whole new throw of the runes. I forced myself to gather my wits; I had to find out all I could and then get clear. I reached to pull the ripped shift to cover her torn nakedness but stopped myself just in time. If wizards were working with the Watch, who knew what they could discover about who had been here and why. I must not touch anything.

I forced myself to ignore the pitiable corpse and looked around the room. It was an office and the invaders had ransacked it comprehensively. Parchments were strewn around the floor, torn, trampled and bloody. I squinted at some, blessing my Forest sight; they were business documents and even to my untrained eye looked significant, detailing percentages, commissions and purchase agreements. I glanced over at the body again; that much work had taken time. She was not gagged or bound, there were no bruises round her mouth to betray a stifling hand; the savage assault had to have made an unholy noise. Why had no one heard her screams? Why had Darni not heard her? I moved to the window; I could see the entrance to the alley where he had kept watch. This had happened while she was dressing for her dinner engagement; where was her maid? I wondered queasily. How had her assailants got in?

A massive strongbox was set against one wall, bolted to it if I'm any judge. The lid was up, though for the life of me I couldn't see how they had got it open; there were no keys anywhere about. More papers were scattered about and a stack of soft leather bags whispered seductively to me. I was not in the least tempted but something looked odd. I had a closer look at the contents, pushing things aside with my dagger point, and then sat back on my heels, frowning. There must have been coin in here; a few coins had slipped between the papers but the rest had gone. There was some jewellery left in the scattered velvet wrappings but those lovely pouches of polished gems had been left alone.

What was this all about? A hit on a strongbox to snatch coin is a fast robbery, in and out and spend the goods that same night, ideally on something you can resell fast. Why leave nice, untraceable gems behind and take highly identifiable jewellery? Torture is a long job and risky in a place like this – why torture at all for that matter? If they wanted information on her business and property, they had left stacks of it trampled underfoot. Come to that, Yeniya was a significant player in her own trade but there were bigger fish. What could she know that was worth this risk in a city where cut-purses got their necks stretched for a first offence? It all smelled very rank. I looked into the chest again; should I search for that chain? No, I'd bet it was long gone with whoever had killed Yeniya. I felt cold; was that what they had been after all along? I had no reason to think so but I was convinced all the same. Stuff this, time for me to leave.

I looked into the chest; should I take something to plant on the nephew anyway? No, he may have been an idiot and greedy with it but he did not deserve to get dropped any deeper into this mire. Was there anything of any use to us at all? Nothing that could be worth the risk of being tied to this crime.

I moved to the door and froze, heart pounding as I heard a soft noise in the hall below. Idiot, I told myself, it's probably just the kitchen cat. Probably, but what if it wasn't? I looked down at my hands, still nice and shadowy, but I cursed myself as I realised I had not been listening out for the chimes. How much longer could I rely on this handy concealment? I moved slowly to a dark corner and leaned cautiously forward until I could just see over the banister. The darkness in the well of the stairs was inky black but a passing lantern sent a gleam through the windows and I saw a shadow move quickly under the stairs. I stood perfectly still and watched as the shadow split and a dark figure ran silently down the hallway towards the kitchen.

I padded up to the next floor on silent feet, heart racing as I forced myself to move carefully round the ornaments. What had seemed elegantly decorative earlier was now just so much inconvenient clutter. I paused to calm my breathing and strained my ears for any sound of pursuit. I could hear nothing, but I was not happy. The doors around me were all closed and I did not want to risk squeaky hinges giving me away, however unlikely in a house so well maintained. I moved down the hallway with agonising stealth on the polished floorboards. Which of the doors at the end led to the back stairs? I pressed my face to the crack of each and was rewarded by the faint kiss of a draught on my lips. I tried the handle and blessed Halcarion as it moved silently and I found the servants' route to the basement.

There was no light at all. Even my Forest sight failed me and I had to feel my way down each step with hesitant feet, forcing aside fears of some unknown hand coming up out of the blackness to grab me. I had to concentrate on getting out of there before Shiv's spell wore off. My right hand was running down the panels of the wall to keep me balanced while I had my dagger ready in my left; an irregularity in the wood caught my finger and I stopped, wondering what it was. No thicker than a knife blade, the line ran round the moulding of the panel and when I pressed lightly on it, it gave a little. I let out a slow breath; could this be the door to the warehouse? It was in the right place and that would make sense. If I got out of here, I'd have to lay off the runes for a season, I was using up luck at such a rate.

I ran suddenly shaky fingers round the panel; there had to be a lock or a catch. Nothing. Stuff it. I rubbed my hands together till they stilled and tried again. This time I found a piece of moulding that slid aside to reveal a small hole. A lock; a catch would have been better but I lost no time getting to work with a lockpick while the dark silence pressed in all around me.

There, I had it. I was through and locking it behind me faster than a rat out of a burning barn. Once I had it secure, I turned to see where I was. The roof was lost in the blackness above but I could just make out tall racks marching away from me in neat lines. I could smell the harshness of new dye and, when I stretched out a searching hand, I felt the reassuring smoothness of broadcloth. I moved fast and headed for the far side where I knew there were doors. I only hoped there were no Watchmen, private or guild-employed; another thing I should have thought to check in advance. A faint scent vaguely like that of a damp dog told me I was among the fur stock and I peered into the gloom for the way out.

A footfall ahead froze me. I almost thought I had imagined it but a few seconds later it came again, the click of a steel-rimmed boot sole on the flagstones. I took a side turning and reached into the furs; was there anywhere to hide? No good. I looked at the racks; were they sturdy enough to climb? Perhaps, but as I weighed up the risks, my head suddenly started to swim. I blinked but the disorientation got worse and worse; it was like having an instant fever. I took a step forward but could not remember which way I had been heading. I turned to go back but that did not feel right either; my knees buckled and my hands started shaking. The tall racks of furs loomed, shifting and crossing in front of me, pressing down from above until I felt like screaming. The smell became a sickening, choking stench and my breath started rattling in my chest. I turned again and fell to my knees as the floor lurched beneath me. I clung to the flagstones as if I was afraid of falling off. The urge to scream was building in my throat but in some sane corner of my delirious mind I knew I must not do it. I bit my tongue hard and the bitterness of blood filled my mouth. The pain seemed to help clear my thoughts and I dived under the lowest shelf of pelts with the last of my control.

As I lay there, shaking my head and trying desperately to get a grip on my scattered wits, I saw a pair of black boots walk silently up the aisle. The rub of leather on leather whispered past and I lay as still as a statue on a shrine. As the almost imperceptible steps receded, my head cleared and I lay there frantically trying to work out which way the door would be. As I racked my brains, I became aware of a faint light ahead of me. I shuffled forwards with agonising care but what I saw made me think I was going under the delirium again. Footprints were gleaming on the stones, not with any of the colours of magelight but with a faint luminescence like the moonfire you get on ships. I stared and then a shock ran though me as I realised those were my steps being outlined for whoever was chasing me. I wriggled round to check my boot soles but there was nothing on them so there was no point in taking them off.

I scrambled through to the opposite side of the racks as fast as I could without making too much noise, but speed was more important than silence now. I stood and looked wildly round. Boots echoed a few rows behind me so I headed away from them, cursing silently as the tell-tale silver footprints followed me. I reached the large double doors and found the postern; my picks slipped in my sweaty hands as I tried to unlock it. My hands, my solid, completely solid and visible hands; I realised with a lurch of terror that Shiv's spell was gone. The scrape of a boot-heel came out of the blackness and my nerve snapped like a bowstring. I wrenched back the bolts of the main doors and shoved them open; I'd take my chances with whoever might be on guard rather than risk ending up like Yeniya.

A shout behind me summoned the hunters and I ran for my life. The streets were dark and silent. My steps echoed back from the blank stone walls of the warehouses. There was nowhere to hide even if I had wanted to. I ran on, heading for the centre of the city, my head clearing in the cool night air, thank Saedrin. Why is there never a Watchman around when you need one?

I saw the dark opening of an alley and slowed a pace; should I go down it or not? That hesitation saved my life as a black-clad man stepped out and swung a sword where my head should have been. I scrambled backwards, drawing my own sword; how in Poldrion's name had they moved ahead of me?

The killer moved and lashed out with his sword. I parried the blow, which made my arms ache, and I had to move fast to avoid the follow-up. I dropped my dagger and drew my reserve from my belt; the good news was this one was poisoned, the bad news was that I'd have to get in close to use it. Thank Saedrin Darni had agreed to practise with me after our Dalasorian encounter. I needed all the skills I'd ever learned to get out of this.

He came at me again with an over-arm stroke that would have split my skull but I was able to dodge it. I watched him carefully and realised he was signalling his moves with his off hand, not by much but even a few breaths' advantage could save me here. We circled and fought and when I saw he was going for the overhead smash again, I darted in and stabbed my dagger into the armpit gap of his hauberk. He spat something at me in complete gibberish and I leaped back to avoid his riposte. That's the trouble with poisons; the ones that are safe to carry around on weapons are not necessarily the fastest.

His next swing was slower and he was licking his lips as the venom started to work. His reflexes failed him and I was able to take out his knees with my next stroke. As he fell, I took his head off with a sweeping cut and it skittered across the street like a ball, helm coming loose to reveal a flaxen head rolling in the moonlight. Blood went everywhere and I swore; that would attract the Watch, if nothing else did.

A shout behind me died into a gasp. I whirled round to see three more men in identical armour heading straight for me. I slipped in the blood as I took a pace back and cursed, scraping my boot-sole on the cobbles as I retreated. I turned to run but the world went weird on me again. You know those dreams when you're trying to run and you can't, when it feels like you're waist-deep in water? It only took a few steps before I turned to face whoever was coming for me. If I was going to die, it wasn't going to be from a sword in the back.

They approached. I saw one grinning, teeth gleaming in his pale face. That made me furious and I spat curses at them as I spread my sword and dagger in a lethal embrace. The poison should be good for one more if I could get a deep thrust, and I'd take as many of the bastards with me as I could. They closed around me as I got my back to the wall, and I wondered how expensive Poldrion's ferry might be tonight.

'Hey, shit for brains! How about picking on someone your own size? Got the stones for it?' Three men emerged from the alleyway with a clash of drawing swords. They were rough and dirty and looked like death in hob-nailed boots; my heroes.

As my hunters froze in a moment's confusion, my own wits awoke and spurred me on. I stabbed the nearest one in the neck and dashed through the gap as he stumbled from the force of the blow.

'Need some help, sweetheart?' The leader of my rescuers stepped up to my side and smiled like a mad dog through his filthy beard. Hardly a Lescari Duke riding to my aid but I wasn't going to criticise his hygiene.

He needed no answer as the hunters in black moved to attack the new threat. They moved together like trained soldiers and attacked as one. My new allies did not have the same polish but made up for it with the savagery born of life in the mining camps. They hacked with their notched swords, driving the hunters back step by step. I was still busy with the one I'd just stabbed, who was taking his own sweet time about succumbing to the poison. His eyes finally rolled and he stumbled forward, so I got my dagger up under his chin. He dropped to his knees at my feet, and I caught the incongruous scent of orris from his clean-shaven face before blood gushed from his slack lips.

I kicked the corpse aside and moved to help one of my new pals. Now we were two on one, the hunters did not last much longer. One died with his brains spread in an arc across the wall as a sword ripped through his skull and tore off his face. The other went down more cleanly when the sudden realisation of his imminent fate made him drop his guard and he took a straight thrust to the throat.

'Move.' Mad-dog had us moving before the man at his feet had stopped gurgling. We ran down the alley and it led to another street of warehouses and trading yards. We ran on through a network of alleys and back lanes until we came out into a quiet street of rooming-houses.

'Thanks doesn't seem to cover it, lads,' I said fervently as we slowed to a nonchalant walk.

'You looked like you could do with a hand, flower.'

'I can't argue with that. What were you doing there?'

'Out for a stroll.' The men exchanged glances and I could see our fragile alliance was fading.

'Good luck for me.' I reached for my purse and wondered how much to give them. Stuff it, they could have the whole lot; I cut it loose with my dagger.

'Get drunk on me and do me a favour, forget you ever saw me.'

Mad-dog blinked. 'You don't have to—' he began uncertainly.

'Cheers.' One of his mates took the purse from me and weighed it appreciatively.

We continued walking slowly along until we had passed a patrolling Watchman. The dark hid the blood on our clothes but I was as nervous as a colt in a breaking yard. I left the miners at the next street corner without looking back and hurried back to the inn as fast as I dared. I slipped through the stableyard and snatched up a cloak some fool had left on his saddle. Wrapping it round me to hide the bloodstains, I went up the back stairs. The parlour door was locked, which threw me, and I rattled the handle angrily.

'Open up,' I hissed into it.

Keys rattled and I fell forward as Darni snatched the door out of my hand in opening it. I pushed past him.

'We've got a demon of a problem on our backs—' I began breathlessly.

'Do you know where he is?' Darni grabbed my shoulder, his fingers digging in painfully.

'Where who is?' I shoved his hand off. 'Listen, this is important.'

'No, you listen.' Darni was a pace away from outright fury and I realised I did not want to see that. 'Do you know where Geris is?'

'Geris?' I looked at him stupidly. 'He's supposed to be here playing runes with What's-his-name the nephew.'

'He's gone.' I looked round to see Shiv kneeling by the coffers we'd been hauling over so many leagues, the now open and empty coffers.

'Gone?' Repeating everything was not very helpful but I could not get my mind round what they were saying.

'According to the innkeeper, he left just before I got back.' Darni's face was set like stone. 'He's taken three seasons' work with him and gone off with a group of yellow-haired men.'

I stared at him, jaw dropped open. I shut my mouth, turned on my heel and ran. I slammed out of the inn, ignoring Darni's outraged bellow and the startled stares of the customers.

Pelting through the dark streets, I found myself muttering the first truly sincere prayer of my adult life. 'Halcarion, please let him be there, please let him be there.' Was the Moon Maiden still going to be listening to me after I'd used up so much luck already tonight?

'Can I help you, madam?' Another of those well-polished Watchmen stepped out of a doorway to bar my path. I registered the gleam of his breastplate just fast enough to stop myself palming my dagger; my nerves were as taut as a bowstring and fraying fast.

'Sorry? No, thank you. I'm late for a meet, that's all.' I stumbled over the words but he just saluted me briefly and stepped back.

I forced myself to walk more slowly; I was still wearing bloody clothes and the last thing I wanted to do was explain that away. No one was raising a hue and cry so it didn't look as if the murder had been discovered yet but it wouldn't take long; the servants would be home soon for a start.

The horse fair was still wide awake; the corrals were full and herders in from Dalasor and Gidesta were camped round fires, singing and drinking with scant regard for anyone who might want to sleep. The Eagle was lit and lively and I pushed my way through the crowd, hampered by the need to keep the cloak wrapped round me.

I scanned the throng for the dark curly head, the long limbs. Finally I saw the man I was looking for; he was playing White Raven with a horse trader, their finely balanced game attracting a circle of people. He looked up as I approached, the lamplight glinting gold in his brown eyes, but now I had found him, I just stood there dumbly, unable to think what to say.

'Is it Grandmother? Has she had another seizure? All right, I'm coming.' He rose and escorted me out immediately, supportive arm around my shoulders, half a head taller than most of the press of people who parted before us.

'What is it?' We paused in the space beyond the horse pens where no one could overhear us.

'You're hunting yellow-haired men. Have you got a lead on them yet?' I demanded.

'Not yet,' he said slowly. 'Why do you ask?'

'Someone I'm travelling with has disappeared and I think they've taken him.'

'Shit!' His composure broke for a moment and I saw real fury in his eyes, his hand gesturing involuntarily towards his sword hilt. 'So who are you? What's your business?'

'I'm travelling with a wizard and an Archmage's agent. They're collecting Tormalin Empire artefacts for some project of Planir's. We had a Vanam scholar with us, Geris. We were out this evening and when we got back, he'd gone, apparently with a group of blond men.'

'He couldn't have gone off himself? Why do you think these men are the ones I want?' His eyes were keen and his face impassive. Not a man to play runes with when drinking.

'On the road here we were hit by a troop of these cornheads, and when I was out doing a job tonight I was attacked by more of them. That's no coincidence. You're looking for them and it has to be something important to bring you this far north.'

'What was the job?'

I hesitated; I did not want to give too much away and I felt strangely reluctant to admit to my role as wizard's tame thief. 'Can we help each other over this?' I persisted. 'I can't say more until I have your word.'

'Surely.' He nodded and swore a binding oath to Dastennin; an interesting choice.

As I told him the bare essentials of the tale, the five chimes of midnight interrupted us. He cursed and looked around. I saw the horse traders dousing their fires and the inns escorting reluctant customers to the doors. I'd only just made it.

'We can't do much tonight.' He ran a hand through his hair. 'How about I see you at first light?'

I nodded and turned to go; I could not think of anything else to do or say and the energy generated by the night's shocks was fading fast. I stumbled on some dried horseshit and would have fallen if he had not caught my arm.

'Are you all right?' I saw him rub his fingertips together, sniffing to confirm the blood.

'It's not mine.' I said tiredly. 'It's just been a pig of a night and I'm exhausted.'

'You can have my bed here if you want,' he offered.

I shook my head. 'I'll be fine. Darni will start taking the city apart if I go missing too.'

'The wizard?'

'No, the agent. Be careful of him, by the way; he doesn't take ideas from other people well.'

'Do you want me to walk you back?'

'No thanks. I'll be careful.'

He nodded and turned to go back to the Eagle. He looked back over his shoulder. 'By the way, what's your name?'

I stared at him for a moment before realising we'd not even introduced ourselves.

'Livak, I'm called Livak.'

'I'm Ryshad.' He winked at me and smiled encouragement. 'See you in the morning.'

He crossed the horse fair with rapid strides of his long legs and I lost him in the press of shadows. I walked slowly back to our inn. Now it was after midnight, the Watch would be taking more careful note of who was out and about. I raised the hood of my cloak and kept to the shadows. Perhaps I should have accepted Ryshad's escort: a couple would have been less noteworthy. I realised he had not pressed the point and I wondered when I'd last met a man who took me at my word when I said I could take care of myself. It made for a refreshing change.

Darni was nearly chewing the table when I got back. 'Don't ever go off like that again!' he spat at me in fury. 'Where the shit did you go?'

'I know someone who might be able to help,' I said curtly. 'He'll be here in the morning.'

I pushed past him and headed for the table where Shiv sat, head hanging over a cup of wine.

'Shiv!' I'd forgotten all about him; we'd been supposed to meet back at the Watch lock-up. 'What—'

He cut me off with a tired gesture. 'I opened the locks on a handful of cells and the main door. With all the commotion there'll be, I don't suppose you'll be missed.'

'Thanks.' I made a mental note to be careful anyway, though one more drunk shouldn't be too memorable, should she?

'Piss on that! Who've you been yapping to?' Darni grabbed me by the shoulder.

I was less than a step from losing my temper too by now. I smacked his hand off.

'Stuff you, Darni. I nearly got killed tonight, do you realise that? Where do you think all this blood came from? You haven't even asked me how I got on, doing your dirty work for you!'

'I didn't have much chance, did I? I wanted to ask you about Geris but you ran out of here like a kicked cat! Don't ever do that again, do you hear me?'

'Don't give me orders, Darni, I'm not one of your dim-witted trail hounds. Didn't you hear me? I nearly got killed tonight; in my runes, that makes us even. I'm not working for you or your precious Archmage any more.'

'Shut up, both of you! This isn't doing anything for Geris!'

Shiv stepped between us and I noticed how tired he was looking. My anger faded and I felt frightened and weary to the bone. I helped myself to a long drink of his wine but it did no good.

'Have you been scrying? Can't you find him?'

'I can't find any trace. I've tried everything I can think of.' Shiv could not keep the fear and frustration from his voice. 'Let's get some sleep and see what we can do once it's light.'

I nodded and left, ignoring Darni completely. Going to my room, I stripped off, dumping the soiled clothes in a heap. I hurried into bed and wrapped myself in the blankets, falling asleep almost at once. I was worried to a standstill about Geris and still fretting about Yeniya, the blond men and everything else. But I had simply had enough. I was too tired even to cry.

CHAPTER SIX

Taken from.

Nemith the Reckless – 7th Year and Last

Annals of the Empire – Sieur D'Isellion

It was in this year that Nemith, last of that line, succumbed to his most foolhardy ambition, the conquest of Gidesta. The year began badly, a double dark of the moons at Winter Solstice is always inauspicious, yet Nemith scoffed at the customary rites to propitiate Poldrion at such a time and humiliated the Auspex who came to take the auguries for the coming year. Relations with the official priesthood deteriorated sharply from this point.

It was at the Imperial Solstice festivites that rumours began to circulate that the Emperor would be acclaimed at Equinox with the epithet 'Reckless'. The delay in his acclamation by the Great Houses was already a source of considerable irritation to Nemith and his correspondence with General Palleras suggests he was even considering the use of military force against some of his more outspoken detractors. While such an idea may seem hard to credit, this would explain his unprecedented decision to retain the cohorts under arms from the previous year, through harvest and on into the autumn and winter seasons. Needless to say, such orders were very unpopular with the troops, leading to considerable unrest in the camps as well as a poor harvest and hardship in the rural areas with so much of the workforce absent. This in turn forced up the cost of bread in the cities and led to growing agitation among the urban poor. The princes of the Great Houses remonstrated with the Emperor on several occasions, until Nemith showed his contempt for Sieur Den Rannion by using his letters as napkins at one of his debauched entertainments. The Princes of the Convocation refused all invitations to the Imperial residence from that point but Nemith merely took this as a sign of their acquiescence.

By Equinox, the cohorts were suffering famine in their encampments and revolt threatened. Nemith sought desperately for a campaign which would both offer the soldiers booty and remove them from the more prosperous reaches of the Empire. Believing Caladhria and Dalasor to be pacified, he ordered the troops north across the Dalas. The tales of distant riverbeds thick with gold and cliffs laced with seams of silver are repeated several times in his letters to his wife, evidently a powerful incentive. As the Imperial accounts for the year show, he was nearly bankrupt by this point and all the Princes of the Great Houses had been refusing him credit for two full seasons. He was indeed acclaimed as 'Reckless' at the Equinox Convocation, an insult all the more galling as he was, of course, unable to retaliate in any way.

The Gidestan campaign began badly as the Mountain Men emerged from their winter homes in the valley fastnesses of the Dragon's Spine and began to fight back. Their ferocity overwhelmed peasant levies used for undemanding duties in Lescar and Caladhria. More crucially, it became apparent that they had far greater numbers to field than had been expected. In alienating princes, patrons and priests, Nemith had left his armies without experienced commanders, essential intelligence-gathering and the means of rapid communication and resupply. As his losses mounted, desertion became a major problem; Nemith ordered ever more harsh disciplinary measures but of course this only made matters worse. The Princes refused to levy more cohorts from among their tenantry and openly sheltered men fleeing the Emperor's own lands. It is debatable whether Nemith could have salvaged his rule at this point by withdrawing back across the Dalas. Perhaps he could, but events in Ensaimin and Caladhria soon made this academic.

It was full daylight when I woke next morning and, for a fleeting moment, I lay there, enjoying the soft bed and the peace and quiet. Then I missed Geris' warmth in the soft woollen covers and the chaos of the day before came crashing back.

'Livak?' Shiv's soft voice at my door saved me from tears.

'I'm awake, come in.' I scrubbed the sleep from my face with my hands.

He entered with a steaming jug and placed it on the washstand. I swung my legs out of the bed and reached for my last clean shirt. It wasn't for modesty's sake; it was getting distinctly chilly in the mornings now we were well into After-Autumn. Well, I didn't have to worry about Shiv making advances, did I?

Shiv opened the shutters and I frowned at him. 'You look shattered. You told us to get some sleep – what were you doing?'

'I thought of a few more things to try,' he admitted sheepishly.

'You can't afford to exhaust yourself,' I said sternly. 'Drianon, I'm sounding like my mother, Shiv. Don't make me do that again!'

He managed a half-smile. 'There's a man asking for you. His name's Ryshad; he said you would know what it was about.'

That got me out of bed and dressing fast. 'Where is he?'

'In the parlour. Darni's organising some breakfast.'

I pitied the poor kitchen maids. When I got to the parlour, Darni was eating bread and meat with single-minded concentration and ignoring Ryshad completely. He was sitting with a mug of small beer and seemed unconcerned at the waves of hostility coming across the table.

'Ryshad, thanks for coming.' I looked at the food on offer: meat, bread, some leftovers from the night before. No oatmeal; I looked at Darni and decided to do without. I took a bowl of some sort of fruit pudding and a goblet of wine, watering it well.

'So, what's your interest in all this?' Darni looked up from his food, his eyes challenging.

'I'm hunting yellow-haired men who attacked a relative of my patron,' Ryshad said in an easy tone. 'Livak and I met a few days ago and swapped a little information. She tells me they seem to have taken one of your friends.'

'You're from Tormalin then?' Shiv looked interested and I was too.

'From Zyoutessela. I'm a sworn man to Messire D'Olbriot.' He reached into his shirt and fetched out a bronze amulet stamped with a crest.

'Which means what, exactly?' Shiv enquired.

'My sword is his,' Ryshad said simply. 'I do his bidding.'

I didn't know the name but the title and style meant old blood and if he was reckoned a patron, this D'Olbriot must be a major player in the complexities of Tormalin politics.

'Do you know him?' Shiv looked enquiringly at Darni.

'I know of him – and carrying a sworn man's insignia without commission is a hanging offence.' Darni's air of belligerence faded a little and he looked at Ryshad with a measuring eye. 'Messire D'Olbriot can trace his line back three more generations than the Emperor and doesn't mind letting him know it.'

'What did these men do to him?' I reached for more water.

'They attacked one of his nephews on his way home from a banquet. The lad was beaten and left for dead; he's blind in one eye now and cannot use one of his arms. His mind is damaged too; he's little more than a child again.' Ryshad's anger showed briefly through his dispassionate words and he unconsciously twitched his cloak away from his sword-hilt.

'Why did they do it?'

'As far as we can tell, robbery. He was wearing some heirloom rings, the only things taken.'

Shiv and Darni exchanged glances which Ryshad noted as he continued.

'My patron wants revenge for the injuries and the return of his property. If I catch up with them in a place where there's reliable justice, I have authority to hand them over. If not, I have orders to kill them myself.'

I didn't have a problem with that and in any case who was going to get in the way of a Tormalin prince's man?

'You're going to deal with them on your own?' Darni tried and failed to keep the sarcasm out of his tone.

'I'm working with someone and we're fairly effective in a fight if we have to be.' Ryshad's voice was assured. 'We generally hire local help if it's required.'

'What era were these rings?' Shiv asked.

'Nemith the Seafarer.' Ryshad looked at me expectantly. 'It looks as if you're not the only ones collecting antiquities.'

Shiv silenced Darni with a gesture. 'I take it Livak told you we're working for Planir?'

Ryshad nodded. There was an awkward silence as everyone wondered what to say next. I broke it by thumping my bowl down on the table. 'Right, now we've established we're all working for really important people, we can all act suitably impressed later on. What are we going to do about finding Geris? What do you know about these people, Ryshad?'

He grimaced and ran a hand over his unshaven chin. 'Not much. They're foreign, I mean really foreign, not from any of the Old Empire countries.'

'Could they be Soluran?' Darni sounded doubtful.

Ryshad shook his head. 'I know Solura quite well; these men aren't like anyone I've heard of from that side of the world. As far as I can find out, they're not speaking in Soluran, any of the old provincial languages, or even Tormalin.'

That was odd; everyone speaks Tormalin as well as their mother tongue don't they? You have to if you want to be involved in trade or learning of any kind.

'How are they managing to communicate with people then?' Shiv looked more concerned than I thought the question warranted.

'They aren't bothering. I've been trailing them up the length of the coast, and I can't find anyone who's had direct dealings with them, not that's still alive anyway. They turn up somewhere, perform a task and leave the same night.'

'What are they doing?' I was starting to think I already knew the answer.

'Taking Tormalin antiquities, mainly,' Ryshad confirmed. 'They don't make any effort to hide what they're doing. They hit someone, beat them senseless or even torture them, and then take some ancient jewels or a sword, heirloom silver, that sort of thing. It makes no sense; what they're taking doesn't warrant the level of violence they're using. When we go after them, they've disappeared like smoke in the breeze.'

'What else are they up to?' Darni's hostility was waning as his professional interest was aroused.

Ryshad sat forward. 'You may be able to make more sense of this. They've been attacking shrines and killing priests.'

He looked a little disappointed as our blank expressions showed our ignorance.

'If they're coming and going like marsh gas, how did you get here ahead of them?' Darni enquired, all business now.

'They've been working up the coast in a fairly direct line and only hitting the big cities. After Bremilayne, there wasn't anywhere else for them to go. We thought we'd got ahead of them for once. We've been waiting here for half a season and now they come out of nowhere again and take your scholar.' Frustration gave a sharp edge to Ryshad's tone.

'That's not all they've done. You'd better all know about Yeniya; we could be in a winter's worth of cowshit if the Watch come looking for us.'

I put down my drink and told the tale of my hair-raising evening. It made me shiver just to remember it, and my breakfast soured in my stomach.

'Was that coincidence, or did they know you were going to hit Yeniya?' Ryshad mused.

Darni looked a little sick. 'They could have got it out of Geris.'

'No, she was dead before we left him here, I'm sure of it.' I did not like to think of Geris in the hands of men who could do what I had seen.

'Tell me more about the disorientation,' Shiv commanded, looking up from some notes.

I went through it again. 'Was it magic?'

'It's nothing I know of.' Shiv sounded positively offended. He dripped sealing wax on to a folded parchment and stamped it with his ring. 'I'll be back in a moment.'

Darni looked at me as Shiv left the room. 'You're not really used to fights, are you? Remember the Eldritch ring; you were in an ungodly state after that. Are you sure it wasn't just fear getting to you?' His tone was carefully neutral.

I shook my head. 'I'm used to creeping about in dark houses, Darni. I don't jump at shadows and I've got Forest sight, remember. I was scared, sure, but that makes my wits sharper.'

There was a pause while we all looked at our hands and I thought seriously about leaving the lot of them to it and heading back for Ensaimin. I'd missed the fair at Col, but I could pick up Halice if she was fit to travel and we could head for Relshaz where Charoleia would be wintering. I sighed. I couldn't leave without knowing what had happened to Geris; I owed him that much at very least. I fought an illogical annoyance with him for getting himself taken like that. That's what comes of playing with amateurs.

Shiv came back in. 'I'm going to contact Planir,' he said abruptly. 'He's got to know what's going on and I need some instructions.'

'There's no need to do that,' Darni objected. 'We could have Geris back by tonight. These men have surely left a trail.'

'I've been after them since For-Summer and I've never found one,' Ryshad said calmly.

'Geris isn't stupid; he could well get himself free,' Darni insisted.

'If he's capable. The innkeeper said he seemed to go willingly with these men. Did he speak to anyone, do you know?' I asked.

'No, but what's that got to do with anything?'

'Oh come on, Darni.' I tried to keep my tone friendly. 'When did Geris last go anywhere or do anything without talking non-stop? He wouldn't go willingly, and that means more magic.'

'We need instructions and the Council has to know what is going on,' Shiv insisted.

'We can handle this ourselves.' Darni's colour was rising.

'I think Livak's right about Geris. Magic is involved here, and that means it's my decision,' Shiv snapped, unaccustomed iron in his tone. He slammed the door behind him. I wasn't going to stay and wait for Darni to find a target for his annoyance, so I stood too.

'I need some money, Darni.'

'What for?' The abrupt change of subject confused him.

'Half my clothes are covered in blood and I don't want to give the laundrymaid that juicy a bone to throw to the Watch. Any more fights and I'll be wearing a dancing gown and slippers.'

Darni reached into his belt-pouch and threw a handful of coins on to the table, muttering something about women and priorities.

I scooped up the coin and smiled at Ryshad.

'Let's go shopping,' he said agreeably.

Morning trade was brisk as we made our way through the streets. I was in my plain skirts and petticoats, and in his unremarkable homespun, Ryshad could pass for a local pretty much anywhere.

'Information,' I said in a low tone. 'Who has information in this town?'

'Let's check the broadsheets first.' Ryshad was clearly heading down the same trail.

The frames in front of the printers' guild-house were attracting a good crowd. When we made our way to the front, I could see why. Yeniya's murder was going to be the biggest news here for a while; no wonder when one of her most eager suitors was a major player among the paper-makers. She had been raped and strangled, according to the broadsheet. Did this mean the writer had faulty information, or were the Watch keeping back details to help them identify the killer?

Ryshad tapped a passage lower down the page. The Watch wanted to hear from anyone who had let rooms to a group of men, possibly brothers, yellow of hair and beard. I was more concerned about the description of four men seen in the area of the murder, miners or trappers by their clothes, one slight in build and red-haired. I hoped my erstwhile rescuers had the sense to keep their mouths shut. With any luck they would still be drinking their way through my money and too soaked to talk to anyone. Whatever, it looked as if I'd better stick to my skirts for a while.

We headed for a draper's stall where Ryshad bought me a shawl.

'So who writes that sheet and where does he get his information?' I wondered as I tucked my hair under the shawl, glad of the warmth as much as the concealment. 'Do we want to let him know we have an interest?'

'Would he know any more than he's written? The guilds run this city and they run the Watch.' Ryshad glanced apparently idly round the square as I pinned. 'They've got to have sources.'

'Let's keep our eyes open then.' I smoothed my skirts and we embarked on a lengthy shopping trip. I was almost enjoying myself until we passed a stall selling hot cups of tisane. I hated to think what might be happening to Geris. I forced myself to concentrate as we continued our masquerade.

'What do you think of this one?' I held out the fifth shirt again and Ryshad glanced at it.

'It's lovely, dear. If you like it, buy it.' His eyes had the glazed desperation of a man taken shopping for linen just perfectly.

'I'm not sure. What about the one with the embroidery?'

'What?' Ryshad looked back from his seemingly aimless staring into the middle distance.

'You're not paying attention, are you?' I grumbled. The

draper tactfully refolded some drawers and I had to struggle to keep a straight face as Ryshad winked at me.

'I'm getting thirsty.' Ryshad raised a hand as I was about to launch into a full-scale scold. 'Buy them both and take that amber silk as well. I'll treat you.'

The draper looked delighted and no wonder, given the price of silk this far north. It was a good colour for me too. Ryshad paid up and we went on our way with yet another parcel.

'Well?' I asked.

'You'll need breeches and I think I'd better go and buy those.'

'What do I do in the meantime?'

'Sit and take a cup of wine and watch that musician.'

Ryshad steered us towards a pleasant enough tavern where I sat outside, ostensibly to enjoy the thin sunshine and the thinner wine. As I sorted my bundles, I kept a close eye on the lute-player. He was propping up a monument to someone or other and playing jaunty Lescari dance tunes. Passers-by were dropping him coppers but I saw a couple of beggars approach him as well. They stopped to talk and he handed them each some coin. Was this just friendly co-operation among the street dwellers? That's about as common as hen's teeth where I come from.

A Watchman came to move him on and the lutenist rose to protest. I watched as they stood toe to toe and argued the point. Odd, that, I'd not seen the Watch bothering with the streetpeople before. The lutenist was not annoying anyone; in fact, he played quite well, well enough to get work in the taverns for a start. The Watchman pushed him back against the statue; I didn't see him pass anything, but I'd have bet Darni's best sword that something got handed over. The musician moved off across the square and I looked around in frustration for Ryshad; I didn't want to lose any hint of a scent.

I breathed a sigh of relief as Ryshad reappeared. I was moving before he reached me.

'You're right, he's definitely doing something for the Watch. Shall we follow him?' I looked round to check I could still see the musician.

'Not just at present. We can find him again and I don't want the Watch to notice our interest in him.' Ryshad led me in the opposite direction. 'They're out in force now and rousting all the riff-raff. Some are just getting a kicking but a few are getting off a bit too lightly and heading off fast.'

'So we let our friend with the nimble fingers gather as much as he can before we ask him a few questions? Offer him the choice of gold and keeping his mouth shut, or a dagger in a dark alley if he rings the Watch bell on us?'

Ryshad smiled. 'I think so. Let's drop this lot off and then we'll go and find Aiten, my partner. I'd better let him know what's going on.'

We stuck our heads into the parlour when we got back to the inn. Shiv was deep in conversation with a nervous-looking young man in an unnecessarily florid robe.

'So who else might be researching trail magic?' Shiv was asking in exasperation.

'No one,' the unhappy youth insisted. 'I've asked everyone I can think of, and no one is doing that kind of work. I can't even think how you'd start trying for that kind of effect. I suppose you could—'

'Never mind.' Shiv looked up at us. 'Any news?'

'Sorry.' I shook my head. 'We'll be back later on. Where's Darni?'

'Out.' Shiv's expression spoke volumes.

I gestured to his companion. 'Any leads?'

'It seems the Watch are asking hard questions among the wizards. They're convinced magic was used to get to Yeniya somehow.' Shiv sighed. 'I daren't make myself too conspicuous asking around; someone could decide to cover their arse by pointing the Watch at me.'

'See you later.' I pulled the door shut and turned to Ryshad. 'So, where are we going?'

'The bear-pits.' He looked at me appraisingly. 'Can you look a little less respectable?'

I let down my hair and arranged the shawl low around my shoulders, unlacing the neck of my shirt. 'Good enough?'

He grinned. 'Fine.'

It took us some while to find his pal among the bloodthirsty crowds at the beast sports. I was very tired of having my bottom pinched by the time Ryshad waved to a face in the mass of people and gestured to the door. The smell of blood and the cries of animals in pain made me think of Yeniya; I've never seen the point in baiting anyway.

'Ryshad! Nice to see you!'

'Livak, this is Aiten.'

Aiten was middling height, middling size and unremarkably brown of hair and eye, the sort of man your eye would pass right over in a crowd. He was looking at me uncertainly so I fluttered my eyelashes at him and looked as cheap as I could.

Ryshad laughed. 'Don't be fooled, Ait. She's working with some Archmage's agents and when she gets bored with that, D'Olbriot could do worse than offer her a job.'

'So, what's the news?' Aiten was all business as we walked to the rail of the nearest arena.

Ryshad gave him an admirably succinct explanation of developments while I watched the hawk-fanciers put their birds through their paces.

Aiten looked unhappy. 'There's not been a sniff around here. The Watch came through earlier and took off a few of the more obvious ruffians, but it was more like a routine rubbish sweep than a search for anyone in particular.'

'So the bastards popped up, ripped that poor bitch apart, dropped back into their hole and pulled it in after them again?' Ryshad's face was hard and set. 'I'm getting tired of this.'

'I'll see what I can find out.' Aiten looked around. 'I'll try the hawking once the competitions get started. I'll need some money for bets.'

Ryshad handed over a plump purse. How come I had never got into business with a rich backer? Because all too often it means taking orders from someone like Darni, I reminded myself.

'Got an eye for a good bird, have you?'

'Piss poor,' Aiten said cheerfully. 'Still, it's amazing what people will tell you when they've just taken your money.'

'Come and find us at sunset.' Ryshad took my arm and we

headed off for a leisurely lunch at a very expensive eating-house, courtesy of Darni's coin. We spent the rest of the afternoon sauntering round the town, idly shopping, taking in the sights and noting the way the Watch went about setting temptingly baited hooks and lines for anyone who might have something to tell them. Whoever ran this town clearly knew what they were doing.

The Chamber of Planir the Black, Hadrumal, 11th of Aft–Autumn, Noon

Kalion swept his parchments into a neat sheaf. 'So you see, Archmage, if we are to be faced with as many apprentices next season, the financial implications are clear.' He sat straight-backed in his chair with the air of man prepared to do battle for his position.

'Thank you for bringing this to me.' Planir smiled pleasantly at the Hearth-Master, leaning back in his own seat. 'In fact, I think we should audit all the Halls' accounts and see if this is a widespread problem. I suspect it will be, and then we can agree a common approach.'

The Archmage closed the various ledgers lying open on the glossy table-top and rose to replace them on their shelf below the narrow lancets of the tall window. 'We can put it to Council next meeting. Now, as long as you're happy with the apprentice rotations, I don't think I need detain you any longer. I am rather busy.' Planir looked expectantly at Kalion but the stout wizard remained determinedly seated.

'There is one other thing that I feel I must raise, Archmage.' Kalion's tone was stern, even faintly disapproving.

'Oh?' Planir reseated himself, narrow eyebrows raised a fraction in polite enquiry.

'I am concerned about the degree of familiarity you allow others to adopt towards you.' Kalion leaned forward in his chair and his jowls wobbled as he shook his head in emphasis. 'The way Otrick addresses you, and Usara for that matter, it is simply not fitting!'

Planir reached for the carafe that stood between them and poured himself a glass of water, turning it idly in a sunbeam as a sudden shaft of sunlight pierced the autumn clouds and washed the stone towers of Hadrumal with gold.

'Otrick is one of the oldest mages in Hadrumal as well as senior Cloud-Master, Kalion,' he said mildly. 'He was a Council member when you and I were both apprentices, if you recall; I hardly feel it would be appropriate for me to insist on deference to my rank from him. As for Usara, he was my first pupil. I consider him a friend as well as a colleague.'

Planir's air of amiable reason was clearly blunting the edge of Kalion's disapproval but the Hearth-Master persisted.

'Well, it's not just Otrick and Usara I'm talking about. I have been told you were seen at the Equinox dances in Wellery's Hall, taking the floor with any female apprentice who lacked a partner. It does not become the dignity of the office you hold, to take and allow such liberties.'

'To be frank, Hearth-Master, of late I am less concerned with the dignity of my office than I am with its effectiveness.' Planir fixed Kalion with a stern eye and a sharpened tone.

'The two are indivisible!' Kalion objected with some heat.

'I think not.' Planir sipped his water, one ringed hand raised to silence Kalion. 'You have been making an excellent case recently in Council for restoring wizardry to prominence in mainland affairs. As I recall, you said mages need to be more visible and less daunting. I agree, and I happen to think exactly the same can be said of the office of Archmage. If I am seen as approachable, to even the rawest apprentice, I can find out more in a day wandering round Hadrumal and chatting in tisane-houses and libraries than I can in a week reading requests and memoranda from the Halls. I need that information if I am to do the duty laid upon me by Council to best effect.'

'There is the question of respect—' Kalion began after a moment's indecision.

'I believe respect is something to be earned, Hearth-Master, not demanded as of right.' Planir cut him off crisply. 'Times are changing on the mainland, you've said it yourself, and our apprentices have grown up with those changes. We cannot expect them to suddenly step back three generations when they get off the boat. This isn't some Caladhrian fiefdom where I only need to wear a short mantle for everyone to take shears to their cloak.'

'Distinctions of rank are essential if you are to maintain authority.' Kalion shifted in his seat and fiddled unconsciously with the ring bearing his insignia.

'Remember that we only hold our ranks by consent of the majority, Kalion, unspoken though that may be. Anyway, have you ever seen me fail to assert my authority, either in Council or among the wider wizardry?'

Planir smiled. His enquiry was mild enough but Kalion coloured and struggled for a reply before dropping his gaze. The Archmage glanced out of the window at the roofs of the halls marching down to the harbour and a slight frown wrinkled his brow. He rose and folded his arms as he looked down at Kalion.

'You know what they say, a dog that barks once gets listened to, the one that barks all night gets whipped. I use my authority when I need to, have no fear, Kalion, but you know as well as I do that Archmages with a taste for tyranny simply find themselves bypassed and isolated.'

There was a polite tap at the door and Kalion turned his head, relief in his eyes.

'That will be Usara for a consultation on his researches.' Planir inclined his head in a brief bow. 'You must excuse us.'

'Of course, Archmage.' Kalion swept his documents into a handsomely tooled folder, rose and smoothed the front of his crimson tunic with an abrupt gesture.

'Hearth-Master.' Usara bowed politely as Planir opened the door to let Kalion leave.

'Do come in.' Planir turned back to the table, leaving Usara to latch the door behind him.

'I managed to see Shannet—' Usara began eagerly but Planir shook his head with a frown.

'In a moment, 'Sar. Tell me, do you know who's feeding Kalion gossip from Wellery's Hall these days?'

Usara shook his head. 'No, do you want me to ask around?'

Planir nodded. 'Discreetly, of course. Now, what did Shannet have to say?'

'First she tried to scry for Geris herself, and then with Otrick augmenting her spell. She had no more luck than we did.' Usara sighed.

'Curse it!' Planir's exasperation was plain. 'Does she want to try with me in the link, now I've finished with Kalion and his wretched arithmetic?' He shrugged off a formal gown and pulled a comfortable woollen jerkin over his shirt.

'No, she said we could enrol half the Council and it wouldn't make any difference. She thinks he's being shielded somehow.' Usara ran a hand through his thinning hair in a gesture of frustration.

'She's the expert; she should know. So we're looking at aetheric magic again,' Planir said, lips set thinly in a grim line.

'That does seem to be the problem,' Usara agreed.

'So where do we find a solution, 'Sar?' Planir demanded, turning to a bookcase and picking out various volumes.

'Otrick's gone to look in the Archives.' Usara took a heavy tome in green leather from the Archmage and set it on the table. 'Shannet said she'd come across something that felt just the same, once before.'

Planir paused, a book open in his hands. 'When?'

'Have you ever heard of a mage called Azazir?' Usara rummaged in the pockets of his ink-stained buff breeches and consulted a scribbled note.

'Yes,' Planir said slowly. 'Why?'

'Shannet said he claimed to have discovered some islands out in the deep ocean, hundreds of leagues to the east. Azazir's pupil, Viltred, was a friend of hers and they tried to scry for these islands, to prove the truth of what he was saying.' Usara looked up from his notes. 'She's certain the same shielding that's concealing Geris is what was hiding those islands from her and Viltred all those years ago.'

'Is she now?' Planir was about to continue when the door swung abruptly open and Otrick appeared, leaning against the jamb and breathing heavily, his face nearly as pale as his shirt.

'I think it's about time we started a fashion that had mages living at ground level instead of up all these unholy stairs!' The old wizard dropped heavily into a chair and fumbled in his cloak pocket for his chewing-leaf.

'Did you find the journal?' Usara handed Otrick a glass of water.

The old man nodded, speechless for a moment, and then took a slim volume out of the front of his jerkin. 'Here. Don't tell the Archivist it was me who lifted it.'

Planir took the book and began to leaf rapidly through the yellowed pages, squinting at the spidery writing.

'Now this is interesting, in light of Shiv's latest news.' The Archmage paused and looked at Usara. 'Listen to this: "The walls of the keep were patrolled by black-liveried sentries and it was apparent our host kept some considerable standing force. When I attempted to leave the confines of the fortification, my passage was barred without word of explanation or apology."' Planir turned the page. 'There's more: "The food was barely adequate and we were made uncomfortable by the persistent stares and muttering coming from the lower tables. I can only assume our dark colouring was cause for such comment, the populace here being universally fair of hair and skin."'

'I told Shannet that Geris was supposedly taken by blond men and that's what made her think of Viltred and Azazir's tales.' Usara nodded.

'So this is where these people are coming from?' Otrick's eyes were bright now and his colour improved. 'Some islands off the edge of the map? They'll need magic to cross the ocean, you know.'

'It's starting to look as if they have it; remember what that Tormalin sworn-man was telling Shiv,' Planir said thoughtfully. 'I think we'd better see what we can find out about these islands and these people. Shiv and Darni are best placed to follow this up, it would seem.'

'What about Geris?' Usara looked up from the book he was searching through.

Planir continued to turn the pages of the old journal. 'We may simply have to accept that Geris is lost,' he said finally. 'Aetheric magic is no longer just some ancient curiosity, not if an unknown people can use it to cross the ocean and work enchantments we can neither detect or counter, not if they're sending agents to rob and kill, for whatever reasons they might have. There's more at stake here than one boy scholar from Vanam. Think about Naldeth's latest theory, those Imperial chronicles he's been researching.'

'Shiv won't want to abandon Geris,' Otrick warned, a scowl deepening his wrinkles still further. 'I wouldn't, in his place.'

Planir shrugged. 'Who says they're abandoning the boy? Surely these mysterious islands will be the best place to look for a lead?'

'You don't really believe that?' Usara's tone was dubious.

'What I believe is immaterial, provided I can convince Shiv.' Planir snapped the little volume shut 'If Azazir found these islands once, Shiv has the talents to do it again once Azazir tells him what he knows.'

'And how exactly is that to be achieved,' Otrick asked sarcastically, 'given no one's heard tell of Azazir in over a generation?'

'I beg leave to differ, Cloud-Master.' A half-smile lightened Planir's sombre expression. 'I have been keeping a weather-eye on the old lunatic ever since I took the Archmage's ring; I can send Shiv to him.'

'What if Azazir won't co-operate? You know his reputation.' Usara paused, a finger marking his place on the vellum.

'We'll bridle that horse when we have to.' Planir laughed abruptly. 'I'll exert some authority, if need be. That'll give Kalion something to think about.'

By the time the sun was setting, I knew the streets and back alleys of Inglis about as well as I knew Vanam. That could be useful if I ever came across a job where the profits outweighed the risks of working here but we'd turned up not a trace of Geris, nor the mysterious troop that had taken him. As we walked wearily back to the inn and started up the stairs, we could hear Darni and Shiv having a difference of opinion from the end of the hall. I hurried to the parlour and slammed the door open.

'Do you want everyone in this place to hear you? I've heard quieter dog fights!'

They were standing across the table glaring at each other. They turned to glare at me but at least I had shut them up.

'What's going on?' I demanded.

'We've got instructions from the Archmage.' Shiv was white with anger.

'I don't agree with them,' Darni began, red in the face and breathing hard.

'You don't have to agree, you're supposed to obey,' Shiv snapped. I wouldn't have believed he could sound so cold.

'So what are we supposed to do?' I sat down and poured wine for us all. Darni and Shiv sat down after a few moments of tension, each reluctant to be the first.

'Planir wants us to go on some hunt for a mad old wizard who's probably dead in a ditch anyway,' Darni said with disgust.

'Shiv?'

'Planir told me that he has heard tales of a race of yellow-haired people. There's this wizard, Azazir, who claimed to have crossed the ocean to an unknown land a couple of generations or so ago. That's where they're supposed to live.'

'That's a bit vague, Shiv,' I said doubtfully.

'There's more to it than that. Planir has confidential Imperial records from the reign of Nemith the Reckless. They mention a blond race too and, as far as Planir can work it out, these foreigners used magic to bring down the Empire. They have powers we don't know about.'

I shivered despite the warmth of the room.

'The Tormalin Empire fell because it grew too big to control. It was logistics, not magic, everyone knows that.' Darni stood again and loomed aggressively over the table towards Shiv.

'So what does Planir want you to do?' Ryshad earned a grateful look from Shiv.

'If we can find Azazir, he can tell us where these people come from. If we can get there, we should be able to find out who they are and what they want.'

'That's a lot of if and perhaps,' I said doubtfully. 'What about Geris? We've found some leads we should follow up here, haven't we, Ryshad?'

He nodded slowly. 'That's true enough, but I've had better leads in other places and they came to nothing. If this wizard could point us at them, we might do better to go straight for whoever's giving the orders.'

'Azazir couldn't point at his own nose without sticking a finger in his eye.' Darni was nearly shouting. 'You've heard the same stories I have, Shiv. He's a mad old bastard who should have been executed the last time he fell foul of the Council. Anyway, no one's heard so much as a whisper of him for years. He'll be rotting in the wilderness somewhere, and good riddance.'

Ryshad and I exchanged uncertain glances. Wizards being executed by the Archmage and the Council? That was not something I'd ever heard tell of.

'So how are you supposed to find him?' Darni challenged Shiv.

'Planir's identified an area where the elements are distorted; a lot of water's been concentrated in a way that can only mean magic. And it's in the region of Gidesta where Azazir was last heard of. I'm a water mage; once we get close, I should be able to follow his influence back to the source.'

That sounded thin, even to my ignorant ear.

'There's no guarantee of that, and anyway, you might just find some long-terms spells and his bones. All right, suppose he is still alive. Why's he going to talk to you? You're going to tell him you're working for Planir, are you? "Please help me because I'm working for the Archmage who threatened to bury you if you came within ten leagues of a village again?"' Darni was back to the top of his voice again.

'What about Geris, Shiv?' I asked, increasingly worried by this turn of events. 'They've got a day's start on us as it is and, if we go off somewhere, the trail will be stone cold by the time we get back.'

'Planir has scryed for Geris himself and used half the Council to augment the spell. If they can't find him, he's not going to be found.' Shiv's face reflected his distress.

'So our best bet is to go for the man who's giving the orders,' Ryshad said calmly. 'Find him and we've got the best chance of finding your friend.'

'Who asked you?' Darni did not look away from Shiv. 'You can't do this, Shiv. We've got to start looking for Geris now and here!'

'I can't disobey the Archmage and neither will you if you've got any sense.' Shiv only controlled his temper with a visible effort. 'I'm setting off at first light. Ryshad, the Archmage would very much appreciate it if you joined us. Livak, your obligation is cancelled but if you want to come, I'd like to have you with us.'

'I need her to help me find Geris,' Darni shouted.

Shiv opened his mouth and then shut it again, stalking out of the room and slamming the door behind him to relieve his feelings.

'I haven't finished talking!' Darni stormed after him and I thought the door was going to come out of its frame when he sent it crashing back.

'Darni's idea of a discussion is to say what he thinks more

and more loudly until everyone else gives up,' I explained to Ryshad as I poured more wine.

'I've met his type before.' Ryshad seemed unbothered. 'So what are you going to do?'

'What about you?'

'Aiten and I'll go with Shiv, no question. This may be a weak scent, but it's the best we've had in nearly two seasons.'

'You don't think we might get a lead to Geris? I hate to give up on him like this.'

'If there's information to be had, the Watch will get it. They've got five of the most important men in the city breathing down their necks over Yeniya, don't forget. If this troop can be found, the Watch will do it just as fast as we would and find Geris themselves.'

'You don't sound convinced.'

'I'm not,' Ryshad said frankly. 'I was starting to wonder if they were using magic long before this. Come on, Livak, you've been around the provinces; Geris could already be dead. If he isn't, it's because they want something out of him, in which case they're most likely to take him back to their leader. Use your wits.'

I sighed. Every emotion and loyalty told me to join Darni in turning the city upside-down until we found Geris, but sense told me Shiv and Ryshad were right. When it came to a hard choice, I realised I trusted Shiv more than Darni, wizard or not.

'I suppose I'd better come with you then,' I said unhappily.

'I'm glad.' Ryshad stood and laid a quick comforting arm across my shoulder. 'I'll see you later. I've got to let Ait know what we're doing and see to a few other things.'

I watched him go and then relieved my feelings by throwing the cups across the room. Why should Shiv and Darni be the only ones allowed to lose their tempers?

I spent the rest of the day busily trying to pick up any trace of Geris' trail around the inn. I achieved absolutely nothing. I finally went to spend a lonely night in my cold bed, miserably going over and over my choices until I fell asleep, exhausted.

We left in the damp chill of the autumn morning. Darni was nowhere to be seen and as Shiv and I saddled up with few words, I realised Geris' horses were gone.

'Where are the bays?' I looked wildly round the stables.

'Darni's making arrangements for them. If necessary, he'll hire a groom to take them back to Vanam,' Shiv said shortly. His expression forbade further discussion, so I turned back to adjusting Russet's girth. I was absurdly relieved that I was not going to have to make a spectacle of myself by insisting Geris' beloved horses were taken care of, but at the same time, I felt angry with Darni for taking the matter out of my hands.

The Licorne Inn, Inglis,
15th of Aft-Autumn

'Now this is more like it.' Casuel drew off his gloves and looked round the neat sitting-room with pleasure. Opening the casement, he drew a deep breath of salted air and smiled as he gazed over the regular lines of the roofs and houses. The fifth chime of the day was just fading away.

'It is good to be back east again. This white stone reminds me of home, you know.' He turned to smile at Allin, but frowned instead. She was standing dolefully in the doorway, sniffing into a grubby handkerchief.

'Why did we have to come here?' she whined. 'I want to go to Hadrumal. I didn't expect to be dragged all through Lescar in a filthy coach. Why couldn't you have taken me to my uncle's house? We passed through the next village to home, things looked peaceful enough. There won't be any more fighting until the spring, now. I don't even know if I want to be a mage any more.'

'That's not a matter of choice,' Casuel said tartly. He was getting tired of this conversation. 'We will be going to Hadrumal soon enough.'

With any luck, he thought to himself, then I can finally get you off my hands. 'I can't be expected to waste time fetching you from some muddy backwater in Lescar. What if I were summoned today?'

Allin began to grizzle into her handkerchief.

'Why don't you go and have a rest,' Casuel suggested in desperation. 'I'll get a maid to fetch you a nice tisane for that cold.'

Allin heaved a moist sigh and took herself off into the adjoining bedchamber. Casuel heaved a sigh of relief; he quickly set up candle and mirror and bespoke Usara.

'*Are you in Inglis yet?*' the sandy-haired wizard demanded without preamble as he sent power back down the spell to establish the connection.

'Of course.' Casuel was indignant. 'Though why we had to come all this way, I really don't understand—'

'*Trust me, Casuel, if I'd had any other choice, I wouldn't have sent you,*' Usara said crisply.

Casuel supposed that was something like an apology. 'All right then, what is it that you want me to do?'

He saw the image of Usara rubbing his eyes and yawning. Why was he so tired? Noon here made it mid-morning in Hadrumal, didn't it? Casuel hoped Usara hadn't taken to carousing with the likes of Otrick.

Usara snapped his fingers over a cup and took a sip once it started steaming, wincing slightly. '*There's been a murder in the city, a prominent merchant, a woman called Yeniya. I want you to contact some of the local mages and find out the latest news. Be discreet, for Saedrin's sake, things will be very sensitive at the moment.*'

Casuel frowned. 'Forgive me, but surely there are scrying techniques you could use—'

'*Don't you think we've tried?*' Usara cut him off, exasperated. '*No, it's eyes in the alley that we need now. You'll have to do the best you can, and use some cursed tact for a change.*'

'Don't you have enquiry agents to do this sort of thing?' Casuel asked. 'This is rather beneath a wizard's dignity, don't you think?' he added distastefully.

The glow of the enchantment flashed briefly golden. '*How about you stop arguing and just do it, Casuel?*' Usara's tone hardened. '*I think you owe me a little co-operation after that fiasco in Friern, don't you? I suppose I could clear it with Planir first, if you'd rather?*'

Casuel hoped the amber tint of the spell hid his sudden blush. 'I'm sorry. Of course we wizards should assist one another. I'll be happy to.'

The spell flickered and Casuel missed the first words of Usara's reply. '*And another thing,*' the Earth-Mage went on, 'we are looking for a group, possibly two groups, of yellow-haired men, a handful or so in each, less than average height and from nowhere in the Old Empire. Now, just ask among the mages, don't draw attention to yourself and above all be discreet. I mean it, Casuel; you don't want these people after your tail.'

'Well, if this is likely to be a little dangerous, perhaps I can find a mage here to look after Allin until she can be escorted to Hadrumal?' Casuel could not disguise the hope in his voice.

'Not appropriate, given the circumstances,' Usara said cryptically. 'Anyway, you found her, you're responsible for her; you know the rules. Now, get on with it and bespeak me tomorrow; after I've had some breakfast for preference.'

Usara severed the magic with an abruptness that left Casuel's hands stinging. He stared at the blank mirror in annoyance for a moment then rummaged in his bag for writing materials. He couldn't very well go trailing round the city, cap in hand, asking to see wizards he'd not been introduced to. After all, he couldn't leave Allin unchaperoned.

'Who are you writing to?'

He turned to see Allin standing in the doorway, dishevelled and miserable. 'Is my tisane coming?' she asked petulantly.

Casuel bit his lip and crossed to ring the bell. 'The maids here do seem to take their time answering.' He sat down and hesitated, pen poised over a scrap of parchment.

'Who are you writing to?' Allin blew her nose.

'I require information from one of the town mages.' Casuel cleaned his nib thoughtfully.

'Wizards live here as well as in Hadrumal?' Allin looked puzzled and Casuel had to remind himself that any sensible mage stayed well clear of the dangerous currents of the Lescari wars. Still, he didn't want her ignorance to reflect on him once she was apprenticed.

'Wizards who can hope to add to the sum of magical knowledge remain in Hadrumal after training,' he explained loftily. 'Those whose talents are more for the workaday, less elevated aspects of enchanting generally return to the mainland and find work. Those of us at the higher levels generally know someone in most cities.'

He frowned. Who did he know in Inglis who'd be likely to want to help him? There were times when it would be useful to have that knack of ingratiating himself with people that Shivvalan used to such advantage. There was Carral, wasn't there? He'd come here to do something involving the river, or was it gemstones? No matter, it can't have been anything important. Casuel wrote rapidly, touched a finger to a stick of sealing-wax and sealed the parchment with his signet.

'Yes?' The door opened and a maid stuck her head into the room.

'Please have a boy deliver this letter.' Casuel rummaged in his pocket for coin.

'Of course, sir.'

'Can I have a tisane, please?' Allin spoke up as the maid went to leave. 'Something for a nasty cold, if you have it?'

The maid looked at her with some sympathy. 'Of course, I'll bring it up at once. You get yourself to bed, pet, you don't want a rheum like that taking to your chest.'

She returned shortly with a fragrant mug and another, older woman. They settled Allin with the drink and a kerchief sprinkled with aromatic oils, all involving what seemed an inordinate amount of fuss as far as Casuel could see. Finally he was left in peace and spread his books over the sitting-room table. He began to read, eager to glean any clue which might explain what Usara was up to. What could possibly be significant about the fall of the Empire? Scholars had been poring over every detail for generations, hadn't they? Occasional sounds drifted up from the street, hooves and steps on the cobbles, shouts and laughter, but Casuel ignored them as he worked steadily on through the afternoon, methodically correlating and cross-referencing.

The door crashed open, hinges splintering the frame as two enormous men with ragged hair and unkempt beards kicked it back against the wall. They stormed in and seized Casuel, slamming him against the wall, their fetid breath moist in his face as they held him pinned. He struggled for words and air, lost for both, panic seizing him as his feet left the floor although he was still left looking up into the wild, ragged faces of his assailants. A surge of dread obliterated every enchantment he'd ever learned from his memory and a feeble gleam died in his fingers.

A second pair of dark-haired ruffians entered, rough leathers stained with old blood and rankly uncured fur jerkins suggesting they were trappers fresh off a river boat. They stood, incongruous, either side of a tall young man whose elegant velvet apparel was sadly creased and stained, expensive fabrics beyond salvage. His face was unshaven and pale, eyes red-rimmed and swollen. Casuel looked at him in dismay, complete confusion hampering any sensible response.

'You, hold the door!' The young man turned to his last hireling. 'Check that room, make sure he's alone.'

He walked slowly round the table and came to stare into Casuel's eyes. His gaze was wide and full of anger, the red-flecked whites of his eyes visible all around the blue.

'Just who are you, you little shit, and what is your interest in Yeniya's death?'

'I don't know what you mean!' Casuel gasped as the men holding him slammed him down against the wall again. He struggled to regain his footing.

The irate man brandished a parchment. 'Don't come the virgin with me! Carral know who cures his bacon, he sent your little note straight to me.'

He gripped Casuel's jaw and forced his head back. 'So, talk to me.' His voice was hoarse and Casuel realised with terror that this was a man whose rioting emotions had evidently driven him beyond the reach of reason.

'Please don't hurt me!' Allin's voice was a desperate squeak of fear.

Casuel had been about to say the very same thing when she emerged from the bedroom in the grip of one of the brutes, bare feet barely touching the floor beneath the hem of her stout shift.

'There's no one else, Evern. Just this little pigeon. Plump enough, ain't she?' He flung Allin down on a chair and she shrank away from the man's leer, his teeth stained and yellow against his dirty brown beard.

'Are you the Watch?' Casuel stammered.

'You'll wish we were soon enough!' The man called Evern laughed harshly. 'No, just call us concerned citizens. You see, Yeniya was a friend of mine.'

His voice cracked and he scrubbed a hand across his eyes. 'Some bastard murdered her and I'm going to kill anyone I can find who had something to do with it!'

'It's nothing to do with me!' Casuel tried to shake his head and got a smack across the mouth for his trouble.

'Then why are you asking questions about it, arse-face? Why are you so interested in finding out what scents the Watch are tracking?'

Casuel gaped, lost for words. Evern nodded to the trapper on his left who promptly punched an iron-hard fist into Casuel's gut. Crying out in agonised amazement that something could hurt so much, he would have doubled up but the men held him firm against the wall. He shifted his weight from one foot to the other, desperately trying to ease the pain.

'Why are you asking questions? Worried the Watch might be on your trail, are you? That's how it reads to me.' The young man took a pair of slim gloves from his belt and drew them on with elaborate care.

Casuel blinked tears from his own eyes. 'I'm simply trying to find out what happened.'

Evern punched him abruptly, hard in the mouth. 'Why?' he screamed, incensed.

A trickle of blood tickled down Casuel's chin. He winced as he licked at the split in his lip and fought to control a whimper as Evern stood before him, slapping a cupped hand around his fist, heedless of the blood smearing the fine leather. The sound of running feet in the corridor echoed in the tense silence and Casuel looked desperately at the door.

'You're a Tormalin, aren't you?' Evern said thoughtfully. 'There've been a couple of Tormalins asking around, but they seem to have disappeared. Who are they?'

'I really have no idea!' Casuel said desperately. 'I don't even know who you are talking about.'

'You're going to have to do better than this, shit-for-brains,'

Evern spat, his face ugly with frustration. 'I want to know what they had to do with it; why else would they disappear?'

He punched Casuel violently under the ribs, leaving him gasping and retching.

Allin broke into noisy sobs of fear, suddenly silenced when she realised that made her the centre of attention.

Evern turned to look at her, contempt plain on his drawn face. 'What have you got to tell me, then?' He twisted a hand in Allin's forlorn ringlets and wrenched her head back.

'What do you know?' He bent his face close to hers and scowled.

'Nothing,' she whimpered, clutching her hands to her breast.

Evern straightened and looked down on her with disdain. 'So you're just here to warm his sheets, are you?'

He turned abruptly back to Casuel, who flinched as far as he was able. His arms were starting to go numb below the grip of the trappers and his jaw ached fiercely.

'She's a bit young for plucking, isn't she?' Evern sneered. 'But you look as if you'd be desperate for it. So, why not share her around? Let's see what she knows that way!'

'Leave her alone, you swine!' Casuel struggled futilely, jumbled thoughts anguished. What would Usara do to him if the silly poult got herself raped! 'She's got nothing to do with any of this.'

Evern pushed his face close and Casuel could smell the expensive scents beneath his rank sweat. 'Convince me!' he snarled in a low tone.

Casuel closed his eyes and mentally cursed the day he'd left Hadrumal. 'I am a wizard, you know.' He groped for some dignity and missed, his voice emerging as little more than a desperate squeak.

'So what?' Evern stood back a little, his face hard. 'Am I supposed to be impressed or something? Wizards do what they're paid to do, in my experience. Going to turn me into a toad, are you?'

He drew a thin dagger and laid the gleaming steel against Casuel's throat. 'They're saying whoever killed Yeniya used magic to get away. Why don't I kill you anyway, on the off-chance you were involved?'

He pressed harder and turned the edge of the blade into Casuel's skin. Casuel began to shake as a burning line of pain crawled down his neck.

'I swear, I had nothing to do with it,' he croaked. 'I'm sorry for your loss.'

Evern closed his eyes on unbearable anguish and a tear beaded his lashes. He turned away with a gesture and the trappers began to beat Casuel with systematic brutality that spoke of considerable experience.

He tried to curl himself around his guts and groin, dimly aware of Allin wailing as his world shrank to a nightmare of pain beyond anything he had ever imagined he might experience.

'I don't think he knows anything, chief. Mel, shut that bitch up or give her something to really cry about.'

Casuel heard the trapper's words through the ringing in his ears after what seemed an eternity.

'He's not the type to hold out, not after a good kicking.'

Tears of relief joined the slime and blood on Casuel's cheeks. He lay still, tense, not daring to move but cautiously opened his eyes. There was a slight sound outside the room and they all turned their heads towards it.

The trapper on the door grunted as the handle rattled, but as he shifted his feet he got the white-painted panels in the face, sending him sprawling to the floor. Before he could regain his feet, a heavy-set man with a dark beard entered and kicked him swiftly in the groin. Sword drawn, he swept his blade round in a menacing arc and glared at Evern.

'Call off your dogs, or I'll have to kill them.'

'Darni!' Casuel tried to get up, halting on his knees as agonising pain lanced through his chest.

'Bet you never thought you'd be so glad to see me, Cas.' Darni smiled wickedly.

Evern took a step back from Darni's sword point, hands low and wide. 'Who the shit are you?' he spat in baffled rage.

Darni sketched a bow. 'Someone telling you that you're making a big mistake here. It's lucky for you that Carral had the sense to let me know about that letter. This sorry pot of piss had nothing to do with Yeniya's death.'

'And how do you know that?' Evern's dagger began to rise.

'Why don't you drop that rat-sticker?' Darni's voice was cold as ice. 'Kick it over here.'

Evern hesitated but then obeyed and Casuel began to breathe again in shallow gasps.

'I know he had nothing to do with her death, because he's working for the same master as me.' Darni looked around at the trappers. 'Why don't you all sit down and we can discuss this sensibly. That's what I would prefer and I am the one with the broadsword, when all's said and done.'

Evern's lips narrowed and a furious growl of frustration escaped him but he finally nodded. 'All right.'

The trappers moved to help their colleague still groaning on the floor as he clutched himself, face grey under his dirt. They moved to stand in a row by the window, leaving Evern between themselves and Darni.

'So, who do you work for?' Evern folded his arms and looked arrogantly at Darni.

'The Council of Mages, of course.' Darni sounded surprised that the man needed to ask. 'Planir is most concerned over the possibility of magic being used in such an appalling crime.'

'He's an Archmage's agent?' Evern stared down at Casuel with patent disbelief.

'No, but I am. Get up, Cas.' Darni drew a thong from the neck of his shirt and Evern looked open-mouthed at the bronze ring on it.

'Show me that,' he demanded. Darni drew the string over his head, tossing it over.

'How do I know this is real?' he asked, flinging it back after a moment.

Darni shook his head, snatching the ring out of the air. 'Do you think someone's going to risk faking that? People don't cross Planir, believe me.'

He looked at Casuel, who had struggled to a chair, still hugging his aching ribs. 'I don't know what he's going to think of this,' he said contemplatively. 'You've made a right mess of poor old Cas, haven't you?'

'I had my reasons,' Evern spat. 'No wizard's going to tell me how to do things in my own city, Archmage or not. I had reason to think this waste of skin was mixed up in this and I'm entitled to find out. Magic helped kill Yeniya and if any mage was involved, we'll drive the whole sorry mess of them into the ocean. What's your precious Archmage going to do if we close the city to you bastards? The guilds don't need you, we run this city and that's the way it'll stay.'

Darni simply shook his head again. 'Don't make pointless threats. You're the ones who'll lose in the long run if you force out the wizards.'

He smiled at Evern, an expression Casuel found the most frightening thing he'd seen so far.

'Anyway, if Planir finds out a mage was involved in this, that sorry bastard won't be able to hide at the bottom of the ocean, inside an ice-field on the Dragon's Spines, or underneath an Aldabreshi fire-mountain. Slow drowning in a bucket of his own shit would be a better fate than the one the Council will put together for him. Isn't that right, Cas?'

Casuel gagged at Darni's disgusting image and nodded mutely.

Evern raised his hands, the gesture cut short as Darni's sword swung up to block it.

'So who killed Yeniya? How do I find the pox-rotted bastards? What's your cursed Archmage doing to avenge her?'

'That's not your concern,' Darni said coldly. 'However, you might like to consider helping me. I'm after some men who I know were involved and I'd say we've got a good chance of catching them.'

'They killed her?'

'No, but they can lead us to the ones who did.' Darni swapped his sword to his other hand and reached out to Evern.

'My word on it. Help me get them and we'll say no more about your little mistake here. Shut up, Cas,' he added as the mage opened his battered mouth to protest.

'So, are we going to co-operate on this, or do I have to organise a little pay-back for my friend here?' Darni glared at the trappers, who exchanged doubtful glances.

Evern stood, hope warring with grief in his face. The silence was broken by a loud thud as Allin fainted and slid gracelessly into a heap on the floor.

'Drianon's tits,' Darni said in exasperation. 'Just who is this, Cas? Whatever you're paying her, it's not enough!'

The tension in the air snapped and Evern lowered his head, blinking away confused tears. 'All right. But you'd better be right about this,' he warned.

'Trust me,' Darni said grimly. 'I want these people as badly as you do.'

Casuel looked up at him and was appalled to realise this was absolutely true. He started to think he could almost feel sorry for these people whenever Darni caught up with them, but the thought evaporated in the mass of aches and pains growing in every part of him.

The Gidesta Road out of Inglis,
15th of Aft-Autumn

Travelling on horseback and camping in the open was soon going to lose its charm as a winter pastime, I decided sourly. I'd take up quilting instead. I poked Russet in the ribs to make him loose the breath he was holding as I saddled him; he wasn't going to catch me like that twice in one day. Some chance I was going to have to forget Geris, riding the horse we'd named together, I thought gloomily.

Luckily, before my mood descended further into dejection, Ryshad and Aiten rode up on their scruffy chestnut horses that looked as if they came straight off the Gidestan steppes.

'So where are we headed this afternoon?' Ryshad swung his mount round to ride with Shiv.

'We need to cross the river and take the northern road.' Shiv kicked his horse harder than was strictly necessary and Ryshad let him go ahead.

We were well on before the sun began to sink. I glanced back over my shoulder to see dusk climbing over the gleaming sea before the hills finally hid the ocean. We let Shiv lead, as he clearly wanted to be on his own. As Aiten regaled Ryshad with a few rather dubious stories, I realised he'd been doing his scouting in all the low parts of town; I'd heard those tales before but only in a brothel. Don't misunderstand me; a lot of whore-houses offer gambling as an additional way of separating fools from their money and I'd spent an interesting three seasons a few years back helping a couple of houses bend the odds in their favour. It had been an illuminating experience which had certainly cured me of any romantic notions about a prostitute's life but it hadn't been much of a challenge; none of the men had been giving the game anything like their full attention.

I listened idly as Aiten was bringing Ryshad up to date with the latest witticisms doing the rounds of the bear pits; Ryshad was laughing and groaning in the appropriate places but his attention remained on the road ahead and the woods around us. Aiten did not seem to find this unusual and carried on with his tales; he had yet to come up with one I had not already heard. Inglis was the town where old jokes came to die. I trailed along behind with the mule carrying our supplies and came to the conclusion that it was probably the most cheerful one of us.

Shiv paused to stick his hands in the river and stare thoughtfully at the tributary we had reached.

'We'll follow this.' His tone was the mildest I'd heard it since we'd lost Geris and I moved up to ride next to him, relieved to see his good humour resurfacing.

'We're following the rivers? Is Azazir a water mage then?'

'Didn't I say? Yes, one of the best.' Shiv gave me a half smile.

'So how did he . . .' I couldn't quite decide how to phrase the question that had been hovering at the back of my mind all day.

'How did he fall foul of the Council?' Shiv moved across the muddy track and we rode on the somewhat drier grass. I let him take his time in deciding what to tell me. When he eventually answered, he spoke slowly and thoughtfully.

'You have to understand that, for a mage like Azazir, his element is the most important thing in the world. He's fascinated by water, by its effects on things, how it makes up part of things, what he can do to affect it. Many of the really powerful wizards are like that.'

'Is he powerful? Is he dangerous, come to that?' I asked a little nervously.

'He's very powerful but I don't suppose he's dangerous unless you get in the way of something he's taken an interest in.'

I'd have preferred a little more certainty, myself. 'So, what was Darni saying about him being executed?'

Shiv frowned. 'Azazir was always a loner. He went off and

did peculiar things like this supposed trip across the ocean. The Seaward Hall is full of tales about him and it's hard to know what is really true. He used to exaggerate half the time and tell outright lies for the rest if you believe some of the Council. What finally got him banished was the flooding of half of Adrulle.'

'What?' Ryshad exclaimed. I turned in my saddle and saw he and Aiten were listening with as much interest as myself.

Aiten laughed and Shiv smiled at him. 'It wasn't funny at the time; it was For-Summer and he drowned a sizeable part of the southern Caladhrian harvest. The price of bread doubled that winter and there were riots in some of the towns.'

'Why did he do it?' I asked.

'He wanted a marsh to study,' Shiv said simply. 'So he diverted most of the Rel into the nearest low-lying area.'

'How low did the river get?' No wonder this wizard was such a menace. The depth and width of the Rel is all that keeps the endless bloody squabbles of Lescar from spilling over into the bland stability of Caladhria.

'Low enough for the Duke of Marlier to send over raiding parties,' Shiv replied.

'What about Relshaz?' Ryshad was looking as stunned as I felt.

'The Magistrates' Convention raised a militia as soon as it became clear the river was falling. They were the first to demand Azazir be executed.'

That was no surprise; the Relshazri take their independence and security very seriously, given their position on the delta between Caladhria and Lescar. Since that depends on the river, any proposal, never mind attempt, to build a permanent bridge carries the death penalty. Not surprisingly, no one ever makes one. Apart from that, it's an easy-going city with plenty of opportunities for someone like me. I was gripped with a sudden longing for warm southern sun and cool southern wines and missed Ryshad's next question.

'No. The Council won't take orders from any other power.' Shiv looked serious. 'Actually, if the Relshazri hadn't made such a fuss, Azazir might well have been executed. As it was, the Archmage wasn't going to do anything that suggested he was giving in to them so Azazir was exiled up here.'

I was still having trouble with the idea of wizards killing each other.

'They really thought about executing him?'

Shiv looked at me, his expression serious. 'The trouble he caused cost many lives, much coin and three seasons' work to clear up. That sort of thing causes wizards to be seriously disliked. We are very powerful, and that can frighten people, so we do our best not to let them see it. When someone like Azazir goes around doing what he wants with no thought for the consequences, people worry. If the Council lets the like of him get away with it, we're heading down the road leading to mageborn children left to die of fevers and wizards stoned out of villages. The Council controls wizards so that no one else has an excuse to do it.'

'Otrick on "Why don't wizards rule the world?"' I murmured to myself.

Shiv heard me and grinned again. 'Most of them could not be bothered. It would be a distraction from the really important business of studying their element. Still, a few have decided to try every now and again, and the Council has dealt with them too.'

We reached another place where streams joined the river and Shiv dismounted to dip his hands in again. I couldn't decide if I was sorry that he had been interrupted or not. Some of these ideas were seriously scary.

A well-beaten track ran along the river bank; with the hills getting steeper and more wooded, it was the natural way to go. We made good progress and hit a mining settlement a few days north of the Dalas. It was quite sizeable for a hill town and possessed an unusual air of permanence, with a stone-built forge and an inn that looked as if it might even offer more than whores and spirits raw enough to make your teeth dissolve.

Shiv led us into what I suppose you would call the market square, though no one looked to be selling anything. Men and women in rough working clothes gave us a faintly curious appraisal. Shiv sat tall in his saddle and stared round arrogantly. I stared back and realised that the bastard was suddenly spotlessly clean, unlike the travel-stained rest of us. Good spell if you can do it, I acknowledged silently.

'I am a wizard of the Archmage's Council and I am looking for news.'

Aiten and Ryshad drew up their horse in a line with mine, shrugged their cloaks aside from their sword arms and rested negligent hands on their blades. The three of us exchanged a glance and waited for the muddy locals to laugh, jeer or throw horseshit depending on their inclination. None of this happened, which surprised me; I'd like to see a wizard try that trick in Vanam.

'What sort of news?' The smith walked forward from his hearth, wiping his hands on a rag. He was formidably muscled and his face and hands were pitted with tiny scars but his voice was calm and assured. I started to think we might get some useful information after all.

'I am seeking an old mage called Azazir; he dwelt north of here some years ago.' Shiv raised his hands and wove a spinning web of blue fire in the centre of the square. The gleaming strands curved around shimmering panels of air, tossing fleeting reflections around the circle. The lines suddenly thinned and flashed into nothingness, leaving an image hanging in the air above the well. About half true size, I saw a scrawny figure in a long green cloak over a mossy robe. Azazir had thinnish grey hair cut off in a straight line at his shoulders and a stoop which brought his narrow face questing forward like a heron, a likeness heightened by his prominent nose. His eyes shone green and, as we watched, the image swept round in a circle, hands spread and skirts flaring, for all the world as if it could see the stunned diggers staring back at it.

I managed to catch my jaw before it dropped too far and I did my best to copy the unimpressed cool of Ryshad and Aiten's poses. I nearly lost it when Ryshad winked at me, but the inhabitants were still so staggered I could have reached down their throats and stolen their guts without them noticing.

'So,' Shiv's voice cut through the silence like a whip, 'does anyone here know of him?'

The crowd shuffled and muttered and a reluctant old woman was pushed forward from the back.

'Can you help me?' Shiv leaned down to her, voice smooth as silk and just as enticing.

The grubby old hag stared back like a rabbit in front of a weasel and then shook herself to what I'd bet was a more usual truculence.

'He did used to come down for flour and the like ten years back,' she snapped.

Shiv gave her a smile, blending gratitude with condescension, and, more crucially as far as she was concerned, slipped her some coin.

The gleam of gold they would not have to dig out of the rocks themselves suddenly loosened tongues all around us.

'He was living up beyond the oak stands, where the beeches come down to the river.'

'That was in my father's time. He had a hut by the trout pools last I heard.'

'He'd gone further than that, idiot. He was living by the lake when Emmer caught that big fish, you know, the one with the green scales.'

'It was Summer Solstice three years back he was last here. I remember it was just before Nalli was born and we'd had that swarm of bees in the thatch.'

'He was older though, he'd lost most of that hair and walked with a stick.'

'My uncles said they'd met him up past the snowline, winter before last. They knew he must be a wizard because he was only wearing a tunic and that was one they'd not give a dog to sleep on. Anyone normal would have been iced solid.'

'Reckon he's probably dead by now.'

Shiv held up a commanding hand and the babble fell silent. 'Has anyone seen him since the spring of last year?'

The crowd, which seemed to have doubled since we arrived, shuffled their feet and looked at each other but no one spoke up.

Shiv bowed from his saddle and then gazed imperiously

around. 'I thank you on the Archmage's behalf. Is there any service I can do you by way of payment?'

If I'd thought they were stunned before, now they were completely poleaxed. The sounds of the rushing river chattered through the silence. Just when I was about to kick Russet on and take us out of there, a voice piped up from the back.

'Can you tell us where the silver lode is headed?' The opportunist was quickly hushed but Shiv smiled and I could see laughter bubbling behind his lordly manner.

'Look for a crag shaped like a bear with rowans above and below.' Shiv distributed a handful of Tormalin Marks and then moved off, Aiten and Ryshad kicking their horses to tuck in behind him like an Imperial escort. That left me holding the mule so I turned to a nearby peasant and adopted Shiv's lordly tones.

'We would be grateful for bread, any fruit you can spare and flour if you have it.'

Several people scurried off and returned with baskets and sacks. I'm sure the mule looked at me reproachfully but I was too pleased at the prospect of fresh bread again to care.

The mule decided to co-operate and I was able to ride out of the little town in fine style. Shiv must have been the biggest thing to hit that place since the last mudslide.

Aiten was waiting for me when I reached a bend in the track above a fine deep pool in the river.

'Didn't want to lose you, flower.' He grinned when he saw the mule's acquisitions. 'Good thinking. Something nice for dinner?'

'Where are Shiv and Ryshad?' He'd better not think the only woman was automatically the cook. I wondered whether to tell him straight or just let him find out by tasting my efforts; even Darni had done better on our trip through Dalasor.

'Shiv's washing his hands again.' Aiten helped me coax the mule over a slippery patch and we headed towards a flurry of rapids showing white through the trees.

'You've spent time up here, haven't you?' I followed Aiten's lead and dismounted to lead Russet over a bank ribbed with exposed tree roots.

'That's right, three seasons in the gold camps, west of the Celiare. How can you tell?'

I smiled thinly. 'If you see me playing the two-Mark thrice-a-night again, then you can call me "flower". Other than that, my name's Livak, all right?'

Aiten waited for me to draw level and I was glad to see he took no offence. 'I'm from a little town near Parnilesse originally.' He offered me his hand over a slippery patch. 'My family are farmers. I didn't fancy life with a hoe so I joined the Duke's militia. We spent one season allied with Triolle against Draximal and the next we were fighting Triolle along with Marlier. I soon worked out that His Grace wasn't going to reunite Lescar short of a major plague killing everyone else off, so I struck out on my own. I made a good bit mining but it's not so easy to keep it up here. I headed south four years back.'

We reached the river bank and saw Shiv studying the trunks of the beeches while Ryshad was poking about in a tangle of wood caught by a fallen tree.

'The high water mark's even further up here,' Shiv was saying.

'Here, look at this.' Ryshad pulled something out of the shallows and we all went over to examine a piece of beam, shingles still hanging from rusted nails.

'I'm sure this is fascinating, but would you mind explaining why to an ignorant town-dweller?' I asked politely.

'This river's flooding on a regular basis and the water's going unusually high,' Shiv said, as if that made everything clear.

'And it shouldn't be?' I hazarded.

'Of course not.' Shiv caught himself and shook his head. 'I'm sorry. No, it shouldn't be doing this amount of damage, not this far up its course.'

'No offence, Shiv, but I've lived in these mountains,' Aiten said hesitantly. 'When these rivers are in spate with the snow melt, they rise like a boiling kettle.'

'I'm taking that into account,' Shiv assured him. 'It's still not natural. Look, there are buildings being washed out further upstream. This is part of a roof! How many people would be stupid enough to build below the high water mark?'

Personally, I've known people stupid enough to set their feet on fire trying to dry their boots, but after the little display at the village, I had to reckon Shiv knew his business. That reminded me of something.

'How did you know about their silver mining, Shiv?'

He laughed. 'Planir told me about it. He thought we might need to sweeten a few people up here. He's an earth mage by affinity, so he sees that kind of thing when he's scrying.'

That sounded a useful talent; I bet he wasn't a wizard short of coin. 'So why can't he just tell us where this Azazir is?'

'There are difficulties with the correlation of elemental combinations with the distances involved. It's complicated.'

Shiv wasn't usually given to such vague answers and did not look me in the eye as he remounted. I followed on thoughtfully as we headed deeper into the increasingly tangled woods.

Shiv's little pageant had been the high spot of the day and, as we headed still further away from any possibility of a real bed and a bath, it began to rain. It was not heavy but a fine drizzle, though I soon discovered it left you just as wet. I stared gloomily at the beads of moisture glinting on Russet's ears and for about the tenth time since we'd left Inglis I started to wonder just what I was doing here. We picked our way along the narrowing trails until the light got too dim for the treacherous going underfoot and we made camp. The temperature dropped like a stone that night and we woke freezing cold, stiff as boards and totally unimpressed. Even the mule was starting to look miffed.

We pushed on higher and further and things went from bad to worse as the rain grew heavier and the air colder. We didn't even manage to finish eating the bread before it developed great smug spots of mould and we lost half the fruit when the mule had a fall when its harness slipped, the sodden leather straps slackening as they stretched. We decided to risk cooking flatbread even though the flour had soaked down into an unappetising gluey mass; the next day proved us wrong as, one after another, we had to dash for the undergrowth with racking stomach cramps. We endured two days where meal breaks were spent drinking and collecting large, moist leaves rather than eating, but once the squits had passed we were able to make better progress.

I must have read a handful of Lescari romances and heard twice that many ballads about quests through the wilderness after this magical amulet or that lost princess and not one has mentioned what a miserable business it can be. I began to dream about hearing cobbles under Russet's hooves again. Unfortunately, I also dreamed about Geris and that was pretty much the only thing that kept me from turning round and heading back towards warmth and dry clothes.

Shiv rode through it all oblivious and I'd swear he wasn't getting as wet as the rest of us somehow. Ryshad and Aiten put up with all the discomforts without visible irritation, which only goes to prove how insensitive men can be. They finally lost their composure one miserable afternoon but it didn't really make me feel any better.

Lips thin with irritation, Ryshad was busy with his usual routine, trying to clean tiny spots of rust off his sword, while Aiten went off into the tangled thickets to try and catch some rabbits or squirrels for dinner. Shiv was off communing with the puddles or something, and I was sorting through the luggage, checking Russet and the mule for harness galls and trying to get the worst of the mud and leaves off their legs.

'Do you really think it's worth carrying this?' I looked at the rusty roll of my chainmail with distaste. Just looking at it made my shoulders ache and I would smell like a bag of old horseshoes besides.

Ryshad shrugged. 'It's no use on the mule's back. Wear it or dump it.'

'It's filthy,' I grumbled. 'I'll freeze in it and it weighs a sack-weight. It stinks too.'

Ryshad waved a wire brush at me. 'Clean it and oil it if you want.'

I looked from him to the chainmail and back again, on the verge of full-scale sulks. I didn't want practical advice, I wanted sympathy, understanding and someone else to tell me it was all right to dump the evil stuff.

'You don't wear mail,' I said accusingly.

He tapped his thick buff coat and I was surprised to hear a solid knock. 'Coat of plates,' he explained, shrugging out of it and letting me feel the metal discs sewn between the leather and the linen lining.

'That looks more comfortable,' I admired. 'Where can I get one?'

'Nowhere this side of the Dalas. I got mine in Zyoutessela.'

'Is that where you're from originally? Tell me about it. Is it true you can see the ocean and the Sea of Lescar at the same time?' I could do with going somewhere warm, civilised and exotic even if it was only on the back of someone else's memories.

Ryshad sat back and forgot his work for a moment. 'Well, you can if you climb a tower the Den Rannions have built at the top of the pass. The two anchorages are in fact quite a way apart, I suppose they're more like two cities joined by the portage way, what with the mountains in the middle. We live on the ocean side, my father's a mason, a tenant of Messire D'Olbriot. The patron owns about a third of the land on that side and has a fifth share in the portage way.'

Perhaps I should think about working for him, after all. Ryshad was talking massive wealth.

'Do many ships risk the route round the Cape of Winds rather than paying to transfer their cargo?' I remembered the sleek Dalasorian ships in Inglis.

'Some do in the summer but a lot come back as wreckage on the autumn tides.'

Ryshad gave his sword one last polish with an oily rag and went to sheathe it. It stuck unexpectedly and he swore as he jarred his arm.

'Now what's wrong?' He stripped off sword-belt and scabbard and examined them closely.

'Dast's teeth!' He wrenched the scabbard free and began peering down the length of it. 'It's warped! Can you believe it? I've had this five years and one lousy trip to Gidesta ruins it.'

He sat and began unpicking the leather covering the wood, cursing under his breath, as Aiten came crashing back into the glade, ripping clinging snarls of vegetation off himself with loud exasperation.

'I can't find a thing out there,' he announced. 'I've seen no tracks smaller than water-deer and a wild goat.'

'I'll eat goat,' I shrugged.

'Not tonight you won't.' Aiten threw a broken tangle of wood and binding on to the fire where it hissed and spat.

'That's your bow!' I objected.

'And the only way I could kill anything with it would be to creep up behind and club it to death.' Aiten rummaged in his saddle bag for a flask of spirits. 'It's as twisted as that mule's back leg. It's all this pissing rain. Where's Shiv? He's supposed to be a water mage, why can't he do something about this ungodly weather?'

He tried to warm his hands by our miserable fire. At least the bow had raised a few feeble flames. I left them to it and went in search of Shiv. He was crouched over a deep pool of water but when I peered over his shoulder, all I saw were complex patterns of ruby, amber, sapphire and emerald light. He stood upright and rubbed the small of his back.

'Did you want me for something?'

'Ait can't find anything for dinner. He was wondering if you could do anything about this weather, stop the rain for a bit.'

Shiv grimaced. 'Sorry, weather magic's well out of my league. It takes a whole nexus of power and at least four mages.'

I sighed. 'It was worth a try. What are you doing?'

Shiv turned back to his pool. 'I'm looking at the elemental distortions around here. The water power's been tied up in some fascinating ways.'

'How so?'

Shiv gave me a distinctly shifty look. 'It's complicated, you wouldn't understand.'

I looked at him, eyes narrowed as lurking suspicion crept up from the back of my mind. 'Are you sure? It wouldn't have anything to do with all the things that have warped or rusted or rotted lately, would it?'

'All right, it does,' he admitted. 'Still, it means we're on the right trail, doesn't it? If Azazir is taking the trouble to try and discourage us.'

'As far as I'm concerned, he's succeeding,' I growled. 'So have you any idea how much further we must go?'

Shiv moved to the river bank and pointed higher into the hills. 'See that double outcrop above the rock fall? I think he's somewhere just beyond that.'

I didn't look at the hill so much as the grey mass of storm clouds seething above it. I frowned as I tried to work out what was wrong with what I was seeing.

'Shiv, those clouds aren't going anywhere,' I said slowly. 'Look, they're just going round and round in circles. That doesn't make sense. The wind's blowing a northerly gale up there, you can see it from the trees.'

'Is it?'

His air of surprise didn't fool me. 'You said a wizard couldn't do weather magic on his own,' I accused him.

'No, he can't.' I really did not want to hear the note of uncertainty in Shiv's voice. 'Well, he shouldn't be able to.'

CHAPTER SEVEN

Taken from:

An Account of the Founding of Hadrumal
Ocarn, Third Flood–Master of Wellery's Hall

Once the domain of Hecksen was laid waste, popular fear of the mage-born increased. Appalling though we may find the folly and ambition of the mages Mercel and Frelt, the claims of the Lords of Pearle and Algeral that they had in fact been ensorcelled can be nothing but lies. Worse, the Elected of Col seized upon this pathetic excuse, purporting to discover their involvement had been forced by a conspiracy of wizards and priests planning to seize power. Rumours inflated this calumny, resulting in wholesale panic among the ignorant; even mere scribes found themselves subject to beatings and the few schools were ransacked. The official priesthood was dissolved and the library of the Temple burned. With Col one of the last remaining Temples to survive the chaos of the Dark Generations thus far, the loss of knowledge this represented is incalculable. It must remind us never to underestimate the dangers of the narrow minds of the mundane populace.

Trydek was then travelling in Caladhria as a tutor. Anti-scholastic bias was not so prevalent, but ignorance was still a pernicious blight. It was now considered enough that a noble retain a scribe, rather than learn to read or write for himself, and many libraries were left to rot and worm. To be mage-born was increasingly considered an oddity if not downright unlucky and many unfortunates became victims of their own untutored powers. A few notable disasters such as the burning of Lady Shress and her baby in childbirth became widely known in a variety of garbled legends. The Duke of Triolle actually declared use of what he termed arcane arts punishable by ordeal and other Lescari nobles followed suit. Of course, all this achieved was to put intolerable strains on already untrained and terrified youths and maidens with inevitable results. Soon any natural flood, fire or lightning strike would be attributed to a mage-born and a frantic search would commence, naturally enough unearthing some unfortunate with a trace of affinity. If lucky, they would simply be driven away; if not, increasingly, killed.

Trydek gathered a coterie of dispossessed mage-born around himself and attempted to settle in various places. As a young man, I heard him speak in his last years, telling most affectingly of the fear and ignorance he and his little band encountered. Various wizards who had contrived to nurture and develop their talents attempted to resist such trends in their localities. With hindsight, we must admit that actions such as the destruction of Gerill Market, the blinding of Lord Arbel and particularly the Parnilesse Rising were ill-judged, if understandable. It was after this last that Trydek finally agreed to remove from the mainland altogether, at the suggestion of Vidella, later First Flood-Mistress of the Seaward Hall.

Rain, rain and more rain. The closer we came to the circle of clouds, the heavier the rain became. That stationary storm soon looked as convincing as a priest's condolences; I noticed Ryshad and Aiten exchanging uncertain looks and slipping dubious glances in Shiv's direction. We struggled on and I mean struggled. The tangles of trees, brambles and ivy got more and more dense and with growing irritation we were frequently brought to a standstill while we cut ourselves and the animals free, or cast about for a path. The rune that tipped the hand came when we stopped to camp and no one could light a fire. I was rummaging in the mule's packs, hoping to find some halfway dry food, I was trying to cut some dry-cured meat with fingers numb with cold when the knife slipped and I gave myself an agonising scrape across the knuckles. I was just about to dissolve into angry tears when I realised Ryshad and Aiten were nearly coming to blows and got a grip on myself.

'Here, let me try. You're doing it all wrong.'

'You're welcome to it. That flint's next to useless.'

'Did you keep the tinder inside your shirt like I told you?'

'For all the good it did. It's as wet as the rest of me.'

'Well, why didn't you wrap it in some oilcloth?'

'Why is it down to me? Why don't you do something useful instead of criticising?'

'I slept with the bloody stuff in my breeches last night. It was dry when I gave it to you.'

I judged it time to intervene. 'Shiv, can you help us get this rotten fire started?'

'Sorry?'

'The fire, Shiv, we need something warm to eat and drink.'

'Are you sure?'

That gave us a spark of sorts; it certainly got Ryshad's temper flaring up.

'Of course she's bloody well sure. We're all soaking wet and freezing cold, at least we three are. Rain doesn't run off normal people like the water off a duck's arse, in case you hadn't noticed.'

I interrupted while he drew breath; he looked like a man heading for something Shiv might regret.

'Just light the fire, Shiv, please.'

Shiv came over to the half-built fire which was already wet enough to wring out and bit his lip as he spread his hands over it. There was a long, cold and tense pause.

'There seems to be a problem.' Shiv looked up at the three of us unhappily.

'Meaning?' Ryshad's tone was ominous.

'It's the elements. Fire seems almost completely closed off in this area.'

'How much is almost?' I was glad I wasn't having to answer Ryshad. We had another of those pauses.

'Enough to prevent anyone lighting a fire, magically or otherwise.'

I waited for the eruption from Ryshad or Aiten but none came.

'So what do we do now?' Ryshad relieved his feelings by kicking the pitiful collection of twigs and tinder halfway across the scrubby hole that passed for a clearing in this undergrowth.

Aiten thrust his hand under Shiv's nose. It was dead white and wrinkled like a wet rag.

'See this? My fingers look as if I've been in a bath for three days. I'm so cold I'm not even shivering much any more. If you don't do something, we'll all be down with exposure by morning, that's if we're not dead in our sleep. I've lived in these mountains, Shiv, I've seen it happen.'

'Maybe we should turn back?' Looks from Aiten and Ryshad told me they were thinking the same way but neither had wanted to be the first to suggest it.

'No, come on.' There was a pleading note in Shiv's voice which surprised me. 'We can't give in. Azazir's doing this to discourage us.'

'As far as I'm concerned, he's succeeding.' Ryshad had got his temper back under control but his face was grim.

'Well?' Aiten's harsh question hung in the air as we all avoided each other's eyes.

'I can't light a fire but I can get you all drier and try to keep the rain off,' Shiv offered.

Aiten looked up from trying to unknot his boot laces. 'Rysh? What do you reckon?'

Ryshad sighed. 'We need to do something to get us through the night. It's too late to set off back down to the valley anyway.'

Now we had something positive to do, we all moved fast. I pulled the driest of the blankets out of the bedrolls while Ryshad and Aiten rigged a canopy out of the largest piece of oilskin. We stripped off our sodden cloaks and tunics and sat in a circle, knee to knee, to share as much of our warmth as possible. It was awkward but we wrapped the blankets around our shoulders, overlapping them and pulling them tight.

'Now just relax and let me work without interrupting.' Shiv gathered faint tendrils of blue light in his hands and closed his eyes. Even I could see the magic was skewed around here; normally his magelight working with air was a clear azure, but now it was shaded like the turquoise the Aldabreshi prize so highly.

I hadn't planned on interrupting, but I soon realised why he'd cautioned us when the shimmering lines of power started creeping over and around us. The water was forced out of our clothes and hair and rose from our huddle in wisps of steam; it tickled horribly. I shut my eyes tight but that just made things worse so I opened them again. It was like the worst case of fleas or lice you've ever had, multiplied by ten. My skin was crawling like a drunk's with the screaming fits upon him and from the fixed revulsion on Ryshad's face, he felt much the same.

I was starting to think this was worse than being soaked when I realised I could feel my toes again. As they itched and burned I told myself this was an improvement but I took some convincing. Aiten shuffled and cursed under his breath but subsided under a stern look from Shiv. I bit my lip and concentrated on the coils of steam twisting out into the gathering dusk. Any passing animal could have mistaken us for a compost heap. Just as I saw the first of the two crescent moons slide up over the tops of the trees, Shiv heaved a sigh and let the magic go.

'That should be better.' I could hardly see him in the dark but I heard the uncertainty in his voice.

I felt my shirt; it was stiff under my roughened hands but pretty well dry and I realised my fingertips had lost their wrinkles.

'Thanks, Shiv.' Aiten rummaged in his belt-pouch. 'Anyone care for some Thassin?'

If I want stimulation, I generally stick to spirits but I decided this was a time for taking whatever was on offer. 'I'll try it, thanks.'

Aiten found my hand in the dark and pressed a small round nut into it. 'Break it up, then tuck the pulp in your cheek,' he advised.

'May I?' Shiv lit a small ball of magelight and held out his hand. 'I didn't know you were a chewer.'

'I'm not as a rule.' Aiten paused to crack the tough outer casing of the nut between his teeth. 'I carry some for emergencies and I think this qualifies. Rysh, do you want some?'

Ryshad sighed and I saw his face tighten in the eerie blue glow. 'I'd better, I suppose. How much do you have?'

'Enough to get you back down gently.' Aiten's face was sympathetic as he handed over a couple of the dark shells.

'I used to be a chewer,' Ryshad explained as he cracked the nuts with practised ease. 'Took me the best part of two seasons to shake the habit.'

I was impressed. 'That's quite an achievement.'

Ryshad grimaced. 'It's not something I fancy doing again.'

We sat and chewed like a huddle of milk cows and I soon found the warmth in my jaw spreading to my stomach and legs. The sour aggravation of days and days spent cold and wet dissolved into a petty annoyance and I began to see why people used this stuff. To my surprise, I began to feel hungry and felt around my feet for the meagre meal I'd managed to salvage.

'When we get back to civilisation, I'm going to buy the biggest piece of cow a butcher can sell me. I'll fry it with onions and butter and eat a day's bread with it,' I muttered with feeling.

'Don't,' Ryshad groaned.

We ate the bits of food, all oddly flavoured by the Thassin, and our spirits rose. We all knew it was artificial but after a while we really didn't care.

'So what's the worst meal anyone's ever eaten? Apart from this one, that is.' Aiten grinned at me, teeth stained and breath bitter from the nuts.

Shiv gave us a highly exaggerated account of student food in Hadrumal; at least I hope he was exaggerating. If he wasn't, Planir could have my report in writing; you won't catch me in a place where someone found a mouse in his stew.

We moved on from disastrous meals to disastrous actions and Aiten had us roaring with laughter with his tales of life as a Lescari mercenary. My personal favourite was the one about the sergeant who led his troop into an ambush one night. 'Come on, lads,' he shouted to get his men going. 'Lads?' All he got was the sound of running feet and the sight of the pennant-bearer's lantern bobbing away at high speed! Another case of death by stupidity.

Ryshad countered with the difficulties of persuading militia levies to use a shield without doing more damage to themselves than to the enemy, and I managed to drive all three of them to distraction by challenging them to guess the single most difficult defence against uninvited entry that I'd ever come across. In case you're wondering, it's not dogs, locks or watchmen, it's those cursed little bells on coils of wire that people hang inside doors and windows. I've won a lot of drinks with that challenge.

Dawn came more quickly than I had expected and we broke up our huddle, stretching cramped legs and preparing for the next stage of this ungodly journey. Shiv had done his best with our clothes and boots but putting on a damp, cold tunic and cloak was one of the nastiest things I had done in a long time. Needless to say the rain was still teeming down and I don't think I have ever seen an animal look quite so pissed off and reproachful as that mule.

Another day of hacking and slipping and cursing through the thickets brought us to a ridge, and when we crested it, we looked down on a totally different scene. It was a valley with a lake in its floor, but where most lakes are fed by one or two streams, this was the focus for hundreds. I know it sounds fanciful but these brooks weren't just following nature downhill, they were aiming for this lake. I'd bet if we'd tried we'd have found others flowing uphill to get here. Water streamed down the steep sides of the valley: few plants had been able to get a foothold here and it looked as if the grass and soil would soon be losing the battle. The lake was a dark murky green and a dense fog swirled above its lurking surface.

'Is this it?' Aiten asked unnecessarily.

Shiv nodded slowly, turning as he scanned the area intently. I followed his gaze but saw nothing. I felt very uneasy and wondered what it was that felt so wrong. The well-spring has always been a lucky rune for me; what was it trying to tell me? After a few moments, I grasped it.

'Can you hear anything? Is it just my ears or are there really no birds here?'

We all stood and listened but the only sounds were rushing water and below that a dull murmur from the far end of the lake.

'This way.' Shiv headed for the noise and we picked our way cautiously along the muddy shoreline. The back of my neck began to prickle and I knew without question that someone or something was watching us.

Russet snorted and paced skittishly as the lake lapped at his feet. I cursed him and had to use all my skills to get him moving again. I had my hands full since I was also leading the mule; the wretched creature had decided I was the only one of us that she'd co-operate with. I'm all for females sticking together, but I felt this was a bit much. I managed to get her moving in a sulky trot, but when I looked forward, the others were quite a way ahead. Tendrils of fog were creeping into the gap and I shivered suddenly.

'Wait up.' I used my heels on Russet and he skipped forward but the fog was growing denser by the second. Shiv and the others were indistinct shapes in a few breaths as clammy whiteness coiled round us.

'Wait for me!' I bellowed but the dead air smothered my voice like a pillow.

I looked down to check for the water's edge but Russet's hooves were already lost in the rising mist. He stopped and snorted nervously, ears pricking forward then laying flat back to his head in turn. I looked at the mule; all I could see now was her head but she was doing the same with her large furry ears, eyes rolling and showing white as something spooked her.

I sat and forced myself to breathe calmly and strained my own ears to try and detect whatever the animals were reacting to. Horrid whispering floated from the direction of the lake but I couldn't make it out. I shook in the chill breeze and kicked Russet hard but he wouldn't move.

Sudden chattering behind us startled the mule into a leap forward that sent her into Russet's rump. He whipped his head round, teeth bared, and snapped at her. She snapped, he reared and I slid gracelessly off his rear end.

'Stop, you bastard horse!' I grabbed helplessly for the trailing reins but the cursed creature vanished into the fog, which was now as dense as rotten milk. I scrambled to my feet and looked wildly round. At least I still had hold of the mule. If there was something out there hoping for a meal, it could have her first. Would there be bears around here? Wolves? Something worse?

'Come on.' I held her by the bridle and leaned into her shaggy shoulder as I took a few cautious steps. I felt water lap round my feet and swore. Back-tracking, I tried what I thought was another way but a few short paces had me paddling again.

As I turned the mule round I caught a glimpse of something in the fog, a dark indistinct shape about man high.

'Shiv? Ryshad? Is that you?' I walked forward slowly but all I could see was fog. There was a scrape on the stones behind me and I whirled round, pressing my back into the reassuring solidity of the mule. I screamed as something or someone tapped me on the shoulder but when I looked wildly round, there was nothing to be seen.

All those fears that you keep locked away in the back of your head started hammering on the doors of my mind. The terror of walking through the house in the dark as a child, the horrors that pursue you back to your bed and the safety of your blankets, the panic of being separated from your parents in a busy street. More adult dreads came crawling up to join them and add their weight; I felt the shock of that near-rape again, the whimpering nausea when I had faced a flogging for theft, the peril and uncertainty when I had been separated from Sorgrad in a riot in Relshaz. I began to shake as the crowding fears made thinking and even walking forward more and more difficult. The mule was shaking now, sweating like a beast facing a predator, head swaying from side to side as shadows in the fog chased around us and evil sounds whispered on every side. I heard echoes of my grandmother scorning my Forest blood, the slap of leather against flesh, the deranged laughter of the would-be rapist. I quailed before the mounting onslaught, sinking to my knees, but still clinging to the mule's reins as if I were drowning.

I don't know how long I crouched there, paralysed by nameless dread in the fog. Eventually a faint voice of reason began to cut through the clamouring terrors in my head. When the fear became too much to bear with my eyes closed, I realised I could see a difference in the fog over to one side. Where it had previously all been white, dead as a pauper's shroud, I could now see faint colour. An almost imperceptible shading of blue was lighting up the heavy wet air.

Shiv, it had to be. I got to my feet and forced my trembling legs towards the colour, dragging the reluctant mule behind me. As I moved, I managed to get a grip on my mind again and hurried the pace. I cannot describe my relief when I saw Shiv standing in a shimmering blue sphere of clear air. The boundaries of his spell were expanding and, as the brilliant blue light swept over me, I felt the fears wash away; it was almost a physical release.

'What's going on?' I hurried to his side and looked round, still apprehensive.

He shook his head and concentrated on his spell. A change in the light made me look up and I saw the fog melting above us. Soon we could see the lake shore and the surrounding valley walls. I drew in deep breaths of clean air until the trembling finally stopped.

'Azazir!' Shiv's roar startled the mule dreadfully but I managed to hold her. 'Your spells are a mighty defence against the untutored. I honour your skills but let us stop this trial! We have urgent business with you; we would not disturb you if it were not a matter of life and death!'

There was a crack like thunder on the plains and in an instant the fog vanished. I blinked away sudden tears as blue sky and sunlight hit my eyes and, for a breath, the valley was bathed in the clear light of a crisp autumn day. It was over so fast I almost doubted my senses; the clouds returned and the rain poured down on us once more, heavier than ever.

'Shiv!' Aiten and Ryshad stumbled towards us through the sheets of rain, feet sliding in the treacherous mud. They had lost their horses too, and each looked white and strained. Vomit stained Aiten's cloak; I didn't want to think what could have terrified him to that extreme. Ryshad's face was set and pale, his naked sword dull and grey as the clouds above us.

'It was a spell.' Shiv held out his arms and we stood in a circle, clasping each other's hands and drawing strength from each other, breath hammering in our chests as we cleared the echoes of the dread from our minds.

Ryshad broke the silence. 'What now, Shiv?'

'We go on.' His tone allowed for no argument and he led the way further towards the head of the lake. We followed, the three of us gathered close to the reassuring bulk of the mule. I realised the rest of us had drawn our swords without stopping to discuss the matter.

The murmur of rushing waters grew stronger and, now the

mist had cleared, we saw a waterfall plunging over a cliff ahead
of us. Vapour floated over the waters like steam, foam roiling
under the onslaught of the cataract.

'Look there.' Aiten pointed over to the base of the cliff.
What I had taken for a heap of rocks proved strangely regular
on closer examination and, as we drew nearer, I saw crude
windows and the dark shadow of a wooden door. It was
definitely a dwelling of some sort.

'Come on.' Ryshad moved out ahead of Shiv and Aiten
followed him.

'Careful, we need to be patient,' Shiv called after them.

I'm not quite sure what Aiten said but I think it was
something along the lines of 'Patience, my arse.' In any case,
he walked swiftly up to the door and kicked it in with practised
violence. He didn't get the impressive splintering crash he'd
wanted, more of a soggy creak; having to pull his foot free of
the rotting timbers spoiled the effect further.

Shiv muttered something uncomplimentary under his breath
and hurried after them. I took my time tethering the mule and
followed once it was clear no maddened wizard was going to
turn them all into frogs. Once inside, it was obvious that this
had once been someone's home but its former occupant was
long gone. Crude wooden furniture stood covered in fungus,
whatever materials had softened the chairs had long since
vanished to line mouse nests, leaving only a few chewed
fragments. Ryshad and Aiten were opening the cupboards
and a chest but found nothing beyond rank leavings sodden
into unidentifiable pulp. Moisture streamed down the walls
and the air smelled dank and unwholesome.

'If this was his home, he must be dead,' I said at last. 'Darni
said he could have left guard spells behind him, didn't he?
Maybe that's all we've found.'

Shiv stood in the middle of the fetid hovel and turned slowly
around. 'No, that magic is alive and that means Azazir must be
too. There must be some clue here.'

'There's something through here.' Ryshad was examining
the far wall carefully and, when he ran his hand around the
outline, we could just make out a door cut from the stone.

'Let me see.'

As Shiv and the others crowded round it, I moved over to the fireplace. It was raised up in the wall with a grill for cooking on and slabs set to either side for warming and simmering. It hadn't seen any activity for a long while, the ashes had been almost completely washed away. I leaned in to peer up the chimney but could see no light; it had to be blocked further up, a nest perhaps, built before the birds fled this unnatural area. I wondered, would a wizard be any more imaginative than the rest of us when it came to hiding valuables?

'There!'

I looked round to see Shiv illuminate the rock door with amber light. It swung open and the three of them looked into the blackness beyond.

'Come on.' Shiv raised a ball of magelight and they went in cautiously.

I reached up the flue and felt around, moving the rusted ironwork built in for smoking and hanging kettles. Nothing unusual there so I rolled up my sleeves and examined the grate. Far to the back, I felt a different sort of stone, smoother to the touch than the rough-hewn rock. I pressed all around it and, somewhat to my surprise, it yielded, pivoting stiffly on a central pin. There was a hollow behind it and I was working at full stretch now, face pressed up against the dirty bars of the hearth. My fingers recoiled from something cold and slimy but I shoved my imagination firmly to one side and forced myself to bring the sodden bundle out.

Once it had been fine, soft leather but that was a long time ago. I pulled the stinking folds apart to reveal a long white rod of some sort and a fine silver ring. I was still alone so I slipped the ring on a thong I keep round my neck for oddments and examined the rod more closely. It was patterned with six-sided shapes like a honeycomb and each had a small carving inside. There were tiny figures, monstrous faces, spider's webs, snow-flakes, all sorts of images. It was a long piece of bone, smoothed and polished with small gems set at one end. I realised this must be something to do with wizardry; they were amber, ruby, sap-phire, emerald and diamond, the jewels of elemental magic.

'Nothing in there.' Ryshad's boots crunched on the rubbish underfoot as he led the way out of the back room.

'I've got something.' I turned and held out the rod to Shiv.

'His focus!' Shiv snatched it from me and peered at it closely.

'So?' Aiten tried to see the rod but Shiv moved it away from him.

'If his focus is still here, he must be somewhere close,' Shiv muttered, speaking more to himself than to the rest of us.

'What is that?' Ryshad asked curiously.

'Sorry? Oh, this is Azazir's focus. A wizard makes one to record his magical training, it's part of the discipline. It's a way of concentrating your mind on what you are doing.' Shiv gazed round the dismal cave-house and frowned.

'Come on.' He led us outside and I shivered as the rain struck us with renewed force.

'Where are you, you old madman?' Shiv scowled, peering through the torrents of water.

'Ait, this way.' Ryshad started to move further round the lake but before he had got more than a few paces things started to change with frightening speed.

The cold became intense and the rain changed to snow, then to hail, and a driving wind roared up from nowhere to hurl it stinging into our faces. I cried out as a hailstone the size of an egg thumped into my arm and then covered my head as more came hammering down. We darted for the shelter of the cave but before we reached it the assault stopped and the air became clear again. We stood and looked uncertainly at each other, rain dripping off our hair and noses. A large bruise was growing on Ryshad's cheek.

My skin began to crawl again, but this time it was the hairs on my exposed arms rising as the air began to crackle with energy. Grey clouds above us deepened to black and billowed menacingly downwards.

'Run!' Shiv's voice galvanised us to action and we reached the cave just before the first spear of lightning blew a shower of mud and water into the air.

'Azazir!' Shiv stood in front of us and raised his arms in protest. 'If you want to continue this, show yourself. If you wish to test me, I'll accept a direct challenge – or none. Come and try my magic, if you dare!'

Ryshad and I exchanged horrified looks. Getting involved with a trial of strength between two wizards seemed like a quick way to a booking with Poldrion.

There was a pause which seemed to last for half a day, but I suppose it was really only a few breaths before the tension drained out of the air and the clouds drew back to their usual task of dropping rain by the bucketload.

I looked at Shiv and saw his gaze fixed, fascinated, on the waterfall at the far end of the lake. An eerie delight lit his eyes and his lips curved in an uncanny smile as he slowly shook his head in wonder. He had never looked so far removed from us ordinary folk and it unnerved me more than I can say.

I licked my suddenly dry lips. 'What is it, Shiv? Is there a cave behind the waterfall? Is he there?'

'Oh no,' Shiv breathed. 'Can't you see? He *is* the water-fall!'

He walked swiftly along the lake shore, leaving the rest of us gaping stupidly as we tried to make sense of what he was saying. Shaking my head, I was the first to move to follow him but none of us got too close as we drew nearer to the cataract.

I stared into the streaming flow and narrowed my eyes; was there something in there, or was I imagining it? One patch of water in the midst of the torrent seemed somehow stationary, circulating endlessly in on itself rather than racing down to vanish into the lake.

'Azazir!' Shiv sent a flash of green power into the waterfall and whatever I thought I could see vanished. I was about to turn away when a figure drew itself up on to the surface of the lake and walked across the water towards us. Initially as clear as the crystal waterfall, the man-shape grew more distinct as it approached. By the time it reached the shore, I saw an old man, naked, no more than skin and bone. His hair and beard were colourless rather than simply white, slicked down with the water; his eyes were pale, piercing and to my mind completely insane.

'Who are you?' The ancient mage's voice echoed with the murmur of the waterfall and he stared at Shiv, unblinking as a fish.

'I am Shivvalan, initiate of the Seaward Hall, adept of water and air. I serve the Great Council and, on the authority of the Archmage, I am here to ask you questions.' Shiv's tone was calm and assured.

A faint frown rippled across Azazir's face. 'Who is the Archmage now?'

'Planir the Black,' Shiv replied steadily.

Azazir's sudden cackle made us all jump. 'Planir! I remember him! A miner's son from the pits of Gidesta, coaldust in everything he owned, down to the scars on his knees and knuckles. Planir the Black! My oath, it was the other apprentices gave him that title when they saw the state of his linens!'

He stepped off the water and I was relieved to see contact with the earth granted him more solidity and colour.

'So what does his eminence want of me?' He fixed Shiv with his fishy stare.

'Let's go somewhere more comfortable.' Shiv turned towards the cave but Azazir simply squatted down in the mud.

'I'm comfortable here.'

I saw his arms and chest were patterned with what I first thought might be scales but I realised they were more of the honeycomb pictures, some tattooed, but most simply scratched into his skin and left to scar over. I shivered, not just because of the cold and the rain.

'You travelled across the ocean in your youth,' Shiv began hesitantly. 'You found the home of a race of blond men. We need to know anything you can tell us about them.'

Azazir turned over a few flat stones. 'Why should I tell you my tales? No one believed me then. Why should I help the Council now?'

He scooped up a handful of snails and popped them into his mouth, crunching them shells and all. Aiten exclaimed in revulsion and turned away.

'These people are travelling to Tormalin and Dalasor. They are robbing and killing people. We need your help.' Shiv kept his tone level and persuasive.

'Nothing to do with me.' Azazir rooted about in the dirt and quite suddenly I lost my temper with him.

'Fine. If you're not interested, after we've come all this way to see you and put up with all your stupid tricks, you can go stuff yourself. Just do me a favour and wrap up this pissing rain long enough for us to light a fire and have something warm to eat. We'll be on our way and you can play mud-castles for as long as you like.'

Azazir looked up at me and I saw the first faint shading of humanity in his cold, dead eyes. 'I suppose if you weren't stupid enough to let the magic kill you, you might be interesting enough to talk to.'

He rose and walked towards the remains of his hovel, glowering at the ruined door. He was looking more and more human the further we got from the lake, and by the time we reached the cave he was starting to shiver slightly. Once inside, the walls glowed with cold green light as the house recognised him.

'Can we light a fire?' Aiten asked hungrily; his face reflected all our relief when Azazir nodded slowly.

'The chimney's blocked.' I stopped him before he tried to get a spark to some tinder and we went outside to clear it from the top. When we came back inside, Ryshad had started a small blaze and was breaking up the remains of the door and stacking it to dry by the hearth. Azazir was wrapped in Shiv's cloak and they were deep in conversation as Shiv explained the events that had brought us here. We ate a sparse meal but I would have paid all my noble coin for a cup of hot soup by now so I wasn't complaining. Even the mule was looking more cheerful as we tethered her by the door and a pile of grass.

'So, can you tell us about your journey?' Shiv asked finally. We all looked expectantly at the old wizard.

He cupped his chin in his hands, elbows on bony knees, and stared into the past. 'I was looking for the lost colony,' he began at last. 'I was born a Tormalin and we don't forget our families, even when magebirth takes us away from our duties to our blood.'

'What was your family?' Ryshad asked, earning a stern glare from Shiv for interrupting.

'T'Aleonne.' Azazir smiled at the memory. 'I was Azazir, Esquire T'Aleonne, Scion of the Crystal Tree.'

I could see this meant something to Ryshad and Aiten but realised I'd have to wait to find out what that was.

'We were a powerful family in the Old Empire,' Azazir went on. 'We had power, wealth; we were related to half the Emperors of the House of Nemith and descended from the House of Tarl. We could have been the founders of the next dynasty at home but my ancestor was caught up in the search for lands over the ocean. When Den Fellaemion took his ships to Kel Ar'Ayen, we sailed with him and helped build the new cities of the Empire overseas. My ancestors sat at the high table with Nemith the Seafarer and sailed the oceans with him. We were going to rule the new lands. We had the right and the blood claim.'

Anger and contempt twisted the old man's face. 'Nemith the Reckless, that's what the historians call him. I suppose Nemith the Whorestruck would be too honest for those arse-lickers. When they appeared, these blond men, the Men of the Ice, the colonists sent message after message asking for help, but none ever came. Nemith the last was too busy running the Empire into the fires to satisfy his lusts for gold and whores. He would rather fight the Mountain Men in his mad ambition to conquer Gidesta. I'll wager he was glad to know he need not face a challenge from a house ten times more fit for rule than his own. My ancestors did what they could. They spent every crown they had, but it was too late. The colony was lost and the Empire fell apart and my family sank into penury while lesser houses grew fat scavenging on the ruins of Tormalin's glory.'

Azazir stared sourly into the fire, brooding on wrongs to his blood, twenty generations past.

'You knew where to find the colony?' Shiv prompted gently.

'We had our archive. My family lost much, but we kept our history, not like the scum who came after us, who had no more ancestry than a street dog.'

Azazir's tone became indignant. 'No one believed us. The other families who had sailed the oceans were long lost and their knowledge was gone. My father was called senile and confused, mocked for his learning. I bided my time while I trained, but I knew that one day I would learn how to cross the open seas like my ancestors and claim what they had bequeathed me.'

He looked around at us, eyes bright with the conviction of the completely obsessed. 'I was born to do this, to restore my family fortunes. Why else would I be a mage?'

Grievance soured his tone again. 'I thought wizards would be different, they're supposed to be open-minded but they're as rotten with jealousy as the rest of them. No one would help me, they worked against me, I'm sure of it. No one wanted me to succeed. I could have been the greatest mage of my generation if petty minds had not thwarted me. I should have been Archmage but no one had my vision.'

'But you crossed the oceans, despite them?' Shiv managed to divert Azazir from his tirade.

'I did!' His tone was triumphant. 'I spent years learning the currents of the ocean and the secrets of the deep. I spoke to the fish and the beasts of the seas and even to the dragons of the southern waters. They taught me their secrets and I finally found an apprentice with the foresight to join his power to mine and make the crossing.'

'Who was he?' Shiv asked before he could stop himself.

Azazir scowled. 'Viltred, he called himself. He came with me but lost his nerve in the end. He was as spineless as the rest when it came down to real magic. None of them have the dedication that noble blood demands of its sons.'

Shiv gave me a rueful look as we sat and waited for Azazir's spite to run its course.

'So you made the crossing?' Shiv was able to ask when Azazir finally paused for reflection.

'I did. They said it could not be done, but I proved I could master the currents and the storms.' The old wizard straightened his shoulders with pride and raised his head high.

'Kel Ar'Ayen turned out to be a land of islands, separated by channels and sand banks and circled by the deep ocean. Those men, the Ice-dwellers, the Elietimm they were called in the old tongue, they must have bred like rabbits. They were everywhere, they had scoured the land nearly barren. I could find no trace of the Tormalin cities, all was lost. All I found were these savages with their yellow heads and fertile loins.' The sadness in his tone made Azazir sound nearly human.

'How can you be sure it was Kel Ar'Ayen?' Shiv asked cautiously.

Azazir looked at him, eyes bright with anger again. 'I found relics of our lost ancestors there even if the cities had fallen. I announced myself to the ruler of the place where we landed and at first he treated us as honoured guests, as was only fitting. The wealth of his house included silver, weapons and other valuables that could only have come from the Old Empire. His ancestors must have despoiled the dead like savages.'

The old wizard drew the cloak tighter around his shoulders and gazed into the fire again. 'That dog soon showed his true blood. We were detained, forbidden to leave our rooms, if you please, and when we protested, we were threatened with chains. He should not have done that, I am not some peasant to bow to a cock on a dunghill. He had no right to detain me or to hold the property of families ten times more noble. I took those heirlooms that I could find and we left. I was not going to be insulted when I should have been ruling those lands with his kind beneath the lash to till the soil and grateful for their miserable lives.'

'You brought heirlooms home?' Ryshad's urgent question made no impression on Azazir, who continued his rambling tirade.

'It's very hard to be sure of Old Empire relics, they're almost certainly just copies,' I said loudly, blending patronising scepticism with just enough pity to annoy.

Azazir took the bait and sat upright, fixing me with a cold

green eye. 'You are an ignorant wench. What do you know of such matters?'

'Don't upset yourself, Grandad,' I soothed. 'If you want them to be Empire treasures, that's what we'll call them.'

Azazir got up from his seat with an oath and stalked into the back room.

'What do you think you're playing at?' Shiv hissed at me. I waved him to silence as Azazir came back with a cloth-wrapped bundle. Wherever he'd been keeping it was well secured, as it was dry and fragrant with preserving spices.

'If any of you have the skills to examine such valuables, you may look for yourselves,' he said loftily as he unrolled what proved to be a cloak a generation out of fashion.

I left Shiv to continue the questioning and looked eagerly at the contents. Ryshad joined me, sorting through jewellery, some weapons, a scribe's case and more of the small, personal items so similar to those Geris had disappeared with.

'What do you think?' I held a set of manicure tools up to the light.

'They're Tormalin all right, end of the Empire.' Ryshad ran his fingers over the crest on a silver goblet. 'This is D'Alsennin's insignia. That's Den Rannion and I think this must be a collateral line of Tor Priminale.'

None of that meant much to me. 'What's this about a lost colony?' I asked in an undertone.

Ryshad frowned. 'That's all a bit odd. There are stories of a colony being set up by Nemith the Seafarer, but all the histories say it was founded in Gidesta, when the House of Nemith were trying to expand the Empire northward. I've read some of the writings; whatever he's saying, it certainly wasn't on any islands. They talk about great forests, new sources for gold and copper, a river with gravel shoals full of gemstones.'

I whistled soundlessly. 'That would be worth finding again, just to break the Aldabreshin monopoly.'

'I agree.' Ryshad sat back on his heels with a sword in his hands. 'How could the histories be wrong?'

'What do they say happened to this colony?'

'It was overrun by the Mountain Men. They were far more widespread in Gidesta then and drove the Empire back. Nemith the Reckless swore vengeance and sent an army across the Dalas, but they got tied up in a campaign with no clear goals in sight. He got so obsessed with adding Gidesta to the Empire that he let the rest go rotten. The Empire fell, magic was almost lost until Trydek founded Hadrumal, and no one ever got to rule Gidesta.'

I pondered this story. 'Have you ever met any Mountain Men, Rysh?'

He shook his head. 'Not to speak of. They don't come south as a rule.'

'I know a couple of brothers who are old Mountain folk. They're pretty much pure blood, from some valley in the back of beyond, up near the Mandarkin border.'

'So?'

'They're shorter than most; the tallest is only about my height. Sorgrad is sort of sandy-haired but Sorgren is much fairer, almost as blond as these mystery men we're chasing. What if those historians of yours were confused, mixed up Nemith's war in the north with the fight for these lands overseas? If these colonies got wiped out like Azazir's saying, there can't have been many people left to put the archive right.'

Ryshad looked unconvinced. 'That's an ungodly leap in the dark, Livak. Anyway, there's no way these islands could be the colony, the description's just too different.'

I was about to answer but something in the folds of the cloak caught my eye. It was a long thin dagger, three blades joined to give vicious triangular wounds.

'What's this?' I turned it over to Ryshad, who shook his head.

'I've never seen anything like that before.'

Aiten looked up at this and came to see what we had. 'There's a nasty mind behind that,' he said admiringly.

'That's not Tormalin and I'd wager it's not Mountain Man work either.' I rummaged among the heap and came up with an oddly curved knife. 'What about this?'

Ryshad shrugged. 'Two unidentifiable weapons don't mean much.'

A sudden commotion ended our discussion.

'So all you came here for was to rob me, is that it?' Azazir sprang to his feet and glared at Shiv.

'No, what I asked was—'

'You don't believe me any more than the rest of them. All you want is to plunder the last of my fortune and enrich yourselves. I don't believe there are any strange invaders. You're lying to me, just like all the rest.'

Shiv winced as Azazir's bony hand slapped across his face. He coughed on a sudden mouthful of blood and swore as he held a hand to his gushing nose.

'I swear we are honest.' Ryshad fumbled under his shirt and drew out his medallion. 'I am a sworn man of Messire D'Olbriot and I seek vengeance on these foreigners for a grave insult to his blood. Here is his crest and my authority to use my sword in his name.'

'D'Olbriot? Of Zyoutessela? Have they risen so high?'

'Messire D'Olbriot is one of the Emperor's most trusted counsellors,' Ryshad said firmly.

'Who is Emperor now? Did Tadriol manage to hold it for his line? Who was chosen from his sons?' Azazir's anger vanished as rapidly as it had appeared.

'Tadriol, third son of Tadriol the Prudent, was chosen. There has been no acclamation as yet, so he has no title.'

I looked at Ryshad with interest. If he had advance knowledge on what the Tormalin patrons might decide to call their ruler, we could win an impressive sum in the gambling houses of places like Relshaz. I would have to discuss it with him further.

Azazir was diverted long enough for Shiv to recover his poise and, between them, they managed to calm down the outraged old lunatic. The price for his good humour was having to listen to more of his rambling spite against everyone and anyone who'd ever crossed him and I soon got tired of listening. I found his dismissal of women as only good for cooking, cleaning and sex particularly irritating and soon decided to get some sleep, if only to avoid the temptation of telling the old bigot exactly what I thought. I settled down in the luxury of dry blankets near a warm hearth and was soon away to the Shades.

The Silverlane, Inglis,
19th of Aft-Autumn

'As far as I'm concerned, my presence here is entirely unnecessary, especially two nights in a row,' Casuel grumbled, sinking deeper into the fur of his hood.

As uncaring as the stars twinkling high above in the frosty night, Darni was staring intently at a narrow alleyway some distance away from their perch on a narrow balcony.

'Oh, stop moaning, Cas, just be ready to slam a ward across that door when I tell you,' he murmured, breath rising like smoke in the crisp air.

'You seem to forget that I have several broken ribs,' Casuel hissed with some asperity.

'Pigswill,' Darni retorted briskly. 'Cracked ribs maybe; if they were broken you'd be flat on your back, crying into a cup of tahn tea. I know; I've done it.'

Obviously nothing could be gained pressing that point; Casuel sulked for a while before trying again.

'Sitting cramped up here in the freezing cold is becoming most uncomfortable. It's past midnight and I'm getting tired and hungry. And stop calling me Cas, you know full well I don't like it.'

'I'd say I've earned the right to call you what I like, if we weigh things in Raeponin's balance. You still haven't said thank you to me for rescuing you, you know.' The grin in Darni's voice annoyed Casuel still further.

'Thank you, then, I'm very grateful, I'm sure,' he said stiffly. 'That doesn't alter the fact that I shouldn't even be here; that apothecary said I could have suffered interior damage as well.'

'Nothing to worry about, those trappers knew their business,'

Darni said in a bored tone. 'You're not pissing blood, are you? Stop fussing.'

'I should be in bed.' Casuel's voice rose indignantly. 'The apothecary said—'

'Keep your voice down.' Darni turned to frown dauntingly at him, eyes shadowed and forbidding in the dim light. 'You've been strapped up, haven't you? You want to take some exercise, put some muscle on; that'll keep your ribs in one piece next time.'

'There's not going to be a next time,' Casuel muttered into his collar.

'I'd say the chances of that depend on how long you'll be working for me.' Darni's teeth flashed in a faint gleam of moonlight.

Casuel shuffled his feet, clenching his buttocks against the stomach-churning notion that he might find himself in such an appalling situation ever again. A pot chinked against the railings, one of a clutter of urns discarded up here to await spring planting.

'Sit still,' Darni growled, low-voiced.

Casuel tucked his hands inside his cloak and cautiously prodded his ribs until a sudden stab of pain made him gasp and fold his arms against the temptation to test any further.

'I still don't understand what we're doing here. Ever since yesterday evening you've been saying you'd tell me in a moment, and I'm still waiting.'

'I want a wizard whom I can trust to seal up that door,' Darni said softly, not shifting his gaze. 'These local boys and girls might suspect I'll rip their legs off and kick them to death with their own boots if they cross me. You know it for certain.' He chuckled evilly and winked at Casuel.

'I don't find that amusing,' the mage snapped crossly. 'And you still haven't told me why we're here.'

Darni moved cautiously back from the balcony rail and scrubbed a hand across his beard to remove the moisture condensing around his mouth in the chilly night.

'That shop down there, the green door you're to ward, it belongs to a money-changer. He had a visit yesterday afternoon from a blond half-measure wanting to trade a hefty sum in Lescari Marks.'

'So someone didn't check the coin down to the bottom of the bag when he got paid for something?' Casuel snorted. 'Being stupid enough to get stuck with more than a handful of lead coins is uncommon, I'll grant you, but it's hardly suspicious.'

Darni stared at him with evident puzzlement. 'Do you ever listen to anything apart from the sound of your own voice? You were there when Evern explained this old coin-clipper is an antiquarian on the side, or did I imagine it? It looks as if he's got some of those antiquities Planir's after. We know these corn-tops are after them as well. So we wait for them.'

'You know, I should have been told about this business with Tormalin artefacts.' Casuel forgot the aches in his chest as this new grievance aggravated him afresh. 'I don't know how I'm supposed to work effectively with Usara if I'm not told what's going on.'

'I'd say everyone's a cursed sight safer, the less you know,' Darni said dismissively. 'You didn't get very far with Lord Armile, did you?'

'How did you hear about that?' Casuel stared at Darni, outraged. 'You can't bespeak Usara, you haven't the talent!'

'Allin told me.' Darni leaned closer and Casuel shrank back into the folds of his cloak. 'It all sounds very interesting. She said you'd been to Hanchet as well; I wonder who you saw there.'

Words failed Casuel, to his intense frustration. He jumped at a scraping sound as the shutters on to the balcony slowly edged open.

'There's no sign of anyone so far.' Evern slid through the gap and hunkered down next to Darni. 'I think this is a waste of time.'

'The Watch commander didn't think so.' Darni's voice was curt. 'He's given us men and permission to keep a vigil for five nights if we have to.'

'You think they'll come then?' Evern persisted.

'Yes.' Darni continued to stare at the distant alley.

'And they'll lead us to whoever killed Yeniya?'

'Yes.'

'You're sure about that?'

'They'd better or they're booked for a quick trip with Poldrion.' Darni stared grimly at the doorway.

A hiss of discomfort escaped Casuel as he shifted in a vain effort to restore some feeling to his numbed behind. Evern turned to scowl at him but, before he could speak, Darni tensed like a hunting dog scenting prey.

'Cas, come here,' he ordered, picking up a dark lantern. 'Light this.'

Casuel succeeded on the second attempt, fingers shaking. 'I'm too cold,' he said unconvincingly.

Darni and Evern ignored him, intent on stealthy movements in the street below. Several men ambled casually along the gutter and, as they crossed a side alley, an uncovered head gleamed pale under the stars.

'There!' Evern pointed at a brief flash of light from a distant window. Darni grunted and drew back the slide on his own lantern in answer.

Casuel struggled to see what was going on. 'Excuse me.' He tugged at Evern's elbow in annoyance.

Evern ignored him but moved to the balcony windows. 'I'll be with the Watchmen.'

Darni nodded, not taking his eyes off the darkness of the alleyway. 'Cas, get ready,' he commanded.

'They've gone past,' Casuel objected. 'They—'

He subsided as Darni raised a warning hand. 'Just do it when I tell you.'

Casuel narrowed his lips and peered through the railings at the door, now no more than a darker patch in a grey wall. He worked a little magic to help him see more clearly, reluctantly admitting to himself that he was somewhat fearful of the consequences of failing Darni. Catching shadowy glimpses of movement, he reached desperately down to the earth that provided his powers, sending that mageborn part of himself into and along the narrow street. The touch of stone and soil steadied and reassured him, restoring his wounded confidence.

His eyes glazed as he felt his way around the stone step of the door, spreading fingers of power into the masonry around it, gathering the magic into himself, poised for Darni's command.

Steps echoed in Casuel's mind as booted feet moved cautiously across the cobbles and halted. Men stood each side of the doorway, another bent to the lock and Casuel's senses tingled oddly as the door opened with no sound of key or lockpick. High-laced boots stepped quickly inside. More followed, iron nails striking sparks from Casuel's magic, walking rapidly across the road and entering without hesitation.

'Now.' Darni gripped Casuel's arm with a vice-like hand. He slammed down the spell with a wordless exclamation, commanding the stone to obey him, to clamp itself silently to the wood of door and window shutters in a bond no ordinary force could hope to defeat. He reached deep into the fibres of the timbers to extend the spell, giving it the strength of rock.

'Come on.' Darni sprang to his feet.

'No, I'll just wait—' Casuel was unable to complete his sentence, gasping as Darni hauled him roughly through the window and down the stairs.

'Run.' Darni moved, fast and surprisingly light on his feet for one so heavy-set.

Casuel hesitated for a moment then scurried after him, even more afraid of whatever dangers might be lurking in the black alleys than he was of what might await him in the house. At very least, he could keep Darni between him and any menace in there.

Evern caught up with them and Casuel saw lamplight shining on breastplates as Watchmen flung back their cloaks to run unencumbered. A squad gathered at the doorway as hammering sounds from inside echoed around the close-packed houses.

'Cas, blanket the noise,' Darni ordered at once. Casuel fumbled with the air, a blue flash escaping him, and the noise was muffled. He heaved a sigh of relief and grimaced at the shooting pain in his side.

Darni nodded at Evern. 'See, wizards do have their uses.'

'You,' Evern pointed at a Watchman and then up to a window where a yellow gleam showed, 'tell whoever that is to go back to bed, that everything's under control.'

'Is it?' Darni demanded.

Evern lifted a silver whistle and blew a short sequence. Answering whistles came from over the rooftops and Casuel noticed another curious candle instantly snuffed in a house across the way.

'Ready,' Evern confirmed.

'Let's get in there.' Darni looked expectantly at Casuel, who laid a trembling hand on the wood of the door. The magic resonated under his fingers and the door flung itself open at his command. There was a thud as it slammed into whoever had been hammering on the inside and the Watchmen followed like an armoured stampede. Darni drew a gleaming dagger and paused on the threshold, barring Evern's grim-faced advance.

'We do this my way,' he warned before raising his arm. 'Cas, stay behind me.'

'I'll wait out here, if it's all the same to you,' Casuel said hastily.

'It's not. Get inside and give us some light,' Darni glared.

Casuel bit his lip and moved hesitantly to the rear as they entered the cramped house together. He winced at the sounds of fists smacking flesh and grunts as returning blows landed on unexpected armour. A hasty spell was sufficient to illuminate the room with bluish magelight and he hovered in the entrance, guts in turmoil at the prospect of more violence.

Now they could see what they were doing, the Watchmen moved to subdue the would-be robbers with practised brutality. Two were already pinned and being bound with cruel efficiency. Casuel exclaimed as a blond-haired youth was clubbed to the floor, blood streaming down his face. Another went down under a hail of blows, scrambling desperately under a table but dragged out to vanish under a heap of breastplates.

Casuel frowned and bit his lip; their resemblance to the man he'd encountered in Hanchet was striking, but he didn't really want to enter a conversation about that trip with Darni; well, it would hardly be relevant now, would it?

'Careful!' Darni snarled. 'We want them fit to talk.'

One at least showed he was still capable of that, albeit incomprehensibly, yelling what could only have been abuse as he fended off three Watchmen with a chair. They lunged towards him but he moved quicker, felling one with a smack in the face that brought the Watchman to his knees. A boot to the face sent the hapless trooper tumbling back into the legs of his colleagues, spitting blood and teeth, jaw hanging helplessly broken.

Darni was moving carefully round to his flank when a flash of silver startled Casuel and a throwing knife came hissing past his ear to bury itself in the pugnacious man's throat. He sank to his knees with a scream cut short into a bubbling gasp as blood gushed from his mouth. He swayed, clawing desperately at his neck, heedless of the cuts to his hands as he groped for the blade, slipping on his own blood as he tried in vain to regain his feet.

'Shit!' Darni darted forward, grabbed the man's hair from behind and cut his throat with a sudden gash reaching almost to the spine. The man collapsed like a marionette, blood spraying everywhere.

'We need them alive, you piss-head,' Darni yelled at Evern.

'Go stuff yourself, I don't take orders from you,' Evern snarled. 'Look what he did to Yarl.'

Darni did not spare the wounded Watchman a glance as a colleague supported him from the house. 'We need them alive to answer questions. Do anything like that again and I'll kill you myself.'

There was a still moment as all eyes went from Darni to Evern and back again, wondering, waiting. Casuel clamped his hands over his mouth, desperate not to vomit, panic-stricken at the thought of just how much that would hurt with cracked ribs.

Evern dropped his gaze first, turning to the wide-eyed captives. 'So, let's ask some stuffing questions,' he demanded.

Darni moved carefully around the gore and filth pooling round the corpse and came to look at the results of the Watch detail's handiwork. The youngest one was hanging limply in his bonds, only upright because of the burly Watchman propping him against the wall.

'What's your name?' Darni waved a hand in front of the white face. 'He's out on his feet, look at his eyes,' he said disgustedly. 'You lads are too heavy-handed for this work.'

The next man was eyeing him warily. When Darni spoke to him, he answered in a rapid scatter of harsh words. The other two stiffened in their captor's hands and their faces hardened. Darni silenced the man with a smack in the mouth but even Casuel could see new determination on the fair faces, eyes fixed on their fallen comrade lying in his own blood, the charnel scent filling the room.

'You can tell us what we need to know and you will be treated well,' Darni announced in a loud voice, taking a pace backwards to look at the captives in turn. 'Keep silent and it will go very hard for you indeed.'

Casuel looked at the blond men, wondering what was going to happen now and desperately hoping it wasn't going to be too messy. The stillness was broken only by a few heaving breaths, chinks and creaks from armour and leather as the Watchmen shifted their grip or their feet. The captives all looked back at Darni in defiant silence.

Darni shook his head and turned his back on them. He glanced at Evern and raised his eyebrows, tilting his head backwards a fraction. Evern frowned, then nodded minutely.

'Oh well, we'll just have to get Cas here to use that magic of his to turn their heads inside out for us,' Darni commented in a conversational tone. 'I'd rather they could keep their wits but we can cut their throats when he's done.'

Casuel opened his mouth, about to deny any such possibility when Evern trod heavily on his foot.

'That one, right-hand end.' Evern stepped up to glare at the man with a hatred that needed no translation. 'He blinked and the others both looked at him.'

'Right.' Darni stood in front of him, beard virtually brushing the shorter man's nose as he slowly wiped his bloody dagger down the man's homespun jerkin, cleaning first one side, then the other. He raised the blade and grinned viciously. 'This is going to hurt you a lot more than it's going hurt me, pal.'

'What are you going to do?' Casuel quavered, looking at the gleaming blade with sick fascination.

'Only what we need to, just enough to get our friend here to talk.' Darni slid the edge of the dagger up behind the man's ear. 'You see, there are all sorts of bits a man doesn't really need, not to talk with at any rate.'

A thin trickle of bright blood slid down the blade and Casuel ducked hastily out of the doorway, gulping down the cold night air as he sought desperately to control his stomach. A yell from inside the house startled him and he hastily wove handfuls of air to block his ears, screwing his eyes shut.

'How did I ever get dragged into all this?' he moaned wretchedly to himself. No amount of recognition or advancement could be worth this, not even a seat on the Council.

He gradually regained some measure of control and, shivering from cold and tension, leaned against the wall of the house, exhausted. Six chimes came faintly from a distant timepiece and Casuel wondered miserably if he could go home to bed. Better not, he decided reluctantly. This didn't seem like a good time to risk annoying Darni.

'All right, then?'

A hand on his shoulder nearly made Casuel piss himself but just in time he realised it was one of the Watchmen. The others followed, dragging along their doubled-over captives, boots scraping slackly on the cobbles.

'Here you are, Cas – souvenir!' Darni loomed out of the doorway and tossed a bloody gobbet of flesh at him.

Casuel skipped backwards with a squeak of revulsion, gorge rising as he saw it was a human ear. 'You didn't?' he gasped, appalled.

'No, I didn't.' Darni picked up the sorry fragment and tossed it back in the doorway. 'Sorry, couldn't resist it, not after I saw your face in there.' He grinned in high good humour.

'Then, then—' Casuel stammered as Evern emerged, followed by a Watchman carrying the last prisoner limp across his shoulder.

'We took him into the back room and told him we'd carve up his mates until he talked.' Darni wiped his hands on a gruesomely stained towel with an air of satisfaction. 'They all screamed pretty convincingly once we had their stones in the log-tongs. And we cut bits off the dead one to show him.'

'You are a nasty bastard, aren't you?' Admiration warred with awe and no little fear in Evern's tone.

'Worst in the pack,' Darni said agreeably. 'Come on, Cas, let's get home.'

Casuel stumbled after him as Darni set off through the silent streets at a cracking pace; he wanted to ask how the man could do things like that but did not dare.

A bleary-eyed maid let them into the Licorne Inn, squeaking with alarm when her candle revealed the blood on Darni.

'Don't worry, chick, it's not mine.' He smiled down at her and she backed away nervously. 'Any chance of something to eat? It's been a busy night.'

She bobbed a mute curtsey and lit a branch of candles on a nearby table before scampering off in the direction of the kitchen.

'You're hungry?' Casuel could not believe it. He hugged his aching ribs and longed for his bed. 'All right. What did you find out?'

Darni waved him to silence as the maid reappeared with a loaded tray. 'Thanks, chick. Here, buy yourself a new hair-ribbon. We'll take this upstairs.'

Casuel led the way with the candles and waited with growing annoyance as Darni chewed on a shank of cold venison, ladling on a fragrant sauce.

'Can I go to bed?' he demanded at length.

Darni shook his head. 'Sorry, I need you to bespeak Usara or Otrick,' he said thickly through a mouthful of bread.

'Not tonight!' Casuel groaned. 'What do you have to tell them anyway?'

'These flax-faces are from some islands, way out deep into

the ocean.' Darni looked up from his food. 'What do you think of that?'

Casuel sat down and reached for a cup of wine. 'I think that's very interesting,' he said at length.

'Why so?' Darni's eyes were keen.

'I've come across a few odd passages in the writings I've been studying, things which would make more sense if there were lands across the ocean.' Casuel looked round vaguely for his books.

'Well, as far as I'm concerned, the important thing is that we've got a lead on where Geris is being taken.' Darni tore at the meat with his teeth.

'Oh, yes.' Casuel looked thoughtful. 'Did they say exactly what they were doing here?'

Darni shook his head, mouth full. 'No, not beyond tracking down and stealing Tormalin antiquities. Only he called it repossessing, kept rattling on about hereditary enemies.'

'These men that Shivvalan and the girl went off with, you said they were sworn-men to Messire D'Olbriot, didn't you?' Casuel fetched a map and unrolled it, pulling the candles closer.

'So?' Darni pushed the tray aside, heaved a contented sigh and poured more wine.

'So, he has an interest. More importantly, he's a leading Prince with interests all along the ocean coast.' Casuel looked up at Darni. 'He could get us a ship.'

Darni gazed at him for a moment before laughing. Casuel gritted his teeth and wished for just one chance to wipe that patronising smile off his beard.

'No, listen.' Casuel fought to hide his exasperation; this was important. 'Of course we'll tell Usara but, whatever they say in Hadrumal, if you want to rescue this boy Geris, you'll need a ship to get you there. The faster we organise one the better.'

The greater his own chances of attracting some positive attention from Usara as well, and perhaps even Planir, he added silently to himself. He needed something to set beside his less than spectacular record thus far. The benefits of such a service to a patron like Messire D'Olbriot weren't to be scoffed at either.

Darni shook his head. 'No, I don't want to involve any more people than we absolutely have to. Anyway, we'd lose the best part of the season trailing all the way down to Zyoutessela.'

Casuel pushed the map across. 'All the Princes will be in Toremal through For-Winter; that's when all the serious politics happen, the harvest is in and the seas are too rough for trade. If we can get to Bremilayne, we can send a message by Imperial Despatch. Those boys cover fifteen leagues a day; we'd have an answer in less than four.'

Darni peered at the map, his expression still unconvinced. 'I can't see the Despatch taking a letter from me, Planir's signet or not.'

'I can send it.' Casuel held up his own seal-ring. 'My father pays enough coin-tax.'

Darni leaned back and sipped his wine. 'I keep forgetting you're Tormalin-born,' he commented, rubbing his beard, dark eyes contemplative in the candlelight.

'Messire D'Olbriot is already involved from what you were saying, with that attack on his nephew or whoever it was,' Casuel went on. 'Surely Planir would be contacting him in due course anyway, if these men of his are working with Shivvalan?'

Darni shook his head and chuckled. 'You're as obvious as the stones on a stag-hound, do you know that, Cas. All right, we'll go for it.'

Casuel paused, momentarily at a loss. 'You mean it?'

Darni drained his goblet. 'Evern's already said we won't get a ship to sail from this far north, not this late in the season. All right, you can go to bed. We'll tell Usara that's what we're doing first thing in the morning. A handful of chimes won't make much difference.'

Azazir's Lake,
20th of Aft–Autumn.

I don't know if Shiv used some magic on the fire but it was still alight when I woke the following morning, banked up with turf from Saedrin knew where. Ryshad, Shiv and Aiten were still snoring. There was no sign of Azazir. I poked the fire into life, added more wood, then took a kettle out to get some water. The mule greeted me with as much affection as she ever showed anyone and neighing from further down the shore proved to be Russet and the other horses, hobbled and making a hearty meal of the drying grass. Azazir had clearly not forgotten all he knew about normal life, for they had been unsaddled and roughly groomed, the gear dumped to one side of the doorway. I checked it quickly. Everything was intact, if covered in burrs and snagged with thorns; Azazir's magic must have caught them as they bolted terrified from the fog. That really was good news, as I'd expected them to be halfway to the Dalas by now.

I was looking uncertainly at the lake, wondering if it was safe to drink from it, when Shiv came out of the cave, yawning and stretching.

'Where's Azazir?' I asked.

Shiv shook his head. 'I don't know. He left just after midnight. I expect he's back in the water somewhere.'

He shivered and not from the cold. 'I've heard about mages becoming obsessed with their element but I don't think I'd ever really appreciated just what it meant. Do me a favour, Livak – if you ever see me going that way, stick one of your daggers in me, one of the rapid-acting ones.'

He stared at the waterfall, his expression now one of distaste.

'So what else did you learn about these Ice Men?' I asked briskly, disliking the fear in his eyes.

'What? Oh, well, I expect the Council will be able to locate these islands after further research. From what he was saying, I think we can be sure that's where these people come from. Ryshad seems to think several of the families targeted in Tormalin are descendants of those who were involved in the Seafarer's colony, so there is a link. I'm not sure where that gets us though.'

'Will the Council do something? What about Geris?'

Shiv's answer was lost in a rush of water as Azazir erupted out of the lake in front of us, naked body pale and unearthly again, eyes mad with rage.

'Did you lie to me, or are you just fools?' he hissed. 'You claim to be hunting these men, but I see they are hunting you! Do you take me for an idiot?'

'What? Show me!' Shiv wove power in an instant and the lake boiled at his feet. I ran for the cave and kicked Ryshad's feet.

'Wake up! Company is coming.'

While the others scrambled for boots, clothes and swords, I hurried back to Shiv's side. He was scrying in a pool of lake water and Azazir was sending his own shower of emerald light into the spell, enhancing the depth and clarity of the image immensely.

We gathered round and watched as the disc of enchanted water showed a group of the now familiar yellow heads bobbing through the tangling brambles and thickets of the forest.

'How did they know where we were?' I scowled down at the water. 'What if they've got Darni; would he have told them?'

Shiv shook his head. 'He'd die first.'

I could believe it; I hoped it hadn't come to that, despite my differences with Darni.

'I'd say they're hunting Azazir themselves,' Ryshad said after a few moments. 'They must be after the Tormalin valuables he stole from them.'

'Why now, after so many years?' I asked, frustrated again by all the mysteries in this business. 'Why, just when we happen to be here as well?'

No one had an answer as we watched the approaching enemies. The main difference between them and us was their direct path, unhesitating as they followed our trail. Even where we'd left no trace or where paths split, they did not even pause to debate the direction.

'More magic,' Ryshad murmured.

'Not that I can feel.' Azazir stared down at the image, face hard and suspicious. 'Let's see what they make of my defences.'

We watched as the invaders' advance was slowed by tangling briars, roots twisting up from the earth to catch feet and hooves, low branches swinging into faces and hair. There was no way to hear what they were saying but I'd bet it was profane.

'Wait a moment.' Shiv raised a hand and Azazir halted his assault. One of the Elietimm, as I suppose we could now call them, was raising a hand and seemed to be chanting something, his mouth moving in a more exaggerated fashion. My own jaw dropped open as we watched the tangle of vegetation unravel itself and part before them.

'What was that?'

Azazir looked mystified. 'It didn't touch my spell, it wasn't a counter-magic of any kind. He was dealing directly with the trees somehow.'

His expression turned to one of indignation. 'Let's see how he likes this.'

As the vicious old wizard threw more and more obstacles in the attackers' path, I studied the little figures in the image. The man with the chants was dressed just like the others, mail over black leather and sword in hand. Metal obviously posed no hindrance to his magic.

'Ryshad, what were the men you were chasing dressed like?'

'They were in local clothing mostly. We found out they were stealing it from laundries and the like.' He frowned at the scrying. 'What about the ones that went for you?'

'The ones in Inglis were in leathers like this lot but the ones in Dalasor were in old homespun and linen.'

'Are we looking at more than one group then? How do they move so fast?'

I was still trying to frame a reply when a shout from Aiten startled us away from Shiv's spell. Aiten had remained watching the lake shore while the rest of us studied the invaders.

'Over there!'

I followed his pointing arm to the far side of the water. A purposeful knot of brown-clad men was heading towards us. Their clothes were homespun but their swords were gleaming in the sunlight and surprise, surprise, so were their heads. A shout rang across the lake and I saw another group of the same make-up coming round the other way.

Azazir and Shiv dropped the scrying and turned to meet the new threat while Aiten and Ryshad moved forward together, swords drawn. Green fire from Azazir's hands flashed across the water and, where it touched two attackers, they halted, frozen, encased in thick, grey-green ice. Shiv wove air above the lake and twisted a great waterspout into the troop. Mud and debris flew into the sky and more of the Elietimm were torn limb from limb, the water blushing briefly red.

I was just starting to think it would all be over before they reached us when Shiv gave a cry. Blood spurted from a gash on his arm and he sank to his knees as some unseen force smacked into the side of his head. I approached him, but felt again the dragging, disorienting slowness that had hit me in Inglis.

'Can you tell who's doing this?' I yelled in desperation. 'Hit them with something. Stop them chanting.'

Azazir's hands wavered in the air, uncertainty on his face as he tried to decide on a target. I swore as a cut from nowhere opened up the back of my hand.

'It's the one towards the rear, with the cowl on his cloak.' I turned to see Ryshad had got a spy-glass out to study the attackers, hand steady despite blood oozing from his cuff.

The Ice Men wavered and a couple sank to their knees, water pouring unceasingly from mouths and noses. They began to choke and splutter and were soon drowning in the open air. My legs began to work again but, though Azazir had halted their magic, we still had to face their swords.

I cursed as I reached for my darts. Another fight and I wasn't wearing that bloody chainmail again. Luckily Ryshad and Aiten had shrugged on their armour and I moved behind them as I looked for targets; these men proved just as susceptible to my poisons and barely a handful of the first group survived to join direct battle.

One made the mistake of heading for Azazir and his sword passed straight through the wasted old body. I don't mean he cut him in half, I mean his sword passed straight through, the flesh opening and closing behind the blade, ripples spreading across the white skin. I could see the shock still freezing the man's face as Azazir plunged a suddenly liquid arm down his open mouth and drowned him where he stood.

I helped Shiv backwards and we watched as Ryshad and Aiten showed just what well-drilled Tormalin swordsmen can do. Evidently long used to working as a team, they protected each other as they cut into their foes with hard, economical strokes, moving in a deft and deadly pattern. Down was as good as dead and the first to reach us were coughing out the last of their lives in the mud while their mates fell back under the onslaught of two Tormalin trained warriors.

I turned to check on the other group and saw them hesitating on the far side of the outflowing river. Azazir raised a hand and their very own hailstorm came hammering down, causing visible consternation. One stepped to the lake shore and threw something into the water. Azazir cursed and ran forward, diving cleanly in, hardly raising a ripple.

The group split. Some started to run away but more headed for us. Ryshad and Aiten came forward but, before they were needed, the waters of the lake soared upwards in an explosion of white foam. Torrents crashed back down to reveal gleaming green scales, a crest of scarlet spines and the sinuous shape of a water dragon. It reared up from the lake and its long head swung from side to side, tongue flickering around gleaming white teeth the size of swords. Wings like the sails of an ocean ship unfolded to shine in the sunlight, beating the air as the dragon curved upwards to stand impossibly on the surface on the lake. A shrieking challenge echoed back from the surrounding hills; everyone froze in shocked amazement.

Aiten broke our thrall. 'Come on, it can only be an illusion. Let's hit them while they're off balance.'

He and Ryshad ran forward and Shiv and I hurried on after. I was a little more wary.

The dragon hissed and darted forwards, snapping at the man nearest the shoreline. The great vicious head shot down and the gleaming teeth shut on his head like a bear trap. It tossed the ragged remains aside like some huge ungodly cat and ripped a second victim in half, then a third.

Ryshad and Aiten skidded to a half and we watched as the remaining Men of the Ice broke and ran in total panic. I nearly joined them as the dragon turned to hiss at us, bloody rags of flesh caught between its jaws. It regarded us with blazing crimson eyes, cat-slit pupils black as pitch. We stood in a still moment of uncertainty, then it folded those massive wings and sank beneath the turbid waters of the lake.

'That's some stuffing illusion!' Ryshad said shakily.

Aiten shook his head in disbelief. 'They killed the last one of those in my grandfather's time, he skippered one of the last dragon-boats. How could it live up here? They're warm-water beasts!'

'Was that Azazir?' I asked Shiv, who was looking as staggered as the rest of us.

He frowned and dipped cautious hands into the lake, whipping them out again as if the water were scalding. 'No, he's in there, but so's the dragon. They're definitely separate.'

'But dragons never came this far north,' Aiten insisted, clinging to what he thought he knew in the face of impossibility.

'I think,' Shiv began hesitantly, 'I think Azazir created the dragon somehow. They're elemental creatures after all.'

'Forget the dragon,' Ryshad said urgently. 'We're losing our best chance yet to catch up with those killers.'

'They're running scared.' I looked at him in agreement. 'They could lead us straight to their base.'

'Shiv, keep track of them while we get the horses,' Ryshad commanded. We left him kneeling over a pool while we ran back and threw gear and harness frantically on the beasts. Russet caught the scent of my urgency and became unexpectedly skittish. I swore at him and yanked on the bridle to settle him; we could not afford delay, these men might even lead us to Geris, if he were still alive.

When we returned to Shiv, he was weaving a complex pattern of amber light among the stones. He looked up and cold triumph coloured his smile.

'I've marked their trail. They can't get away from us now.' He looked past me to Ryshad. 'You've got the relics?'

Ryshad nodded as we mounted up.

'Azazir gave you his treasures?' I asked, incredulous. 'How did you manage that?'

'I pointed out that if I were busy studying them and pursuing the Archmage's orders, I'd be unlikely to have time to tell Planir about Azazir's tinkering with the rivers and messing about with the weather up here.'

Shiv's tone was as grim as his face. 'That's before we knew about the dragon of course, I'm not sure I can keep that a secret.'

I shuddered and looked nervously at the lake. 'Let's get a move on, shall we?'

Shiv rode ahead to follow whatever magic he was using and I found myself riding next to Ryshad. I noticed something different about him.

'You're using one of those swords from Azazir?'

He grinned a little uncertainly. 'Shiv said I should. I can't say it feels comfortable having a couple of thousand Crowns' worth of somebody's heirloom strapped to my side.'

That raised my eyebrows; I knew old swords were valuable, but that valuable? I wondered if I could claim a share of its worth, like the ink-horn. Probably not, I decided regretfully.

We soon reached more normal-looking woodland and halted as Shiv raised a hand. 'We're nearly on top of them,' he said quietly. 'I'd better take some precautions.'

The air around us shimmered like sunlight reflecting off a stream.

'Are we invisible?' Aiten asked hesitantly.

Shiv shook his head. 'Not as such, just difficult to see. If we stay at a distance and keep quiet, they shouldn't notice us.'

The day passed slowly as we picked our way after our quarry. Their initial panic-stricken flight slowed after a while but they continued at a steady pace considering the terrain.

'We're heading east, aren't we?' I asked Ryshad, trying to see the sun through the golden autumn leaves of the dense forest.

'At the moment,' he agreed. 'I'd say they're heading for the coast.'

I was beginning to wonder if they were ever going to stop as dusk deepened into night and they kept up their steady march, though both moons were virtually at full dark by now. I saw Shiv signalling us to stop and breathed a quiet sigh of relief.

He dismounted and walked back. 'They're making camp in a little glade just over that rise,' he said softly. 'We'll take turns to watch them, but I don't suppose they're going anywhere.'

Ryshad looked up from hobbling his horse. 'I'll take first watch, if that's all right.'

'I'll join you.' I gave Russet a final pat and we crept towards the ridge.

Ryshad moved through the woodland debris almost as quietly as me and I grinned at him approvingly when I caught his eye. We dropped to hands and knees for the final stretch and lay down to peer over the top of the rise. It was a cool night but dry and still, we weren't uncomfortable.

Our quarry were gathered around a small fire but I frowned as we watched them.

'They're not talking to each other much, are they?' I murmured to Ryshad.

He nodded agreement. 'They seem to be doing everything by drills.'

I soon saw what he meant. Half of the ten survivors ate while the others stood guard, they took turns collecting wood and water, and even stripped off and washed in unison, five by five. It made me shiver to watch them; I'm reckoned to be a bit obsessive about personal cleanliness, but even I'd pass on an open-air wash in this weather.

The squad wrapped themselves in their blankets in unspoken agreement and two sat in silent watch, staring out into the blackness of the forest night while their companions slept. Some instinct or training woke another pair some time later and they took over the guard, all without a word.

'They've lost their officer,' Ryshad said softly after a while. 'No one's giving orders, no one's discussing what they should do. There's no one in charge.'

I bit back a curse. 'We forgot to check the bodies, didn't we?'

The dark shape of Ryshad's shoulders shrugged. 'No time, was there? I reckon the ones throwing that weird magic around are the leaders in this outfit. This mob are just following their training, they haven't got anything else to do.'

'So where does that get us?'

I saw the gleam of his teeth in the dark as he smiled. 'I'll bet they're heading straight back for whoever's in command, or the quickest way home. Want to put a few Crowns on it?'

I shook my head before remembering he probably couldn't see me. 'No wager, Rysh.'

Nothing happened that night apart from the Elietimm getting more sleep than the four of us, which I mentally added to their debt against me. I sat and ate a cold breakfast while I watched them prepare for the next day's march and the others sorted out our gear. It was almost becoming boring, until I reminded myself just what these men had been doing. I wondered how men so lacking in initiative could have made such a calculated ruin of Yenlya; if they had just been following instructions, what kind of man could give those orders? I decided I was glad that we had probably killed him at the lakeside.

That day and the next few passed in similar unremarkable fashion as we trailed the increasingly dispirited squad further and further east. Their pace slowed and their routines became ragged. The trip was no hardship, the weather was cold but sunny and dry, and then we caught the salt scent of the ocean on the breeze and I realised we were nearly at the coast.

CHAPTER EIGHT

Taken from:

D'Oxire's Precepts of Navigation
The Ocean Coast

Sailing off the ocean coast is a totally different proposition to navigating the Lescar Gulf or the Aldabreshin Archipelago. Any mariner coming to the ocean must relearn all his seamanship or perish. The weather is much harsher, storm-force winds coming straight in from the deeps. The waves are both bigger and more forceful, which means vessels are narrower, deeper in draught and carry a greater variety of sail and rigging. Galleys cannot be used with any confidence in these waters, since fierce storms can blow up from nowhere. However, given the lack of coastal routes on land and the length of time it takes to move goods via the inland routes, a mariner who learns what he must to survive will make impressive profits quickly. Those who don't bother will drown.

Ocean currents are the major danger to shipping on this coast. Any mariner venturing out of sight of land must be alert for the danger of being carried off his planned route. Obviously, it is relatively easy to tell if you are too far north or south, but this may be of little help. There are relatively few anchorages along the cliffs of the coastline and most of those that exist are limited to fishing vessels. Hiring a pilot with personal knowledge of the coastline, its hazards and landmarks and the points where fresh water can be taken on is essential. Not all harbours are easy to approach, especially with contrary winds, and many have shoals at their entrances. Experienced crews are worth paying for. Former pirates are useful crew members as long as their numbers are limited.

Being carried too far east will almost always prove fatal one way or another. The currents move fast and dead reckoning is of no use in calculating daily rate of travel. Any harbourmaster will be able to list ships lost in any season, where no trace ever returned to land, even in the winter storms. The currents that circulate south of Bremilayne are particularly rapid and can carry a vessel tens of leagues out of its way. If a ship gets favourable winds and escapes such a current, the danger then is that the prevailing winds will drive it rapidly west and wreck it on the ocean coast, especially if landfall is made at night. This happens sufficiently often that most fishing families earn extra coin recovering cargoes washed inshore.

The weather deteriorates fast once south of Zyoutessela and the currents become highly unpredictable. Attempting the passage of the Cape of Winds is for the mad or the desperate, not for serious seamen. Portage of goods across from one side of Zyoutessela to the other is less expensive than losing a ship and cargo. Most traders make portage a condition of any agreement with a mariner. No one reputable will lend money against purchase of a cargo unless portage is written into the contract.

Sholvin Cove, Gidesta,
26th of Aft-Autumn

The cries of seabirds came winging over the tree-tops, followed, after a while, by sounds of human activity – the creak and splash of vessels, hammering, snatches of voices swept towards us by the strengthening wind.

'Careful,' Shiv cautioned us as we tethered the horses and moved to the edge of the trees to look down the steep hillside.

'Sorry,' he said as I shot him an irritated look.

We saw the Elietimm heading openly into a village sitting in an irregular inlet cut deep into the rocky coastline by a vigorous river that Azazir would have been proud of. Fishing boats were tied to a jetty of dark grey stone and drying nets fluttered in the breeze, which was now bringing us a powerful mix of weed, fish innards and mud, the usual delightful scents of the seashore.

I frowned as we watched our quarry head straight for a large three-masted vessel tied up at the far end of the quay, some distance from the nearest boat where a handful of grubby locals were heaving baskets of fish out of the hold. The crew did not even look up from unloading their catch as the Elietimm passed by in two even-paced ranks, discipline having suddenly reappeared.

'Shiv, are they using magic to hide themselves too?'

'Not that I can tell.'

'But no one's even noticing them, let alone speaking to them. What's going on?'

We watched as the orderly squad marched to the side of the boat and went through what must have been some kind of identification.

'Saedrin, this is peculiar.' I ignored Shiv and Ryshad's objections and slipped carefully down the path, keeping as much cover as possible between me and the boat until I reached the muddle of stone-built cottages around the river where there were enough people to hide me.

None of them had any trouble seeing me; they looked at me as if I were a travelling fair.

'Morning.' A grizzled old gaffer, sunning himself on a bench, eyed me suspiciously.

I tried the bright smile, cute but dim, even if it didn't go with the stained cloak and breeches.

'Can you tell me anything about that boat over there?' I pointed at the three-master.

He looked at me in complete mystification. 'A boat, you say?'

'Yes, that one, the one with the green pennants,' I said slowly, wondering if I'd managed to find the village idiot at the very first attempt.

His eyes narrowed as he peered out to sea, completely ignoring the huge ship right in the centre of his field of view.

'Is it coming in then? My eyes aren't what they used to be.'

'Never mind.' I was about to move away when a woman with hands like leather and a face to match opened the door of the cottage.

'Dad? Who're you talking to?'

She looked as sharp as the gutting knife she was holding so I abandoned any attempts at charm. Women rarely fall for it, at least not from other women.

'Can you tell me if you've seen any strangers round here lately?'

The gleam in her eyes reflected the silver she saw appear smoothly between my fingers. 'Who might they be?'

'Fair, like Mountain Men. Foreign, keeping themselves to themselves.'

She eyed the coin but shook her head after a moment. 'Sorry, I've seen no one like that.'

'How about ships you don't know? Ocean-built, like a Dalasorian.'

'We've seen no one new since a trader sailed up from Inglis for the Solstice.'

Disappointment coloured her tone but there was no doubting her sincerity. I would have believed her absolutely if only I hadn't been able to see the ship with its crew busy doing whatever it is that sailors do.

'How about that boat at the end of the dock, when did they come in?'

She looked rather puzzled as she followed my gaze and her eyes lit upon the fishing boat. 'That's Machil and his brothers. They got back from the fishing grounds just after dawn.'

I pressed a couple of Marks into her slimy palm to distract her from wondering just who I might be and walked briskly back through the village with enough self-assertion to dissuade anyone who might have accosted me.

Ryshad looked none too pleased with me when I got back to the others. 'Well?'

'It's peculiar. No one seems able to see that ship or the men from it,' I said simply.

Ryshad and Aiten looked puzzled but Shiv looked dismayed.

'You're sure? Sorry, stupid question.' He was looking as if his dog had just died.

'Why's that such bad news?'

Shiv rubbed a hand over his tired face. 'One of the magic disciplines in the Old Empire was mental control: they could do this kind of thing. We've never been able to duplicate it in Hadrumal. Do you reckon they know something we don't?'

There was a moment's silence before we all turned to Shiv at the same instant.

'So, what do we do now? Can you tell if they've got Geris in there?'

'How do we get to your mate if they have him here?'

'Can you get him out the same way you got me out of the lock-up?'

'Give me a moment,' Shiv snapped. He closed his eyes and frowned as magelight of several different colours flickered round his head. 'Shit. There's something blocking me, I can't see inside the hull at all.'

I sighed. 'I think that proves a different sort of magic is at work here.'

We stood in a indecisive circle until Aiten looked down into the anchorage and cursed. 'Dast's teeth, they're not wasting any time. They're casting off.'

We watched helplessly as the crewmen loosed the lines to the quay and long oars moved the ship out of the shelter of the inlet.

'Come on,' Shiv snapped. 'We need a boat.'

Oh, wonderful; things were just getting better and better. I wondered yet again which deity I'd offended to get landed with this.

We hurried down the hill and out on to the quay, ignoring the curious stares of the locals.

'Machil!' The sun-browned sailor looked up from the deck of his boat, clearly wondering how this strange redhead knew his name.

Shiv cast his instant-respectability-for-dealing-with-peasants spell again and looked down imposingly from his horse.

'I am on urgent business for the Archmage and require a vessel. Are you for hire?'

Machil looked sadly unimpressed as he turned to continue washing fish guts and scales off his deck. 'No.'

Ryshad drew out his amulet. 'I'm working for Messire D'Olbriot of Zyoutessela. He would be extremely grateful for your co-operation.'

Machil shrugged. 'What's that to me? I'm not going that far south, not at this time of year.'

Since appealing to the man's better nature was clearly failing, it looked like my turn.

'We'll make it worth your while.' I didn't bother with a smile, just a rattle of my belt-pouch. He wasn't to know it only held Caladhrian pennies; I just hoped Shiv had collared some more of Darni's expense money before we started on this mad trip.

Like they say, you can always get to a man's hands through

his pockets. Machil put down his bucket and raised his eyebrows, still unsmiling. 'How?'

I looked at the boat, the size of its cargo and the size of the village; an idea struck me so I ran with it. 'You don't sell all that fish here, do you?'

He looked suspicious. 'What of it?'

'So, you salt it, smoke it, whatever, and take it inland? How about the mining camps? I bet they'd pay top coin for it?'

He looked at me, silent but expectant. The others had the sense to sit still and look as if they knew exactly where I was heading.

'Do you move it yourself, or sell it on to a middleman?' His eyes flickered to a long, low building on the other side of the river and I knew I had him. I gestured to our horses and the mule.

'With three saddle horses and a pack-mule, you could cut out anyone else and take the profits yourself.' Now I grinned at him and, to my relief, received a thin smile back.

'Four horses and we might have a deal. I'm not taking a horse on board ship, so you'd have to leave it here anyhow.'

No chance of keeping Russet then; it had been a slim hope at best and I stamped down hard on my regret. Whenever I caught up with Geris, he was going to pay for landing me with all this sentimental nonsense.

I looked appropriately reluctant so he'd feel he'd won a round and then nodded slowly. 'I suppose so.'

'You've got a hire, then.' He yawned. 'I'll be ready on the dusk tide. Where are we heading?'

I shot Shiv a questioning glance. He nodded almost imperceptibly and I smiled at Machil. 'We'll tell you later.'

He didn't look too happy at that, and I thought we might have trouble when we turned up that evening with as many potentially useful supplies as we'd been able to buy in such a small place. Luckily, he didn't want to display his own ignorance before his crew and he curtly beckoned us to follow him down to the cramped cabins while our gear was loaded and stowed.

'So where are we heading?' he demanded.

'Straight out to sea,' Shiv said baldly. 'I'm tracking a ship that left the coast this morning.'

Machil gaped. 'You must be joking. They'll be long gone by now.'

Shiv gestured negligently and lit the gloomy wooden walls with magelight. 'I'll be able to find them.'

'Can you guarantee the winds and currents too?' Machil asked sarcastically.

'Of course.' Shiv looked as if he were mildly surprised the fisherman bothered to ask.

'Sorry, there's no way I can take on enough stores for a voyage when I don't know how long it will take, not by this evening. Anyway, I'd need to know how long we were going to be out so I'd know how much fresh water to take.'

A hint of steel edged Shiv's voice. 'The ocean is full of fish and I can take the salt out of as much water as anyone could need.'

Machil ran a hand through his greasy hair, clearly disbelieving but, not unreasonably, reluctant to call a wizard a liar to his face. He shook his head, his face set.

'No deal; you can have your animals back. I'm not risking the open ocean for anyone.'

'How far do you usually go out?' Aiten asked mildly, knotting a piece of twine as he spoke.

'There's good fishing on some banks about three days out,' Machil said after a moment's suspicious pause, watching Aiten's hands.

'How about you take us that far? If we've found the boat we're looking for and the weather's holding, we can see about going further out then.'

'That's got to be a fair deal for five good beasts and their gear.' I thought a little reminder would do no harm.

'All right. As far as the fishing grounds, then I decide if we go any further.' Machil left without giving anyone a chance to answer and we heard him shouting orders at his brothers.

Aiten gave Shiv a grin. 'I take it you'll be able to keep the winds in the wrong direction, if we need to go on.'

'That's all very well, but I'm no sailor,' I pointed out.

'We'll still need them to run this tub; what if they won't co-operate?'

Aiten threw his knotted piece of twine to me. 'I learned more than good sea stories from my grandfather. Why do you think he decided to trust me?'

I was saved from having to find an answer by a sickening lurch of the floor.

'Looks like we're under way.' Aiten climbed up the ladder and out to the deck while I drew a deep breath and sat down, gritting my teeth.

Ryshad looked at me sympathetically. 'Are you not a good sailor?'

I looked at him and forced a smile. 'I did the trip from Relshaz to Col once and threw up all the way, and coastal waters are supposed to be calm.'

Casuel bit down on his vexation as Darni started pacing the room yet again.

'I don't see why we have to spend all morning waiting around for this man to call,' the warrior repeated irritably.

'A Tormalin Prince sees people at his convenience, not theirs,' Casuel said wearily for what felt like the fiftieth time.

'All we want is permission to ask one of his sea captains for a charter.' Darni went to look out of the window. 'I'd like to know why he decided to come here himself.'

'How should I know?' Casuel wiped his pen clean and put it away. There was clearly no point in trying to do any work. He stoppered his inks and stacked his books neatly on one side of the gleaming, if elderly table.

'I could be doing other things, making enquiries.' Darni turned to look the other way down the street, twitching the muslin drape aside. 'I don't like being ordered to waste time to suit the convenience of some nobleman who's decided to get nosy.'

'Messire D'Olbriot is one of the leading patrons of Tormalin life,' Casuel said, exasperated. 'He is used to running the affairs of his household, his wider family, his tenants and their clients and overseeing the business of about a twentieth share of the country, at last taxation. If he wants to see us, it's because he thinks this is important, not because he's just at a loose end!'

Allin looked up from the corner seat where she sat with her sewing. 'Is he like a Duke, then?'

'No, he's far more important. When he says it's about to rain, everyone from the Emperor down puts up their hood.'

Casuel looked at Allin; she was neatly turned out today, he'd made sure of that, but he was still uneasy about having her here. He had planned to send her out with a handful of copper to amuse herself shopping or something but typically it turned out to be the guest-house washday so no maid was free to accompany her on the one occasion when he would have been glad of her unquashable tendency to befriend servants at the spit of a candle.

'He's the most important man you'll ever meet, so sit still and keep quiet,' he said forbiddingly. Her Lescari accent would sound appallingly commonplace in such company.

'He might be the most important Tormalin.' Darni looked round. 'I'd say Planir's the most important man of all.'

Allin jabbed nervously at her seam with her needle. 'Will I have to meet him as well?'

'Yes, but don't worry, he's very approachable.' Darni smiled at her. 'We'll get you to Hadrumal soon, I promise. I'll introduce you to Strell, my wife. She's an alchemist so she knows lots of fire-mages; she'll soon get you fixed up.'

'Thank you for your interest, Darni, but I shall be arranging Allin's apprenticeship,' Casuel said firmly

'Surely there's no harm in looking at all the offers?' Darni tried to look innocent. 'You can help her choose the best.'

Allin looked from one to the other, faint surprise animating her round face, eyes brightening. 'I'll be able to choose?'

'I should say so.' Darni nodded. 'New fire affinities are in demand at the moment.'

'I think we should concentrate on the matter in hand,' Casuel said repressively. Allin ducked her head over her sewing again but a small, pleased smile played around the corners of her mouth.

The business of the morning carried on outside their window; visitors came and went, people came to make offerings at Ostrin's shrine and distant calls could be heard from the market beyond the wall. Allin worked her way through most of Casuel's mending and Darni must have examined every bit of the sparsely furnished waiting-room, its handful of chairs, the table and the series of engravings depicting various of Ostrin's travels in disguise to test the hospitality of kings and princes. At last they heard the jangle of the front bell.

'At last,' Darni exclaimed.

'Remember what I told you about conducting yourself properly, Allin.' Casuel smoothed his hair with nervous hands, hastily tucking books and workbasket under the settle.

The door opened and a liveried youth entered. 'Messire D'Olbriot awaits you in the reception room,' he announced in a condescending tone.

'Does he, indeed?' Darni's face hardened and Casuel stepped hurriedly forward.

'Thank you, my man.' Casuel swept past the flunkey, pressing a coin into his hand. The lackey stared at it in momentary puzzlement, so effectively disconcerted that he had to scramble to get past Allin as she trotted obediently after the wizard. Darni sauntered after them with an appreciative grin.

'Messire D'Olbriot.' The lackey bowed them all through the door, still taut with outrage. Casuel acknowledged the footman with a superior nod and then bent low in a servile obeisance before the four men seated before them on elegant chairs set around a gleaming table bearing a vase of fresh flowers.

'Messire, I have the honour to be Casuel Devoir, mage. My companions are Darni Fallion, agent to the Archmage, and Allin Mere, apprentice.'

Allin's petticoats swept the floor as she dropped so deep a curtsey she nearly fell over. Darni caught her elbow and steadied her as he inclined somewhat stiffly from the waist.

The four men rose and bowed politely in return.

'May I introduce my elder brother, the son of my first sister and my youngest son.' The Prince indicated his companions in turn, to Casuel's profound relief. He bowed again, studying this leading patron and his advisors covertly.

Messire D'Olbriot was well into his prime, a stout man with receding grey hair, a plump face and deceptively watery eyes. His brother was definitely on the verge of old age, deep wrinkles drawing his jowls into a lugubrious expression though his expression was keen. The nephew was some years the senior of the younger man, both already showing a tendency to excess weight although expensive tailoring concealed this fairly effectively thus far. As well as a considerable family resemblance, the four faces showed all the self-assurance of wealth and influence.

'Devoir?' The nephew spoke suddenly. 'Would your father be a pepper merchant in Orelwood?'

'Indeed.' Casuel forced a nervous smile; his father would not thank him for attracting this kind of notice if he made a mess of things.

'Then you are a brother of the composer, Amalin Devoir?'

All eyes turned to Casuel with new interest and he bowed low again, suffering a stab of pain from his damaged ribs, scarcely less painful than his chagrin. Would he ever meet a cultured Tormalin who recognised him for himself, not just in relation to his bumptious little brother?

'I heard your brother's new composition in Toremal; your father must be very proud,' Messire D'Olbriot said politely.

'My father is no one in particular and I have no brothers but I answer personally to the Archmage.' Formal courtesies were clearly not to Darni's taste. 'May I know your answer to our request?'

All the blue-grey eyes turned to the warrior. Messire D'Olbriot drew a parchment from one of his wide sleeves.

'Your letter came as something of a surprise,' he commented. 'I was concerned at not hearing from Ryshad for so long but I was aware his enquires could take him beyond the reach of the Despatch. Do you know where he is at present?'

'I have scryed for him and our associates.' Casuel took a cautious pace closer to Darni. 'At present all we can tell is that they are on a fishing boat, somewhere deep on the ocean.'

'Then we've seen the last of him and Aiten,' the brother observed dourly. 'We shall mourn their loss.'

'Not necessarily,' Darni replied firmly. 'Our colleague is a wizard with considerable experience and many talents over water.'

'Do you know where they are heading?' the nephew asked, leaning forward, clearly intrigued.

'A group of islands, far to the east.' Casuel tried to rub his sweating hands discreetly on the back of his jerkin.

'And what do they hope to discover there?'

'We believe this to be the home of a race of yellow-haired men who are responsible for a series of thefts and violent attacks.'

D'Olbriot looked at his relatives in turn, eyebrows raised in question; the brother shook his head, the son shrugged and the nephew pursed his lips.

'We need a boat to enable us to pursue them.' Darni's impatience was becoming evident. 'We hoped you might assist us.'

'Garbled tales for children and contrary legends speak of islands in the east,' the brother stated grimly. 'The only thing they agree on is the ill fate that befalls anyone who reaches them.'

'In that case, we can only hope Ryshad and Aiten fail to find them.' The nephew looked thoughtful. 'They are in some considerable peril whether they make a landfall or not, that much is certain.'

Messire was rereading the letter. He looked up. 'You evidently know of the crimes against our blood of which these men are guilty. What is your interest, beyond a natural love of justice?' His voice was neutral but there was a glint in his eye.

'One of our colleagues has been abducted by a group of these fair-haired men. He is a scholar working on the Archmage's business; he is also my friend.' Darni stared down at the seated Prince.

D'Olbriot returned his gaze steadily. 'What is this business of the Archmage that is so vital? Does it affect this strange blond race?'

'That is for the Archmage to tell you, should he decide you need to know.' Darni's tone was courteous enough but Casuel winced at his bald words.

'It is very important and I am sure that Planir will want your counsel, Messire. It certainly pertains to the security of Tormalin territory and—'

Darni cut him off with a glare. 'The immediate question is that of a ship. We need a vessel to enable us to find these islands, to assist our men and yours in recovering our colleague. I have heard much of the loyalty owed a sworn-man in Tormalin; I had assumed you would wish to help.'

'I don't think you can teach a D'Olbriot anything about loyalty, mage's man.' The nephew looked at Darni with faint hostility.

'I'm sure he meant no insult—' Casuel began hastily, subsiding as Messire D'Olbriot raised a hand.

'What do you think, brother?'

The older man shifted in his seat. 'Two sworn men in a fishing boat is a reconnaissance, but an ocean ship with the D'Olbriot pennant at its masthead could be construed as a hostile act. There is also the question of allowing wizards to become involved in politics. I think we would do better to leave well alone.'

'You may do as you choose but I don't believe these men are going to leave you alone,' Darni said in a level tone. 'Make your own enquiries, my lords; you will find many others have been robbed besides your nephew. I'm sure you have had reports of recent events in Inglis. When you hear Ryshad's account, I think you will find this violence is only a prelude to something worse.'

Casuel wondered how Darni could make a guess sound so convincingly like a plain statement of fact.

'We have an obligation to secure vengeance on my cousin's behalf, Father.' The son spoke up for the first time. 'And we do owe a duty of loyalty to our sworn-men.'

Messire D'Olbriot looked at him consideringly then looked back at Darni. 'You intend to go, irrespective of my decision?' It was barely a question.

'I do,' Darni replied firmly. 'I cannot abandon colleagues in such a situation. I have contacted Hadrumal and obtained the Archmage's permission.'

'You intend to tackle this unknown race on your own, do you? A man, a mage and a maid?' the brother asked with delicate sarcasm.

Darni did not rise to the bait, to Casuel's intense relief. 'No, sir, the Archmage said he would send both wizards and fighting men to support us. They will be arriving soon. I would prefer to have a ship ready and waiting, to lose as little time as possible.'

'Then you are planning an invasion,' the old man said with crisp disapproval. 'Most certainly a hostile act.'

'They committed the first aggression, in attacking people such as your nephew and in abducting my colleague.' Darni's voice was under control but icy cold. 'I would term it retribution.'

Messire D'Olbriot had rolled up the letter and was tapping it absently on his knee, looking thoughtful. 'We cannot ignore the fact that we have a personal interest in this matter, gentlemen.' He crushed the parchment in his fist. 'Associating ourselves with wizards will doubtless cause talk but I think, in this instance, we can tolerate that.'

He indicated his nephew with a wave of his hand. 'Esquire Camarl will arrange interviews with my sea captains for you. The decision whether to sail must rest with them but I will let it be known that I am supporting your endeavour.'

'That is most gracious of you, Messire—' Casuel swallowed his fulsome gratitude as the Prince continued.

'What I require from you is this.' He fixed Darni with a piercing eye. 'Planir or one of his close associates is to visit me personally to explain this business in full, no later than Winter Solstice. If there is any threat to Tormalin territory or interests, I want to know in plenty of time to take appropriate action. Do you understand me? This is a condition of my assistance, and is not open to debate. Do I have your assurance that this will be done?'

'Of course, sir.' Darni bowed politely, shooting a venomous glance at Casuel as he did so. 'I'm sure the Archmage will be only too eager to give you all the information you require.'

'I can't see any sea captain being too eager to set out into the open ocean at this season.' Messire's brother folded his arms with an air of finality.

'We'll find out who has the greatest faith in Dastennin,

won't we?' Humour enlivened Messire D'Olbriot's face for the first time, lightening the tense atmosphere. 'Perhaps you had better make some offerings at the Sea Lord's shrine, before you embark on this voyage.'

'An excellent suggestion.' Casuel forgot his ribs and bowed low, wincing as the noblemen rose, but Darni only laughed and offered his hand.

'It couldn't hurt, could it? Thank you, Messire.'

'Esquire Camarl will contact you later today and escort you to the docks.' Messire D'Olbriot paused to bow courteously to Allin, a gesture echoed by his family. She blushed scarlet and curtsied, mute with confusion, Casuel was grateful to see.

'Let me escort you.' He hovered anxiously as the noblemen made their way out. Darni looked after him with an expression of faint contempt.

'Do I have to go on a ship over the ocean?' Allin whispered, her plump face crumpling with worry.

'No, chick.' Darni put an arm round her shoulder and gave her a quick hug. 'It'll be all right. There will be some proper wizards here soon; they'll look after you.'

The Far Reaches of the Ocean,
Latter Half of Aft-Autumn

I can't say much about this particular stage of our nonsensical journey because I was soon staring continuously at the bottom of a bucket. None of the others were affected but the jokes at my expense soon faded when they realised it wasn't just a case of a few hours heaving before I'd get my sea-legs. A handful of days vanished in a blur of nauseous misery.

Ryshad came to see how I was as one dusk darkened into night. He held my head and then helped me wash my face. Lemon oil in the water cut through the sour smells of sickness and I managed to force out a thanks.

'Don't mention it.' He wiped my face gently with a clean, damp cloth. 'Here, drink some water and chew this, it might help.'

When a few cautious sips stayed down, I held out my hand. 'It's not thassin, is it?'

'No, sugared ginger.' He passed me a sticky lump. It cleaned my mouth, which was a relief, but as the motion of the ship mounted again, I was back to my bucket. I soon lost interest in everything else and couldn't even summon up the curiosity to listen when Shiv came down into the cabin. Well, not until I realised they were discussing me.

'She's not even keeping water down now,' Ryshad was saying. 'This could get serious.'

'You should have fetched me earlier,' Shiv fretted. If I hadn't been feeling so dreadful, I'd have been touched by his concern.

'You were too busy. How's the helmsman taking the magical effects?'

'Oh, he's happy enough, though I can't decide if it really

doesn't bother him, or if he's just pretending, to put his brothers on the wrong side of the river.'

Shiv came over to the bunk and put gentle hands on each side of my head. I screwed my eyes shut at a sudden emerald glimmer; it didn't help much since the light seemed to come from inside my head which was such a peculiar sensation that I quite forgot to feel sick. The glow faded and I blinked to clear the shimmering from my eyes.

'What was that?' I croaked.

'There's water inside your ears,' Shiv explained. 'It's part of why you're being so sick. What I've done should help; try to sleep now.'

I realised the racking nausea had faded. I drew a deep breath and regretted it as I felt the rawness in my throat, the ache in my stomach and shoulders and my head started to pound like Misaen's own anvil. 'You'd never think I had the southern sea-wind in my birth-runes, would you?' I managed to joke feebly.

'Here, try the ginger again.' Ryshad passed me a small grease-paper parcel. It did seem to help; I took a long drink and, when that stayed down, I had another and some dry biscuit. After a while I thought I probably could sleep. To my surprise, I woke to a bright sunny day, an empty cabin and a peaceful gut, thank Drianon.

Ryshad appeared after a while with some dry bread. 'Come out on deck,' he advised. 'You'll be better for some fresh air.'

I followed him, my legs still shaky on the steps of the ladder, but there was no return of the racking nausea so it looked like Shiv's magic had worked. I looked round the boat and saw Aiten stripped to the waist despite the cold, helping the crew with a net. Shiv was deep in discussion with the helmsman.

'Sail ho!' A shout made me look up and I saw a skinny lad clinging high up the mast as it swayed from side to side. That was almost enough to set my stomach off again so I peered out to sea.

'Where is it?' I asked Ryshad.

'You won't be able to see it from down here.' He looked back at Shiv, who nodded and I realised the boat was slowing.

'Are we stopping?' I asked nervously, looking around at featureless water in all directions.

'No, just making sure they can't see us. We'll stay far enough back so the curve of the ocean hides us.'

'Pardon?'

'The ocean is curved.' Ryshad drew an arc in the air. 'If we stay here, they can't see us. They're a taller ship, so we can follow the tops of their masts.'

I must have looked totally blank so Ryshad squatted down to draw a picture in water on the deck. 'This is the surface of the ocean; some say it's like the curve on top of a full glass, some even reckon the world is a sphere. Anyway—'

I raised a hand to silence him when he looked up. This was starting to sound like a conversation with Geris and I decided the less I knew about oceans, the happier I'd be.

'I'll take your word for it. All I want to know is when are we going to see dry land?'

No one could answer me but none of them seemed bothered. Machil agreed to continue sailing out into the open ocean once he realised how well Shiv could control the winds and water around the vessel and when it became clear he would look very foolish in front of his brothers if he backed out; Aiten had done excellent work getting them on our side. None of them asked what we were doing and since Shiv did not volunteer any information, the rest of us kept our mouths shut.

So our voyage grew longer, another ten days, another handful. My main problem was soon boredom since there was little I could do to help, even if I'd wanted to. The weather grew greyer and stormier but no one else seemed bothered so I had to believe we weren't in immediate danger of sinking; at least I didn't get seasick again. Shiv was concentrating on keeping track of the enemy ship while Ryshad and Aiten helped the crew. I managed to get a few games of runes but once I'd netted the ship's supply of crabshell betting tokens for the second time, interest waned.

By the time the moons showed us the arrival of For-Winter,

I was starting to wonder if we'd be sailing on until we saw the Elietimm ship fall off the edge of the world when the lad up the mast shocked the whole ship to silence with a cry of 'Land ho!'

Machil scrambled up the mast efficiently if gracelessly; the wind snatched away his words so we couldn't hear what he and the look-out were saying. When he came down, his face betrayed an odd mixture of wonder and fear which was reflected on his brothers' faces.

'There is land out there.' He obviously hadn't believed we would find anything.

The sailors all looked at each other; something was bothering them but no one seemed to want to be the first to say it out loud.

'Let's put on more sail and get closer then.' Aiten made a move towards the ropes but no one followed.

'I don't want to.' The watch boy, the youngest of the brothers, blushed red as he spoke out abruptly. None of the others hushed him as was their usual habit.

'Why not?' Shiv asked cautiously; I could tell he was worried by this turn of events.

The lad set his jaw. 'If there's land out this far, it must be where the shades live.'

He looked round the circle of his brothers, challenging them to contradict him. They exchanged a few impenetrable glances but none spoke.

'Shades?' I asked, fighting to keep my voice no more than mildly curious.

The lad opened his mouth but shut it again. There was an awkward silence until Machil finally spoke up.

'There are old tales about islands where the shades of the drowned live. They say if you land there, you can't leave again.' He looked at us defiantly and I realised we had a problem.

'You don't believe children's stories, surely?' Aiten's amused tone was a mistake and I saw the faces around us harden.

'There are shades, sometimes they get in the nets if you go too far beyond the northern fishing grounds.' One of the older brothers spoke up now, the sort of man you wouldn't expect to have the imagination to bake fish instead of fry it.

'I see. What do they look like?' Shiv looked entirely serious.

Machil shrugged. 'Like any other drowning, but you can tell they're shades because they don't have hardly any colour, not to their hair or skin.'

I didn't have to look at the others to know we were all thinking the same thing. Why hadn't we told these people what we were doing and asked if they knew anything useful? Whatever we said would sound like lies crafted to suit now this idea of shades and drowned men had gripped the crew.

Shiv looked at the set faces round us and made a rapid decision. He gestured to the ship's little rowing-boat. 'Put us off in that. You can go home.'

'Oh no, we need you to give us the winds we want.' Machil's tone was uncompromising.

'I can set a spell that will get you home.' Shiv matched him with a mage's authority.

Machil turned away, muttering something about a whole mule train not being worth this trip, but ordered a couple of his brothers to unlash the row-boat. I followed Shiv down to the cabin.

'Shiv,' I began nervously. 'Just what are we doing here?'

He looked up at me from a letter he was scribbling. 'Oh, I'd never intended taking this ship right inshore; I think it would be better to land unseen and spy out the land before we decide just what to do. This is a bit further out than I'd planned to take to the row-boat but that won't be a problem.'

'I'm really not sure about this.' His calm reassurance was having entirely the contradictory effect on me. 'How are we supposed to get home? This lot will be heading west before we've got the oars out.'

'I'll get us home. If we can get a boat, it'll be easy. If worst comes to worst, I can translocate us, like I did for you in Inglis.'

I gaped at him. Out through one stone wall and a half a

street away is one thing, but how many leagues was he talking about here?

A sudden thought distracted me. 'You mean you can do this sort of trip by magic? I needn't have been heaving up my guts like that after all?'

Shiv shook his head as he sealed his parchment and addressed it to Planir. 'Sorry, I can only take us somewhere I've already been. I'll be no use to anyone for a full day afterwards either. A complex spell like that really wipes you out.'

I cast about for another objection to stop Shiv abandoning this suddenly charming boat and its delightful crew in the middle of the ocean. To my intense annoyance, I couldn't come up with anything I didn't feel he would be able to set aside with similar ease. I remembered this was one of the many reasons that I preferred to avoid dealing with wizards.

So off we set in the cockleshell of a row-boat which put me entirely too close to the water for my peace of mind. At least Ryshad and Aiten were looking nervous as well, though this was down to the fact they had decided to wear their armour in case of trouble when we landed. This meant they would be able to swim with all the efficiency of a sack of corn, but at least that would mean I had company if we all went over. With Vanam about as far from any seas as you can get, I've never got round to learning to swim.

At least we didn't have to row. Shiv sat in the prow of the boat and trailed one hand in the water, intense concentration on his face. The vessel slid quietly through the waves and I soon saw the grey shapes on the horizon take on colour and substance. Dull green hills above slate-coloured shores looked completely uninviting. We glided noiselessly into a flat gravelly bay and sat for a moment looking at each other, suddenly unsure what to do next.

'Come on.' Ryshad stood up decisively and stepped out of the boat. 'We came to get some answers; let's go looking.'

Aiten insisted we pull the boat up above the tide mark and secure it with some rocks. If I had any choice, we'd be going home the fast way and Shiv could sleep it off for however long he needed. I didn't say anything though; we were all too nervous to risk starting an argument. Still, it felt good to have solid ground under my feet and a task to turn my mind to.

'So what now?' I asked as we found a sheltered hollow in the banks of shingle and cached our supplies.

'We need to get a feel for the place before we can make any plans,' Ryshad asserted. 'Let's see how these people live then perhaps we can identify who's in charge.'

This was more to my liking. 'If we can find his house, I'll go in and see what I can find out.'

'I'm not sure we should split up . . .' Shiv began uncertainly.

Ryshad waved him to silence. 'We'll discuss that when the time comes.'

He led the way through the shingle banks and we crossed an uncomfortably exposed stretch of scrubby grassland. I looked around and frowned.

'There's precious little cover here, Rysh.' The few trees were sparse, twisted down by the winds; they might just have hidden an undernourished pig.

He didn't waste time answering and led us towards a long ridge of broken rock which, while hard going, was at least more concealing. After a lengthy hike, smoke ahead indicated people. We moved with greater caution.

'Dung fires.' Aiten wrinkled his nose at the smell but I just shrugged. What else were they going to burn here?

From a vantage point high on a crag, we looked down on a small settlement clinging to the rugged shoreline. People were working all around beached boats. Something else which I couldn't make out lay immense and black on the grey sands.

Ryshad got out his spy-glass and couldn't restrain an exclamation. 'Dast's teeth; it's a fish.'

'May I?' Shiv took the glass. 'No, it's a whale, a sea-beast.'

'Like a dragon?' I asked nervously; at least I hadn't thought to worry about that while we were still on the boat.

'No. They're built like fish but they're animals, red-blooded. They suckle their young.' Shiv passed me the glass and I was able to see a group of blond-haired people busy stripping skin and flesh from a massive bloody carcass. My stomach was feeling none too strong so I turned the glass to see what else was going on. The place was a hive of activity; meat from the whale was drying on racks, children were digging for something in the sands beyond the village, adults mended nets, gutted fish, sorted out ropes.

Shiv reached for the glass and I surrendered it reluctantly.

'Azazir was right when he said they bred like rats; there must be three times the population of that place we sailed from,' I commented.

Aiten was keeping watch in the other direction. He looked back over his shoulder. 'Come and see this.'

I moved to look down the coast and saw men and women busy on rocks exposed by the low tide. Some were gathering shellfish while the rest were filling baskets with seaweed for others to lug inland, where still more people dug it into mean fields terraced into the hillsides with grey stone walls.

'They move like slaves,' Aiten murmured. 'It's like Aldabreshi.'

'Apart from not being boiling hot and covered in jungle, you mean?' I said, half-teasing.

Ryshad joined us. 'They're not slaves,' he said slowly. 'There are no overseers, are there? No one with a whip or a staff. They're doing this because they want to.'

I looked round at the barren landscape and shivered in the continuous chill breeze from the sea. 'They're doing it because if they don't they'll starve. Misaen, what a place to choose to live.'

'It's not a question of choice.' Shiv spoke up as he passed Ryshad back his spy-glass. 'There's no way off these islands without magic to beat those currents and winds.'

So we sat and watched the grim-faced people going about their tedious tasks. The arrival of a flotilla of small one-man boats created a flurry of activity and excitement; nets strung between the craft were laden with fish. A couple of larger two- and four-man vessels came in soon afterwards and I couldn't restrain an exclamation as I spotted what looked horridly like bodies strapped to them. Ryshad reassured me they were seals, explaining something similar lived off the southern Tormalin coast. I decided I disliked having my ignorance of the seas and their animals exposed every time something new appeared; I'd keep my mouth shut from now on and work things out as we went.

'Where do they get the wood for the boats?' Aiten mused to himself as we watched the craft being hauled up the shore and secured in long, low buildings.

Ryshad was peering through his eye-glass again; I decided I really must get one for myself.

'I don't think they use wood,' he said after a while, snapping the glass shut. 'Those boats are leather over bone frames.'

We looked at the carcass of the whale, now reduced to a bloody framework of massive ribs.

'They do make use of everything, don't they?' Shiv's admiration was tinged with concern and I could understand why. These people had little enough but made the best possible use of it. Poverty and ingenuity is a dangerous combination. We moved stealthily into the shelter of a grey crag. Getting out of the wind was a relief, but we were still cold; if it started to rain we would be in trouble.

Noon came and the shifting wind carried us tantalising scents of cooking fish.

'I'm starving,' Aiten groaned. 'Smell that!'

He looked at me speculatively. 'I don't suppose there's any chance you could slip down and lift us something?'

'Be serious!' I spared him a rueful look. 'I'd stick out like a eunuch in a brothel.'

'I thought the whole point about eunuchs was they didn't stick out, not in brothels or anywhere else,' Aiten grinned.

'Will you two be quiet,' Shiv hissed, unamused. I suppose this wasn't the most appropriate time for silly jokes.

'Look over there!' Ryshad was still studying the village and we all followed his gaze. A group of men had gathered on the landward side of the houses and were loading up with packs heavy enough to make me wince even at this distance.

'Let's follow them.'

We worked our way carefully round the stone ridge that encircled the little settlement, looking down on the men as they formed themselves into an orderly line and headed off up the coast. We kept roughly parallel with them and found ourselves moving into a flatter, less rocky stretch of land. Cover became more scarce again and we had to sprint from stone walls to ditches cut in the close-cropped turf, trusting Shiv's magic to keep any casual gaze sliding over us.

There was a delay when the pack-men reached a river where yet more people were out on the estuary mud, dealing with nets fixed to catch fish brought up by the tides. A cliff rose high on the far side; small figures on the ledges gathered eggs from the nests of the seabirds who were shrieking their indignation and attacking with beak and claws. I shivered. That was an ungodly climb to attempt on damp rocks, with your hands busy and birds shitting on your head.

We waited until our pack-men were safely over and then picked our way cautiously over the wet sands, Shiv leading the way to keep us out of hidden pools. My boots kept out the water, but we were all getting thoroughly cold now and I was relieved to see we were heading inland once we'd crossed the river. Hills rose to give shelter from the wind and we hit a levelled road, which made the going much easier, although we still had to dash for the cover of the scrubby bushes which lined the route whenever Shiv's questing magic revealed that somebody was approaching.

As, on one of these occasions, I sat sucking a hand skinned by the vicious thorns of the local vegetation, I noticed something on one of the stone posts that marked out the road. It was a crude device of lines and angles set in a square. Where had I seen that before? Had it been on the fishing boats? I'd thought it was just decoration.

We moved on and, now I'd noticed it, I spotted the emblem on all the road posts. I was so busy wondering what it could signify that I nearly walked straight into Ryshad's back when we turned a curve in the road to be greeted by a cluster of buildings. The pack-men had arrived at a compound. A large house stood two storeys high in the centre, surrounded by a high wall lined with smaller buildings. It was as busy as the village we had just left but the buildings were not nearly so crammed together; I guessed space meant wealth in a place where every scrap of usable land had to be tilled. A slab carved with the emblem I had been following was set high above the gate, where brown-liveried guards stood alert.

'Looks like we've found the chief's house,' I murmured, moving next to Ryshad.

He was looking around with a frown. 'It's not a very defensible site. Attackers could get on this high ground and simply pour rocks or arrows in.'

'You don't know what magic defences they've got,' Shiv remarked, a reminder I could have done without.

We crouched in a secluded niche in the rocks and watched as the pack-men waited patiently in line. None of them sat down or slipped off their packs. They just stood until they were called forward to have their loads taken by men from the compound. People were busy in stores and workshops; I heard the ringing hammer strokes of a smith at work and there was another sound that I couldn't place until I saw men dusted with flour carrying sacks out of a low building. What was missing was any sound of water or sign of smoke from a forge.

'How are they powering a mill?' I whispered to Shiv.

He frowned and closed his eyes, hands spread flat on the rocks. Confusion wrinkled his brow for a moment then he opened his eyes. 'Heat is coming up from under the ground, hot water too, and steam. They're using that somehow.'

We looked at each other, wide-eyed; these people were certainly inventive.

'Fire mountains must have made these islands,' Ryshad breathed. 'Like the Archipelago, after all.'

The line of pack-men shuffled forward and I remembered what I was supposed to be doing. A man was making some sort of list on a wooden tablet and I watched him carefully; we wanted information so I wanted to see where this particular piece was taken. Eventually he put a cover over his list and headed for the main house, entering without challenge or ceremony.

'Do you think you can get in?' Ryshad passed me the spy-glass and I studied the settlement.

'If all I have to worry about are the walls and the windows, it'll be no problem.' I turned to look at Shiv. 'Have you any way of telling if there are magic defences?'

He shrugged helplessly. 'Nothing elemental, but I can't say if there's anything aetheric.'

I frowned. 'I don't mind taking risks but I prefer to do it when I know I'm after something worth the gamble.'

Ryshad got the obvious question out just ahead of me. 'Can you tell if any of the things you had stolen are in there?'

Shiv held up a hand, already rummaging in his pack for his scrying oils. 'Let's see.'

We kept up our watch while Shiv muttered and gestured over his little silver bowl, all magelight extinguished for safety's sake. Finally he tapped me on the back and I wriggled back to his side.

'I think I've found some of Darni's books, a couple of volumes of a history by Weral Tandri. They're in a study of some kind, I think it's on the far side, top floor.'

'Any sign of Geris?' I asked, hoping vainly for a win on this first throw of the runes.

Shiv shook his head with a sigh. 'None.'

'Any areas shielded like the boat?' Ryshad looked back over his shoulder.

'No, I was able to scan the whole place.'

'Could you show me the inside? It would make things a lot quicker when I go in.'

Shiv looked reluctant. 'I'd rather not, if you think you can manage. A quick scan is one thing, a detailed survey takes time and power. Remember, those people at the lake were able to pick me out as the magic-user so I suspect they have some way of detecting elemental magic, even if we can't pick out theirs.'

Sadly, I had to agree with his reasoning.

'If there are no shields, I'd say there are less likely to be any aetheric defences,' Ryshad said encouragingly. I raised my eyebrows at him and gave him a sceptical look; it was a pretty thin argument but I suppose it was better than nothing.

So we sat and waited the rest of the day out, getting bored, cramped and hungry. Ballads about great adventures leave out an ungodly amount, I decided. When was the last time you heard a minstrel put in a few verses about his hero getting bored rigid waiting for something to happen, or soaking wet in a rainstorm? Well, at least we didn't have that problem; I nearly remarked on it to Ryshad but decided, given the luck we'd been having on this particular quest, that would just be too much like tempting Dastennin.

The Guest-house at the Shrine of Ostrin, Bremilayne, 1st of For-Winter

Darni vented his irritation on the handle and the bell jangled frantically.

'Organise some lunch,' he snapped over his shoulder at the startled acolyte opening it.

'Good afternoon, do forgive my associate.' Casuel made a hasty bow and hurried past. Esquire Camarl followed slowly, his expression thoughtful.

'What's wrong?' Allin asked, nervously clutching her sewing as the three men shed cloaks damp from the persistent drizzle.

Darni began pacing. 'We can't find a single captain willing to go out on to the ocean with us.'

Casuel looked gloomily at a list of names. 'We've been given every excuse from the state of the currents to the dangers of sea-serpents.'

'I must confess that I am getting a little tired of being treated like an idiot by men who smell of seaweed.' Camarl ran a hand through hair sticky with wind-blown salt.

'They're just cowards,' Darni spat.

'No, just cautious, and rightly so at this season.' The Esquire shook his head. 'We're asking these men to risk their lives.'

A sudden gust rattled the window as if to emphasise his point.

'We're offering them enough coin!' Darni dropped heavily into a chair. 'Why can't Messire D'Olbriot just order one of them to take us?'

'They are his clients and many sail in boats he owns.' Faint irritation tinged Camarl's voice. 'However, they make their own decisions and Messire has neither the means nor the desire to coerce them.'

'We've got to get a boat organised before Planir's people arrive.' Darni's frustration drove him to his feet once more.

Camarl looked at Casuel, who was sitting morosely hugging his ribs. 'Do you know when that is likely to be, Esquire Devoir?'

Casuel shook his head tiredly. 'They've got to get a crossing from Hadrumal and that's always a problem in winter. They should make good time overland through Lescar though – there won't be any fighting at this season.'

'The roads are going to be in an unholy state at this time of year.' Darni was not mollified. 'Shiv and the others could be in all kinds of danger.'

'Alternatively, they could be heading home as we speak.' Camarl frowned. 'I would not land on an unknown shore without means of escape. Surely they will have retained their vessel?'

'I don't suppose it's occurred to Shivvalan to worry about how to get back again,' Casuel muttered sourly.

'Do you know what's been happening to your friends?' Allin finished her neat darn and bit off her thread.

'Well, Cas? You've been scrying them, haven't you?' Darni loomed over the table at him.

'Not as such, not since the last time you asked and they were still on that boat.' There was a defensive edge to Casuel's indignation.

'Do I have to tell you to do everything?' Darni threw up his hands in disgust.

'You've been telling me to bespeak Hadrumal at every new chime,' Casuel retorted with a flash of spirit. 'How do you expect me to have the energy for anything else?'

'Show some initiative, Saedrin curse you!' Darni's voice was beginning to rise.

Allin hurried to answer a knock on the door, revealing a startled maid.

'The Esquire asked for tisanes.' She bobbed a nervous curtsey.

'Thank you.' Camarl watched the girl place her tray on the table and scurry out.

'I don't think arguing with each other is going to prove very productive,' he observed as he reached for a tisane ball, spooning tiny amounts of dried herbs from the little china bowls on the tray. He snapped the hinged sphere shut with a decisive click. 'I will talk to my uncle and see if he can think of any other mariners we could approach.'

Camarl placed the pierced silver ball in a cup and added hot water from the jug.

'I really don't want to spread our business about any more than we've had to already.' Darni reached for a cup. 'We know these blondies have been in this part of the country. Who's to say they haven't still got spies here?'

'There aren't any yellow-haired people around at the moment.' Allin spoke up unexpectedly. She put her mending aside and began to make herself a tisane.

'How do you know that?' Darni looked at her, bemused.

'I've been talking to the maids.' Allin coloured and pushed her tisane ball around in her cup. 'I said my mother's looking to buy some fair hair for a wig and I asked them to let me know if they saw anyone with really pale hair. I said it didn't matter if it was a woman or a man, because I could always ask a man if he had a sister who might be willing to sell her hair, if she was getting married soon.'

She peeped up through her eyelashes to see the three men looking at her, their expressions ranging from Casuel's irritated disbelief to Darni's surprised approval.

'I just wanted to do something to help.' Allin hid her face in her cup as she sipped her fragrant drink.

'I've spoken to you before about gossiping with maid-servants—' Casuel began heatedly.

'Oh shut up, Cas, and make yourself a tisane.' Darni shoved the tray towards him.

'What if she's put us all at risk of discovery?'

'You know, you—' Darni caught sight of Camarl's politely disdainful face and clearly changed his mind about what he was going to say. 'If you were any wetter, you'd have ducks landing on your head, Cas.'

Allin grinned and Camarl rubbed a hand over a sudden

smile. Casuel busied himself making a drink, filled with sudden longing for his mother's elegant sitting-room and her tisane tray, complete with everything to the same design, new from the silversmith last Solstice. He was accustomed to better than this collection of mismatched antiques, he sulked.

Esquire Camarl coughed. 'If there's no word of our adversaries, that's one worry that we can leave simmering on the hearth. However, I do think it would be useful to find out what Ryshad and your friends are doing. Esquire Devoir, are you sufficiently rested to attempt a "scrying", I think you called it?'

The urge to withhold his talents out of sheer spite warred with Casuel's desire to ingratiate himself with such a potentially influential gentleman.

'I can try, but I am very tired,' he said after a pause.

'Thank you.' Camarl made him a courteous bow.

Casuel rubbed his hands. 'I need a broad, flat bowl and cold water.'

Allin hurried off obediently to obtain them.

'Do you have anything that belonged to Shiv or that woman?' Casuel went on. 'I'll need something to focus on, working at this range.'

Darni rummaged in his pocket. 'Here.' He handed Casuel a rune-bone. 'I took this off Livak when some Dalasorian goatherders were getting a bit irritated with her.'

'What's he doing?' the Esquire whispered to Allin as they watched Casuel place the oddly heavy rune in the bowl and add water, leaning over and drawing a deep breath which he instantly regretted as pain lanced through his ribs.

'He's going to bring an image to the water, of the people you're looking for, a sort of reflection.' She watched closely.

'Can you do this?' Camarl was intrigued.

'Not yet. But I'll learn.' Allin's eyes were bright with determination.

'Can I have a little silence?' Casuel snapped.

Dull green light gradually gathered at the bottom of the bowl, growing brighter and clearer as it rose towards the surface of the water. It shone up into Casuel's drawn features and flickered, casting strange shadows against the bones of his face.

'That's got it!' Casuel set his jaw determinedly and hung on to the image grimly. 'They've landed, anyway.'

Darni, Allin and Camarl leaned forward eagerly to see a jumbled vista of grey rocks.

'There,' Darni said after a long moment. 'In that hollow.'

Camarl scanned the image. 'They're hiding, but I can't see from what.'

'Geris isn't with them.' Darni's voice was heavy with disappointment.

Allin drew her shawl around her shoulders unconsciously. 'It looks very gloomy and cold.'

Camarl nodded. 'The question is, are they much further north or simply a very great distance further east?'

'Show us some more, Cas,' Darni commanded.

'I'll try,' Casuel said through gritted teeth. The image moved slowly, harsh rocks, bleak screes, cowering houses defying the bitter weather, the scrying rising gradually to reveal more of the surrounding land.

'Do you suppose they're watching that?' Camarl reached to point at the house.

'Don't touch the water,' Casuel said with some effort and the Esquire pulled his hand back hurriedly.

Darni hissed through his teeth, thinking. 'I wonder if Geris is in there. If they get him out, they need a way off those rocks and soon. Saedrin, this is so frustrating!'

'Can't you bespeak them?' Allin asked hesitantly.

'Not with this spell, not at this distance,' Casuel said shortly; sweat was beginning to glisten on his forehead.

Darni muttered something under his breath but the others all caught the word 'useless'.

'Would you like to try doing this yourself?' Casuel snapped, the light of the spell flickering and dimming.

'It is certainly remarkable,' Esquire Camarl interjected smoothly. 'I've never had occasion to employ a wizard and I had no idea you could perform such wonders.'

Casuel lifted his chin and shot Darni a look of triumph

mixed with contempt before bending his will to the enchantment again.

'Can you show us any more of these islands?' Camarl began to make notes on a scrap of parchment. 'For when we land.'

'We?' Darni looked enquiringly at the young nobleman, who grinned back.

'I feel I should represent D'Olbriot interests when you reach these islands. Messire will be expecting me to look for any opportunities that the family might exploit in this situation.'

'The idea is to rescue our friends, not to make your Prince even richer,' Darni scowled.

'The two aims are not incompatible,' Camarl replied firmly. 'The seas are obviously fertile, there might be other resources.'

'Is anybody watching this?' Casuel demanded crossly and everyone hastily returned their attention to the image in the water.

An ice-clad mountain fell away, its sides hidden in snow. Below that, long screes of broken rock stretched into bleak valleys with a threadbare covering of scrub and poor grassland. A scatter of lights was virtually all that distinguished a small settlement from the surrounding rocks in the deepening dusk. Any people and animals were out of sight and out of reach of the frost already glistening on the bare faces of the cliffs. Faint tracks were scratched around a patchwork of ragged fields spreading down towards the shoreline where the cold grey sea lapped on the shingle.

'We need to get an ocean boat inshore.' Camarl frowned.

Casuel took a shaky breath and the image began to slide along the coast. An inlet appeared, a long bank of stones protecting a lagoon. A second island came into view, a headland and a narrow strait with a chain of little eyots.

'That's not rock, that's fortification.' Darni pointed. 'Look, that must be a patrol.'

They watched as a file of tiny figures crossed a causeway over the shallows and disappeared into the irregular precincts of the little watchtower.

'What are they so keen to defend, I wonder?' Camarl mused. 'Esquire Devoir, could you follow that strait?'

Casuel nodded silently, now taking short, abrupt breaths. The sea shimmered beneath the moons but the grey land was increasingly indistinct as the twilight deepened to night.

'Look, shipyards!' Camarl exclaimed suddenly.

They peered down at the enclave fenced in on the shore; timber stacked around long low huts, a square mast-pond at one end, tiny dots of light bobbing along, suggesting patrolling guards. A clutch of tall ships lay moored at the end of a long jetty.

The two men looked at each other. 'Where are they getting the wood for ships that size?' they asked at the same moment.

'Gidesta or Dalasor?' Darni's lips narrowed.

'Are they taking it or buying it?' Camarl wondered grimly. 'Just what sort of foothold have they got over here?'

The image wavered suddenly as Casuel carried it high up the side of a cliff. An ice-field shone beneath them, and a reddish glow began to lift the gloom.

'Fire-mountains!' breathed Darni.

'Like the Archipelago.' Casuel wiped his forehead with a shaking hand.

The land sped beneath them until it fell away into a boiling sea. Great gouts of steam rose from the margin of land and water as a river of fire belched molten rock into the seething foam. A little further out to sea, an islet rose up, the graceful symmetry of its cone in stark contrast to the chaos of the waters around its base.

'Misaen's still busy here,' Camarl commented.

'I can feel the power of the earth coming back to me through the spell.' Casuel blinked sweat out of his eyes. 'This place is alive with raw elements, the fire, the seas, all of it.'

Darni stared. 'Is there no way you can translocate me there, Cas?'

'You know full well a mage can only translocate to places he's physically visited,' Casuel snapped, the light of the spell beginning to dim inexorably.

'Otrick's combined it with scrying,' Darni objected, hands hovering in impotent exasperation.

Casuel shook his head and the water was suddenly empty. 'How Otrick hasn't killed himself yet is one of the great unsolved mysteries of modern magic.' He cupped trembling hands around his tisane and drained it.

'At least they look safe enough at the moment.' Darni's face was twisted with frustration.

'You're just annoyed that they got there ahead of you,' Casuel said spitefully.

'That's not the point and you know it,' Darni replied furiously.

'Surely—' Esquire Camarl raised his voice to speak over them both. 'Surely the important thing is that we find a means of making sure assistance is at hand, when they need it.'

Darni and Casuel looked at him. 'How?' they said almost in unison.

Camarl looked thoughtful. 'Just at present, I'm afraid I have no idea.'

The Islands of the Elietimm,
1st of For-Winter

Dusk drew in and the guards on the gate changed. A new contingent marched out from a barracks on the near side of the compound, which I made a note to avoid. As the officers exchanged what I guessed might be the keys, one hapless soldier was stripped, marched over to a wooden frame and tied to it. I winced as the crack of the lash echoed around the hollow in the hills. Even without Ryshad's spy-glass, we could see the blood streaming from the lad's back. When they finally left him, he was hanging with a stillness that spoke more of death than simple unconsciousness.

'And you still reckon this isn't like Aldabreshi?' Aiten muttered grimly.

Ryshad shook his head. 'Flogging troops is discipline, however brutal. Flogging the locals would be more like the repression the Warlords go in for and there's no sign of that. If you're thinking we might get help from the peasants here, I reckon you can forget it.'

This reminder of our isolation and the danger we could find ourselves in silenced us all and we sat and watched glumly as the night deepened around us. It grew colder and colder and I began to worry about how I would go about picking locks with such stiff, icy fingers.

'Here.' Shiv passed me a small rock and I was surprised to feel it warm my hands.

He grinned at me. 'I'm not much good at earth magic but I can do a few tricks.'

I peered up at the stars and moons; Halcarion's crown was in a different part of the sky but I watched it carefully. When I judged we were well after midnight, I got slowly to my feet, grimacing as I stretched the stiffness out of my limbs, and changed my boots for soft leather shoes.

'I don't want you scrying after me in case it alerts someone,' I whispered to Shiv, 'but can you enhance your hearing at all?'

He nodded and I gave a sigh of relief. 'If I get caught, I'll scream the place down. If you hear me, get me out of there fast.'

I crept carefully down the slope. Loose stones lay every-where and I didn't want to betray myself with the slightest sound. A straggle of one-roomed houses around the road and the gate provided useful cover and I made full use of the shadows as I slipped round to the side of the compound furthest from the barracks. The walls were all dry-stone-built which gave useful hand- and footholds and I was able to scale it with no real difficulty. I clung there like a squirrel for a while, peering over the top of the wall while I checked it was safe. When I was sure all was as still as a miser's strongroom, I rolled over the top and dropped silently inside. No one shouted or pointed. All the guards seemed to be gathered in the gate-house and I didn't begrudge them the warm brazier glowing through the doorway, not if it kept them inside with no night vision to speak of.

The main house had long narrow windows with what proved to be horn panes set in wooden lattice. I shook my head in wonder; this was doubtless the local standard of luxury. At home even yeomen are getting glass in their windows these days. I moved round to the side where Shiv reckoned the study was located, and tested the lowest casement. It shifted but I'd bet there were shutters on the inside, if only for the warmth in this inhospitable climate. I frowned, not keen to risk it when I had no idea what might be on the other side. Even the dimmest servant is going to make a fuss if someone comes through the window and treads on them in the middle of the night. I moved on to a side door and found a crude lock which I could probably have opened with a stiff piece of straw. Since I had my lockpicks, I was inside in a few breaths and closed it quietly behind me.

The hallway was silent and black and I moved cautiously, not wanting to bump into anything. As my eyes grew accustomed to the darkness, I could make out a few alcoves in the walls and doorways on either hand. I listened at each as I headed for the stairs but heard nothing, not even the minor noises of people sleeping. The alcoves held what the locals must have reckoned treasures, metal mostly, goblets, a ewer, some mean-looking ceramics; nothing I would have reckoned worth lifting for the price of an evening's ale back home. The only things I liked were the wall hangings, the same pattern as the gate, neatly woven in soft wool.

One door was ajar so I gave the room a cautious glance. It was stacked with chests and I found myself inside before I really stopped to think; locked boxes have that effect on me. Should I open one? I tried the lid and it proved to be unlocked so I peered inside. It was full of scrap metal, broken bits and pieces of old iron and bronze. I recalled the village, where everything was made of stone or bone, and looked at junk that would be discarded by a smith at home. Here it was stored in the leader's house like silver or gold. If this was what these people saw as wealth, they were more dangerous than I had realised, now they had some way of beating the ocean and reaching the mainland.

My feet were no longer cold and I put a cautious hand on the stone floor. Rather than striking up cold, it was warm to the touch, which puzzled me until I remembered what Shiv had said about heat from underground. I left the boxes and peered carefully up the flight of stairs where a dim glow suggested a light on the floor above. It was not shifting about so no one was carrying it, but if you leave lights burning at night, it's because you're expecting someone to be moving around at some point. I crept stealthily up the stairs and once I turned the corner was pleased to find a carpet underfoot, so much better for silence than flagstones. A small oil-lamp stood on a highly polished stone table in the middle of the hallway and I realised this was the noble's living quarters. I paused to get my bearings and headed swiftly for the study to get out of sight before someone went looking for the privy.

It was not locked either. I was struck by this man's confidence in his security, especially given the relaxed approach of the gate guards. These people just didn't expect trouble, at least not the sort we were bringing. Well, I always aim to be ready for trouble so I locked the door behind me anyway. I looked round the neat room with its stacks of documents and orderly records. This was no idle ruler, like Armile of Friern, say, grinding every mite he could out of his subjects to spend it on a pretty militia and fancy whores. The peasants tilled the land and caught the fish or whatever, but this man ran the mill, the forge, the stores and did a lot of the organisation too. Co-operation meant survival for everyone here, and that made for a still more dangerous enemy. I shivered despite the mild air as I began a thorough search of the room.

With everything else left open, whoever ran this place should have realised that locking a box is as good as sticking up a sign that it holds something important. The ancient oak chest was open in a moment and I pulled out a book. There were others. It was too dark to read anything so I reluctantly reached for a small lamp full of a fishy-smelling oil. The shutters were closed and with the lamp in the hall, there would be no betraying glow under the door so I judged the risk worth it.

In the golden glow of the lamp, I could see the books were written in Old Tormalin and halfway down I found the histories Shiv had mentioned. There was better to come but it is a real shame when something happens to prove you were right about something important and there's no one with you to look impressed when you say 'I told you so.' What got me so pleased were the notes on slips of parchment tucked between the pages. They were written in the Mountain Men alphabet, or something almost identical. Sorgrad and Sorgren had taught Halice and me the script as a means of writing letters no one else would be likely to read, so I knew I wasn't mistaken. I couldn't make much sense of the words themselves; my vocabulary in the Mountain tongue is rather specialised, dealing mainly with gambling, valuables, houses and horses. Still, I was able to see this language bore a resemblance to the Mountain tongue, about the same as, say, Dalasorian to Caladhrian, or Tormalin to Lescari; if you know one, you'll probably be able to get the gist of the other if it's spoken slowly.

Charts were folded beneath the books and I was getting more and more interested so I dug them out and spread them on the desk. As I painstakingly spelled out the names on what looked like a family tree, I recognised several of the Tormalin noble houses mentioned by Azazir and Ryshad. Some had the names of cities beside them, along with other unidentifiable notations. A couple had been crossed through and I wondered what that might signify. Other closely written sheets might have been reports. They were headed with what looked worryingly like the names of Aldabreshi Warlords. I know very little about the Archipelago; it's another place where no one uses money and, besides that, they have a nasty habit of executing uninvited travellers. Still, everybody knows the Warlords have been known to attack the Tormalin and Lescari coasts when they think they can get away with it, and I didn't like to think of these Elietimm looking for allies down there. It was starting to look as if much more trouble was brewing for Planir the Black than he knew about. I looked around for something to make copies on, but found that ink and writing materials were precious enough here to have their own little, locked cabinet which meant they would probably be missed. I didn't dare do anything which might alert anyone to my visit so I tried to commit as much as I could to memory.

There were maps on the table and I studied them too once I noticed they depicted this island, identifying the village and the road we had followed. I gave a soundless whistle as I saw the detail. Almost every rock was drawn in. The island was divided between three owners and I realised the symbol we were seeing everywhere was a badge of some kind. Each domain was marked out with its own insignia and I made a mental note of the landmarks around what seemed to be the main stronghold of each one; if we were ever going to find Geris, I'd bet it would be in one of these compounds.

I ran through the charts, careful to keep them in order, until I found one drawn to a larger scale which showed the whole island group. My heart sank as I saw the extent of the land area and roughly calculated the population, if every village had as many people as the ones we had seen. These islands might have less than half the land of Caladhria all told, but I'd bet they had more than four times the population of Ensaimin, and we're reckoned to be crowded by local standards. The only good news was the extent of division here; even sand banks in the shallower channels between the islands were marked with badges of ownership, sometimes with several. Careful erasing and redrawing of insignia was quite common on the borders of each domain and several of the changes looked recent; with land this poor, even a few plough-lengths would be a valuable addition, wouldn't they? This evidence of conflict was about the only bright spot I could see in an otherwise very gloomy vista.

This faint spark of good news was stifled when I realised the next map showed stretches of the Dalasorian and Tormalin coasts, I was able to find Inglis and, in a separate sketch, Zyoutessela. The Dalasorian coast was drawn in some detail with numerous lines and notations on the sea which I suppose would mean something to a sailor. I frowned; with Inglis the only real centre of power and organisation in those parts, it would be a tough job to drive these people out if they decided to all get on a fleet of ships and help themselves to some decent land for a change. I could only hope they had very few ships, ideally just the one we had seen. Sinking that – and any other similar vessels – would have to be a priority. Shiv would just have to get us home by magic.

The sound of a door opening down the hallway froze me to the spot. I pinched out the lamp and crouched behind the desk, sucking my scorched fingers. No one approached so I knelt down to peer through the crack of the ill-fitting door; a small child in a long night-gown was padding down the hall, trailing a woolly animal of some sort. It went into a room at the far end and I heard a low murmur of adult voices, hushing the child when a rising wail threatened. I crouched there, heart pounding, for what seemed an age. Finally I decided they must have decided to let the child join them rather than try returning it to its own bed. Still, parents of young children are notoriously light sleepers so I decided I'd better get clear as fast as possible. I replaced everything as precisely as I could and let myself out with ten times the caution I'd used before. Luckily, Drianon must have decided that particular mother deserved a decent night's rest and I was out of the house without anyone rousing.

I went over the wall at the closest point and took a long route around the back of the compound to get back to our observation point. Safety was more important than time now I had such valuable information. Ryshad was looking out for me as I crept towards the hollow in the hillside and I took the cloak he offered me gratefully, shivering in the cold breeze.

'We've got to—' I began, rummaging in my gear for something to eat.

He hushed me with a finger to my lips. 'Later. Let's move out while it's still dark.'

He turned to Shiv and Aiten and had them awake in a few moments. Aiten was none too keen to move on but Shiv agreed and we were soon creeping through the scrubby grass and bushes. We found another little hollow and Ryshad and I got our heads down while Shiv and Aiten kept watch. I woke cold and stiff in the grey light of dawn and while we ate I explained what I had found.

'I reckon we should try and find that ship, the ocean-going one, and sink it,' I concluded.

'We're going to have to cut back to get more supplies before we do anything else,' Aiten said sourly as he chewed on a strip of dried meat.

'I want to contact Planir and tell him what you've found out,' Shiv decided. 'This information's too important to wait.'

Too important to lose if we get captured, I thought grimly.

Shiv held a blue crystal between his palms, eyes closed and concentration knitting his brows.

'Can you make some kind of map for us?' Ryshad asked me thoughtfully. 'Show us where these other nobles are for a start.'

'I'll try.' I was busy scraping lines on the turf, using small stones for hills and villages, when I heard Ryshad and Aiten swear at virtually the same time although they were keeping watch in different directions.

I looked up, mouth open. 'What is it?'

'Men. A big sweep's coming this way.' Ryshad slid down the slope, face grim as he crossed to Aiten.

'Could it be a hunting party?' Aiten said hesitantly.

'What's to hunt out here, apart from us?' Ryshad gripped Shiv's shoulder and shook him. The mage swore as he opened his eyes.

'What is it?' he said crossly. 'I'd barely got the link made.'

'Trouble,' Ryshad said shortly, shouldering his pack. 'And it's on our trail.'

We crept as fast as we could along a shallow valley leading away from the pursuers. I risked one look back and could just make out two packs of dark shapes. They moved with silent purpose, fanning out as they came down the slope. Despite the dim light and the fact I would swear to any god of your choice that we'd left no trail, they were headed straight for the dell.

'Wait,' Ryshad breathed and we crouched among a scatter of boulders in the sparse stream. As we watched, the hunters attacked the hollow from all directions in a sudden rush of violence. There was little or no sound: their discipline was as hard as the rocks around us and they drew up in watchful ranks as two men began to quarter the area like hounds casting for a scent. Faint on the still, cold air, a rhythmic chant crept across the silent landscape.

'Move.' Shiv led the way and we picked our way carefully along the stream bed. Faint wisps of mist rose from the water, but I could see them swirling round Shiv's hands in a way that disclosed his control. The vapour seemed to glitter at the edges of my vision and while I guessed it was another concealment magic, I found it horribly distracting, like a tune on the edge of hearing that you can't quite make out.

'Shit, flower, watch what you're doing,' Aiten hissed as I trod on his heel. I mouthed an apology and we hurried after Ryshad and Shiv as the valley fell away to leave us

horribly exposed on a grassy plain. Ryshad looked around
in a moment's uncharacteristic indecision then led us up
a rise covered in a scrawny shrub that offered at least the
possibility of concealment. My back was starting to ache from
running in a half-crouch but we dared not get sky-lined, even
helped by Shiv's enchantment. The light was strengthening
now and the first gold of the sunrise was colouring the edges
of the hills. I wasn't scared, not as such, not quite yet, but the
knowledge that I might have reason to be seriously frightened
very soon prickled round the back of my head like an itch you
can't scratch. I certainly disliked being caught somewhere so
isolated; no quick escape over a border possible here.

'Down.' Ryshad dropped flat into the scrub and we followed
him as the tinkling of goat bells came up from the far side
of the rise. Ryshad edged forward and I had to resist the
temptation to move up too; the more movement, the more
chance someone would get spotted. I was surprised to realise
how much I trusted Ryshad but I hate leaving any part of
my fate to someone else at the best of times, and this was
promising to be one of the worst.

I managed to unclench my jaw as Ryshad beckoned us
forward and used elbows and knees to move through the
berry bushes, ignoring damage to skin and clothes. Drawing
level, I looked down to see a lad yawning and knuckling his
eyes as he drove a flock of remarkably shaggy goats out from
crude pens off to our left. A couple of women were milking
the nannies there and the lad was heading up the far slope,
so we continued our agonising crawl down to the right. The
good news proved to be that the valley's shelter had allowed
some larger trees to grow, which gave enough cover for us to
stand up; the bad news was that the only reason the goats had
left them alone was the finger-long thorns which ripped into
us at every opportunity. We ignored them and moved faster.

'Hold it.' Aiten was covering our backs and we froze at his
warning. I looked back and saw our pursuers hit the goat-pens
with the same precision they'd used earlier. The women raised
their hands to show they were unarmed but, once they had
identified themselves, they stood straight and unafraid and

there were no raised swords or voices as the leaders of the hunt came forward to question them. As the first sun lit the valley, I saw glints from gorgets of steel round the necks of these two. Not quite time for real fear, I decided, we could settle for serious apprehension for the present.

'See the insignia?' I breathed to Aiten. 'Those had better be the first ones down if this ends up in a fight.'

Shiv was considering a question from Ryshad and I turned to catch his answer.

'You're right. They must be somehow picking up on live bodies, identifying people at that, since no one's headed for the goats.'

'So we need to be among people,' Ryshad said grimly.

'That's bloody risky,' Aiten murmured dubiously but I had to agree with Ryshad; the thief who hid the pearl in a jar of sugar drops is an old story but it worked then and it works now.

I scanned my mental map of the islands and cursed myself for not taking better note of where we had been heading.

'There's a village down that way.' I led us off and we were able to make good speed but full daylight was nearly upon us and it wasn't long before we began to see where the trees were being coppiced, opening up the woods too much for comfort. We headed for the denser growth on a slope, and our pace slowed on the slippery leaf mould underfoot.

The everyday sounds of a village making an early start on the day came filtering through the leaves and we crept closer, bent like gaffers with joint evil. I saw rough stone roofs with stubby chimneys and Ryshad motioned us all to stillness as he moved ahead, step by agonisingly cautious step. I held myself motionless, forcing myself to keep my eyes fixed on Ryshad's back.

'You can't hear them behind you, you won't be able to see them, so don't risk someone spotting you moving, you daft bitch,' I scolded myself silently. 'Ait's guarding the rear, trust him.'

Shiv's face was taut and I realised the faint sound I could hear was the grinding of his teeth. The tiny noise grated on my nerves like the scrape of a knife-blade on earthenware and

I cringed where I stood. Just as I thought I could not stand it any more, Ryshad beckoned to us and I breathed a silent oath of relief.

We picked our way through tangled saplings below the lip of a rise sheltering the village, and I realised Ryshad was heading for a small cluster of standing stones. We had to do the last bit on bellies and elbows but once we were among the dolmens we had a degree of cover and, more importantly, we could see the whole village, the way we had come in and the other road out of the settlement. Aiten moved to cover the far approach and Ryshad crossed to lie next to me.

'Make out that map again, will you? They may lose us for a while but we need to have some idea of where we're going.'

'We should head for a coastal settlement when it gets dark.' Shiv said softly, looking back from his vantage post. 'If we can get hold of one of those whale-boats, I can get us home.'

'Couldn't you just magic us out of here?' I tried and failed to keep the pleading note out of my voice and scowled at the map I was scoring into the turf.

'Can you?' Aiten looked over hopefully but Shiv shook his head regretfully.

'If I'm not forced to perform any other enchantment between now and dusk, I might be able to send one of you back.'

Aiten looked uncertainly at Ryshad, who shrugged.

'It had better be Livak,' he said simply.

'No!' I exclaimed incautiously, blushing, furious with myself, as the others hushed me.

'You're the one with the information Planir needs.' Ryshad fixed me with a stern eye and I swallowed my confused objections. To be truthful, the long-held instincts of looking after myself first and last had leaped for joy at the prospect of getting out of this mess, until the more recent habits of working in this kind of team had kicked me in the shins. I couldn't decide if that made me a callous bitch or a sensible agent for Planir, but I did know I hated the idea of leaving these three behind to Poldrion only knew what fate.

Still, time enough to worry about that when Shiv was sufficiently rested to regain his strength for the magic, which was not something I was going to offer good odds on. I couldn't think what to say so I moved over to survey the village from a post between two of the great sarsens. The tension eased away but I knew relaxing would be a seriously stupid idea. I forced myself to study our surroundings in detail to keep myself alert. Script was carved into the stone and I wondered what significance this enclosure had, that such good land was set aside in such a poor country. After a while, deciphering the letters in between keeping watch on the village, I decided they were lists of names. A horrid suspicion grew in the back of my mind until it could no longer be ignored. I felt around the turf I was sitting on, running my fingers under the tangle of dead summer's growth, crawling round on hands and knees. Sure enough, I found the regular lines of cutting and lifting which gave a rounded outline about man length and half as wide. I threw up a quick prayer to Misaen, hoping no one in the village had a sudden urge to come and commune with an ancestor today.

I realised Ryshad was looking at me with open puzzlement and I crept over to sit next to him.

'We're in a grave circle,' I said quietly.

He looked momentarily perplexed and I remembered Dastennnin's followers bury at sea rather than burning their dead like the rest of us.

'Peculiar people.' His face mirrored my own distaste; Saedrin grant I die somewhere civilised and get a good hot pyre and a pretty urn in a shrine for whatever's left while I find out what the Otherworld has to offer.

CHAPTER NINE

Taken from:

The Lost Arts of Tormalin
Argulemmin of Tannath Lake

Chapter 7: Priestly Magic

Before the fall of the House of Nemith brought the Dark Genera-tions to our unhappy world, many and wondrous were the arcane arts of Tormalin priests. While we may lament the loss of much that brought grace and beauty to the life of the lost Empire, such arts as these are best left hidden in the darkness of the Chaos.

It is said they could look into a man's mind and read his very thoughts. Most could do this face to face and, more terrifying yet, some adepts could do this from rooms apart from their target, or even, hard though it is to believe, from some leagues away. What the priests could read was dependent on their level of proficiency. A novice might gain merely the sense of his victim's mood, his fear or pleasure. One more skilled could see where such emotions tended and identify the object of terror or lust. The most accomplished priests could pick the very words out of their hapless subject's heads, repeating their innermost thoughts and secrets back to them. Some could even invade a man's dreams, searching his memories and desires, leaving their victims sickened with pain.

By such methods, the power and influence of the priesthoods, particularly those of Poldrion and Raeponin, grew and spread. When brought to answer charges of some crime, few men would have the hardihood to deny evidence given by a priest and if one should, how was he to be believed, when all present knew the powers of their magics? Can we believe that this power was never abused, that false witness was never given when no man could be believed if he gainsaid a priest? Alas, the fallibility of human nature is one thing that has not changed through the generations.

Once a youth had joined the priesthoods, his life was lived at the commands of the higher priests. Dreadful oaths were sworn in rites now lost to us, doubtless so terrible that no record was kept lest it should be revealed to profane eyes. Fasting and privation was used to purify the body and to break the spirit, bending the will of the acolyte to his master's behests. Should a youth repent of his decision and seek escape, the priests had many magics with which to weave a net around him.

It is said they could speak with each other over many leagues, from shrine to shrine. That which one priest was seeing could be revealed to another, and the face of a man sought by the priesthoods could be carried across the Empire in days. His very steps could be traced by sorcery immune to the vagaries of weather or attempts at deception. The emanations left by his very spirit would be revealed by mysterious means, an unbreakable trail. Small wonder that so few left the priesthood in those days.

The sun rose higher and we saw no sign of our pursuers which was a relief and also something of a puzzle. The village buzzed with activity and luckily it seemed the demands of living in this place outweighed honouring the dead. This close to Solstice and this far north the days were shorter than any I had known. As noon came and went sooner than any of us expected, I began to wonder if we might be able to wait until the early onset of night and scout out to find a boat. We sat and watched teams of men dragging ploughs across the stubborn ground beyond the village and I realised I had seen no sign of any beast larger than the goats anywhere. No wonder the men attacking us back home had had no horses. Groups of women were gathering what I thought was spite nettle, apparently oblivious to the stinging leaves, and dumping it in a long stone trough. Others were emptying a similar trough and I observed they were retting the stuff in the same way we would treat flax to make linen at home. There was something disquieting about seeing such industry devoted to making cloth out of a weed that everyone at home simply ignored or hacked down as a nuisance.

The children, even the very smallest, were busy – cleaning, fetching, carrying. I could see down into the neat yards behind one group of houses and every one had a pen for some sort of furry animals, not coneys but something about the same size with long bushy tails. Cisterns for rainwater were being skimmed for leaves and the like and every dwelling had a small patch of yard where I could just make out older girls and boys tending greenery. These gardens backed on to each other, separated by thick walls with flues running through them, wisps of blue smoke rising into the sheltered air in lazy curls. No wager, but they weren't growing exotic flowers like the fiercely competitive botanists of Vanam. These people weren't spending fuel to flower lace-purples a week earlier than anyone else, this was survival. Thinking about Vanam brought my ever-present worry about Geris charging to the front of my mind and our inactivity began to press still more heavily on me, the more irritating because I knew it was the most sensible thing to do. The sun marched relentlessly across the sky and I began to worry that I might be forced to go back alone after all.

Ryshad must have seen me fidgeting and came to sit by me.

'Busy, aren't they?' he murmured, nodding down at the village.

'There's something odd about this place but I just can't place it,' I said as one aspect of my discomfort came into focus in my mind's eye.

We stared down the slope and now I was looking for it, I saw what was wrong. 'Where are the old people?' While we could see a few bald heads here and there, a couple of grey and white, as busy as everyone else, there was no sign of the oldsters sitting and gossiping on benches that you find in the smallest village at home.

'Come to that, where are the cripples or beggars?' Ryshad was leaning forward now, frowning as he peered at the bustle of people. He passed me his eye-glass and I saw he was right; there were no twisted limbs, no deformities from old illness or accident, no sign of the everyday bad luck that Misaen puts in so many birth runes.

'I'd say they have either very good medicine or very bad.' Activity caught my eye and I swung the glass over to a group busy around a midden. A gleam of white in the muck shone on the sun and, as I looked through the lens, I saw a spread of bones that looked horribly like a little hand. The implications of this were so unpleasant that the appearance of brown-liveried men over the far crest came as a welcome diversion.

'Don't move,' Shiv said unnecessarily. We crouched in the long grass like leverets afraid of a coursing party.

All activity stopped as the hunting party came into the centre of the village. The men with the gorgets shouted something and the villagers gathered without protest but, for all that, there was no fear in their movements, no doffing of caps and tugging of forelocks like you would expect back home. The leaders of the hunt spoke briefly and I was relieved to see shrugs and shaking heads answer them. The pack stood in a moment's tense indecision then, at a word from their handlers, they spread out among the villagers, visibly relaxing as they drank deeply from proffered jugs. I really wished they hadn't done that since I immediately developed a raging thirst.

'Time to leave,' Ryshad murmured. We crawled towards the far side of the circle, bellies flat to the grass.

Shiv was the first to reach the gap facing the coastal road we'd identified earlier, but a flare of white fire suddenly flashed between the stones. The cursed things rang like temple bells, a great hollow sound like Misaen's own hammer blow. Shiv recoiled with an oath, hugging his hands to himself, face screwed up with pain.

'Arseholes!' Aiten ran at the gap full-tilt, like a man charging down a door. He disappeared unexpectedly over the lip of the rise as no resistance halted him.

There was a moment's confusion as Ryshad and I both went to grab Shiv's shoulder and then stopped to let the other do it.

'Stuff this, move!' Shiv spat at us and we ran all together, heading down the path to find Aiten dusting himself off after what had evidently been a lengthy tumble. He was upright and conscious which is all I needed to know, so I sped past him and led the way down the coast road. The sounds of alarm and pursuit faded as the land fell away before us but I knew we had scant time before the hounds were on our trail again.

Shiv was muttering to himself as he ran. 'How did that happen? There was no magic, those stones were as dead as the bones they put under them. I know I'm not an earth adept but I can tell that much. What did they do?'

'Does it really matter?' I turned to snap at him, my voice suddenly shrill. 'Just run.'

We turned a curve in the road and I nearly ended up wearing a goat as we met another of those inconvenient herdboys. Aiten drew his sword with a steely rasp.

'It's not worth the time.'

'Forget it. They know our direction anyway.' Ryshad and I spoke in the same instant and Aiten settled for swearing at the lad and pushing him into a thorn bush.

I spared a glance for him and realised that Aiten at least had decided the time to be seriously frightened had arrived. I was hard put to disagree but I saw Shiv was still more concerned about his stinging hands and injured pride, and Ryshad was managing to keep his customary cloak of composure, even if it was a little ragged round the edges. I decided I could wait until panic struck the majority before I cast my lot.

The grass gave up in the face of shingle and sand and we came out on to an open strand where the westering sun gilded the shallows of a broad channel split with sand banks. I realised the tide was out; Dastennin must had decided to send Ryshad or Aiten a lucky throw.

'Wait a minute.' I cast around, looking vainly for any distinctive landmarks in scenery at first glance as varied as a field of corn. Curse it, I had seen a map, hadn't I? I forced myself to slow my breathing, ignore my racing heart and concentrate. In a few breaths, I had it – a line of cairns marching down from the forbidding hills opposite and a massive stone something-or-other in the middle of the channel.

'Spy-glass!' I demanded. I used it to study the stones; I was right, the insignia were different.

'If we can cross this channel, we'll be in another domain,' I said crisply.

Ryshad nodded in rapid comprehension. 'Breaking a boundary won't be something done lightly. Even if they don't turn back, they'll need to send word or get orders, surely?'

We were moving as we spoke and Shiv led the way into the icy sea water, eyes intent on staring below the surface to find us a safe path.

'Arseholes!' Aiten had regained some of his usual poise as he took up the rearguard so I stifled a smile when the others momentarily paused for a deep breath as the bitter water reached groin level.

We pressed on. I fixed my gaze between Shiv's shoulder blades, resolutely ignoring crawling fears about where I was putting my feet on the softness of the unseen seabed and how to avoid the unnerving tug of the current. The water level dropped after a while but this was not much of an improvement as the dusk breeze pressed against our wet clothes and chilled us like muslin-wrapped meat in an ice-house. Still, as soon as we were out on the sandbank, we could run, clumsy in wet boots and clothes, but at least it got our blood moving.

The clatter of boots on the shingle made me look back and realise the runes had just landed for the other hand. Shouts rang out over the water. Chief Gorget and his pal were sending men into the water after us. I hated the triumph on their faces but just as I was wishing to kick in their smirking teeth, the two in the lead disappeared, dragged below the surface without so much as time to scream.

'Shiv!' I looked round but he was not facing my way, his hands were still by his sides. His expression was one of numb horror and as I turned right around, I saw why. A spearhead of men in gleaming black leathers had crested the ridge line above us and a white-haired man with a black mace was standing at the tip. His arms were raised above his head and, as the wind shifted, it brought us a dissonant, ringing chant. Dread sank like a stone in my stomach as I recognised the studded patterns and cut of the livery from our encounter in Inglis.

Any panic in our original hunters evaporated faster than I would have believed possible. Crossbows appeared from nowhere and I flinched as quarrels hissed overhead. Some got through but more bounced uselessly off some invisible canopy. The leather-wearers replied with bows of their own and surprisingly effective slings but as a second volley came in, their reply was scattered as a handful fell to the ground like poleaxed cattle, bleeding from ears and nose.

The man with the mace shouted and some sort of acolyte

joined his chanting. Suddenly a squad of his men disappeared and yells of outrage pulled me round to see them
now somehow on the other side of the water, hacking into
the bodyguard around Junior Gorget. Several of them fell
back, faces exploding in showers of blood but Junior Gorget
was forced to do his own aetheric leap a good way back up
the hill. Now he was exposed, the mace-wielder sent blasts of
power directly at him. Earth and stones flew into the air and
one unfortunate soldier was ripped quite literally limb from
limb. White-hair seemed oblivious to the fate of his squad, who
were suddenly held motionless and cut to pieces where they
stood. Once he'd dealt with them, Chief Gorget tried to hit
back directly at his enemy with shafts of blue-white fire. These
flared wildly in all directions as they hit some kind of shield
around the mace-holder, but a few men took minor wounds
from this and, as I watched, surface cuts ripped themselves
open into ragged gashes and grazes disintegrated into open
sores. Another acolyte stepped forward and redoubled the
chant, the tone harsh and bloody.

'Move.' Sword drawn and ready, Ryshad made to lead the
way off the sandbank as troops were advancing from either
side. I hoped forlornly that they would be more interested in
killing each other than us. Perhaps moving was a mistake; we
were certainly noticed.

I screamed in sudden shock as irresistible, invisible hands
began to pull me upwards. Ryshad seized my thigh as my feet
left the ground and I grabbed wildly for his shoulders and curly
head. Blue-white sparks crackled in my hair until an icy blast of
wind knocked me back to the ground. Strange angular beams
of light darted from side to side but were foiled on each pass
by the brilliant blue fire shooting from Shiv's hands. Green
gleams around us shoved at the advancing soldiers; wherever
they stepped, the sand turned liquid and treacherous under
their boots.

'Try your old book-magic then,' I heard Shiv mutter savagely. 'I'm in my element.'

Unaccountably dizzy, I clung to Ryshad. We huddled
together as Shiv wove a shimmering net of power around

us and Aiten drew his sword with an awkward gesture of defiance. Men in brown and black were advancing from both directions now and Shiv began to throw spears of lightning at them, sending them reeling back blackened and hissing as their charred flesh landed in the water pooling on the sands. Now I heard a sob of frustration in his voice as he cursed them; for every one he blasted to Saedrin, the aetheric enchanters were simply lifting two more over the channel, abandoning attacks on each other in favour of the real prize. As I realised this, I wondered if this was the time for abject terror but somehow, it didn't seem worth it.

We stepped back, shoulder to shoulder, facing oncoming death, swords drawn and hands steady. My bowels were turning to water inside me and a scream was trying to rip its way out of my chest without bothering with my throat, but I felt a mad surge of pride.

Shiv let his assault falter for an instant and, in that breath, an invisible hand knocked him backwards, clean off his feet. As a massive purpling bruise erupted across his forehead, he landed, boneless as a rag-doll, on a scatter of rocks hidden in the shallows. Blood stained the water behind his head and I took a futile step towards him.

My feet slipped and stuck under me. I twisted wildly and was held in an impossible position, hanging in the empty air, pinned like a fish gutted and racked for smoking. I waved my arms helplessly but felt like I was struggling in thick honey; I soon lost any ability to move at all. With the last of my strength, I twisted my head to an agonising angle and was just able to catch sight of Ryshad and Aiten. They were caught like me, held motionless halfway through a step and a fall. In Aiten's case, his head was only a hand's breadth above the water; I could see the ripples of his breath on the surface.

Battle cries screamed around us as the real fight was joined, now we were immobilised. The sands blushed red and the charnel smell of slaughter mingled with the salt scent of the sea and the sweaty reek of fighting men. High above I could hear the seabirds crying, attracted to this sudden unexpected bounty. Whatever magic had numbed my feet was creeping up my body; I was feeling increasingly remote from the mayhem all around me. My mother had once dosed me with an Aldabreshi pain-syrup after the surgeon had cut an abscess from my back. I had woken fleetingly in the depths of the night to see her by my bed, face drawn tight as she watched every breath I took, but I had been as far away from her anguish then as I was now from the men dying all around me.

I vaguely realised that the screams were changing, losing any sense of words or coherence. I saw one man in brown turn on his neighbour, and abandoning his sword, attack like an animal with teeth and nails, oblivious as they drowned together in the foam of the returning tide. The wavelets rolled a corpse past me, hands clasped tight on the dagger the man had used to tear open his own throat. Two men staggered across my bleary gaze, each bleeding from a handful of mortal wounds as the madness in their eyes drove them to fight on.

Rough hands grabbed me and I was slung across some leather-clad shoulder, my head bouncing helplessly, studs scoring my cheek. In a brief moment, as I was passed to someone else, I saw the path we had come down such a little time before. Brown-liveried corpses were strewn across the shingle and Senior Gorget was moving among the wounded. Some were being helped up but, as I watched, he came to his junior and with a brief shake of his head and a dagger through the eye despatched him to whatever Otherworld awaited these people. Bloody-handed, he screamed a curse that chilled even my numbed and uncomprehending mind but the pace of the black-clad men carrying us did not so much as falter as they turned their backs on their defeated foes, kicking the enemy dead aside with evident contempt.

I realised dimly that this should frighten me but as I was trying to work out why, the creeping insensibility finally reached the last of my mind and everything dissolved into nothingness.

It was quite some time before it occurred to me that I was conscious again. I could not move, not even my eyes, and it took a while for me to realise the featureless white expanse that I could see was actually a plastered ceiling. That thought hung in my numbed mind for a while and then, as my wits slowly awoke, I began to notice tiny cracks, missing flakes, a spider's web clinging optimistically to an inaccessible corner. I was just getting interested in the textures of the ceiling when I realised my hearing was coming back, not that I'd realised I'd been missing it until then. Footsteps marched briskly along wooden boards some way off to the side and an unidentifiable clatter rose from somewhere below. As I tried to establish what these sounds might be and what they might mean, all with my wits as useless as a three-day drunk's, a tearing scream ripped through the silence, ending with shocking abruptness.

It woke me up more thoroughly than a bucket of stable water. That had been a man's scream, not a yell or shout of outrage, but a scream of pure terror. An instant of fear for my companions filled me but vanished in fear for myself; mentally, the shock of that scream might have made me jump twice my height in the air but in reality, I hadn't moved a muscle. I was as helpless as a stunned hog waiting for the butcher's knife.

In the same instant, almost as if my thought had been a signal, the door opened and I heard the soft scrape of boots on the floorboards. I strained uselessly to turn my head but need not have bothered; the newcomer came over to where I lay and leaned over me so I could see his face.

It was the white-haired man from the beach, the mace-wielder. He was handsome in an angular sort of way. The long bones of his face carried no spare flesh and the skin was drawn smoothly over them, patterned with tiny wrinkles and a few small scars. His eyes were deep brown, almost black, pitiless and as alien to me as an eagle's, dispassionately regarding its prey.

He spoke but his words meant nothing. They carried something of the cadence of Mountain speech and a few similar sounds but, at that speed, I was going to make no sense of anything. I tried uselessly to shrug, to widen my eyes, to turn down my mouth to convey my incomprehension. Unpleasant amusement flickered in my captor's eyes and he spoke a slower mouthful of gibberish with a subtly familiar metre.

Sensation returned to my arms and legs. I felt restraining bands around ankles and wrists anchoring me to a hard table. Twisted muscles all began to protest at once and I found I could now grimace with the pain. The confusion inside my skull began to subside, leaving me with a feeling like the worst morning-after head I've ever suffered and I had to concentrate on not throwing up, a bad idea when you're flat on your back. White-hair was still leaning over me, supercilious amusement in his eyes, and I decided that if I were to vomit, I'd do my best to give him a faceful.

'So, I must welcome you to my home. I hope we can reach an accommodation over your visit here.'

He was speaking Tormalin, not the Old Tongue of books and parchments that he might have pieced together from first principles, but the everyday language of that country, accent flawlessly of the south, dialect that of the merchant classes. Any ideas of petty gestures of defiance seemed suddenly ridiculous.

'You have come uninvited to my domain and I have rather strict rules about that sort of thing,' he continued pleasantly. 'However, you are from Tren Ar'Dryen and that is presently an interest of mine. Information useful to me might well count in mitigation of your offences.'

I frowned over the unfamiliar term: Tren Ar'Dryen? Mountains of the Dawn? Something like that anyway; it struck me as odd that these people should have a Tormalin name for our homelands.

He struck the table by my head with a leathern fist, mail-links scoring the woodwork. 'Please pay attention when I am speaking to you.' His mild tone contrasted chillingly with the violence of his gesture. 'You are travelling with a wizard of Hadrumal and two mercenary warriors,' he went on calmly. 'What is your purpose here?'

I could not think of any useful reply so kept silent. He raised an eyebrow in eloquent disappointment.

'You are working on a commission for Planir the Black. Please tell me what it is that you are doing for him.'

I kept as mute as a statue on a shrine.

'You made contact with the thief Azazir. What did he tell you about the lands of Kel Ar'Ayen?'

As I still made no reply, he leaned closer and I could smell soap and bath oils on him. His breath was fresh with herbs, teeth even and white as he bared them in a threatening snarl.

'If you co-operate, things will go well for you. If you resist, you will wish you were dead a thousand times before I let them release you to the shades.'

This might sound like one of the speeches every black-cloaked villain makes in a Lescari drama but he meant every word and I knew it. He must have seen the fear in my eyes; he smiled in calm satisfaction and turned away to pace the room in measured steps.

'What can you tell me of Tormalin politics at the present? Who are the patrons with real influence? Who has the Emperor's ear?'

Why ask me that? I had no idea and couldn't even have come up with a convincing lie.

'What about Planir? What are his relations with, say, the Relshazri, the Caladhrian Council, the Dukedoms?'

What did I know about any of that? Shiv and Ryshad might have some idea but—

As I framed the thought, his boots scraped to a halt. 'Good, so at least some of you have the right connections. Now, what do you know that's of use to me?'

I tried frantically to empty my mind but he crossed the room in a few swift paces and seized my head in his hands, fingers pressing into the sides of my skull, his breath warm on my face, flecks of spittle stinging my cheeks.

'Don't try and fight me, young woman. I can walk in and out of your mind as I please and take whatever I want. If you resist, you'll just get hurt, so be a good girl and keep quiet, and perhaps I won't kill you just yet.'

The words were those of a rapist and he violated my mind more thoroughly than that perverted bastard in Hawtree could ever have dishonoured my body. He tore away the self-possession of my adult life and stripped bare the child

I had been, frightened and rebellious by turns as I sought to fit in with a world where others had whole families and their own homes. He ripped through precious memories of the happy times with my father and mother, defiling them with his own derision. Having reduced me to a weeping child, he turned to my meeting with Darni and Shiv, forcing apart my memories to extract whatever knowledge he might find useful. His contempt for my ignorance of their plans seared through me but before he could pursue my activities further, I felt a salacious curiosity invade me. The intimacies of my time with Geris and others were laid open before him and I felt his lascivious amusement penetrating my mind; I felt soiled beyond belief. My very mind throbbed, bruised, swollen and torn, but he continued to force his questing intellect into me until I feared for my reason. It felt like an ordeal of hours though I doubt it took more than a few breaths.

The shock of release was almost a physical pain. He stood over me for a long moment, a repellent satisfaction and satiation curving his thin lips. I clamped my teeth together to stop myself begging, pleading with him not to hurt me, not to do it again, but I could not control the tears that ran down to dampen my hair.

He leaned down again and whispered confidingly into my ear like a lover, 'There's more I want from you. Now decide if you're going to tell me yourself. Or whether you want me to try and find it inside your head again. Or whether you'd prefer I turn you over to my guards.' He pinched my nipple in merciless fingers and I gasped at the pain. 'There are more ways than one to make people talk and, believe me, I use them all.'

He left abruptly and I heard the door lock behind him. As it did, the bands around my wrists and ankles loosened but when I sat up to rub them, there was no sign of any restraints. I stared at the red lines denting my flesh where I had struggled against the cuffs and shook as I realised they had existed only in my mind. I fought to control the hysteria that threatened to overwhelm me, my breath coming in shallow pants like a cornered animal's. I don't know how long I sat there, incapable and incoherent, but eventually the fear receded and I began to hear more normal sounds filtering up to the narrow window of my prison. My grandmother had called it bloody-mindedness, my mother had called me stubborn; I have always preferred to call it strength of character. Call it what you will, it finally dragged me to my feet.

I crossed the room and examined the casement; it was barred, so offered no chance of escape, and in any case, I saw I was four storeys high up a sheer stone wall. It belonged to a keep, square and defensible from the little I could see by craning my neck all around. Below I saw a busy court surrounded by a thick wall, topped with parapet and walkway and regular patrols. We seemed to be some distance from any high ground and on a rise as well; whoever had built this place understood defensive architecture.

I tapped the glass of the window. It was uneven and discoloured but it was still glass. Down beyond the compound, I could see the glitter of a whole range of hot-houses on the south-facing wall of an enclosed garden. I looked down on the patrolling guards, their black leather uniforms patterned with gleaming metal studs. By local standards of wealth, we had to be in the hands of a major player, which had all sorts of worrying implications – for us in our present predicament and later for Planir and whoever else might find these jokers on their seafront. I realised the tall things sticking up in the distance beyond the wall were ships' masts, ocean-going vessels at that.

So what now? I have to admit I came very close to simply giving up. Part of me could see no way out beyond telling what little I knew and hoping for a quick death. Luckily, the larger part of me is the gambler, and that kept reminding me that the game's never over until all the runes have come up. Eventually, I began to listen. I crossed to the door and examined the lock. It was good, but I reckoned I was better. I was about to detach the tongue of my belt buckle, which is incidentally a useful lockpick, when I heard footsteps in the corridor. I shifted quickly to a corner and sank down, head on knees and buried in my arms, the very picture of fear and despair.

It was not the white-haired man but six of his foot soldiers;

this had to be an attempt to intimidate me since they surely knew by now that I worked no magic. I looked suitably terrified and believe me, it was not hard. They marched me off wordlessly and we descended three flights of stairs and featureless, whitewashed corridors. In another empty room, an older man in a soft grey robe stripped me with impersonal disdain and gave me the most thorough search I've ever had. The guards watched with occasional flickers of lust but, by this stage, rape was way down the list of things I feared. I'd had worse when I'd had to visit an apothecary with a dose of the itch in my younger, more ignorant days. When the man with the grey robe and the cold fingers was done, they marched me down more stairs and threw me into what had to be the cleanest dungeon I'd ever seen. I was not chained; I suppose they figured a stark naked redhead would be easy to spot if I were to escape.

I examined my new prison. It was about the size of a stablebox and lit by a grating open to a yard high up on one wall. The walls were whitewashed and scrubbed but stains told me blood had once pooled on the floor and spattered the walls. There was a pail, a pitcher of clean water with bone beakers and a basket of bread and cheese; I noticed the floor was warm here too. I had just decided I would have preferred a filthy Lescari forgettory where I might have stood some chance of being overlooked and thus escaping when the door opened again and Aiten was shoved through it.

'Livak!' He was as naked as me but in a far worse state; fresh bruises and cuts stood out starkly across his pale skin and one eye was purpling. He stared at me and the unbruised bits of his face went scarlet as he waved his hands vainly in an attempt to cover himself.

'Don't be a fool,' I snapped. 'Neither of us has anything new to hide, have we?' It was typical that Aiten, with his store of dubious jokes, would turn out to be as shy of naked flesh as a virgin sworn to Halcarion.

The awkward moment was broken by Ryshad's arrival; he had no obvious injuries but looked shaken and drawn and, like me, behaved as if lack of clothes was the last thing he had to be concerned about. His few days' growth of beard stood out starkly black against his unaccustomed pallor.

'Are you all right?' Aiten and I spoke as one as we helped Ryshad to sit down. I fetched him a cup of water but he waved it away with an expression of nausea.

'Have you been taken to that white-haired man yet?' he asked us shakily, unable to meet our concerned glances.

'I have.' I could not keep the tremble out of my voice. Ryshad looked up and I saw my own ordeal reflected in his warm amber eyes. That instant of shared experience somehow gave me strength and I saw an answering spark of determination rekindled in Ryshad's gaze.

Aiten looked at us, fear in his face. 'I take it this is bad?'

'Yes,' Ryshad said slowly. 'And I guess we're supposed to tell you how bad so that the fear will make it ten times worse.' A trace of the usual steel strengthened his voice. 'So I won't. It's bad, Ait, very bad, but nothing you won't be able to handle.'

I wondered at the conviction in Ryshad's tone and from the fear remaining on Aiten's face, he did too.

'So what happened to you?' I wanted to distract him and to find out what I might be facing when the next set of games were played.

Aiten shrugged. 'I was handed over to a handful of them who did their best to knock me senseless. They must have thought they'd softened me up so some rump – some old man started asking questions about why we were here. I didn't say anything so I was stripped and – and searched,' he blushed furiously, 'and thrown in here.'

'Don't feel bad about it, Ait.' I could see it was bothering him. 'Six guards can swear I'm a genuine redhead now. They're just doing it to try and break us down.'

Ryshad looked up from the floor as if our naked state had only just occurred to him. He stared at me rather like a thoughtful horse dealer.

'Did any of them try anything? Do you think any of them might be persuaded—'

'Rysh!' Aiten's tone was outraged.

'It's all right, Ait, honestly.' I put a reassuring hand on his arm. 'Don't take this the wrong way but I'd let them stuff me six ways to Solstice if I thought it would get us out of here. But none of them did so much as help themselves to a quick handful.'

Ryshad flashed me a half-smile. 'Well, that tells us their discipline is better than most troops I've ever met.'

'Sadly,' I agreed with a faint grin.

Ryshad got to his feet and began to examine the cell. As he was looking up at the grating, the door opened once more and Shiv was thrown unceremoniously in. Luckily Aiten was in position to catch him since he was unconscious, hair still matted with blood and clothes stained with seawater.

'How come he keeps his breeches?' Aiten muttered crossly as he laid Shiv gently down, stripping off his jerkin to pillow his head.

'Because there's not much point in humiliating an unconscious man.' Ryshad knelt beside him. 'Which means he's not come round since we were taken.' He looked grim as he examined the wounds to the back of Shiv's head, gentle fingers teasing apart the long black hair crusted with blood.

I shivered. 'I'd be happier if someone wasn't taking the trouble to think things like that through.'

Ryshad sat back on his heels. 'Whoever's in charge here is a clever bastard. Why do you think we're being put together one by one like this? Assume everything is being calculated to disturb us, to eat away at us. And fight it.'

I don't know if we were being listened to somehow, either our words or what we were thinking, but I can't believe it was coincidence that the door opened again a breath later and the guards threw in another limp body.

I recognised the fur-trimmed cloak before Ryshad rolled the corpse over to reveal what was left of Geris's kindly, freckled face. I choked on something halfway between a wail and a scream and clapped my hands to my mouth to stifle any further outburst.

Ryshad came and put his arm around my shaking shoulders.

'It's Geris?' he asked softly, already knowing what the answer must be.

I nodded numbly and then broke into shattering sobs. I had been dreading this moment. Logic had told me to expect it but my gambler's blood had kept urging me on to hope for the kind of improbable ending Judal used to stage at the Looking Glass. I had lost friends before but the danger had been part of the wager, part of the game, and we'd all gone in eyes open. I had not been able to shake the conviction that Misaen would somehow look after Geris, in the same way he cares for drunks and little children. He was too nice a person for anything really bad to happen to, surely?

Grief for Geris welled up inside me and flooded my mind. It fed on fears over my own fate, the shock of the violation I had endured, the sense of failure of our mission for Planir and biting dread at what might happen when this white-haired man led his cursed yellow-heads over the ocean. Irrational guilt that this was somehow all my fault lashed at me; I knew how the world works, I should have taken care of an innocent like Geris. My defences, my hard-won optimism, the hope that we might somehow survive this crumbled utterly. I wept as I had never wept before, sobbing like a little girl whose world had collapsed over a broken doll. I cried until I felt hollow inside, trembling with spent emotion, my head pounding, eyes swollen and sore, insensible of anything beyond the all-encompassing pain of the moment.

Gradually, the storm passed, as all upheavals do. I reached the point where wailing was an indulgence rather than a relief and I became aware of Ryshad's strong arms around me, his masculine scent and the fine curled hairs of his chest that I had soaked with my tears. I drew a deep, shuddering breath and allowed him to sit me against the wall. In some remote corner of my mind it occurred to me that we should all be finding this acutely embarrassing but I really could not be bothered. Ryshad fetched me water and Aiten wordlessly handed me a scrap of linen torn from Shiv's shirt. I wiped my face and leaned back, exhausted. That was when I again wondered if we were being spied upon and a faint spark of anger began to fight back against the chill deadness of grief in my mind.

I looked over at Aiten and saw he was glancing between Shiv and Geris, shame and defiance confused on his face. He felt my eyes on him and bit his lip but met my gaze squarely.

'They don't really need all their clothes, do they? To be honest, I'll be able to think a lot straighter without my stones swinging about in the breeze.'

'True enough.' I fought to keep my voice calm when inside I was screaming at him to keep his stupid hands off my friend and my lover.

Ryshad gave me a glance which made me think he understood my feelings. 'We can't give Geris any kind of burning but we can lay him out and say the rites over him,' he said softly. 'He deserves that, at least.'

So we stripped Geris, washed his poor broken body as best we could and wrapped him in his good wool cloak, achingly redolent of the herbs he'd used to sweeten his linen. I wept again as I saw the ruin of the fine delicate hands that had given me so much pleasure; all his fingers were broken and one had been completely cut away. Nails were missing on hands and feet while soles and palms showed the thin welts of repeated beating with some hard, fine rod. Blisters and burns showed where hot irons had been used on his face, the insides of his arms, and thighs, and groin. His firm, full lips, so well suited to kisses and being kissed, were split and bruised. One of his arms was broken in a couple of places and his jaw and several of the bones in his face were too. He had lost most of his teeth, either smashed or ripped bodily from the gums. Slow tears ran down my face as I closed those soft brown eyes that I had grown used to seeing alert with curiosity and keen with innocent goodwill.

My sorrow was not diminished but my anger mounted as we did not find the one thing I was looking for, the final dagger stroke, the mercy blow that would have released Geris from his agonies. It was not there and I began slowly to burn with a determination to somehow repay the white-haired, ice-hearted bastard responsible, to strike back in some way before I died.

Looking at the shattered corpse that had once been Geris, I finally realised we would never get out of this alive.

None of us had any coin, of course, so we pried dirt from the treads of Geris' boots and made mud to write our names on his palm so Poldrion could record the debt to us. I added Shiv's name and, after a moment's hesitation, Darni's; I didn't think he would mind. We spoke the words of farewell over him, Dastennin's rites proved similar enough to the ceremonies of Drianon that I was used to and I figured Poldrion would know what we wanted. I covered his face for the last time with the hood of his cloak and sat, head bowed, at his side. It was the lowest point of my life.

'Tell me about him.' Ryshad handed me Shiv's over-tunic as he laced on Geris' breeches and sat beside me.

I shook my head in mute pain but Ryshad gripped my arm and I looked up to see intensity in his face and tears standing in his eyes.

'Talk to me, tell me what he was like, remember the good things, the happy times.' A single tear fell down his cheek, unregarded. 'If you don't, you'll only ever be able to remember him like this. I sat with my sister while she sickened and died with the dappled fever and believe me, I know. I couldn't see her past her death pains for a year or more. That's what started me on Thassin.'

I could not think what to say but Ryshad persisted. 'I never knew him. Do you think we would have been friends? What was he like?'

'He was a good lad, genuinely good-willed,' I said eventually. 'Quite innocent in some ways; no idea of the real value of money and too trusting for his own good. He was loyal, loving.' My voice shook.

'Were you . . .' Ryshad did not know how to continue but I knew what he meant.

'We were lovers but more by accident than anything else,' I said frankly. 'I think it meant more to Geris than it did to me. He's from a big family and from what I saw, he loved children. He may have had ideas about settling down with me but it would never have come to anything.'

Regret for the loss of something I'd never actually wanted was stupid but it still cut me like a knife.

'Saedrin, who's going to tell his family?' Fresh tears tumbled down my face; I would not have believed I had any left in me.

'Were they close?'

'I think so. He talked about them a lot.' I was suddenly uncertain. How much had I really known about Geris? It hadn't seemed important before; now I wondered what I might have found out, if I'd taken the trouble.

I told Ryshad about Judal and the Looking Glass, about Geris' endless curiosity, his artless chattering on about everything and anything, Calendars and Almanacs, different systems of electing kings, writers ten generations dead and burned. As I talked, I realised how incompletely I had known Geris; where had his fascination with his stupid tisanes begun? I wondered. I recalled the fight at the Eldritch ring, Geris' bravery and his unexpected coolness in a crisis; where had he learned such courage?

When emotion threatened to choke me, Ryshad countered with his own stories, talking about his brothers and his lost sister, about horses he had owned and scholars he had met, anything that followed on from what I had been saying.

I don't know how long we talked. The room darkened and later was illuminated by the glow of torches from the yard above but, at the end, I was calm and Geris was at least alive in my memories again; I could see him as I had known him, not as the broken thing at the side of the room. Geris had told me the Aldabreshi reckon no one is truly dead until the last person who knew them is dead as well. I realised I might have some idea now of what they meant.

The Guest-house at the Shrine of Ostrin, Bremilayne, 2nd of For-Winter

Allin sighed at the triangular rent in the knee of Darni's breeches. She was sitting in the window seat, knees drawn up, glancing intermittently out into the narrow rain-dark street. She thought she'd escaped tedious tasks like doing everyone's mending and she did miss the hard, clear winters of Lescar, so unlike this drizzly place. A knock at the door startled her and she hastily put her feet to the floor, straightening her skirts.

'Come in.'

'Good day.' A man about Allin's father's age opened the door, lowering a wet hood to reveal neatly cut dark hair and a clean-shaven face. 'Are you Allin?'

'Of course she is.' A shorter man pushed past to warm himself at the meagre fire; he shed a tattered cape to reveal disordered grey hair and a ragged beard, and turned piercing blue eyes on Allin.

'This is a piss-poor fire, lassie. Ring for more coal!'

Allin didn't like to admit she hadn't dared to.

'Never mind that.' The dark man smiled at her, his grey eyes kindly 'We're here to see Casuel and Darni.'

Apart from the Gidestan accent, he reminded Allin of her Uncle Warrin. 'I'm afraid they're both out at present, sir. Can I tell them you called? You could leave a note.'

She put her sewing aside, remembering the social graces her mother had striven to teach her. 'Shall I ring for wine or tisane?'

'Thank you, wine would be very welcome.' The dark man hung their cloaks on the pegs and went to warm himself. His hands were white with cold, nails blue-tinged.

Allin clasped her own hands tight together and went to

ring for a maid. The echo of the distant bell rolled around the silence in the room.

'Are you seafarers?' Allin hazarded an attempt at polite conversation.

'Of a kind.' The little man shot her a wicked grin and, to her chagrin, Allin felt her inevitable blushes rising.

'We are wizards, colleagues of Darni and Casuel.' The dark man smiled at some private amusement.

The door rattled and saved Allin from having to find an answer.

'Fine, tell me something I don't know, Cas!' Darni stormed in.

'Good day.' The dark man turned from the fire and Allin was treated to the rare sight of Darni at a loss for words.

'There's no—' Casuel's words trailed off as he entered. 'Planir?'

He swept a hasty bow and Allin managed a ragged curtsey before her knees failed her and she landed on the window seat with an audible thump.

'Archmage, Cloud-Master.' Darni made the deepest and most sincere bows Allin had seen him perform yet. 'You are very welcome.'

'What have you done about a ship?' Otrick scowled at him.

Darni scowled right back. 'No one's prepared to risk the currents, the storms, the sea-monsters, you name it.'

'Messire D'Olbriot is going to see if he can negotiate something for us,' Casuel added hastily.

'I'm sure someone would change his tune if Messire started issuing a few direct orders,' Darni grumbled.

'That's not how things are done in Tormalin,' Casuel snapped, before he remembered himself and looked nervously at Planir. 'Pardon me, Archmage.'

Darni ignored him and turned to Otrick. 'Who else is with you? How many swords?'

'At present, it is just the two of us. We thought we should come on ahead,' Planir answered with a glimpse of authority which stifled the waiting questions on Darni's lips. 'I was concerned about the potential problems of acquiring a ship at this time of year.'

'I'm sure we'll manage, I mean, Messire D'Olbriot has offered us every co-operation and I'm sure he'll get permission for us to approach other sailors,' Casuel insisted.

'If D'Olbriot's mariners won't sail in this season, I can't see any others agreeing.' Planir's tone was gentle enough but Casuel still looked as if he'd been kicked in the shins.

'Right, then we'd better try someone else.' Otrick rubbed his hands together gleefully.

'Who else is there?' Darni was clearly puzzled.

'Pirates!' Otrick said with relish.

The door opened before anyone could respond and the maid looked curiously round.

'Wine, please,' Allin said faintly. 'And more coal.'

'May I ask how your discussion involves pirates?' Esquire Camarl stepped around the maid and took his time hanging his wet cloak over a chair.

'Oh, Esquire, that is, well, my, that is . . .' Casuel looked from Otrick to the young noble in an agony of indecision.

'Esquire Camarl D'Olbriot,' Darni stepped forward, 'may I introduce Planir, Archmage of Hadrumal, and Otrick, Cloud-Master of the New Hall.'

Camarl swept a low bow which Planir returned while Otrick contented himself with a curt nod.

'I was saying that the only way to get a ship at this season is to ask a pirate.' Otrick's eyes shone with a challenge.

'That is an interesting proposition,' Camarl said cautiously.

The wine arrived and Camarl took his time adding warm water and honey; Planir joined him, which effectively silenced Darni.

'It is certainly possible that a pirate would agree to put to sea when a regular mariner will not.' The Esquire sipped his drink. 'However, we should have to pay an extortionate price for that rather dubious privilege.'

'Coin's not a concern,' Darni said robustly, refusing water for his wine and tossing it down.

'I confess I would not know how to contact a pirate.' Camarl shook his head with a slight smile. 'My acquaintance has been limited to watching them swing on dockside gibbets.'

'Oh, I can take care of that. I've sailed with half the rigging-slashers in these waters.' Otrick grinned with relish at the shocked expressions all around him.

'I can see that you find this a startling proposal,' Planir said smoothly as he looked around the room. 'However, unless any of you have new thoughts, I fear it is our only remaining option.'

There was a glum moment while everyone exchanged enquiring glances and rueful shakes of their heads.

'But what's to stop some pirate just taking us out of sight of land, cutting our throats and dumping us overboard?' Casuel burst out suddenly.

'Me, for a start,' Darni snarled. 'Saedrin's stones, Cas, what kind of a wizard are you?'

'Caution is all very well, Casuel.' Planir moved swiftly to fill the awkward silence. 'However, your colleagues are in some considerable peril and we must act swiftly to have any chance of saving them.'

'What do you mean?' Darni looked at the Archmage in consternation before rounding on Casuel. 'Haven't you been scrying them?'

'They've been captured, you oaf.' Otrick was barely Casuel's height but he still shrank away from the old mage's contempt.

'I've been, that is, I meant to, but there's been so little time . . .' Casuel's voice rose to a despairing bleat.

'It does seem to have happened rather suddenly.' Planir moved to sit at the table, breaking the circle which was closing in on the hapless Casuel. 'That's why we've come on ahead.'

'That, and so you could avoid all sorts of awkward questions in Council!' Otrick sniggered as he refilled his cup.

Casuel looked horrified as Darni and Camarl laughed with him.

'Sadly, that is also true.' Planir winked at Allin, who was watching the whole conversation wide-eyed. She giggled, caught by surprise, and clapped her hands to her mouth, mortified.

'Right, if you've quite finished flirting with the new talent, oh revered Archmage, let's go.' Otrick drained his goblet. 'You'd better stay behind, blossom. If I take a pretty girl like you to the places we're going, I'd like as not have to pay to get you back!'

Otrick caught up his cloak and marched out. Planir swept Allin a florid bow and sauntered after Darni and Camarl, leaving Casuel hovering in the doorway like a badly trained footman. He lifted his chin and tried unsuccessfully for a look of quelling disapproval.

'Don't you get yourself into any foolishness,' he snapped.

Allin managed to wait until he was out of earshot before she laughed.

Casuel looked wildly round until he saw the valiant green of Esquire Camarl's cloak heading down the hill. He made after them hastily, nearly slipping over on the wet cobbles of the steep street.

'This way.' They followed Otrick down a narrow alley where the houses looked like heaps of boulders that had unaccountably sprouted chimneys. The ordure underfoot grew more and more acrid, while heaps of refuse whispered with the rustle of rats. Inn-signs were clearly out of fashion in this neighbourhood but the doorpost formed into a crudely carved woman holding a flagon between her naked breasts conveyed her message clearly enough.

'Here we are.' Otrick gave the whore a familiar slap on her smooth wooden buttocks.

The others followed, Darni scowling blackly, Camarl's expression a well-schooled blank, Planir smiling as if he were enjoying some private joke and Casuel patently horrified.

The buzz of conversation stopped dead. Casuel trod on Darni's heel as the bigger man stopped, folded his arms and glowered at the assembled company.

'Stop looking as if you're daring someone to spit in your eye, Darni,' Otrick said acidly. 'If I wanted to start a dog-fight, I'd have brought a mastiff.'

Darni transferred his gaze to the assorted women hovering around the rickety stairs and his look became more of a leer. One came over, her bodice sporting a frill of dirty lace which patently failed to conceal the rosy jut of her nipples.

'Hello, old man. Haven't seen you here for a good few seasons.' Closer, the daylight betrayed the wrinkles beneath her whore's rouge.

'I've been busy, sweetheart.' Otrick waved an expansive hand.

Darni sat stiff-backed on a settle against the wall; the Esquire and the Archmage took stools, conveying an impression of being completely at ease, although Camarl did betray a certain loss of poise when he turned in response to a tap on his shoulder to find himself looking straight down the cleavage of a rumpled blonde, bending down to offer him a cup of wine.

'Thank you.' He took the cup and offered the girl a copper which she dropped between her grubby breasts with a slow wink.

'This is certainly a side of Bremilayne I haven't seen before,' Camarl murmured to Casuel who was sitting, knees together and cloak clutched round him. Casuel nodded and sipped absently at the wine, astonishment replacing his expression of distaste.

'What did you expect, Cas?' Otrick laughed. 'Free trade is all about getting the best goods without paying coin to all the middlemen!'

The harlot in Otrick's lap giggled like a girl and stroked his beard. 'We certainly offer the best here.'

'Our time is limited, Otrick,' Planir reminded the old wizard, with a touch of steel in the velvet smoothness of his manner.

'Now then, sweetheart, I'm looking for Sanderling.' Otrick clasped the trollop round the waist.

The whore's eyes were wary. 'He was in here a few nights ago but I haven't seen him since.'

Otrick squeezed her thigh with a knowing grin. 'Just tell him Greylag was looking for him.'

'If I see him, I'll tell him.' The woman nodded.

Planir rose and bowed. 'Thank you for the wine, madam.'

He handed her a discreet handful of silver which caused a rustle of petticoats round the stairs. Otrick slid the whore off his lap and stood for a farewell squeeze of her buttocks and a lengthy kiss. The others made their way outside and waited for a moment, blinking in the daylight.

'Fancy coming back later, Darni?' Otrick wiped his beard, eyes bright blue with mischief.

'I'm a married man, Cloud-Master,' Darni laughed. 'I don't think Strell would thank me for the sort of gift I could get for her in there.'

They soon regained the wider streets of the more savoury quarter of the town and were able to walk abreast.

'I'm curious, Cloud-Master Otrick,' Camarl began hesitantly. 'Sanderling and Greylag are birds' names, aren't they?'

'Would you use your real name if you took to free-trading?' Otrick's eyes flashed at the young noble.

There was another silence.

'What exactly was your involvement with these pirates?' Planir asked delicately. 'Everyone's curious but I'm the only one with the rank to ask and I feel it may not be a tale fit for young Allin's ears.'

Otrick chuckled with an evil grin. 'You don't get to be called Cloud-Master by sitting under trees and throwing handfuls of leaves into the breezes. Out there on the deep ocean I've learned more about the winds than any mage alive. How else do you expect we're going to go after Shiv and your men?'

Camarl looked at Planir. 'I've been meaning to ask you about that. I really can't see how we can hope to arrive at these islands in time to be of any assistance.' The Esquire's face was serious, the unconscious authority of rank in his words. 'I can't see how we can hope to make such a crossing in under twenty-five days.'

Planir looked casually around before answering. 'Trust me, Esquire, if need be we can cross that ocean in as many chimes.'

His voice carried absolute authority.

Camarl nodded. 'So, what do we do next?'

'We hope Otrick's old shipmate makes contact and all prepare for a sea voyage,' Planir replied crisply. 'In the meantime,
I contact Kalion and a few others in the Council and we hope
they find this minstrel's tale sufficiently intriguing to come
and join in the fun.'

The Ice-man's Keep, Islands of the Elietimm, 3rd of For-Winter

We might have gone on talking round the chimes but Shiv began to stir and groan. Aiten had been sitting silently by him after borrowing his breeches, checking his breathing and heartbeat from time to time and squeezing water into his mouth from a scrap of linen.

'How is he?' I held Shiv's hand, feeling useless once more.

Aiten shook his head. 'We won't know till he wakes, that's the problem with head injuries.' His calm tone reassured me. 'Still, I can't feel a skull fracture and, to be honest, if he were going to die, I reckon we'd be seeing him sinking, not stirring.'

It still seemed like half a day before Shiv finally opened his eyes and they were blurred and lazy when he did. His pupils were different sizes and when he tried to sit up he began retching helplessly. Some water helped and we managed to make him more comfortable but it was a while before he could talk.

'Just relax, go with it,' Aiten said firmly. 'Your wits have been knocked halfway to Saedrin and it'll take a while for them to get straight again.'

I could see the helpless frustration on Shiv's face so I gripped his hand. 'We're not going anywhere.' I hoped no Elietimm soldiers would turn up to make a liar of me.

He coughed. 'I take it we're in some dungeon?' he said with a weak flash of his old humour.

I shrugged. 'Compared to some of the lock-ups I've been in? I've stayed in worse inns but yes, we're locked in.'

Shiv focused on Aiten with obvious difficulty. 'Either you've fallen under a herd of pigs or they've been trying to get information.'

'They are keen with their questions, I'm afraid.' Ryshad hesitated. 'They've got ways of getting inside your head too.'

Shiv groaned and not from pain. 'So they're users of aetheric magic? We were right?'

'Sorry.'

'So what do we do now?' Ryshad looked around at all of us questioningly.

I held up a hand. 'Should we talk? I'm sure the Ice-man, that white-haired bastard, was somehow listening in to my mind.'

Aiten and Ryshad looked at each other and at me uncertainly.

'It's well past midnight,' Shiv said weakly, eyes closed. 'I can't find a wakeful mind anywhere close. Anyway, what choice do we have? I don't fancy sitting here in silence until they come for us again.'

'Can we get out of here?' Aiten stared dubiously at the grating, now just a pattern of paler shapes against the darkness as the torches above had been quenched. 'Where do we go if we can?'

I went to examine the door and found another lock, well secure by local standards but only a challenge to me since I'd be working without tools. I looked thoughtfully at the bone beakers and wondered how much effort and noise smashing one would take.

Shiv shifted himself with an effort and grimaced. 'If we can get out of this room we need to find a hole to hide up in until I can contact Planir. Once I've made the link he can get the Council to meld power through him so I can get our warning across at very least.'

'Could they get us home?' I tried not to sound too beseech-ing.

Shiv sighed. 'Perhaps, but it's unlikely. I can't lie to you.'

Aiten and Ryshad covered their disappointment well but I actually felt my spirits rise. Some chance is better than none and I'm a gambler. As long as I didn't ask Shiv the odds, I could kid myself they were worth the throw; after all, it's only the long runes that get you the heavy coin.

'Could you hide us, Shiv?' Ryshad asked after a moment's thought.

'I think so,' he replied slowly. 'I've been thinking about how they might have been tracking us and I reckon I can create some illusions to throw them off the scent for a while at least.'

Ryshad nodded. 'If we stay in or near the keep, they shouldn't be able to pick us up so easily.'

'Every castle I've ever been in has dead space and places to hide.' Aiten's expression had finally lightened a little so I did not see any profit in pointing out the basis of this plan was about as solid as a horse-trader's warranty.

'We need to reconnoitre.' I looked at Shiv. 'You're not going anywhere fast so we need to know where we're going. If I can get out and scout the place while they're all asleep, I can look for a good place to hide up.'

Ryshad did not look convinced and I wondered if he was making a guess as to my real intentions. I did not meet his eye but crossed over to the door and peered at the lock again.

'Ait, can you try and break one of those beakers? I need long splinters, not too fine at the ends if that's possible.'

Shiv coughed weakly. 'I think we can do better than that. People clearly don't do much by way of breaking out of lock-up round here; any Watch back home would never have let me keep my boots.'

He chuckled softly and I looked down at him with faint exasperation.

'Check the seams, Livak, inner and outer.'

Sudden hope warmed me as I picked at the stitching with careful nails and slid out four fine steel probes with neatly shaped ends.

We turned our head to the door in a single movement to see if any eavesdropping bastard was going to come bursting in but, after a long moment of still silence, I dropped a soft kiss on Shiv's forehead.

'I'll be able to go anywhere in the place with these. We may even be able to get right out of here.'

'Be careful.' Ryshad looked sternly at me.

I gave him a faint echo of my old smile. 'When am I anything else?'

Before Ryshad could pursue me or his suspicions, I was

out of there and padding noiselessly in my bare feet along a corridor lined with more cells to either side. We seemed to be White-hair's only guests at present, which was a relief. Cold draughts reminded me I was still only wearing a woollen tunic but that was an irrelevance at the moment. I had more important things to think about and, with Shiv's lockpicks in my hands, I could do a lot more than I had been hoping.

I would certainly look for a place where we might hide, and more importantly I would find the quickest route out of there. Whatever Shiv might say, I had no faith in his ability to conceal us for any length of time. It was not that I did not trust his capabilities, but these people had skills we knew nothing about. How in Saedrin's name was Shiv supposed to counter them? The Ice-man's confidence had me convinced of his pre-eminence in this strange magic and we were in the heart of his lands. Even if we did get out of here, where would we go? His hounds would be after us before we had gone half a league and, with Shiv so weak on his feet, we would be wounded deer waiting for the final arrows.

Drianon might be smiling on us so it was worth a try, but I intended to make more valuable use of my time while I was loose in the sleeping keep. I climbed swiftly up the back stairs, resolutely quelling fear as I passed the room where I had been held; there was no time for such luxuries. Pausing at each door, I listened carefully for sounds of any sleepers within. This was easier than most places I work where I have to contend with the night sounds of a busy town and I was soon confident none of the rooms on this level were occupied; these were rooms for business, not living. My confidence was returning after so long feeling like a spare horse tied to the wagon tail; Shiv could spell rings round me if he chose and I was never going to equal Ryshad or Aiten with a sword, but I'm still the best I know at discreet investigation.

Still, no harm in checking; caution keeps you alive. I went up one more flight of stairs with agonising caution and felt the carpet under my feet grow thick and softer at the turn. I swept careful toes from side to side and found it reached the walls here. This was luxury – were these living quarters? By now my Forest sight was used to the faint light filtering through the narrow gaps in the shutters and as my eyes reached the level of the floor above I made a brief survey of the hallway. I could see the warm sheen of polished wood, a bright glimpse of blue ceramic, the rich sparkle of a bronze mirror hung on a far wall. Our host might only have been reckoned middling wealthy back home but I judged he was the biggest cock on this dunghill. So, he not only had ambition but the talents, magical and otherwise, to make things happen his way.

Moving with all the stealth I could muster, I listened at the nearest door. After a long moment of silence, I heard the faint rustling of bed linen as someone stirred, the creak of a bed then stillness once more. Was it the white-haired, ice-hearted bastard who ran this place? I flexed my hands in preparation before remembering I had no blade. Had I had a weapon, I would have been in there and slitting his throat without a moment's pause. Perhaps it's a good thing I was unarmed but I'm still undecided on that one. I would probably have lost my life but I would give a sack-weight of noble coin for a chance to sink a blade into that evil neck, then and now. Would one of the lockpicks through an eye or ear do the job? Perhaps, but it wasn't enough of a certainty to be worth the risk. A good gambler knows when to throw and when to hold the runes. Anyway, I had no idea who else lived here; I could find myself having to silence some woman or child and I don't like unnecessary killing.

I stamped down hard on pointless frustration and slipped silently down the stairs again, ears alert for the slightest sound. There wasn't so much as the hint of a patrolling guard within the keep and when I pressed up against a crack of a shutter to squint down into the compound, I could only see a couple of sentries doing little more than stamp their feet occasionally against the cold. On an impulse, I promised myself that if by some god's grace we got away from here, I would come back with Halice, Sorgrad and Sorgren, Charoleia too if she was free, and pick this place clean, just to show the bastard the point in taking decent precautions.

Indecision hovered around me for a few breaths and then I

set to work on the door next to the room where I had been held. For White-hair to hear my thoughts and reach me so fast, he must have been somewhere close. Perhaps, but it hadn't been in that room, I decided, after opening the second set of ledgers. Saedrin knows what they where about but numbers are numbers, whether they're Tormalin or Mountain script. I investigated the door on the far side and this looked more hopeful. This lock was the best I'd seen outside Relshaz, decent steel and well oiled. It was good but I am better and my efforts were soon rewarded. The room was a study or library; I slipped in and carefully locked the door behind me; I didn't want to be disturbed.

Tapestries of undyed wool softened the walls and muted the draughts. It would have been churlish to criticise their limited range of colour as they were beautifully worked, intricate patterns in all shades of brown from nearly black to palest beige. Thick rugs caressed my painfully chilled toes and the furniture was smoothly carved wood, glowing with beeswax and seasons of devoted polishing. The gloom was a problem and I wondered about light; I soon found a candle-end in a fine Gidestan silver stand and decided to risk it. Was any sentry going to question a light in his master's study? I didn't think so, not here, whatever the hour.

I looked around in vain for steel, flint, spark-makers, anything. Impotent with frustration, I tried all the desk drawers but found nothing beyond pens, ink and knives. I took the sharpest; it wasn't much but it was better than nothing. The smell of beeswax teased at my memory and I had a sudden inspiration. Staring hard at the wick, I whispered at it, 'Talmia megrala eldrin fres.' Glee quite inappropriate to our plight thrilled me when it leaped to life. Get a grip of yourself, I told myself sternly, you wanted light, now use it. My spirits rose absurdly for what seemed like the first time in seasons.

Now I could see better, I studied the packed bookshelves. Volumes of Old Tormalin histories were arranged by reign; there were collections of letters, works of natural philosophy, ethics, drama, endless volumes. I recognised some of the names I had heard Geris mention and realised much of the trove of books and treasures that the Ice-man had stolen from us had to be here. I was hardly in a position to reclaim anything.

I turned my attention to the desk and sat in the softly padded chair to examine the neat stacks of parchment. I was not too concerned about leaving any traces; what was the worst that could happen to me, after all? I could be captured and tortured? That was hardly news. I was still convinced we were all going to die here; what I wanted to do was somehow knock the axle-pins out of this caravan before it got on the road. This was partly for Planir, and partly in a general sense for all my friends and family who might fall foul of these people if they invaded. But mostly I was looking for revenge, to pay the bastards back for what they had done to me and for Geris' lonely, agonised death. I ignored the small voice in the back of my head that wanted to remind me that looking for revenge was what brought me here in the first place.

I was considering setting fire to everything but I decided to wait until I had scouted a way out of the keep for us all, when we could make best use of the distraction. I would take a quick look and see if I could glean any useful information. Tidy minds seemed to be bred into these people like long legs on a deerhound and I soon identified the different stacks of notes. Ice-man had much the same information on the Inglis coast as the commander of the brown liveries but less on the Tormalin coast, which was the faintest suggestion of good news. What he did have was a large sheet dedicated to the collapse of the Empire, the years marked down the centre and events noted on either side. This was clearly something he'd been working on for a good while; the edges were a little ragged and the entries were written in a variety of inks. He seemed particularly interested in the activities of the various noble families Azazir had said were involved in the founding of Kel Ar'Ayen. Underneath I found genealogies and other records, clearly pieced together over a long period.

Another sheet had names of various Tormalin, Dalasorian and even some Caladhrian cities on it. Each city had its own list of people attached and numbers beside each name. It meant nothing to me initially and I put it aside for another list of the

Elietimm domains here in these islands with what I eventually decided must be personal names associated with them. Some were crossed through, with numbers written by their sides.

I stared at both lists until a new picture emerged, like one of those Aldabreshi carvings that are a tree from one side or a face from another. If I were looking to leave these rocks in the middle of the ocean, I'd be looking for information about the place I was going to; I reckoned White-hair had quite a network of informants back home and, by the look of it, was paying them well. I looked thoughtfully at the second list. Rivalry here was intense and since no one seemed inclined to take an enemy on face to face, I'd bet assassination was a popular option. Maybe, maybe not. Wouldn't that mean they'd have guards up to the rafters, like a Lescari noblewoman trying to avoid 'marriage' by abduction? I'd seen no sign of that. Perhaps they had magic defences they could use? I shrugged and put the lists aside; there was no time for this.

Another stack proved to be sheets each headed with the name of an Elietimm domain. I couldn't make any sense of them even though I was regaining familiarity with the angular Mountain alphabet, so I moved these to one side and reached for a pile I judged more recent by the shade of the ink. A chill crept up my back as I recognised Ryshad's name and picked out the names Zyoutessela, D'Olbriot and Tadriol in the notes. I couldn't blame him for giving up the information, knowing the Ice-man's methods, but I was concerned to see just how much the bastard seemed to have picked out of Ryshad's head. The sheet headed 'Aiten' had a few terse lines and it seemed he had not got much of real worth out of me either. I didn't exactly know much worth having, did I?

I turned over the page and my hand shook suddenly as Geris' name leaped off the page at me. I could not face trying to decipher the record of his interrogation so put it quickly aside and stared stupidly for a moment at what I had uncovered. Several sheets were covered in neat Tormalin and I recognised Geris' expensively educated script. What had I found?

'Calm down,' I scolded myself. I quelled my trembling hands and forced myself to breathe more slowly until the words emerged from meaningless jumble in front of my eyes. It proved to be a carefully presented discourse on the collapse of the Empire. I skipped the references to writings and people I knew nothing about but, in the careful argument, I could hear Geris' enthusiasm and learning so clearly that it brought tears to my eyes. I blinked them away crossly and began scanning through the document for anything useful for those of us still alive. A mention of aether caught my eye and I read that passage more fully.

Having studied the works of Trel'Mithria and the annals kept by the Order known as the Hammers of Misaen (now lost in the Western Lands), it is apparent that magic in the Old Empire was predominately that which we now refer to as aetheric. Elemental magic was a subordinate science deemed of little practical use. This aetheric magic draws on the potential for power contained within the minds of individuals which explains its affinity with forms of mental communication and control which are unusual in elemental magic.

'Stick to the point, Geris,' I breathed as I skipped a few paragraphs speculating on mental powers in legend and tradition.

The power is enhanced when a number of minds are focused on one object. The evidence of Argulemmin and Nemith the Learned proves that religion provided that focus in both the Old Empire and the Ancient Elietimm cultures, which explains why priests were the main practitioners of such magic in those days.

And explains why these bastards were razing every shrine they came across back home. There was a complicated passage of Rationalist argument and Geris was even speculating that our ideas of gods may have originated in no more than early and especially proficient wielders of aetheric magic. There was more in the same vein but I scanned ahead until a mention of Kel Ar'Ayen halted me.

From these passages, taken from the Elietimm histories, the existence of an eastern continent and the location there of the Tormalin colony of Kel Ar'Ayen cannot now be denied. If the following evidence from the Annals of Heriod *can be taken as accurate, it suggests the battle for control of these lands was bitter and heavily reliant on magic.*

I skipped swiftly through the densely detailed argument proving this, it meant little to me and I was prepared to take Geris' word

If we accept the amendments of Gar Pretsen and add the Elietimm record, it is clear that when the Tormalin settlers were finally trapped they struck not at the magic the Elietimm were wielding but somehow at the source of their power. However in doing so they not only removed the foundations of their enemy's magic but those of the Tormalin Empire back home. Aetheric magic in the western lands never recovered in the chaos that followed the disintegration of the Empire or in the subsequent Dark Generations. The Elietimm clan system, however, continued to provide a mental focus for the loyalties of the inhabitants and so a reserve of power, albeit seriously diminished, for the practitioners of aetheric magic who were both priests and rulers.

I ignored the passages which followed, detailing the state of religion in Tormalin and elsewhere at home. If we needed priests and faithful to give us aetheric magic to fight these bastards with, we were lost before the Elietimm had even landed. I couldn't think of anyone I knew under middle age who did anything more devout than keep a few festivals and make their oaths by some or other deity. Priests didn't need to worry about the arguments of the Rationalists turning people away from religion; apathy was doing a fine job on its own.

I ignored the rest of Geris' neatly argued treatise, intensely depressed. So now I had answers. Did that help me? Would it help Planir, even supposing we could get any of this information to him? Would he be able to get any co-operation from the Emperor? If he did, could Tormalin and the wizards hold off an invasion backed by unknown magic? Half the Dukes in Lescar would probably ally themselves with the Elietimm just to get an advantage over their rivals and, by the time the Caladhrian Council of Nobles had debated the matter, they'd have the Elietimm camped at their gate houses. Saedrin knows what the Aldabreshi would do but I'd swear it would be anything but co-operate.

As I straightened the piles of documents, a new thought ignited fierce anger inside me, driving away these fruitless musings. Geris had spent time here, he had been given the run of these books, had been asked to write down his conclusions. He had to have co-operated. There was no way he could have done this kind of work with his skull full of the Ice-man's control. I could hardly blame him, given the situation he found himself in. Had he bargained his learning for freedom? Perhaps, but I guessed being let loose among so much information had been a powerful temptation in itself.

Had he expected to be killed once he'd finished the job? I hoped not; I would have anticipated it but I would probably have still gone along with the game, hoping for a lucky throw of the runes to get me out. If I looked at it from White-hair's point of view, killing Geris made sense; no point risking him telling all to a rival or getting free to take Elietimm information home. That was all very well but if Geris had been co-operating there had been no point to the torture, no reason for it that I could see other than black-hearted sickness of mind. Stuff it, I just didn't have time for this. I seized any papers that I thought might prove useful – might as well be flogged for a loaf as a slice after all – and snuffed the candle end and left.

I stood in the corridor wondering which way to go when I noticed another fine lock. Given my history with secured doors and boxes, it can come as no surprise that I was in there in a few breaths. A smile cracked my dry lips when I saw I had found our clothes and some of our gear. You'd have thought these would have gone as booty but Ice-man obviously kept his troops on a tight rein, or he was keeping our presence a close secret. A number of items had been unpicked or cut apart but it seems shirts and breeches are the same the world over and were of little interest. I was in my breeches and boots faster than a lover who's heard the husband's horse ride up and quickly sorted out Ryshad's and Aiten's.

Saedrin seize it, there were no weapons. I looked around the room; there had to be some close at hand, I was certain of it though I could not have told you why. Crossing to the window to crack open the shutter for some light, I found a deep wooden coffer in the embrasure. Once I had it open, steel, silver and gold glinted in the starlight.

'Thank you, Poldrion,' I breathed in exultation.

The swords were not our own but anything with a handle and sharp edges would suit me. There were two good blades, heavy and longer than the usual, as well as a handful of daggers. Lack of scabbards and belts was going to be a problem but we'd just have to live with that; a sword in each hand certainly improved my morale.

A noise outside froze me to the floorboards. Through the crack in the shutters, I saw the sentries meet at the top of the stairs to the parapet. A second pair were coming up and they paused, presumably to swap notes, before the original two hurried down, doubtless to warmth, food and sleep. I squinted round the edge of the shutter to follow them and saw the bright glow of a brazier as they went into the gate-house. I scanned the stars; Trimon's Harp was directly overhead and if guards were changing the shift again we had to be well on the way to dawn. Nights here might be long but I didn't have time to waste. I quickly rummaged among the velvet packages at the bottom of the coffer. One turned out to be full of rings and I shoved two or three on to all my fingers; there had to be some people around here who'd take a bribe.

I swept quickly round the room in case I'd missed anything but all I found was a privy closet in a niche behind a curtain. I had turned to ignore it when a thought struck me. I looked at it, at the ewer of water standing ready to sluice it, and then peered down into the privy itself where an open drain fell away into darkness. I'd heard of water closets, though never seen one, but this seemed to be halfway between that and the seat, pail, box of ashes to shovel in after yourself arrangement that I was used to.

Water. I racked my brains but I couldn't think of any standing fresh water that we'd seen on our trip. Come to that, the streams we'd crossed had been mean little things and that village had had rainwater cisterns on every roof whereas I couldn't remember seeing a well, not in the open anyway. This was a rich household but while they might have water to spare for rinsing out the privy, I'd wager that it was put to further use after they were done with it. I decided to follow both that thought and the drains.

I found my way rapidly to the lower levels, moving cautiously in case of wandering servants. They were conspicuous by their absence and I wondered briefly why this was but came up with no answers. A cat prowling for vermin nearly gave me a seizure when it silently rubbed round my legs but other than that the place was deserted. I don't know where the kitchens were; the lowest levels of the keep were bathing and laundry rooms. As I had hoped, these all had large drains set in the middle of sloping floors and it was quick work to prise up a cover. I checked a few and sure enough, they were all heading south. It took me a few moments to get up the courage to crawl along one but the pressure of time was now beating relentlessly on the back of my head.

These drains were large, and I supposed they had to be in a place so obsessed with washing. Small hand- and footmarks in drifts of silt also suggested that hapless maids or children were sent down here to keep them clear. I could move along easily enough but I was a little concerned about the others. Aiten should be all right, as should Shiv, despite his height, given his skinny build. Ryshad might find it a squeeze but if it were a choice between risking a few grazes and getting out of this cursed place, I felt sure he'd opt for the former. I pressed on, hopes rising as the drains joined and continued to head south. My nose told me when a foul-water sluice joined the flow but I could not let that stop me. I tried to keep out of the mire and made a mental note to warn Aiten; we couldn't risk him getting this shit in his cuts, else they'd fester in no time.

With the load I was carrying and the necessity of walking bent double, my back was aching fiercely and my eyes straining uselessly in the dark when I came up against what I first thought was a corner. I felt carefully round the walls but it soon became apparent it was a dead end. So where was the water going? I reached reluctantly under the surface and discovered a spread of smaller pipes; this was clearly as far as I could follow. So why have such a large space here? Why not spread the pipes out before this?

After racking my brains for what seemed like an age, I felt above my head. After a few false starts, I found what I suspected must be there – a hatch. I pushed at it cautiously but it had no fastening and when I had it open just enough to see out, I found I was in the walled garden with the hot-houses. I bit down on an exclamation of success and concentrated on looking all around to see where we might go from here. We would have to be careful over a route, I realised. The tall winter-killed stems of a corn crop were coiled around with the remnants of bean plants while the ground was covered with the flat leaves of something I didn't recognise. Three crops on the same ground; in other circumstances it would have been admirable, but here all that concerned me was the potential for noise in such a dense mass of dry vegetation. I identified the outer wall and was delighted to see a postern gate in it. It was barred and bolted against intruders but that was no problem since we would be leaving, not entering. The unwelcome scrape of boots on the wall walk reminded me of the sentries and curbed my elation. I frowned; would Shiv be up to masking us with a concealing illusion, if only long enough for us to get through the gate and clear of the walls?

Delay gained us nothing. I hurried back as fast as was silently practical and scolded myself sternly as I felt optimism rising irresistibly within me. I had a route out, we had clothes and weapons, and I was starting to think we might actually have a chance of getting out of this bear-pit.

'Be realistic,' I told myself. 'Whose bell are you ringing? What you've got now is a chance of dying on your feet with a blade in your hand and that's the best you can say.'

Maybe so but that would be a cursed sight better than dying at Ice-man's hands with him ripping through my head, or under his tame torturer's irons. I shivered as I remembered some of the passages in Geris' writings, the bundle cold against my skin as if the inhumanity of the words had soaked into the very parchment.

CHAPTER TEN

Taken from:

The Last Work of Geris Armiger,
Late Scholar of the University of Vanam

Prepared with annotations by Ornale Scrivener, his mentor and friend.

While incursions by the Elietimm into the lands of the western continent are comparatively recent, they have known of our existence since the battles for the lands of Kel Ar'Ayen and their historical record has a continuity we can only envy. The following letter was written by the Clan-chief of Blackcliff to the Clan-chief of Fishsands at some point in the two years between the death of Feorle the Last and the Anarchy of the Blood-Axes. The attitudes it illustrates do not seem to have changed to any great extent, up to and including the current generation:

> *The final failure of the priests and their magic has led many of the people to doubt the gods, my brother, but do not let yourself be swayed. We are the Hammers of Misaen and we must remain true. To be confined to these isles for so many years has indeed been hard, especially for those of us whose elders can remember tasting the sweet green of Kel Ar'Ayen. Do not forget that broad and fertile land, my brother, rather tell your grandfather to polish his memories and keep them bright, the mirror of Misaen's promise to us. Do not let doubt poison your mind. Misaen is testing us, refining us, scouring our mettle clean of the impurity that led to our downfall at the*

hands of the accursed men of the Dawnlands. The gods remain true, Misaen remains the maker. He continues to bring fire from our mountains; shall we let the fire in our hearts die? I shall not, nor my sons, nor my sons' sons, not until my line is extinguished in the cold ashes of the Last Storm. Our steel will be tempered in his fire, not shattered by the cold bite of the seas.

I make you this promise, a sacred vow on the graves of my forefathers who once trod the golden sands of the East. We will regain mastery over the Ocean. We will take the powers of mind and spirit from the puling priests who have betrayed us. We will travel to the east and throw down the cities of Kel Ar'Ayen until no stone is left standing upon another. We will travel to the west and hunt down the Tormalin invaders until their clans are scattered upon the winds.

The age of the priests is past; we are not children needing nursemaids. Misaen awaits an age of warriors who can wield swords of the hand and of the mind. Such warriors will have lands to conquer on either hand; the emptiness of Kel Ar'Ayen to fill with their sons and the rabbles of Tren Ar'Dryen to enslave. Do not think that Misaen has cast us down; he has not. Rather he has shown us our destiny and locked us away, like athletes before a contest, to make sure we train ourselves to obtain the victory and to deserve it.

It is curious that the Elietimm names for Tormalin all include a reference to 'dawn' given their islands are themselves to the east. See Section 8 for further argument suggesting this race originated in the lands of the Mountain Men.

The Ice-man's Keep, Islands of the Elietimm, 3rd of For-Winter

I returned to our cell rapidly. The others were lying in a close huddle, Shiv's boots and a fold of tunic giving the impression of enough feet and heads for any curious guard. I saw them tense as I opened the lock.

'It's me!' I whispered and Aiten and Ryshad were on their feet at once.

I tossed Aiten his clothes; his initial gratitude dampened slightly when he found them more than a little moist and smelly.

'Where've you been?' Ryshad was dressing fast, ignoring the state of his breeches.

'The drains,' I said succinctly. 'We've got a way out.'

I looked past Ryshad to Shiv who was slowly relacing his boots. 'Are you up to hiding us for a short stretch? We need to get through a gate.'

Shiv looked up and grinned. 'I'm fit enough.'

I was relieved to see his eyes were focusing properly on me but his face still looked unhealthily drawn.

'Come on then.'

Aiten moved out, sword at the ready, and Shiv flexed his fingers in the way I'd come to realise was preparation for working magic as they covered the angle of the corridor while I worked on relocking the door. As I did so, I caught a glimpse of Geris' shrouded body and a sudden pang of grief made the picks slip in my nerveless fingers. What would these bastards do to him now? Bury him in the cold earth for the worms or just dump him in a midden? I wondered miserably. Why could they not use the cleansing of fire like civilised people?

Ryshad's firm hand on my shoulder made me jump.

'That's not Geris, Livak,' he said softly and I looked round into his sympathetic eyes. 'He's escaped already.'

I nodded, not trusting myself to speak, then shook myself mentally and led the way into the nearest scullery where I had left the drain cover slightly askew. Once we had all climbed down into the drain, I breathed easier, despite the fetid smells, and concentrated on the job in hand.

Aiten cursed as he slipped, and his voice echoed harshly in the confined space. Ryshad hushed him before I had a chance to and we scrambled awkwardly onwards in comparative silence. I hoped no one was anywhere above to hear the scrapes of boot and sword when Ryshad met a narrow corner but it was too late to worry about that now.

I had to slow down as the others got disoriented in the blackness and for one awful moment became confused myself when I met a junction.

'Make a decision and stick to it, right or wrong,' I told myself silently and, not too many paces later, was rewarded with the sting of scraping my outstretched knuckles on the end wall of the drain. I could see a pale thread in the darkness showing where I had left a root of a plant wedged in the trap door. I breathed a deep sigh of relief. I was going to owe Drianon half my next year's profits at this rate.

'Ait? Shiv?' Ryshad's questing hand touched my shoulder and I grabbed at it. Sudden weakness plucked at my knees but his reassuring grip answered the tremor in my fingers and gave me new heart.

We wedged ourselves awkwardly into the cramped stone box.

'What sort of cover do we need and how long for?' Shiv worked his way round to stand next to me and we raised the lid of our drain cautiously together.

I pointed out the gateway and then the wall walk with the desultorily patrolling sentries. Shiv made a careful survey of the entire garden and nodded slowly.

'We'll need to get out one at a time, slowly. Once we're out, we can move faster. How long will the gate take you?'

'How long is a piss? I don't know, Shiv!'

'Sorry, stupid question. Let's wait until our friend in the dressy leathers is at the far end of the parapet then.'

The idle bastard took his own sweet time to move back along the wall but, once he was gone, I was first out, lying under the frost-wilted leaves of some crop still in the ground. The fresh smell of the cold, damp earth cleaned out my nostrils and I welcomed the scent of a little normality. Once we were all out and crouching like rabbits in a salad garden, Shiv drew some silent patterns in the dirt and nodded for us to move. It was a short dash to the shelter of the wall. No warning shout split the night to betray us.

I unslotted the bar and reached eagerly for the bolts but luckily stopped myself just in time. They were stiff with rust and muck and would have screeched like a night owl. I stared at them in impotent fury for a moment then got to work on the lock, my mind working frantically at the problem. I could hear Ryshad and Aiten shuffling impatient feet behind me and I had to quell an urge to swear at them.

'Shiv, these bolts are going to make a stuffing noise. Do something.'

After a moment's incomprehension, he laid quick hands on the top set and, as I reached down to the bottom ones, I felt the air go soggy and dense around them. I looked up, nodded and we drew them in one swift and blessedly silent wrench. We were through the wall and across the killing ground surrounding the keep at the run. I looked up at the slowly paling sky and wondered how long we had before our escape was discovered. Elation at freedom warred inside me with the fear of pursuit and recapture.

'Stuff it,' I told myself. 'He's got to find you first.'

We ran on, habit soon easing us all into a regular pace. I was concerned that we should be moving faster but I was bone tired by now, only fired on by emotion. I looked at Shiv and Aiten with concern as they fell to the rear. Shiv was still unusually pale in the washed-out light of the early dawn and Aiten was clearly suffering from the beating he had taken. Dark stains on his shirt showed where some of the wounds had reopened.

'You have to get clean as soon as we get a chance, Ait,'

I told him firmly. 'Sea water's good for healing, you know that.'

He nodded, eyes tired and mouth set in a thin line that spoke of his discomfort.

Ryshad had taken the lead and was heading for the thicket of tall masts silhouetted against the pale rose sky that heralded the rising sun. He led us off the main path and we went to ground in a thicket of tangled bushes overlooking the harbour. It was an irregular inlet bitten deep into the coast, evidently carrying a deep-water channel from the size of the vessels moored out from the shore. Despite the early hour, figures were already at work on the decks and the harbour side where cargo was being moved and sorted. Splashes carrying clearly in the cold air spoke of rowing-boats that we could not see moving between ship and shore against the blackness of the water. I had no knowledge to tell me what the tide was doing but I guessed it was at an important point in rising or falling or whatever as many of the huts around the harbour had warm yellow lights in their windows.

'I won't give good odds on us getting a boat here,' I remarked dubiously.

A burst of pipe music startled us. We watched with unanimous dismay as a door spilled a group of soldiers out of what was evidently a tavern. We sat in silence as they marched a little way up the track and watched them relieve a second detachment hidden in an otherwise unremarkable hut. I cursed under my breath; if you're trying to get in somewhere, you want to be going for it when the guard is at the end of its shift, tired and bored, not when it's just been changed and they're all as keen as a slaughterhouse dog at the start of the day's business.

Ryshad reached for his spy-glass and cursed briefly when he realised it was now a prize for White-hair, back at the keep.

I had seen enough. 'There's no way we're going to get to a boat there. We'll have to try for a fishing village or something.'

'No, wait,' Aiten said.

I didn't bother turning my head as I surveyed the coastal

paths leading away from the harbour. 'We've got to get clear of here. It's going to be dawn sooner than you think.'

'We do need to talk this through,' Ryshad said slowly. 'We need to have a plan.'

I looked round and heaved a mental sigh; one of the few things my mother had been proved right about was her assertion that men will always come up with inappropriate ideas at the most inconvenient times.

'We have to get out of here first. Come on!' I hissed at him.

'And once they find we're gone? We'll have them on our trail in no time and we'll be back where we started,' Shiv countered.

'We're going to need a distraction,' Ryshad said firmly. 'It has to be a good one too.'

'All right, it would help, if we can manage it without digging ourselves any deeper into this shit-hole,' I admitted. 'I was thinking along the lines of a little judicious arson, myself.'

Shiv shook his head. 'Fire's going to be hard for me at the moment. I really should save my strength in case we need another covering illusion.'

I raised a hand to silence him. 'Remember Harna's table? I found Geris' list of little spells – I can do it myself.'

'The aetheric cantrips? What about his notes? The books? What else did you find?' Shiv asked hopefully.

'Later,' Aiten interrupted him. 'We need something more than bonfires. I know what I'm talking about; there are some Lescari tricks we should use. We need to cause trouble and we need to have them think it was their own enemies. You were saying how much strife there seemed to be over borders here. We can make this bastard think the ones in the brown did it.'

'This is too complicated,' I objected. 'We don't have time for anyone to waste proving how clever they are.'

'Just listen, will you?' Aiten's voice was rising so I shut up. I was beginning to regret giving him back his boots. Warm feet were obviously draining the blood from his head.

'When I was fighting for Parnilesse, a group of us were

trapped between Triolle's men and a fort held by a contingent from Draximal. We would be cracked like a nut come daylight, so five of the old hands slipped out and found the Triolle camp followers. They butchered the whores and left some Draximal insignia from our booty lying around. So you see, while Triolle's troops were ripping into the Draximals they thought had done it, we were able to get clear.'

'You just want to pay them back in their own coin, Ait. Revenge is a fool's game.' Since Halcarion decided not to strike me down for hypocrisy, I continued, 'I'm not starting some needless slaughter. I'm not into random murder and, anyway, I can't think of a quicker way of rousing the keep, short of finding a hunting horn.'

There was an uncomfortable silence until Ryshad spoke.

'It doesn't have to be a killing, does it?' he mused. 'How about taking a hostage? We could take a woman or a child or, if it looks possible, one of those with the gorgets, an officer.'

I stared at him in disbelief. 'I thought it was Shiv got the knock on the head? Have you any idea how much trouble a hostage can be? One hostage means one of us taken up completely looking after him. There are only four of us and Shiv still hasn't got all his pieces on the board, has he?'

'If we've got a hostage, we've got something to bargain with,' Ryshad insisted. 'If they catch up with us, we might be able to deal our way out.'

'If we do get clear, a hostage could give Planir invaluable information,' Shiv said thoughtfully and I realised with a sinking feeling that he was starting to dance to the same tune.

I pulled the documents out from the breast of my tunic. 'These are aetheric spells.' I brandished the sheet at him. 'I can do them, Rysh, I can set fires from a distance according to Geris' notes. How about I start on those ships over there? Won't that make them think a rival's been busy?'

I was making no impression.

'Let's get out of here first,' I pleaded. 'You've all played Raven, haven't you? You don't take on all the Forest fowl at once, you deal with one flock at a time.'

I could see the sky growing brighter and urgency lent authority to my voice.

'All right. Let's get clear and then we can take on whoever they send after us.' Ryshad's crisp agreement broke the sullen silence and if I were closer, I would have kissed him for it.

A long estuary carried the sea away to our right and a stretch of higher ground rose to hide the shoreline from the keep. We moved rapidly over the close-cropped turf and sandy tracks, my skin crawling as I waited for the shout that would betray us, but Shiv's magic kept any casual glance sliding over us once again. We reached the meagre shelter of a row of hillocks and dunes and crouched down as we paused to reorient ourselves.

'This way. We'll have more chance of finding a boat.'

I have no idea what made Aiten so confident, but he was the man from the coast so we followed his lead. As the curve of the shore and the height of the dunes rose, we headed down for the beach where we could make better speed across the firmer sands.

'Wait a moment. I need to get my breath.' I turned and was shocked to see how far back Shiv had fallen. His colour was still grey while the rest of us were now rosy-cheeked in the brisk breeze.

'Are you still keeping the illusion up?' Ryshad asked abruptly and I cursed myself for not realising how much the magic was draining him.

'We'll have to risk moving without it,' he said decisively as Shiv nodded tiredly. The air around us crackled briefly as Shiv dropped the spell. I felt uncomfortably exposed.

'Let's get closer to the dunes.' I led us back to the boot-catching sands above the tide line and we ploughed on. Shiv was still lagging behind and I saw he was caught in a no-win game; slogging through the sand was going to tire him as thoroughly as working magic.

'Dast's teeth, you're stuffed, aren't you?' Aiten caught Shiv under one arm and Ryshad moved to support him from the other side and looked over at me with a grimace of frustration.

'Scout ahead a bit, Livak. Find out what we're heading for.'

I nodded and put some distance between me and the three of them, climbing a little higher into the tussocks of spiny grass to get some vantage on the terrain around us.

We made better speed this way but the reverse of the runes was the worrying inability of the others to react fast if someone came upon us. My eyes were going like a frog's in all directions as I tried to keep watch everywhere at once. I might as well have saved myself the effort since it was my nose that alerted me to potential danger ahead when I caught the sickly-sweet smell of dung fires on the fitful breeze. I stopped and waited for the others to draw level with me at the base of the dunes.

'I think there's a village or something up ahead. Come up here – I'll go and take a look.'

Shiv sank gratefully on to the soft sands and I exchanged a worried look with Ryshad before starting to work my way through the clumps of grass, back down on my belly and elbows as I recalled every lesson I'd ever learned in moving without being seen. I found a hollow at the edge of the dunes and peered cautiously through the tussocks.

A stream wound its way across the sands and just looking at it made me thirsty. I forced myself to concentrate and saw the rivulet made its way through a break in the line of hillocks which rose again on the far side, soon climbing much higher and marching off to join a chain of steep outcrops. On the landward side of the rising ground, early morning smoke spiralled from a couple of chimneys jutting out of roofs thatched with the coarse grass that was surrounding me. That made sense, the village was well in the lee of the higher land and so sheltered from storms coming in off the water. I looked hungrily at the long low stone building exposed on the seaward side of the rise. No one was going to be living there, not with a cosy little village tucked away round the corner. It had little, unshuttered windows and huge broad doors taking up most of the facing end; it positively shrieked boathouse and I crept forward, one alert eye towards the village as I did so.

Once I was right at the edge of the open ground, I saw three long grey-brown shapes huddled together above the high water mark next to the boathouse. I grinned; Dastennin had just earned himself a share of whatever I had in my purse next time I passed one of his shrines. They weren't whale-boats but looked more like the vessels we'd seen bringing in seals what seemed half a lifetime ago. I wasn't going to quibble; they were boats and I was at the point where I'd seriously have suggested we try putting to sea in a hollow log

I shuffled back through the sands and grasses and found the others.

'Well?' Ryshad was looking anxious and I saw Shiv was looking far from well.

'There are a few houses, they're away behind the shelter of some little hills. The important thing is I can see some boats, seal-hunters' I think. They must be secured somehow, so if you come to the edge of the cover, I'll get over to them and see if I can get one free before we all risk the open.'

Everyone's eyes brightened at this news: even Shiv looked better. We made a cautious descent to the edge of the tussocks. Aiten and Ryshad spread out to get a better view of the village and I circled round so as to find the shortest route across the exposed stretch of beach.

I looked back at Ryshad, he nodded, I took a deep breath and, keeping as low as I could, sprinted for the shelter of the boats where the rise of the land would hide me from the houses. The cold shock of the stream's splashes spurred me on and I went to ground by the leather boats, heart pounding and cold air rasping in my chest. I looked back towards the others and noticed with a twinge of disquiet that I could see the distant battlements of the keep beyond. A pale line scored in the turf suggested a track down from the main harbour on the inland side of the dunes; it forked with one arm heading for the village and the other coming straight for me.

I dismissed it as irrelevant and examined the boats lying upside-down on the shingle. To my land-bred eyes, they all looked seaworthy, which was a relief since this could just as easily been a salvage or repair yard. There was no sign of paddles or such like as I peered underneath but we had Shiv so I hoped that would not be a problem. What was going to present more difficulty was the braided rope of oiled leather which tied each of them to an iron ring set firmly into a little stone pillar. I gnawed at a split in my lip as I tested a dagger on it; the knot was so complicated and tightened that I didn't even consider trying to undo it. I huffed with exasperation; the stuff was as hard as dried meat and about as easy to cut. It was not going to be fast work.

As I shifted my grip on the dagger to get more pressure, a stinging pain on the side of my head made me look up, startled. I looked round to see Ryshad kneeling up and readying a second pebble to get my attention. When he saw I was looking his way, he gestured frantically back round behind himself and I saw the reflection of the rising sun on metal-studded livery. I was round behind the boats in a moment and, with an annoyance that drove out any thought of fear, saw a detachment of black-clad troopers making their way down the main track at a steady pace. They vanished behind a rise in the ground and I considered my limited options hastily.

I could not rejoin the others; the incoming enemy would see me if I tried to cross the open ground on either side of the stream. As soon as they reached the fork in the track, they'd see me by the boats unless I hid under one. That was an idiot's choice since I'd bet they had been sent to guard the boats, which meant our escape had to have been discovered by now. I looked at the distant towers of White-hair's keep; there didn't seem to be any commotion over that way but then that wasn't really his style.

I dashed for the better cover of the boathouse and worked my way round to get it between me and the approaching peril. There was a little door at the far end and I was through it like a cat fleeing ratting dogs. It was indeed a boathouse; the skeletal framework of a new vessel stood on trestles down the centre and benches either side were cluttered with carved sections of bone, glue pots, binding, needles and scraps of leather. I moved carefully down to the main doors and peered through the crack.

The Elietimm were coming down the track at a fair pace but, now I could see them more clearly, I saw all was not the highly trained efficiency we had come to expect. They were being led by an individual in a long black cloak whose very posture proclaimed arrogance, and he was being shadowed by a burly hulk with silver chains gleaming round the upper arms of his jerkin and the natural swagger of a second-in-command. This was all very impressive and the four following them looked suitably alert and well trained. What let their parade down was the lard-arse puffing along at the rear. He moved with the grace of a pregnant sow, though rather more slowly, and he was falling further and further behind.

As I watched, the others halted and the one I would have called a sergeant was clearly shouting at Fatty, reminding me of every reason I've ever had for avoiding working in an organised militia. I caught snatches of the guttural abuse and realised the breeze was coming off the land, which would work to our advantage. Any noise we made would be carried away from them and the long shadow of the boathouse stretched away to my left, which meant the sun would be in their eyes as well. We had to make use of every possible advantage and I quickly scanned my surroundings for anything useful.

I pulled a nicely tanned skin down off a rack in a moment and grabbed some shears to cut a sling. It wasn't the same as poisoned darts but at least I'd have something to hit the bastards with before we met hand to hand. I paused for a moment, hacked off another strip, sliced a hole in the centre and produced myself an instant leather tabard which had more chance than a woollen tunic to turn a blade. The only other potentially useful things I could see were a clutch of heavy spears lashed together out of sections of wood, bone and leather. I picked one up and, keeping an eye out through the crack in the door, weighed it dubiously in my hand. I'd be better off trying to throw one of the paddles but perhaps I could use it as a sort of pike, which is a useful weapon so long as you can keep the bastard trying to slice you up at the pointed end.

I propped a handful of the spears against the door and bent to feel around for sling-sized pebbles on the shingle floor as I watched the sergeant move back along the track to give Fatty a personal kicking. Movement in the long grass on the seaward side of the dunes caught my eye and Ryshad risked a brief glance over the tussocks. I slipped the bar from the door, cracked it open and waved him down, thinking fast. The Elietimm had to be coming to guard the boats and, as far as I was concerned, alone and discovered meant dead. The four of us might have been able to take the seven of them but Shiv was out of the game for a stand-up fight. What we needed was to get together and hold them off just long enough to push a boat into the water and escape. This was the time for a distraction and I just hoped Ryshad would be able to hold Aiten back long enough for me to manage one.

A side window gave me a view towards the huts and I could just see the grey-green thatch of a roof. Setting a fire has always been a favourite option when I've needed to divert unwelcome attention and this would have the added advantage of occupying whoever might be living in the little settlement since I didn't fancy adding men used to putting spears through swimming sea-beasts to the opposition.

I concentrated on the patch of roof with all my might and sang out the words of the cantrip, drawing on every Forest rhythm bred in my bones. Nothing seemed to happen for a sickeningly long moment, then I saw a grey haze spiral skywards and greedy snatches of flame licking at the thatch. I eased the door open again and saw the others were all now crouching cautiously at the very edge of the cover. Saedrin bless them, they were obviously going to make a break to support me, whatever the risks.

I held them still with an open palm and watched the Elietimm detachment carefully. The sergeant was now nose to nose with Fatty and prodding him in the chest to punctuate his words. The officer in the cloak was watching with proud aloofness while two of the others were clearly enjoying seeing someone else get a poke in the stones for a change. All three jumped when one of the others caught sight of the fire spitting up over the roofs of the huts and shouted; I very nearly laughed despite the dangers of our situation as they moved, halted, looked wildly at each other and then started up the right-hand fork of the track.

I flung the door open and waved the others in, heart racing as I stood helplessly motionless, sling in hand as they raced across the open ground. Aiten and Ryshad had Shiv between them, his arms over their shoulders, and I swear his boots stayed dry as they crossed the little stream. I really thought they were going to make it but as they passed the cluster of boats, some alert bastard looked back to the sea and saw them, his yell silencing the rising murmur of panic from the huts.

As the others reached me in the mouth of the boathouse, the soldiers turned to face us and I saw a gold gorget at the throat of the officer flash in the sunlight.

'Thank you, Lord of the Sea,' Aiten breathed with savage satisfaction.

'How so?' I asked nervously as I saw him tighten his grip on his sword in a purposeful manner.

'That's the bastard who was in charge of trying to kick my stones up through my ribs earlier.'

I could see he was spoiling for a fight and I suppose it was hard to blame him.

'Look, Ait, we just need to hold them off until we can get a boat in the water,' I warned him. 'We can't take them on in a straight fight.'

'I'll deal with the boat.' Shiv was looking strained but alert and I flashed him a quick smile.

'I'll help.' Ryshad passed the spears to Aiten. 'Try and spoil someone's day with these.'

Aiten grinned with a savagery I'd never seen on his good-natured face before and he hefted the solid missile with an ease which spoke encouragingly of experience. I sorted out a good handful of stones and we crouched in the doorway as the enemy drew closer.

'I don't think they can see us,' I murmured with wonder as they came onwards, the one who'd raised the alarm gesturing to the rest as they looked all around the boats and the boathouse. The sergeant was still to the rear, giving Fatty a hard time, and this was clearly distracting the others.

'We're in shadow, aren't we? They have the sun in their eyes.' Aiten narrowed his eyes measuringly then rose with an explosive shout to hurl his spear.

'Catch, shit for brains!'

I don't know if it was the surprise or the sunlight dazzling him but the first one just stood there till the heavy spear ripped right through his chest, sending him crashing to the ground in a welter of blood and gurgles. The shock halted the others long enough for Aiten to launch a second spear into the air but they were soon moving when they realised what was coming their way. Much good it did them; Aiten had clearly done this before and another one went down screaming like a pig with the head of the spear embedded in his leg.

Harsh yet oddly musical syllables rang out over his screams and I realised the officer was starting a chant as Ryshad and Shiv broke for the boats. Shiv worked on the rope of one while Ryshad put his sword through the bottom of the others.

'Dozy bitch, a gorget means magic, doesn't it?' I muttered angrily to myself as I rapidly wound up the sling with an egg-sized stone. You can forget any nonsense about hitting him between the eyes, I aimed for his chest. The stone flew hard and true and he doubled over, sinking to his knees with a screech that promised a cracked rib at the very least.

'Right, you bastards, I'm going to kill you!' Aiten launched himself out of the doorway, sword in one hand, dagger in the other.

'Wait!' I yelled pointlessly. I looked at Shiv and blinked as I saw the complicated knots unravelling themselves under his hand. Ryshad helped him flip the boat right way up and then ran to back up Aiten, who was closing with the two leading Elietimm.

'Dast's teeth!' Since Shiv was getting the boat into the water rapidly enough, I ran after the two bloodthirsty idiots. Ryshad went for the sergeant and Fatty was backing off with an expression of horror so I looked for an opening to help Aiten, who was hacking down the guard of the remaining two foot soldiers.

A guttural hiss alerted me to the officer, who was looking up from his agony with hatred in his eyes. I stared at him and froze in unreasoning terror as I recognised him. His hair was dark and his skin unlined but every bone of his face told me this was what the Ice-man must have looked like a generation ago.

He spat something at me in measured cadences but before he could get to the end of his spell, I was on him, daggers drawn and bowling him to the ground with the unthinking strength of panic. He cursed and managed to grab one of my wrists while my other dagger scraped uselessly at the mail on his back. With a thrust of his hips, he managed to roll us over but I've done more dirty fighting than I usually care to admit and I was out from under him, doing my best to kick into the side of his knee joints as I carried on over and back to the top. I ducked down and butted him in the nose, and felt a warm gush of blood in my hair as his attempts to speak choked on it. A scaring pain in my scalp meant he was biting back but I managed to get my free hand round and raked up toward his eyes with my nails. In a convulsive movement, he nearly threw me off; I managed to hook a leg round him but lost my free hand to his vice-like grip. We rolled over and over, sand in my eyes, my nose, my mouth as we each struggled to find an advantage over the other.

His greater weight was beginning to tell and I was starting to think I had caught a wolf in a rat-trap when he suddenly choked and released his grip on me to claw at his throat. He turned a peculiar shade of blue and slumped across me, completely unconscious. I heaved his body off and scrubbed my face vaguely clean. Shiv was standing a little way off looking at the collapsed officer with a remarkably smug expression.

'What happened?'

'I took the air out of his lungs,' Shiv said with vicious satisfaction.

I stared down. 'Is he dead?'

'Not yet, not if I don't want him to be.'

I looked over to Aiten and Ryshad, who were standing over Fatty. He had evidently thrown away his sword and was down on his knees, belly wobbling like a skin of ale as he spread his hands in supplication.

'He'll tell them where we went!' Aiten was clearly all for killing him.

'He can tell them we've got your pal with the gold necklace,' Ryshad countered. 'I told you a good hostage would be worth having.'

Aiten spat something at Fatty and they left him cowering in the sand as I helped Shiv drag Gold-gorget into the boat.

'So you've got your hostage, Rysh, and Ait got to kill people. If everyone's happy, can we please leave this pissing place?'

Ryshad and Aiten grinned at me as they got in and it was impossible to keep up my pretence of irritation.

'You get more luck than you deserve!' I shook my head at Ryshad.

'Dastennin favours me, what can I do?' he asked, wide-eyed.

'You can keep praying and keep on his good side.' Shiv ran his hands along the sides of the boat and it began to move rapidly through the water. 'We've got half a stuffing ocean to cross before we're anywhere near safety.'

Bremilayne Docks,
3rd of For-Winter

Casuel stamped across the quay, his face clouded with a sufficiently forbidding scowl so that even the idling dockers gave him room to pass. He clutched the wax-paper packets of herbs and dried fruit with impotent anger. He was a wizard, he fumed; he was due more respect than this. It was all very well for Esquire Camarl, he had grown up used to ordering menials around and doubtless he didn't mean anything by it, but Casuel was not a footman and Camarl really shouldn't be sending him out on errands like this. Why wasn't Darni running up and down the steep streets, collecting pointless packages like a maidservant? He looked across to the far side of the harbour and the distant ship riding gently at the quayside, a tall-masted, rangy vessel with steep sides and a questing prow, the tiny figures of Darni and Camarl busy with the crew as they prepared to sail.

A ragged skein of crab-trapper boats rounded the long arm of the sea-wall. They bobbed over the gleaming waters of the harbour and began to tie up. People with baskets on their arms started to gather on the dockside, eager for first pick of the catch. Casuel's mood lifted a little at the prospect of fresh lobster: they were so much better on the ocean coast. The food at the guest-house had been a pleasant surprise, if the accommodations were a little old-fashioned and sparse. He pushed his cloak back over one shoulder and tucked the parcels under his arm. At least it wasn't raining today; the sky was a freshly washed blue and a gentle breeze was bowling fluffy clouds overhead. He wasn't exactly looking forward to risking the open ocean but hopefully their voyage wouldn't be too rough, not with Otrick to control the winds.

'Casuel, we meet again!'

Casuel halted and turned, astonished to be greeted like this. A short, blond man stepped out from behind a rack of drying nets, all smiles.

'You have the advantage, sir.' Casuel tried to look unconcerned but his mind was racing. This was the enemy! How could he summon help? Darni? Camarl?

'We met in Hanchet, don't you recall?' The fair-haired man smiled cheerfully. 'You were most helpful; spite and envy make a mind so very easy to read.'

Casuel gaped and turned to run but the man gripped his arm with fingers of iron and steel flashed in his other hand. A shocking pain lit through Casuel's head and his eyes were held, frozen, helpless in that icy green gaze. A disdainful touch scoured the surface of his mind, rough and superficial.

'So that's the ship and those are your allies; thank you, that's all I wanted to know.' The enemy glanced at the purchases in the crook of Casuel's elbow with a brief, contemptuous smile and then stabbed him abruptly above the belt buckle. Casuel folded around the hammer blow of the knife stroke and was pushed with one swift movement into the tangle of nets. He clasped frantic hands around the hilt, whimpering as an ominous thread of blood welled from his guts, gasping for breath. The blond man looked down for a moment then vanished in the gathering throng.

'Help,' he croaked. 'Help me!'

Casuel managed to get himself to a sitting position, half hanging in the nets, muscles cramping brutally in a vain effort to do something about the red-hot agony spreading from his midriff. Warm blood on his fingers was sticky and slippery at the same time. Yelping like a kicked dog, Casuel managed to shuffle forward on his buttocks, biting clean through his lip as the pain seared him. He rested, panting, his boots clear of the nets, blood trickling through the cobbles to pool around the scuffed leather, glistening drops scarlet on the wrappings of his little parcels.

Steps rang on the stones and Casuel looked up with relief. 'Help me, I've been—'

He stared, uncomprehending, as the fisherman stepped over his feet and went on his way regardless. 'You bastard,' he croaked despairingly.

The knife was a white-hot rod running from his stomach to his spine, an iron bar of scorching agony, his torn body melting around it. The rest of him was growing colder by the breath, clammy sweat freezing on his brow.

Casuel screamed in fresh anguish as someone stepped on his ankle, wrenching his leg and sending new torment to his abdomen.

'Watch where you're stepping!' the fishwife said cheerfully to her companion as their skirts swished past Casuel's disbelieving eyes. They could not see him! They did not realise he was there! How could that be? There was no magic worked round him! He leaned against the post, eyes blank with fear. He was going to die here!

Movement on the dockside caught his eye; the boats were unloading baskets of sluggishly moving crustaceans and the fishwives and townsfolk were stepping forward to argue the prices. A whimper of fresh despair escaped him, nothing to do with the agonies in his belly. Pushing through the throng, Casuel saw several blond heads heading for the distant berth of the pirate ship. He reached for the earth, a futile effort, the iron in his stomach twisting and dispersing the magic. He clutched at the wound in hollow terror; it felt as if his whole stomach was tearing apart inside him.

'Casuel!' Allin's white face peered through the netting, her expression one of horror. 'Halcarion help me!'

'The enemy, here!' Casuel struggled for more words, light-headed, shuddering as every sense in his body screamed in confusion over the wound.

Allin moved round to kneel in front of him, dumping her basket and ripping at her petticoats.

'Hold still,' she commanded, as she folded a pad of linen. A faint scent of lavender floated to Casuel's nostrils, rising above the charnel smell of blood like a ghost of summer.

'Here.' She pressed the linen against the wound and Casuel

gasped. After a moment, he grasped the hilt of the dagger but Allin gripped his fingers tight, heedless of the blood.

'No, not until we've got you to a surgeon.' She removed his hand with absolute authority and looked around, her round face pale and set.

'Look!' Casuel pointed to the ship, arm jerky and unco-ordinated, desperation in his faint voice.

There was trouble aboard the pirate vessel. Allin stared as one of the great booms came crashing down, sails tearing with a sound like thunder, the screams of a crushed man mingling with the shrieks of the gulls. A sweep of torn canvas landed on two men to become an active, smothering thing, their muffled struggles increasingly frantic as they grappled with it, ragged edges rippling with malice as it wrapped itself tighter and tighter. A body fell from the highest mast, ropes coiling after it like snakes. A second man fell but was caught up before he reached the deck, a killing noose looping around his neck; he hung in the shrouds like a broken-necked bird. A little crab-boat at the next berth bobbed against the jetty, its crew oblivious as they haggled cheerfully with a knot of eager customers.

'Get Planir,' Casuel gasped but Allin was already tying the rough dressing tight to his wound with her sash.

'Don't move and for Saedrin's sake, don't touch the knife,' she commanded and ran full-pelt across the quay, heedless of the surprised glances of the populace calmly going about their business.

Casuel leaned against the net-post, sucking in feeble breaths, eyes wide with dread and despair as he watched the chaos on their vessel. He could see Darni now, unmistakable in his red cloak and dark hair. The cheerful sunlight danced on Darni's sword as he flailed at some invisible enemy, swinging this way and that at another unseen foe. Wheeling swiftly round, he lunged, lashing out and felling some hapless seaman, heedless of his unintended victim as he pursued the phantoms only he could see. Swaying and jumping, his sword swung, all his attention on the empty air before him. He lunged but less smoothly this time, his moves becoming more and more ragged, panic threatening as he looked round, assailed now on two sides, three and more.

Camarl was backing slowly along the stern rail, dagger held before him, half bent in a fighting crouch, one hand reaching backwards to check his position, eyes fixed on some unseen threat. He darted forward, then back, leaping to one side to avoid an imaginary thrust. Flinching, he clapped a hand to his shoulder, body angling to protect the injury his mind was seeing, arm hanging uselessly by his side, blade falling from numb fingers. Moving backwards once more, he suddenly ripped off his green cape and dived over the rail, plunging into the busy waters of the harbour. Casuel saw his head reappear briefly but realised with consternation that the young noble's attempts at swimming were failing, the skills of his body foiled by his mind's conviction that his arm was useless.

Several more white gouts of foam in the dull green water of the harbour signalled the fates of men falling from the rigging. The booms and canvases of the ocean ship swung wildly to and fro, flailing as if they were caught in some manic whirlwind while the gaily coloured sails of the little fishing boats hung gently flapping in the light breezes. Ropes lashed out at impossible angles to tangle around legs and arms, tools and spars rose from the deck to stab and club unprotected heads. A water cask pulled itself from its rack and bowled down on a couple of lads cowering by the deckhouse, crushing them mercilessly. All the while, the everyday business of the port hummed merrily around the carnage, unseeing, unheeding.

'Stuff me!'

Casuel managed to lift his heavy head to see Otrick staring down with a expression of mingled horror and wrath. He raised a blood-stained hand to point to the crowded quayside.

'Fair heads.' He forced the words out through gritted teeth.

Otrick leaned forward, eyes narrowing. 'I'll have the bastards.'

Women waiting their turn to pick over the baskets of blue-grey shells began to look around as fingers of wind plucked at their scarves and shawls. A couple of fishermen glanced up at the clear blue sky with puzzled expressions. Gusts of air snatched at skirts and cloaks and the press of the crowd began to loosen and spread out. Water began to seep across the quayside, exclamations rising as women cursed suddenly damp stockings and looked to see who could be so carelessly discarding slops, whether garbage had choked one of the sloping drains that ran across the quay. Several stumbled, cobbles unaccountably loosened, rolling underfoot. One nameless figure slipped and fell, a circle of confusion rippling outwards as someone else tripped over her, basket rolling round to catch another unwary victim. The cheerful mood of the morning began to waver as people looked round, puzzled and disconcerted.

'Right.' Otrick cracked his knuckles and bright blue fire crackled in his eyes as they glinted in the sunlight. The fair-haired men had almost reached the ocean ship but the growing disquiet among the quayside crowd was slowing them, although still no one seemed to see the foreigners, surely unmissable with pale heads shining above their stark black livery, silver studs dull with sea salt. A sudden, smacking wave wrenched a clutch of the little crab boats away from the dock, ropes snapping, the waiting townsfolk recoiling from the spray and leaving the black-clad men exposed. Water bubbled up around their feet, foam seething through the cobbles. Cracks opened up in the dock as their boots came down, catching their iron-shod heels. The men staggered, buffeted as if by a winter gale, when women just strides away could move without hindrance. Cries of alarm and annoyance from the people rose above the slapping of the water and the cries of the gulls. A dark cloud boiled up from nowhere and hid the sun.

'Just knock them down, I don't want anything too dramatic.' Planir appeared with Allin at his heels and raised a hand as Otrick gathered sparkling blue light around his fingers. 'We don't want to start a riot and I don't want too much to have to explain to Messire! This is bad enough as it is.'

The old wizard snorted with disapproval but the blackness melted away and the fair-haired men simply dropped to the cobbles as if they'd been clubbed. Shouts of consternation rose as the fishwives and sailors suddenly noticed the interlopers; some began forcing a path away, others moved closer then hesitated to approach, gesturing with wondering hands.

'The ship!' Allin pointed a trembling finger.

The chaos on the vessel showed no signs of abating; knots of terrified men were huddling together, fighting off ropes and sailcloth, spars and cargo as the lifeless objects around them continued their assaults. Some were trying to reach the rail and take their chances in the harbour but loose timbers swung from ropes, scything viciously down to fell anyone who made the attempt.

'So, who's doing that?' Planir murmured, lips thin as he set his jaw, turning to scan the dockside and the rise that led up to the town.

'I can't feel a thing; just how are the bastards working it?' Otrick's face was sour with frustration.

'There.' Planir pointed and a nondescript figure half-hidden behind a stall suddenly doubled over. 'Look for someone else who's not moving, towards or away.'

'Someone will have Casuel's blood on his hands.' Allin spoke up. 'Could you find that?'

Otrick rubbed his hands together and scowled. 'I've got one, there by the inn.'

A woman screamed as a man measured his length on the cobbles and nearly tripped her. She kicked him in passing, half by mistake, and continued to hurry away. Real panic was starting to run through the crowd now and the hapless man disappeared under a mass of booted feet and homespun skirts. When the press parted, he was lying like a trampled doll, cloak soiled, footprints clearly visible on it, fair hair dull with dirt and bloodied around his face.

The chaos on the pirate ship halted abruptly; Darni emerged from a gang of sailors and ran down the gangplank, sword naked before him. He ran along the dock, arms spread, head shaking, startled fishermen falling backwards out of his path. Darni ignored them, alternately searching the crowd for anyone he could legitimately attack and glancing down into the water for any sign of those who'd fallen or jumped.

'Darni, here!' Planir did not seem to raise his voice but the warrior evidently heard him halfway across the harbour and headed their way.

'Where are the stuffing bastards?' he demanded, face scarlet, drenched in sweat, seemingly oblivious to the chill of the season. 'I'll have their stones for this!'

'We'll take care of them in a while.' Planir knelt beside Casuel, concern plain on his face. 'Let me see that.'

He loosened the dressing with careful fingers, maintaining the pressure on the wound and mindful not to touch the bone hilts of the dagger. He snatched a quick look beneath the sodden linen and then tied it on tightly again.

'We need a surgeon and fast,' he said grimly.

'Bespeak Hadrumal,' Darni insisted. 'Talk to someone who was working with Geris; they'd been working on healing.'

Planir looked at Allin, who was folding another pad from strips of torn linen. 'You did well.'

'You learn a lot when stupid men spend half a summer dying in your hedgerows,' she said unhappily, kneeling to apply the new dressing. 'How are we going to move him?'

'Here.' Darni removed his cloak and spread it on the ground. 'We'll take a corner each and go slowly.'

'Let me help. What's happened to Cas?'

Casuel opened bleary eyes to see Esquire Camarl looking round Darni's shoulder, sodden hair in rats' tails, dripping water down his face.

Casuel wanted to say something, anything, a last message, but all he could manage was a tearful whisper. 'Tell my mother I love her.'

'Tell her yourself, I'm not a messenger-boy,' Darni said, his robust words at odds with his careful hands as he lifted Casuel on to the thick wool. 'It's a good thing this cloak's red, Cas, but you can still pay the cursed wash bill.'

'Where's the best surgeon?' Planir demanded of Camarl.

'Cockleshill,' the Esquire answered after a moment's thought. 'This way.'

'Shit!' Otrick's curses halted them after a couple of awkward steps.

Allin followed his pointing arm and saw the remaining crew from the pirate ship had gathered around the fallen foemen. Arms were raised with improvised clubs and the occasional flash of a blade, boots were going in with concerted, bone snapping determination. One gang rolled a ragged bundle to the dockside and dumped it lifeless into the scummy water lapping rubbish round the slimy wooden piles.

'Saedrin's stones!' Planir shook his head. 'Oh well, they're just the spear-carriers, aren't they. Camarl, it's those two we want. Find something to tie them up in.' He shifted his grip on the cloak to one hand, to point with the other.

Casuel could not stifle a low moan as he was rolled sideways.

'Of course, I see them.' Camarl moved and Casuel heard him calling for assistance in the commanding tones of a Tormalin noble. 'You and you, those men are criminals. Hold them! You, bring me rope, fast as you can. Captain, get me a runner, I need to contact the Patron D'Olbriot!'

'Let's get going.' Darni could not hide the concern in his voice. 'Cas is in a bad way.'

They moved, slowly, awkwardly, taking small shuffling steps over the uneven cobbles.

'Cheer up,' Otrick said abruptly. 'Young Cas here's finally managed something useful.'

Casuel stared muzzily at the old wizard, blinking as he swayed between the four of them, looking up into a dizzying pattern of backs, roofs and clouds, concerned voices echoing around him, words meaningless as his wits bled out.

'What are you talking about?' The exasperation in Planir's tone betrayed his worry.

'You were wondering how to persuade the Council to back you, weren't you?' Otrick was starting to puff a little as they began to climb up the steep street. 'There'll be no questions now. These people have attacked a mage, and not some backstreet philtre-maker, one of our own, even if it is Casuel. When did something like that last go unpunished? Not since the Chaos, if I remember my history right!'

Otrick's thin cheeks were scarlet with exertion as he looked down into Casuel's grey, drawn face.

'There you go, Cas, you've done something not even the Archmage could have done. The Council will follow us across any ocean and back again now, just to make sure everyone learns they can't get away with this kind of thing. We'll have the bastards for this, don't you fret.'

'What about the ship and the crew?' Darni asked grimly. 'We're going nowhere without them and they look in a pretty shitty state to me at the moment. What's your pal the birdman going to do about that?'

'Shit!'

Casuel felt himself slipping away under waves of pain and dizziness but could not shake a sense of outrage that the last thing he should hear was the Archmage swearing like a five-year mercenary.

The Ocean Approaches, Islands of the Elietimm, 3rd of For-Winter

The seal-boat hurried out to sea with Shiv's magic urging it on. We bounced unnervingly over the foaming breakers as we left the shore but were soon out among the great, rolling swell of the open ocean. I looked back with relief to see the black sands and sere grasslands disappear behind us. Soon the towering summits of the grey mountains were only intermittently in sight as our fleeing boat rose and fell among the peaks and troughs of the sombre green seas. I turned away from the sight, which was threatening to make me queasy. Ryshad was managing the steering with a reassuring display of competence while Shiv knelt in the nose, all his attention questing ahead as he used every fragment of his power to get us away.

It had to be the first time ever I was glad to find myself in a boat, which only went to prove how much I was dreading recapture. The spray from the tops of the swells was caught by the wind and we were soon all wet and chilled but none of us was about to complain. I sat behind Shiv and when the oscillating view of featureless ocean palled, which was pretty rapidly, I turned to see Aiten prodding our prisoner thoughtfully with a foot. He had been dumped unceremoniously in the bottom of the boat and, as far as I was concerned, he could stay there all the way home.

'He's still out of the game, I take it?' I wasn't going to get anywhere near Gold-gorget if I could help it, unconscious or not.

'Totally off the board,' Aiten said cheerfully, grinning broadly at me. 'You know, I really didn't think we were going to get out of that one, flower.'

'Me neither.' I shook my head, which was still ringing with disbelief at our luck.

'We're not out of it yet,' Ryshad reminded us a little sharply, a frown of concentration on his face as he guided the vessel through some turbidly coiling seas.

'We're off those cursed islands and that's good enough for me,' Aiten said robustly and I found myself smiling too.

'You know, Rysh, the only convincing thing I ever heard a Rationalist say was "enjoy the moment when it happens". This one feels pretty good to me.'

That won a reluctant smile from Ryshad and, when Shiv turned to catch what we were saying, I could see the strain was lessening in his face too.

Whatever he was about to say was lost in a sudden gurgle from Aiten's belly.

'Dast's teeth, I'm starving!'

Now he'd mentioned it, I could see us all thinking the same thing. Fear fills the belly while it lasts but we'd need more than fresh air to see us across however much ocean there was in front of us.

Shiv rubbed his hands together and the boat slowed.

'What's the matter?' I asked, more alarm in my tone than I cared to hear.

'I can't keep us moving, keep our friend unconscious and call for fish at the same time,' Shiv explained. 'I'm just not fit to do it all yet.'

Ryshad frowned. 'I'd say we need to keep moving as fast as you can send us. If we tie him up,' he prodded the prisoner with a toe, 'can you just keep his mouth shut so he can't spell us?'

Shiv nodded, his eyes brightening. 'I can put bands of air round his mouth. If I don't have to keep him down, we should be able to get on a lot quicker.'

I reached for the braided leather tether. 'Why didn't you say so?'

I doubled the rope, twisted a slip knot into the centre to go round his neck then used each end to tie Gold-throat's hands and feet. The more he struggled, the sooner he would strangle himself and that would end any threat he might be thinking of posing.

Aiten whistled with admiration. 'You know a thing or two about tying beasts, don't you?'

I tugged on an end to make sure it was fast. 'I'm a woman of many talents.'

My cool pose was spoiled when I jumped as a fat fish dropped past me into the floor of the boat.

'How are you at gutting?'

I turned to see Shiv tossing another dripping offering over his shoulder.

'Useless, since you ask, on fish at least.' I looked at the flapping thing with distaste. 'I suppose there's no way of cooking it?'

'Fish this fresh? No need!' Aiten drew his dagger, looked approving as he tested the edge and cleaned the fish with a few deft strokes. He laid it on the seat across the middle of the boat and sliced wafer-thin mouthfuls from the meat.

'Try it.' He offered me a piece. There was nothing for it, I folded it into my mouth and did my best to swallow without chewing. Actually, it wasn't too bad but I didn't relish the thought of raw fish and plain water all the way home.

Aiten turned to pass some to Ryshad, who ate it without comment or expression. He saw me looking at him and laughed for the first time since we'd escaped.

'I'd rather have some pepper sauce with it, or a decent wine, but I'm quite partial to fresh fish.'

'They have a lot of ways of preparing it in Zyoutessela, don't they?' Shiv reached for some, without any real enthusiasm, I was glad to see.

'Thin sliced with herb paste, soused in sour wine or citrus, rolled with pepper sauce and black salt.' Aiten looked dreamy-eyed for a moment. 'When we get back, I'll take you all to the finest fish-house on the east coast.'

I coughed on the aftertaste of the sea. 'Can you sweeten some water for us, Shiv?'

We all looked around in vain for something to use as a bucket.

'There's always our boots,' Aiten said dubiously.

'We can just use our hands,' Shiv said firmly and as we dipped handfuls from the sea he filled the water with blue light, leaving it free of salt and fit to drink. It was a slow process and the water tasted oddly dead and flat but I wasn't about to complain. As Ryshad leaned forward to take his turn, it occurred to me we should be sharing the steering.

'Can I give you a break?'

Ryshad shook his head. 'Don't get me wrong, but you've no experience with boats, have you? Ait and I'll manage between us.'

I wasn't about to argue or take offence. Cold water and raw fish weren't sitting any too easily in my stomach so I tucked myself down to shelter as best I could from the wind and spray and carefully unfolded Geris' notes. If I could do nothing else, I could find if there was anything we could use to defend ourselves or speed up our journey.

After what must have been most of the morning had passed, I thought I might have found something but as I looked up from the parchment, I saw Gold-throat staring intently at me as he lay uncomfortably in the belly of the boat, outrage shouting silently from his vivid green eyes. I stared back at him, throwing a challenge at him, but he did not drop his gaze.

I looked beyond him to Ryshad, who raised an eyebrow at the intensity of my expression. I nodded at Gold-throat.

'What do you reckon we should do with him then?' I asked casually.

Ryshad paused for a breath and winked at me before replying in the same easy tone. 'We could cut him up for fish bait if you like, or just eat him ourselves if you fancy warm meat.'

'What?'

I ignored Aiten's surprised exclamation; I'd seen fear flare in those grass-coloured eyes as Gold-throat stiffened uselessly against his bonds.

'I'd say our friend here speaks Tormalin.' I turned to Shiv. 'Can you stop up his ears as well?'

'I should have done that earlier, shouldn't I?' Shiv bit his lip with annoyance at the uncharacteristic lapse and wove a tight band of sparkling blue around the man's helpless head. As it faded, I saw real fear in his face that anger could not drive out and I bent closer to stare into those pale eyes with all the threat I could muster. This time, he turned his gaze aside and closed his eyes.

'He's all right. Anyway, Shiv, one of the rest of us should have thought of it as much as you.'

Satisfied, I returned to my notes. 'Listen. There's something here we should try. It's described as a concealment, a way of hiding your tracks.'

'What use is that on water?' Ryshad frowned.

'I don't think it means real tracks but whatever it is that the aetheric spell casters pick up on.' I scowled at the document. 'I'm pretty sure that's what it signifies.'

Aiten shrugged. 'Can't hurt to try it.'

I cleared my throat a little self-consciously and ran through the words silently to find their metre.

'Ar mel sidith, ranel marclenae.' I chanted the words but nothing seemed to happen.

'Has it worked?' Ryshad asked curiously.

I felt more than a little foolish. 'I've no idea.'

There was nothing anyone could say to that. We settled down for a tedious afternoon watching grey waves rolling up to meet a grey sky as the boat scooted over the billows. We were all starting to look and feel more than a little grey ourselves by the end of the day.

I hadn't realised I'd fallen asleep but it was morning when Shiv patted me on the shoulder and I blinked up at him, disconcerted.

'Look, my magic's working anyway!'

I turned to see some enormous fish leaping clean out of the water as they headed straight for us. I swallowed my instant of fear when I saw the smile on Shiv's face and wondered what on earth, or in this case, in the ocean, these could be.

'Dastennin's hounds!' Aiten greeted the creatures with a

glad cry and I saw Ryshad was smiling broadly as well so I bit down hard on my own nervousness.

The huge fish frolicked around the nose of the boat and I had to admit they had very friendly faces; long, almost beak-like snouts with engagingly curved mouths. They made peculiar squeaking noises as they reared out of the water to look at Shiv and I saw their mouths were full of effective-looking teeth. I told myself not to worry until the others did but could not help jumping when one surfaced next to me and showered me with warm, fetid spray from a hole in its head.

I tried to restrain myself but I had to ask. 'What are they?'

Shiv looked round from feeding a large one. 'They're dolphins, sea animals, like the whale, but smaller.'

I looked at the sleek bodies thronging the waters, triangular fins cutting through the foam.

'You called them?'

Shiv nodded. 'They can tell me a lot about the waters we're in. I need to know when we're going to reach that main current heading south for a start; crossing that's going to take every scrap of power I've got. If we hit it before I realise, we could find ourselves taken right past the Cape of Winds without knowing it.'

'I think proving there's one new continent is enough for this trip.' Ryshad reached over the side to rub an inquisitive head.

'What did you call them?' I was getting more used to the cheerful creatures but kept my hands well inside the vessel.

'Dastennin's hounds. They're sacred to him.' Aiten was feeding them scraps as well. 'They're supposed to be able to travel between here and the Otherworld whenever they want to, not just in dreams or death.'

A cheerful face popped out of the water and looked at me with a convincing air of intelligence.

I bowed and addressed it in formal tones. 'If you've any way of reaching Dastennin or any of the gods, please ask them to get us home.'

The others smiled but no one laughed. As Aiten had said, it couldn't hurt to try.

I gaped as the creatures abruptly ceased their antics and all dived deep into the waters; I looked questioningly at Shiv.

'I've sent them to find out where we are in relation to the currents around about,' he explained. 'They're going to come back from time to time and make sure we're keeping on course.'

He pointed to the unbroken cloud cover above us, the monotony of the heaving ocean and did not need to explain further. I ate a breakfast of cold, raw fish without enthusiasm and wondered how we were going to survive an ocean crossing in an open boat on such a diet.

Shivering involuntarily and not just from the cold wind, I huddled back down into the meagre shelter afforded by the sides of the boat. I glanced over at Gold-throat and saw a studying look in his dark brown eyes. I had seen that look before and the memory chilled me more thoroughly than wind or water. He met my gaze and hatred burned in those black depths, spitting furious, helpless fire as I lunged desperately over the seat to knock him clean out with a blow to the jaw. I can't usually do that, not even to a bound man, but the fistful of gold and silver rings I'd taken from the keep lent a lot of weight to my argument.

'Livak!' Everyone was staring at me as I wrung my hands to ease my stinging knuckles.

'It wasn't him,' I stammered. 'It wasn't him. Those weren't his eyes; his are green, I was seeing brown, nearly black. It was that bastard, the Ice-man, the one from the keep, his father or whoever he is.'

We all looked uneasily at the motionless body and I wondered how much damage I had done with that punch; you just never can tell and that's got more than a few men hanged.

'The leader, the man who interrogated us, he was looking out through this one's eyes?' Ryshad asked after a long silence.

I nodded emphatically. 'I'm sure of it.'

'So he knows where we are?'

'I've no idea.' I shrugged. 'I just didn't want him looking at me like that.'

'Perhaps we should drop this one over the side,' Shiv said dubiously.

'If they are going to catch up with us, he could be the price for our freedom,' Ryshad reminded him.

Aiten half turned, opening his mouth as if to speak, but said nothing as a puzzled expression crossed his face. He blinked and as I looked at him, I saw the light of his genial brown eyes snuffed out like a candle. Dead blackness looked back at me as his face went slack and unknowing.

'Ait!' I screamed in horror as I dodged a sword blow that would have split my skull like a turnip. I fell backwards on to my bottom, which saved me from the follow-up.

Shiv was moving but was a fraction too slow and the next slashing down stroke bit hard into his arm, snapping the bone like a dead branch. He screamed; I braced myself on the seat and kicked out with both my feet to send whatever had been Aiten just moments before stumbling back down the vessel.

Blue light flared all around me as Shiv pulled me backwards through a spell woven from pure instinct. As the dazzle cleared, I felt a wall of air protecting us.

'Ryshad, he's got Ait, the bastard's got into his head.'

Ryshad had not waited to be told before grabbing his blade but the thing that had been Aiten was already turning to face him, sword rising.

They stood poised in a moment's stillness but when the Ice-man made his move, he did not send Aiten's sword at Ryshad; he had him drive it down right through the bottom of the boat, slicing through the oil-hardened leather like calico.

'You bastard!' Shiv spat as he clutched his shattered arm. He grimaced in pain, gasping with the effort, but I saw a tangle of green lines knit the gash in the hides together again, keeping us afloat for the moment.

I cut my sleeve free and sliced it into crude bandages for Shiv's arm. Blood was streaming down his fingers to mingle with the water sloshing around our feet.

'Let me to it,' I ordered curtly.

Shiv moved his hand, I clamped the linen down hard on the spouting gash. He whimpered with the pain and I cursed helplessly.

'Ait, Ait, fight it, throw the bastard out, fight him.'

There was agony in his voice as I looked up to see Ryshad's sword come up to meet Aiten's, a clash that raised sparks from the blades.

I watched with horror knotting my guts as the puppet that bastard Ice-man had made of his friend continued to lash out at Ryshad. There was none of Aiten's usual finesse; the strokes were signalled like those of a first-season militia recruit and I prayed that this meant Ait was fighting to regain control inside his own skull.

Ryshad's face was twisted with pain and I saw blood on his shirt. I watched with a sinking feeling as I saw Ryshad was not attacking; his sword strokes were all purely defensive. As the Ice-man tightened his hold on Aiten and drew on more of his skills, Ryshad was too slow to respond. Fear of hurting his friend was paralysing him, dooming him.

It was going to have to be me. If Ryshad went down, I could not take on the experience of a trained warrior face to face, whoever was controlling his mind. Shiv was barely conscious now and I shied away from imagining what might happen if he lost control of his spells.

I drew a dagger and moved to the edge of Shiv's barrier, glancing anxiously behind me as I did so. Shiv nodded, face taut with the effort of clinging on to consciousness, knowing what I had to do. I edged forward, as much to ensure I didn't fall out of the wildly rocking boat as to make sure I didn't alert the enemy.

Ryshad lunged forward and I was nearly trodden underfoot as Aiten staggered backwards from a blow to the face. Ryshad had hit him full with the pommel of his sword, blood blew back into my face with the sea spray. I saw the despair on Ryshad's face; that blow should have knocked Aiten clean unconscious into the Otherworld. It had to be the aetheric hold keeping him on his feet. Despair nearly cost Ryshad dear. Aiten's sword flicked forward with something like its old speed and tore a bloody rent down one arm.

I gripped my dagger and wished uselessly for some of my poisons, some of the narcotics I knew could drop a man in his tracks. There was no time. I studied Aiten's back but a heart stroke was too risky; with the boat jouncing underfoot and Aiten lunging back and forth, I chanced hitting a rib, which would be more likely fatal for me. It would have to be a blood stroke, the great vessels in neck or leg. It would drop him fast but would it be fast enough? I just had to pray Ryshad was quick enough to realise what I was doing.

Aiten's feet spread as he steadied himself in the frantically tossing boat. He went to launch a smashing blow at Ryshad's head. As he moved, so did I. Between his legs and up to the inner thigh, I sliced deep into the artery as it left the groin. He stumbled and as Ryshad saw the scarlet gush of life blood, he lunged forward to pin Aiten's arms to his side in a fierce embrace. They sank to their knees in the little boat and Aiten's struggles soon ceased. His head lolled forward on to Ryshad's breast and then sideways; I saw the blackness of possession fade from his eyes, the familiar easy brown returning to pierce my heart. His brow wrinkled faintly and he half opened his mouth as if to speak. Whatever it was went unsaid as he breathed his last in a puzzled sigh and closed his eyes like a tired child.

The agony in Ryshad's face was too much for me to bear and I closed my eyes to blot out the sight of his helpless tears for his friend.

'You bastard, you stinking arsehole, you scum-sucking son of a pox-rotted whore, you're a shit stain on the arse of the world, you'd stuff a pig for pleasure but none would have you.'

I poured out my hatred for the Ice-man in futile obscenities but got no relief. I went to open my eyes again to face the hardness of reality but found I could see nothing.

'You have quite a turn of phrase for a common slut. Still, it enabled me to find you, so I shan't complain.'

The gloom around me lightened with eerie, colourless fire

and I saw the Ice-man coming slowly towards me through coiling darkness. I gasped with a terror that almost stopped my heart. What had he done? Where was I? I clutched frantically at my dagger and held it out to ward him off but it was pale and insubstantial in my hand. Shaking like a tree in a gale, I realised he had trapped me inside my own head. I don't know how I knew, I just did.

'You're very astute,' that hated voice agreed, sounding as if he were standing next to me, and I saw the lips on the image move as it floated towards me. I scowled, anger keeping terror barely at bay now the initial shock had passed. I saw the shape was indistinct, fuzzy at the edges; that gave me some measure of strength but, as I watched, it grew lighter against the blackness, more whole, more dreadful.

'I should have paid more attention to you,' he sighed. 'It's just that Geris took such pains to convince me you were nothing more than a bed-warmer, a little feminine comfort servicing him and your conjuror friend.' A revolting anticipation coloured his tone. 'I shall find a lot more to interest me in your mind and your body now I know the truth, shan't I?'

The fear of him let loose inside my mind again was beyond any terror I had known. He could do what he liked to my body; flesh heals and at worst the Otherworld beckons, but to imagine the feel of him in my very intellect again was not to be borne.

'Talmia megrala eldrin fres.' I spat the words at him and the gloom flared scarlet, the image fading for a second.

'Impudent bitch!'

I winced as a lash of pain scored through my head but I repeated the words, screaming at the top of my mind. The darkness lifted for a moment this time and I racked my brains for anything else I could use as I threw the incantation at him again and again.

'You pitiful thing. I have been inside you once, I can do it again.'

I pushed at the coils of malice that threatened to entangle me and walled my reason against him. He knew my mind but that rune reversed meant I knew his; I fought instinctively, not knowing how or why but with all the strength I could summon. What did I have to lose?

I cursed myself for just skipping over the spells in Geris' list, ignoring the unpronounceable words. What I could remember I gasped out and, gibberish though it might be, as I stumbled through the fragments, I felt the whip of his intellect deaden a little, the questing grip on the edges of my mind slipping. The rhythms spoke to memories buried deep inside me and I felt a new surge of hope.

'Marmol, edril, senil, dexil, wrem, tedren, fathen, ardren, parlen, vrek.'

I chanted out the number song of the Forest, nigh on nonsense to the Folk themselves in latter generations but still taught as my father had passed it to me. I shouted out the ancient words and then found a song naming the birds of the Forest; Raven was a game of the Folk long before the rest of the world knew it. I repeated myself over and over as I searched my childhood for meaningless words and cadences that somehow kept the nightmare that was the Ice-man from invading me again.

I could feel his wrath and, more faintly, his confusion; to him I was no more than a child sticking its fingers in its ears and singing a defiant song to drown out a parent's rebukes. It was all I could do but, as any three-year-old can tell you, it's a difficult tactic to beat.

The darkness around me retreated and the terrifying image of the Ice-man drifted for a moment like smoke in a wind. I could feel burning in my wrists and cold in my feet and redoubled my efforts as my senses told me I was still in command of my own body.

'Livak! Livak!' Ryshad's hoarse voice rang in my ears and the Ice-man's curses echoed through my mind in a last burst of fury.

My vision cleared to show me Ryshad's pain-racked face, nose to nose with me. I gasped at the pain of the vice-like grip he had on my wrists.

'Is it you?'

'My eyes are my own, aren't they?'

He stared deep into me, suspicion fading after a long, tense moment.

'It was him?'

'If he tries for you, say the fire chant, old ballads, ancient prayers, old liturgy if you know any. There's power in the words, I don't know why.'

The wind's chill was biting through me and I realised I was wringing wet with sweat, trembling and exhausted like a beast that's been running for its life. My knees buckled and I sank on to the seat, the sickly-sweet smell of blood revolting all around me as the little boat was swung hither and yon by the uncaring seas.

'Rysh? I had to, you do realise that? It wasn't him, it was that bastard who did it but it was the only way.'

I looked up as I stumbled through the broken words but Ryshad was not looking at me. Complete despair such as I have never seen, other than on the face of a man on a scaffold, filled his eyes. I turned to see what he was gaping at and, as we were carried up on a high hill of green water, I saw a thicket of masts coming out of the pale eastern skies. Sails bellied with a full wind as they sped towards us and long pennants bearing the Ice-man's insignia licked towards us like greedy tongues.

'Trimon save us.' Shiv breathed a heartfelt oath to the god of travellers and I saw him grip the side of the little boat, white-knuckled with effort. My spirits wavered upwards as he turned the nose of the vessel and we skimmed the foaming crest of one swell, then another, then another.

'Oh, Pered,' Shiv said softly as his head sank forwards in total collapse. I lunged forward to keep him from falling clean out of the boat but though I had hold of him I dared not move again in case I upset us all completely. The boat was now broadside on to the rolling waves, rocking sideways and threatening to spill us out. Aiten's body sloshed around in the water steadily gathering around our feet; I saw we were starting to sink as Shiv's spell began to lose its radiance.

'They won't get all of us.' Ryshad moved with sudden fury and heaved the pitiful corpse over his shoulder, his friend's last blood staining his back as he dropped him into the vastness of the ocean.

'Dastennin take you, Ait. Travel well and follow his hounds to the Otherworld, where your deeds will go before you. We'll keep your memory bright here until we join you.'

He choked on the words of farewell and I reached out with my free hand. He grasped it, I held him and we clung together, wordless, helpless, hopeless.

We both jumped as our prisoner suddenly vanished, carried off by some aetheric spell I suppose but to be honest, I really didn't care. I moved to support Shiv as the boat bucked and spun with the gathering winds whipping up the seas around us and finally I wondered if we should just give ourselves up to the greedy waves to spite the Ice-man at the very last. I shivered; it was going to be a dreadful way to die.

The masts came closer and now we could see the long dark hulls of three Elietimm ships. Our boat bucked again, but the jolt did not come from the waves. Another came and I saw a lithe shape slide through the water alongside.

'Dolphins!' Ryshad looked at me with wonder as the pointed fins cut through the spume and began to push our little craft towards the west. A sleek head poked out of the water near Shiv and nodded fruitlessly at him, lunging as if wanting to touch him. I was afraid the beast was going to get us all drowned so I held out Shiv's limp hand to the questing nose.

'Who in Saedrin's name are you?' A ringing voice filled the air around me as the dolphin touched Shiv's hand.

I stared round wildly and saw from Ryshad's startled expression that he had heard it too.

The air above Shiv's senseless head shimmered blue and grew opaque; I saw an old man's face, a sharp-featured man with wind-tossed hair and an unkempt beard, blurred and distorted as if seen through thick glass.

'Who are you?' I could not think what to say.

'I am Otrick,' the face said crisply, as if that said it all. 'Who are you and what are you doing with a mage's ring of power on your hand?'

I looked stupidly at the collection of rings I had gathered and noticed for the first time that I had the silver band purloined from Azazir.

'I didn't realise—'

'Put it on Shivvalan's finger and then put his hand in the water.'

I struggled with the ring, my cold, wet fingers and Shiv's nerveless hands. When I finished my task, green light rose up from the depths all around us and drove the boat forward at a startling pace. A surge of foam gathered at the nose and the dolphins gave up pushing to race alongside, leaping across the bow wave in a manner that I found quite frankly terrifying.

I did not have enough hands for this; I was still keeping Shiv balanced and Ryshad had my dagger hand. I was glad of the reassurance but really wanted to hang on to the side of the boat myself. Ryshad must have seen the insecurity in my face; he moved to sit beside me, putting his arm around me as he gripped the seat for the two of us. The rolling seas drew aside as the boat carried us on the wildest ride of my life. Shaking with whatever fear I had left, I promised myself I'd never set foot on so much as a river ferry after this, not even if finding a bridge took me half a season out of my way.

'What's that?'

As Ryshad spoke, I opened my eyes; I'd been seeing if things were better or worse with them shut.

'Fog?' I tried and failed to keep sarcasm out of my tone. 'Seen much fog like that, have you?'

A spark of life relit Ryshad's eyes and I looked with new interest at the mist. It was a dense bank and I suddenly realised it was moving, ignoring the wind and waves as it swept towards us. I looked over my shoulder but the Elietimm ships were approaching remorselessly. Individual figures could be identified in the rigging now, I could spot the heads of people on the decks. Would we make the shelter of the fog before we were caught? Was this something Otrick had sent?

With a speed that took my breath away, white mist shot towards the enemy ships and I saw it was borne on fists of punishing winds. The Elietimm ships halted like reined-in horses, sails flapping uselessly as the surge of the sea spun them into chaos.

'Look!'

I always seemed to be facing the wrong way. I turned to see the predatory lines of a Dalasorian ocean ship emerge from the bank of fog and our little boat headed for it as if drawn by a rope, green light shining up from the water all around us.

Dead white light startled us, reflecting back from the forbidding barriers of mist, and the Elietimm ships surged forward again. Blue light danced around them, intricate webs of power were woven in the skies, the colour vivid against the dull grey clouds. I groaned. Though the network of spells grew thicker, we could still see some kind of barrier was protecting the ships; if the wizards could not get through, they could not touch the Elietimm.

Our boat rocked as a massive wave gathered the seas to itself and bore down on the pursuing ships. Crashing foam spilled emerald light over the Elietimm prows and one of the ships reeled helplessly under the blow. As it heeled away from the others, taken way beyond the aetheric shelter, air and water combined to raise a spiralling spout which ripped clean through the middle of the hapless vessel. Sails and masts flew high into the sky, decking split like firewood under the axe, while bodies and nameless flotsam scattered far and wide over the dark seas. The prow went down in a roar of white foam, screams abruptly silenced as that half of the stricken vessel headed for the distant ocean floor. The stern rose high in the air, all manner of debris falling as it hung impossibly still for a moment before plunging down to join the rest of the ship. The waters seethed as it vanished, nameless tatters and fragments boiling up from the depths.

The aetheric defences of the Elietimm faltered at the sight and no wonder. The probing blue light coiling round the other ships found a weakness; lightning flashed down from the glowering clouds to shatter the tallest mast on the second ship. The sails were alight in an instant, all three masts blazing like trees in a forest fire. The fires burned brilliant orange but did not die back to the wood once they had devoured the canvas. Now flaring anew with the deep red light that proclaimed wizardry, the greedy flames raced to and fro across the decks, engulfing everyone they snared. Fire sprang vigorously across impossible gaps to snatch at ropes, clothes, hair, devouring all it touched, consuming everything down to ashes with hopeless speed. I swallowed on a suddenly dry mouth as the enchanted blaze took a death grip on the stricken ship, even pursuing those who jumped overboard in a vain effort to escape the inferno, burning them alive as the waters refused to quench the elemental fires. The clouds reflected the light in a horrific parody of sunset and I wondered if it was my imagination or whether I could really feel the heat on my face. The smoke coiled high into the sky, twisted into unnatural patterns by winds doing wizards' bidding as they sought to halt the third ship, which still pressed on, untouched.

'Look, Rysh, dolphins.' I pointed at triangular fins cutting through the chaos of debris on the waters.

Ryshad frowned and drew in a long, slow breath. 'Er, no, I don't think so.'

I looked again and saw something was indeed different: the fins were paired, smaller ones showing a trailing tail.

'Sharks!' Ryshad sprang to his feet and turned to the wizards' ship.

'Halloo, get a rope to us quick,' he bellowed. 'We've wounded aboard and sharks are gathering.'

I watched, not quite understanding until one of the long grey shapes came seeking the source of our tantalising trail. As it passed by our fragile craft, it heeled over and I saw the gill slits of a true fish, cold dead eyes with no spark of intelligence or compassion and a curved mouth with row upon row of teeth like barbs on a man-trap. The boat rocked as it passed and I noticed the shark was longer than our thin-skinned little boat by more than an arm span.

'Will it attack?' I called to Ryshad, who was standing by the rudder, sword poised to smash into any questing nose.

'It's been known,' he said grimly. 'They'll follow the blood in the water.'

His shouts had spurred activity on the wizards' ship; men were lowering a net over the side and I saw a tall figure in rough clothes swinging a coil of rope around his head. It came singing through the air and, as Ryshad caught it, the gang of sailors began hauling us in. I turned to see the sharks were more interested in the easier meat struggling among the wreckage of the other boats and tried to shut my ears to the choking screams.

The third boat pressed on, ignoring the drowning men even as they were sucked down into its wake. It came closer and closer, unslowing despite the multi-hued network of light around it as wizards of every talent fought to penetrate the power that protected it. It loomed above us; we were nearly at the Dalasorian ship but, as I moved ready to catch a rope, I saw sailors suddenly fall from the rigging like frost-killed birds. The men on deck ran this way and that, complete panic threatened by something I could not see as the Elietimm struck back with aetheric magic.

A crack of thunder split the heavens and I saw an instant of blue skies as the clouds above the Elietimm ship were rent apart. The gap closed in a moment but, as we watched, the clouds began to circle, roiling, darkening, coiling down towards the ship. A second thunderclap made my ears hurt and a bright white flash shot down from the heart of the cloud.

It was a dragon, a dragon of air, a creature of clouds and thunder. It was huge, twice the size of Azazir's water dragon, and it dwarfed the black ship as it circled overhead. Its belly was silver rippled with faintest gold like the fine clouds high on a winter's sunrise, and the rest was the pure white of the soaring mountain-high clouds of the plains. It flew down and around the wizards' ship, face questing towards it. We were close now, close enough for me to see the spines on its crest, transparent as icicles, the grey-blue line of scales down the middle of its back rimed with frost, the startling azure of its eyes which narrowed as it suddenly darted towards the hapless enemy ship. Soaring high above and hovering impossibly on broad sweeps of its translucent wings, it lashed at the masts with its massive tail, sending wood, sails and rope crashing down in a hopeless tangle. The screams of the doomed Elietimm were lost in the unearthly howling of the triumphant dragon as it flew upwards, circled and stooped like a hawk, diving to rend anything it could see in its shining white jaws. Claws with the size and brilliance of swords batted the futile defiance of a few soldiers aside into bloody fragments.

The downstroke of its wings battered the water, driving the waves aside to send us crashing into the side of the wizards' ship. I grabbed the netting and clung to it like a miser to his purse strings.

'Help!' I screamed. 'Saedrin's arse, help us!'

Faces appeared over the rail and hands reached down to haul me up into the ship. I shivered in the cold wind as shock finally worked its claws into me but I pushed aside solicitous hands that would have wrapped me in blankets and taken me away.

'We've an unconscious man—'

As I forced the words out between chattering teeth, two lithe mariners were over the side without delay. Ryshad's dark, curly head appeared over the rail and he half climbed, half fell into the boat.

'Livak!'

I turned incredulously to see if I was imagining things or the owner of that harsh voice was really standing behind me.

'Hello, Darni,' I said, having difficulty believing I was seeing him again.

He looked past me to the sailors, lifting Shiv carefully on to a blanket, and I was pleased to see genuine concern in his eyes. A hatch opened and as Shiv was lowered carefully below to waiting hands, Darni heaved a sigh of relief. He moved abruptly to look down into our frail boat.

'Geris?' There was a catch in his voice.

I shook my head wearily. 'We found him but he was already dead.'

The words threatened to choke me. I brushed at my eyes, suddenly full of tears from the biting wind, exhaustion and that abiding sorrow.

Darni's face fell and I could not think what to say. I

reached into my shirt and pulled out the documents I'd been cherishing, sea-stained and sweat-smeared though they were.

'I found some of his work. It's important – one of your wizards should see it.'

Darni ignored the parchments. 'I'd rather have had Geris back,' he said gruffly.

I fought a very real urge to ram the documents down his throat and was about to give him my opinion of his ingratitude when Ryshad draped a blanket over my shoulders. I huddled into it gratefully.

'How do you come to be here, just when we need you? It's a cursed lucky coincidence.'

He clasped his hands tightly round a steaming cup and I reached forward eagerly as a warmly clad sailor offered me one. It was spiced wine and the welcome warmth seared straight down to my toes.

'Coincidence, my arse! This isn't some bard's fantasy ballad.' Darni lifted his head with a trace of his usual arrogance. 'I said we could find a trail in Inglis, and I was right. Those bastards in the black leathers cleared out at the same time as you lot but I took the time to make some contacts in Inglis. Everyone was trying to earn the reward for ringing the bell on Yeniya's killers and we tracked down that group who were trying to blend in by wearing local clothing. You remember, Livak?'

I remembered his scepticism when Geris and I had said that was what they were doing but I kept quiet. It wasn't important now.

'I reckoned they'd be desperate enough to try for another hit when they'd lost out to the other lot. I had details of other prospects with Tormalin artefacts in the city, so I went to the Watch. I'm an Archmage's agent, don't forget, with the insignia to prove it and the Council to back me up. The Guild leaders were as keen as Planir so we kept a close watch on all the likely targets.'

Darni paused for breath, pride in his achievements evident, the desire to say 'I told you so' apparent though mercifully unspoken as yet. I was not interested; he could be as smug as a horse at stud for all I cared. We'd reached the islands before him and we'd found Geris, albeit too late, while he was probably bullying underlings with the threat of someone else's magic. I squeezed my eyes shut on tired tears.

'So how do you come to be here, just when we need you?' Ryshad's tone was curious but sadly lacking in the admiration Darni was clearly expecting. An older, harsher voice answered him

'Shivvalan is my pupil. Once I knew I was looking for him out here, finding those islands was comparatively easy.'

I recognised the skinny white-haired man coming towards us as Otrick. He was shorter than I had imagined, barely my height, dressed in rough canvas breeches and a short, grubby blue cloak. To me, he looked more like a pirate than an eminent wizard. I curbed my desire to ask how come he hadn't managed it sooner, if it was so easy; a handful of days would have made all the difference to Geris, finding us before daybreak would have saved Aiten. I thrust away the sudden memory of his warm blood spilling over my hand.

'How did you find our boat?' Ryshad asked, evidently glad to have someone other than Darni to thank, a sentiment I wholeheartedly shared.

'That was a little more difficult, I have to admit. I've had every whale and dolphin this side of the Cape of Winds searching the seas.'

Otrick grinned toothily at us and I was struck by the brilliance of his sapphire eyes.

'That dragon,' I said suddenly. 'Was it real or an illusion?'

Otrick looked at me, cunning and amusement mingled in his smile. 'That would be telling, my lady. It did the trick, didn't it?'

We all looked at the wreckage-strewn sea, the screams of the dying Elietimm now replaced by the thin cries of seabirds summoned from who knew where to pick at the spoils.

'Planir's compliments, Otrick, but could you come below?' A thin man dressed in a warm cloak appeared at his elbow. His tone managed to be both obsequious and aggravated at the same time; his expression of disapproval looked to be habitual, given the lines it was carving into an otherwise handsome enough face. His colour was pretty sickly and he moved like a man with belly-ache so I supposed he might have some excuse for his mood.

'What do you want, Casuel? Oh, I suppose so. Come on, you two, you'd better get dry too.'

Ryshad and I followed Otrick, leaving Darni standing dissatisfied on the deck. Getting out of the buffeting wind into a warm, dry cabin was one of the greatest pleasures I have ever experienced, and that includes Summer Solstice at the Gilded Rose in Relshaz. A sturdy, pink-faced girl with long brown hair, maybe ten years my junior, found me dry clothes and while I'd have preferred breeches, thick woollen stockings and four petticoats went a long way to keeping out the chill. I shrugged into an over-large shirt and bodice and wrapped myself securely in a serviceable shawl.

'Where to now?' I could not stop myself yawning now the wakefulness of fear was deserting me. I glanced longingly at the feather-bedded bunk.

'I think you'd better see Planir,' my benefactress said apologetically. 'He did ask to meet you.'

'Are you a wizard?' I asked curiously; she looked as if she should still be in a schoolroom somewhere in the Lescari backwoods her accent betrayed.

'Not yet.' She blushed even more pinkly. 'But I'm going to be.'

I suppose I would have got excited about something like that at her age, but then I'd been busy trying to keep alive long enough to prove to my mother that I didn't really need her.

'Lead on, then,' I said with the limited enthusiasm that was all I could muster. 'Sorry, I didn't catch your name.'

'It's Allin.' She led me through a maze of ladders and wooden walls to a large cabin where five figures were bent over a table as others hovered attentively around. Two raised their heads as we entered, and one came forward, offering me his hand.

'I'm Planir. I'm so glad to meet you.'

The Archmage was not overly tall, and was dark-haired

and lithe in build with angular features softened by warm grey eyes and an engaging smile. His voice was soft with the lilting accents of his Gidestan youth and had an intimate quality that rippled through me. I was suddenly aware of my matted hair and the fact that I must look like an unmade bed. He could have been anywhere from forty years of age to sixty; fine lines fanned out from his eyes and his hair was receding but I'd bet he could talk any woman he wanted inside his bed-curtains. What he didn't look like, to my mind, was an Archmage.

I forced my mind back to business. 'We couldn't save Geris but I found some of his work. It might help.'

'Usara?' Planir beckoned with a commanding hand.

A thin wizard in brown came forward and took the crumpled parchments eagerly.

'Where exactly—'

One of the other mages interrupted him abruptly.

'Planir, we need you.'

They both turned back to the table and, since no one said otherwise, I followed. An image was now floating above the rough wood. I gasped. If I had thought Shiv and Harna's duck pond was good, it was a child's drawing in the sand compared to this. I recognised the islands of the Elietimm but this was no mere map; perfect in every detail, I saw every beach, village and fortification. I shivered as I spied tiny figures frozen in the image; was this what it was like to be a god?

'Now, if you can break that fissure, Kalion can bring up the molten rock and I'll work on the glacier.'

The wizard doing the talking was a robust-looking woman in the clothes of a Caladhrian farmwife, with the slack belly and gappy teeth of someone who's done more than her fair share of child-bearing. For all that, her eyes were keen and her face commanding as she peered down at the tiny ice-clad landscape in front of her.

Planir was leaning over and frowning as he studied the crater of the fire-mountain.

'Usara, can you open up that channel for me?' Amber light crawled over the image and Usara nodded confidently.

I stood silently as the mages bent over the miniature world they had created and worked ruin for the Elietimm. The side of the mountain quivered under Planir's magelight and gradually began to slip aside in a series of jerks. The wizard called Kalion cleared his throat and cracked his knuckles to send brief flashes of red down into the opening. Brilliant white fire emerged, the boiling rock cooling to red as it trickled down the mountainside. Sparse vegetation flared to ashes as the fire crept towards an unknowing hamlet.

'Usara, can you thin this out a bit?' Kalion murmured. Sweat beaded his forehead as he concentrated and he wiped it absently away on a rich velvet gown that would have looked more at home on a Lescari money-lender.

'Not so fast,' the woman commanded. She was doing something to a wall of ice further round the mountain where Planir was opening another channel in the rock. I watched as an orange glow surged under the ice and shuddered at the thought of so much water let loose to wash away the meagre settlements of the hapless peasants. I hoped some of their carefully hoarded stores would survive; the Elietimm were facing a bleak and hungry season.

I jumped when the door behind me opened. The man called Casuel looked in hesitantly, evidently relieved when he saw me.

'It's Livak, isn't it?' he enquired in low tones.

'Who wants to know?' I asked cautiously, not keen to answer a summons from Darni, for example.

'I need to hear about your experiences. Come with me, please. I want to prepare a report for the Council, to save time.' He shot an anxious glance at the wizards huddled over their enchantments but they were oblivious to our presence by now.

I drew a reluctant breath; I wasn't about to start taking orders from another wizard, let alone a cloak-carrier like this one. On the other hand, I didn't have the energy for a row.

'Can't it wait? It's not as if I'm going anywhere!'

He pursed a mean mouth in my direction; I stared back at him, expressionless.

'I suppose so,' he said finally with ill grace. 'I'll see you after I've spoken with Shivvalan.'

'Casuel!' The fat wizard called Kalion looked up. 'Send Allin in here, will you? I'd like her to see how this is done.'

Casuel sketched a bow. 'Of course, Hearth-Master.' He offered me a thin hand and I shook it briefly. 'I'll see you later.'

'Not if I see you first, you charmless lout,' I said silently to myself, pushing past him.

I followed my nose and my instincts to the galley; I soon found a quiet corner on deck to eat the bread and meat I'd scrounged from the agreeable ship's cook.

'I was starting to wonder what they'd done with you.' Ryshad appeared round a barrel and sat down next to me. I passed him a hunk of bread.

'I met Planir but he was rather busy. They're trying to sink those islands, from what I could see.'

Ryshad nodded as he chewed hungrily. He passed me a lidded pewter flagon of ale and I drank deeply before remembering I don't really like beer.

'It looks like everyone's got things to do except for us, then?'

'Oh, I think we've done enough for a while, don't you?'

I managed a half-smile to answer Ryshad's rather strained grin.

'Did anyone say where we're going?'

'This ship's headed for Hadrumal but I reckon they'll have to make landfall somewhere before that, Tormalin probably. They can put me off there,' he said firmly.

'You're going home?' I was oddly reluctant to face the prospect of losing Ryshad. 'I thought we would all be kept in Hadrumal till they'd wrung every last detail out of us.'

'That could take half a season. No, I don't take orders from wizards, even Archmages. My first duty's to make my report to Messire D'Olbriot; his scribes can take a copy for Planir.' Ryshad grimaced and reclaimed the ale. 'After that, I must go and tell Ait's family how he died.'

We sat in silence for some moments.

'How about you?' Ryshad asked after a while. 'I'd like to show you Zyoutessela and I'm sure Messire D'Olbriot will want to reward you.'

'For what?' I looked at him curiously and he pointed to my hands.

'These are his rings, the ones with the flame-tree on the crest.' He took my hand and rolled the gold bands gently round my fingers. 'These are worth a prince's hire.'

I laughed as I slipped the rings free and handed them over. 'Who'd have thought it? I don't know, Rysh, I've a life to get back to as well, you know. Halice will be thinking I've dropped off the end of the world, and we were supposed to meet some other friends at Col. The best place for me to head for would be Relshaz. Perhaps the wizards could take me to the Spice Coast, I could go up the Pepper Road.' I yawned, despite the stimulating chill of the wind. 'I certainly don't want to go to Hadrumal, I'm not spending the winter with wizards and scholars turning my mind inside out. They can pay me the money they owe me and I reckon I'll be adding a percentage for undue risk but, beyond that, there's nothing for me there.'

We sat in silence again for a little while.

'I have to say I don't like leaving a job half done, though,' I admitted. 'This isn't over, is it?'

'No, I don't suppose it is, but my mother always used to say the only thing in life with no loose ends is a new tapestry.' Ryshad sighed. 'I know what you mean, I feel the same, but I've other loyalties to meet.'

I reached out and held on to Rysh's hand; we sat there, wondering what to do for the best. A long, low rumble drifted over the ocean towards us and we looked at each other, eyes wide and questioning.

'Shiv!' I waved a hand as he went past, attention elsewhere.

'I didn't expect to see you on your feet!' Ryshad offered him the ale with a broad grin of relief.

Shiv joined us in our sheltered nook and rubbed at his thickly bandaged arm.

'One of those scholars has been looking into the healing magic they use in Solura. It seems that's aetheric as well. Whatever, it's put me back together so I'm not arguing.'

I studied his face; his colour was better but he still looked drawn and strained and Ryshad wasn't much prettier. I wondered what I'd find next time I chanced on a mirror.

'We were just wondering what to do next. Any ideas?'

Shiv shook his head wearily. 'I'm needed back in Hadrumal. Piecing together the whole story of our little adventure is going to take a lot of work. The Council will have a lot to discuss and then they'll have to decide what action to take. Some will think we should deal with this all ourselves, another faction will argue for alliance with Tormalin, and there'll be every shade of opinion in between. Some will favour blowing the Elietimm islands out of the ocean, others will want to wait and see and hope they'll just go away. Planir will have his work cut out getting a decision this side of Spring Equinox.'

He heaved a great sigh. 'Still, that's his problem. I just want to go home to Pered and lock the door till the turn of the year.'

That was a more cheerful prospect. 'Will we be home for Solstice? I've lost count of the days.'

Shiv smiled. 'Yes — what shall we do to celebrate? How about a trip to one of the gaming-houses in Relshaz?'

I was about to laugh but the wizard called Casuel popped up through a hatch, looking all ways like a startled rabbit.

'Shivvalan, there you are! Quickly, we need your help.'

Several other wizards appeared and we rose to our feet. I watched, open-mouthed, as a massive wave came sweeping across the ocean at us. Enchantment wove a shining emerald curtain around the ship; we rode the huge swell like a floating seabird and my heart stopped trying to hammer its way through my ribs. The wizards all watched for a moment then returned to whatever they had been doing, their matter-of-fact attitudes taking my breath away.

'You really should keep yourself ready for the Archmage's instructions, Shivvalan,' Casuel reprimanded in a lofty tone which would have had me planning to stitch a fish into his mattress if I'd had to spend any time with him.

'You forget, Cas, I'm Otrick's pupil.' Shiv gave Casuel a charming smile which seemed to annoy him out of all proportion. He snorted but noticed Usara emerging on deck and went scurrying off to hover attentively round him. Shiv shook his head and I caught him flicking his fingers after Casuel in that peculiarly Caladhrian gesture of disdain as we sat ourselves down again.

'You two don't get on, I take it?' Ryshad had watched this little exchange with amusement.

'No, we don't.' Shiv shook his head with a rueful smile and reached for the ale. 'Well, he's not the most likeable type in the world, but it is partly my fault.'

Shiv's faint air of shame was intriguing. 'How so?' I asked.

Shiv shrugged for a long moment before deciding to answer. 'It was a couple of years back, at Solstice. I'd had a bit too much to drink and I had one of those ideas which seem so good until you sober up.'

Ryshad and I both agreed mock-solemnly and Shiv laughed.

'The thing is, no one had ever seen Cas with a girl, he's always been very reserved and it occurred to me that he might be – er – of my persuasion. I'd happened to hear his family are pretty Rationalist in their thinking and you know what they're like—'

'If nature intended men to lay with men, why have women at all and so on and so forth.' Ryshad nodded.

I gaped at Shiv. 'You made a pass at him?'

'No I did not!' Shiv retorted indignantly. 'Pered and I don't stray. All I did was offer to introduce him to a friend of Pered's who was staying with us for the festival . . .'

'But what's-his-name took this as a calculated slur on his manhood?' Ryshad hazarded a guess, grinning broadly.

'He took a swing at me!' Shiv admitted ruefully. 'He missed – but I didn't and, what with one thing and another, it all got a bit out of hand.'

I laughed and shook my head. 'You idiot!'

'Look!' Ryshad pointed back in the direction of the distant

islands. An ash-filled plume of smoke was climbing high into the uppermost skies. The sight dragged us brutally back to the present.

'I'd better go,' Shiv muttered and slipped away.

'I'd say Planir and the others have given Ice-man something to keep him busy for a while,' I joked shakily.

Ryshad nodded, his expression strained. 'It won't stop him though. I reckon Messire D'Olbriot will have the look-outs watching for black ships on the Spring Equinox winds.'

I shivered. When Ryshad opened his arms to me, I leaned into his embrace. I rested my face on the warm, dry wool of his jerkin and shut my eyes, relaxing for the first time since before Inglis. He tightened his arms around me, and buried his face in my hair with a long breath. It was the most natural thing in the world to raise my face to his kiss and then we simply sat there, taking what comfort we could from each other as the ship soared over the seas towards home.

CHAPTER ELEVEN

Taken from:

Travels in the Unmapped Lands of Einarinn

BY

Marris Dohalle

The Number Song of the Forest Folk

That the Forest Folk are an ancient race is clear from this song. It is used to teach children the words once used for counting; marmol, edril and so on, now meaningless in themselves as the language has changed over the generations.

> One is the Sun, soaring in the height,
> Marmol, the hearth-circle we all share.
> Two are the moons in their dance of might,
> Edril, their web woven in the air.
> Three races share mountain, plain and wood,
> Semil, on all is the sun's face warm.
> Four are the winds, bring they ill or good,
> Dexil, the life-breath of calm or storm.
> Five are the fingers for harp and bow,
> Wrem are the days of a minstrel's wake.
> Six are the rivers that foil the foe,
> Tedren, when hoofbeats the greenwood shake.
> Seven, the Wise Ones the windrose spin,

Fathen, the empty, the seat of fears.
Eight are the seasons, each one begin,
Adren, new wood on the Tree of Years.
Nine are the Holy, the Three of Three,
Parlen, the fate-sticks the foolish mock.
Ten are the fingers of weapons free,
Vrek, double handclasp of friendship's lock.

Much of the original meaning of this ancient rhyme has been lost as the Forest Folk have only an oral tradition of history, and that varies from clan to clan, each concentrating primarily on its own members. Concepts once familiar become blurred with repetition and changing circumstance. Forest Folk are not troubled by this, seeing history as an ever-changing, ever-spreading framework for life, rooted in creation and expanding with each new season – the Tree of Years, in fact.

Spreading and dividing is seen as healthy and natural; family groups travel the vast reaches of the Great Forest, joining together at some seasons, separating at others. Bonds are rarely permanent and it is entirely acceptable for family members to leave their own kin for a season or more, travelling with another group or leaving the Forest altogether. It is this tradition that keeps Forest Folk minstrels a familiar sight on so many roads, combining their incorrigible wanderlust with the race's love of music, which stems from their reliance on song and epic poetry in place of a written history.

Given the abundance of the Great Forest, the Folk are able to supply all their needs easily, sharing without conflict between themselves. Accordingly, this results in a lack of understanding of more formal boundaries and concepts of ownership. For similar reasons, Forest Folk are rarely proficient in physical combat, concentrating on those skills of eye and hand needed for hunting in a wildwood rather than for direct confrontation over land or resources. However, the incautious traveller leaving the highroads through the Great Forest risks inadvertently stopping an arrow tipped with deadly venom if he blunders into a chase.

The Forest Folk are largely a tolerant people, living close to nature. Harmony – between races, between individuals and of course, in music – is highly prized. When they need to decide any question of dominance or authority among themselves, this is usually done in a contest of poetry or song. It is considered far more damaging to humiliate an opponent than to actually kill him. However, when faced with dire peril, the Forest Folk display a doughty determination few races, ancient or modern, can equal.

Shanklane Cottage, Middle Reckin,
40th of For-Winter

It wasn't a long walk and it did me good after spending the best part of six days in carrier's coaches. The tapster at the Green Frog had no trouble remembering Halice and her broken leg and gave me clear directions to the little cottage she'd been renting since the turn of the season. I thanked him and took the road through the broad open-fields with a spring in my step. The weather had turned crisp and dry, there was snow underfoot and, once night fell, the frost would be iron-hard. But, for the moment, there was no wind and the afternoon sun was warm on my face.

Every league of my journey was enabling me to put more distance between myself and my experiences, but I was still suffering odd pangs of guilt and wondering how things were working themselves out. I caught myself hoping Ryshad had been sympathetically received by that patron of his. I didn't want to think about what reception he might get from Aiten's family. Should I have offered to go with him? Only that would have meant going over the whole horrible experience time and again; it had been bad enough the first time and it wasn't going to improve with retelling. No, Aiten had crossed over to the Otherworld and nothing was going to bring him back. His family could grieve for him well enough without my help. People live, people die; Misaen makes them, Poldrion ferries them, that's the way life is.

I wondered how Ryshad was faring. Did he find himself thinking about me? Were sudden rushes of desire warming his blood in the same way as mine? Something had turned that warm kiss of friendship into a scorching blaze of lust that had left us both trembling like eager virgins. Privacy is in fairly short supply on an ocean boat crowded with nosy wizards, but we'd managed to find enough seclusion to gratify the unexpected passion that had seized us. Still, good as the sex had been, even in those cramped and uncomfortable conditions, I'd waited at the stern rail and watched Ryshad disembark at Zyoutessela. Had I made a dreadful mistake or saved us both from something we'd have lived to regret, like my parents? That was something else I didn't want to dwell on too much. I slipped and stumbled where a patch of shade had kept a puddle frozen solid through the brief noon warmth and smiled ruefully at myself. A man hadn't affected me like this any time in the last ten years.

It was proving difficult to shake off the dust of this unexpected adventure though. There were all the various questions about the Elietimm, that lost colony, the dreams and all the other parts of Planir's puzzle. I couldn't help being curious but as my mother always said, 'Curiosity got Amit hanged.' Forget it, I told myself firmly; Tormalin princes and all the wizards of Hadrumal can sort it out between themselves, without your help. This isn't your fight, it nearly got you killed. Yes, it would be nice to pay a little something back for Geris but revenge is for fools; that's what started all this and look where it got you! Walk away from it, Livak, I ordered myself sternly; walk away and don't look back.

I turned off down a shaded, muddy track, the edges of the ruts rock-hard in the frost. A straggle of snug cottages nestled under their wheatstraw thatches and I looked for a green door. If Halice was looking after herself, her leg couldn't be that bad, could it? I began rehearsing all the arguments I'd been preparing to explain why I'd gone off the way I had. The only problem was that they all sounded a bit thin, apart from the muffled chink of the hefty pouch of coin that was plumping out my jerkin. I patted it affectionately, the way some women do with a season's child-belly on them. I'd got a wax-sealed flagon of irreproachable wine in my backpack as well; that should help, whatever Halice thought of me.

I knocked on the door and lifted the latch; my cheerful words of welcome died on my lips as I saw Halice in a chair with two short, blond men standing over her, arms raised.

'And then I said, "Look, how much damage do you think I could do?"'

Halice roared her familiar barking laugh as the fair-haired pair turned to see who had come in.

'Livak!'

Sorgrad and Sorgren hurried to embrace me but I took a step backwards, shaking, struggling with the fears that had come clamouring out of my memories. They halted, concerned.

'Are you all right?' Sorgrad's familiar voice dispelled the horrid illusions and I was able to manage a more normal smile.

'Sure, sorry, just caught a draught from Poldrion's cloak.'

'Come and get warm.' Halice did not stand up and I saw a crutch resting against her chair. I could not see her leg under the blanket over her lap and wondered how it was healing. Well, she'd tell me how bad it was when she was good and ready but I could see she had put on weight through sitting about waiting for the damage to heal.

I moved to the hearth and rubbed my hands over the glowing coals, breathing in the familiar scents of baking bread, meat spitted and roasting, home and safety.

'So, where did you get to?' Sorgren poured me wine from a jug standing in the fender and I savoured the spicy warmth for a moment.

'You know that one gamble, the one you always talk about when you're drunk, the one that's going to set you up for an honest life?' I grinned at them all.

'You found it?' Halice's dark eyes reflected the firelight, amusement warring with hope on her weather-beaten face.

'No.' I shook my head and reached inside my jerkin. 'I thought I had but it wasn't to be. Still, it paid quite well, for all that.'

I dropped the washleather bag and it landed on the table with a thud that simply shouted out noble coin. Sorgren weighed it in one hand and a wondering look crossed his face.

'How much is here?'

'Enough to give us all a Solstice to remember! How about we hire a fast team and head for Col?' I drained my cup and reached for more wine. 'We could make the last of the Solstice.'

'Sounds like a fair plan.' Sorgrad smiled at me, eyes bright. 'So, what exactly have you been up to? Halice said she'd had a message from some wizard, saying you were off working for the Archmage.'

'It's a long story and I don't want to tell it now,' I said firmly. 'Maybe later, I don't know. It wasn't like some half-arsed ministrel's ballad, I'll tell you that much. It was bloody dangerous and I nearly didn't make it back.'

'You did, though, and it looks to have paid well,' Sorgen said cheerfully, opening the bag and beginning to stack the white-gold coins into gleaming columns. He always likes to live in the present.

'Coin's only worth anything if you're alive to spend it, 'Gren.' I shook my head at him. 'That's my share and a dead man's. His gamble only won him passage with Poldrion.'

A tremor ran through me and I turned it into a theatrical shudder. 'I'll take an honest job before I work for the Archmage again!'

Halice looked closely at me for a moment. She may look like the village idiot's older sister but she's no fool. 'Let's head for Col then, spend his gold and forget him,' she said cheerfully. 'The lads have got some interesting ideas for turning a few coins in Lescar.'

'All right.' I turned the spit and fat crackled in the flames. 'Let's eat this piglet and make some plans. I'm in favour of something involving warm tap-rooms, a familiar set of bones in my hand and some well-controlled games of runes with stupid farmers. There's just one thing I want to make clear: whatever we do, it's to have nothing to do with wizards!'

THE SWORDSMAN'S OATH

The Second Tale of Einarinn

Juliet E. McKenna

'An enjoyable debut brimful of magic and adventure'
Starburst

When Ryshad, a sworn man, is instructed to assist a wizard
in his fight against the strange magic of the Elietimm, it
seems the perfect opportunity to seek revenge for the death
of his friend. And the chance to renew his acquaintance
with Livak – gambler, thief and former lover.

But Ryshad will have to overcome far more than his
personal grief, for the Elietimm's threat to the Empire is
increasing at an alarming rate. He will journey to far-off
lands and encounter treachery and terrifying visions.
He will witness incredible wonders and terrifying visions.
He will fight to the death to stay true to his oath. And for
much of the time his sword will be his only friend – in more
ways than he can possibly imagine.

With spellbinding characters and non-stop action
The Swordsman's Oath is an unforgettable adventure from
a captivating new storyteller.